35

YANKEE DOODLE DANDY

By Noel B. Gerson

YANKEE DOODLE DANDY
THE SLENDER REED
OLD HICKORY
THE GOLDEN LYRE
THE TROJAN
THE LAND IS BRIGHT
THE HITTITE
THE YANKEE FROM TENNESSEE
THE EMPEROR'S LADIES
DAUGHTER OF EVE
THE SILVER LION
THE CONQUEROR'S WIFE
THAT EGYPTIAN WOMAN
THE HIGHWAYMAN
THE FOREST LORD
THE IMPOSTOR
THE GOLDEN EAGLE
THE CUMBERLAND RIFLES
THE MOHAWK LADDER
SAVAGE GENTLEMAN

Nonfiction

SEX AND THE ADULT WOMAN
   (with Ellen F. Birchall, M.D.)
KIT CARSON
SEX AND THE MATURE MAN
   (with Louis P. Saxe, M.D.)
BELGIUM: FUTURE, PRESENT, PAST
ROCK OF FREEDOM
FOOD
VALLEY FORGE
THE LEGEND OF POCAHONTAS
NATHAN HALE

Yankee Doodle Dandy

A Biographical Novel of *John Hancock*

By NOEL B. GERSON

1965

DOUBLEDAY & COMPANY, INC., GARDEN CITY, NEW YORK

For
Dr. Sidney S. Greenberg

This new nation we have forged with the hammer of freedom on the anvil of justice is neither the first nor the last to fight for her liberty. But the United States of America is unique. For the sake of principle—and of principle alone—we have waged our battle. Every family has suffered losses. My own health is somewhat impaired, and my fortune much reduced, but I am fortunate and do not complain. No sacrifice is too great for the cause of liberty.

JOHN HANCOCK

YANKEE DOODLE DANDY

ONE

1754

1

"John Hancock, you're a jackass!"

It was very quiet in the modestly furnished second-floor office overlooking Boston Harbor. The silence was broken only by the creaking of a weather-beaten sign, THOMAS HANCOCK, DRYGOODS AND SHIPPING, that was hanging from a wrought-iron standard outside an open window. Scores of ships, their sails furled, were loading and unloading merchandise at the Long Wharf, some distance away, and a square-rigged brig was gently maneuvering toward the nearer, new Hancock Wharf, directly opposite the whitewashed warehouse and retail store.

Thomas Hancock, a portly, handsomely dressed man with a long nose and piercing, dark eyes, half-stood in his cushioned chair to glance out at his ship, the *Lydia*, and then returned his full attention to his seventeen-year-old nephew. "Harvard College may have given you the smattering of an education, boy—"

"It did far more than that, Uncle!" The red-faced youth ran a clumsy hand up over his brown hair, smoothing it, then tugged at the double rows of lace cuffs that emerged from the sleeves of his silver-buttoned coat of maroon velvet. "If you'll permit me to quote Horace, '*Aut virtus nomen inane est. Aut decus et pretium recte petit experiens vir.*' Translating rather freely, one might say it means that virtue is either a mere name, or else it is a thing of glory and value which a man wisely pursues." Pleased with himself, he smiled brightly, exposing two rows of strong, unusually white teeth.

The man behind the desk clutched his wig in despair. "I warn you, if you quote the classics to me once more, just once, I'll tan your backside. Even if you are a Master of Arts and have become a living fountainhead of learning."

The boy's eyes were as dark and unyielding as his uncle's, his long, bony face set in lines equally stubborn. "I'm sorry you don't appreciate Horace, but I was merely trying to express myself."

"You're not just a jackass. You're pompous. Above all, you're a disgrace to me. Look at you!"

John studied his reflection in an oval mirror above the mantel at the far side of the room and preened. His tailor had assured him that his suit was a duplicate of one worn by the Prince of Wales, his stock was made of linen so expensive that Uncle Thomas hadn't bothered to import more than three bolts of the stuff, and his stockings of the purest white silk were faultless. What was more, his square-toed shoes with three-quarter-inch heels and silver buckles had come from France, and had been made by a bootmaker formerly in the personal service of King Louis XV.

"If you think the buttons on the swallowtail of my coat are a trifle gaudy, Uncle," he said earnestly, "I assure you that His Royal Highness himself wears them."

"You're no damned royal highness!" Thomas roared, striking his desk with such force that two models of merchant ships toppled onto their sides. "No, and you aren't a dashing gallant spending the autumn at a fashionable English watering resort. You're a Boston colonial who starts here today as an apprentice. And on top of everything else, you're two hours late reporting for work!"

John thought he understood the reason for his uncle's ire now. "I'm afraid I haven't quite overcome my summer holiday habits yet, Uncle. I overslept this morning."

Thomas' face became livid, but he managed to control his fury. "You're impossible. However, if it happens again, you'll be penalized. Any of my apprentices who fail to put in a full day of work lose a full month's wages." He studied his nephew for a moment,

2

shook his head and rang a small bell of silver that stood at one side of his cluttered desk.

A moment later his chief clerk, Elias Wheaton, hurried into the room, pushing his spectacles onto his forehead.

"Here's a new hand for the unloading crew. Send him down to the wharf foreman."

Wheaton looked at John's finery and opened his mouth to protest, but changed his mind. No one in Boston, much less in the employ of Master Hancock, ever disputed his direct orders. He beckoned silently.

John followed him downstairs, and they walked without speaking through storage rooms piled high with crates and barrels, stacks of muskets recently manufactured in England, and bolts of wool from England, silk from France and cotton from India.

The clerk walked quickly to the front, where the retail establishment was located, and made his way past plain wooden counters heaped high with merchandise. A few women, hoping to pick up bargains, were already strolling through the place, even though the store had just opened its doors for the day.

John wanted to linger, and slowed his pace. Ever since he had been adopted as a small boy by Uncle Thomas and Aunt Lydia, he had been fascinated by the rich and bewildering variety of goods for sale here. The pungent odor of spices from the Far East created a romantic aura, and as a child he had loved to inhale their scent as he had fingered the products made by master craftsmen in a dozen lands. Uncle Thomas was said to be the only man in the American colonies who sold Spanish poniards, wine and cloth, carved marble statuettes from the Italian states and cooking ware from Sweden. It was rumored that he gladly bought merchandise from any sea captain, not caring whether a master was a freebooter who had obtained the goods by committing acts of piracy on the high seas. John had never believed these vicious stories. He and Aunt Lydia knew, as no one else did, that there was no stricter moralist in the entire colony of Massachusetts than Thomas Hancock.

"Come along," Wheaton said, trying to conceal his annoyance with his employer's young ward. Halting at the bookkeeper's counter, he scribbled something on a small sheet of paper with a frayed quill pen, dropped a blob of hot wax onto the paper and

3

imprinted it with the Hancock seal, two crossed keys. "Here," he said, "take this down to Dan Fowler on the wharf."

John accepted the paper, unable to understand why Wheaton looked at him with such pitying sympathy.

The *Lydia* was securely tied, resting at her dockside berth, and a huge, cumbersome crane of wood and iron, the largest machine of its kind in the New World, was already dipping its long neck of reinforced oak into the stern hold. John made his way rapidly up the wharf, surreptitiously studying three painted trollops who were walking arm in arm and laughing loudly to attract the attention of the *Lydia's* seamen, who would be hungry for female companionship after spending more than five weeks at sea.

One of the women returned John's gaze coldly. "That one will be ripe for plucking," she said, "in about five years. After he turns into a man."

John flushed and pretended he hadn't heard the remark. Some day, when he attained a position of authority in Uncle Thomas' company, he would ban all harlots from the wharf. Ladies and gentlemen from King Street were already appearing to watch the unloading of a merchantman, which was always an occasion, and it did the Hancock name no good when such creatures flaunted themselves on family property.

Dan Fowler, the wharf foreman, was a husky blond in his late twenties who had worked on the docks all of his life. His calf-high boots were scuffed, the leather apron he wore over his homespun breeches was spotted and soiled, and the sleeves of his coarse shirt were rolled high above his elbows, revealing thick arms and bulging muscles. He was bellowing orders to several straining men who were carrying a large crate down a frighteningly narrow gangway from the main deck of the ship to the wharf, and was unaware of John's existence until the boy twice cleared his throat.

At last Fowler turned to him, obviously irritated at being interrupted by a young gentleman.

"I was told to report to you," John said, handing him the paper.

Fowler glanced at it, then looked again at the immaculately attired dandy.

"I'm to begin my apprenticeship working for you," John said.

4

Fowler scratched his head with a ragged fingernail, then grinned. "I thought I seen all kinds," he muttered. "Name?"

"John Hancock."

"You're the old man's pup?" The foreman scowled when John nodded, and spat into the water of the harbor. "Damn the eyes of that Wheaton! I got enough worries!" Again he scratched his head, and then jabbed a finger in the direction of the ship. "You'll work with the gang in the forward hold. I need extra hands there. You'll stay until you're relieved." Suddenly, inexplicably, he started to laugh.

John knew he was being mocked, and realized his clothes were responsible. "I didn't know my assignment when I started out this morning," he said. "May I go home to change into something more appropriate?"

"And lose the whole morning?" Fowler shouted. "Get to hell on board! The *Marion* is due from the West Indian islands before the day ends, so we've got to finish unloading the *Lydia* by sundown!"

He looked so ferocious that John instinctively took a single step backward. His apprenticeship would last for seven long years, and his life would be miserable unless he won the respect, if not the friendship of the men who worked for Uncle Thomas. So, rather than argue, he walked to the ship. The gangway was still being used, and he leaped from the wharf to the deck. Afraid of falling into the sea between the dock and the *Lydia's* hull, his jump was too energetic, and he landed with a crash on the smooth deck, falling and tearing a hole in the right knee of his new breeches. Two cargo handlers who had joined Fowler laughed raucously, and John's temper flared, but he held it in check.

He couldn't blame the men for feeling as they did. It would be useless to explain that he had expected to be given a position in Uncle Thomas' office. And it was no one's business that he felt insecure on board any ship. Some of his friends at Harvard had loved sailing, and he had been ashamed of himself when even a slight swell in the outer harbor had made him queasy. He had preferred to become expert in the art of dueling and the handling of firearms, which were the pastimes of gentlemen. But

5

the Hancock fortune was based on ships, so he supposed the time had come for him to conquer his distaste for the sea.

" '*Beatissimus is est, qui est aptus ex sese, quique in se uno sua ponit omnia,*' " he said under his breath. "He is the happiest man, who depends upon himself and is entirely self-reliant." He couldn't remember whether the quotation was from Horace or Cicero, and was astonished he had forgotten his Latin so quickly.

However, it really didn't matter. Squaring his shoulders, he started toward the forward hold.

2

The October breeze that blew across the waterfront from the west was crisp, but the air in the dark hold was stifling. John had been assigned the task of hauling down barrels from neat, tight piles and rolling them to a hatch, where others hoisted them onto the deck and carried them ashore. He lost all semblance of time in the gloom and, aware that the cargo handlers regarded him with suspicious scorn, worked twice as hard as anyone else.

His arms were so tired that it was an agony just to lift them, excruciating pains shot through his back every time he doubled over and sweat poured down into his eyes, blinding him and ruining his shirt. But he continued to work doggedly, no matter how great his discomfort, and it no longer mattered that his finery was in a sorry state.

His own carelessness had been responsible for the destruction of his handsome coat. Soon after he had removed it and thrown it aside, he had rolled a heavy barrel of English-brewed ale over it, flattening its expensive buttons and ripping the fabric irreparably in two places. His breeches of the same material were coated with dust, his silk stockings were black and snagged, and the silver buckle was missing from one of his new shoes. But the endless rows of barrels still to be unloaded from the *Lydia* drove everything else from John's mind.

Gradually it dawned on him that he was ravenously hungry, and a short time later he realized that half of the cargo handlers had gone off for their dinner, returned and sent the rest of the crew for food. John could hear his insides growling, and won-

6

dered whether he had been forgotten. But he continued to work for another quarter of an hour, and when no one came to relieve him, he finally decided to take matters into his own hands.

He left his tattered coat in the hold, climbed up to the deck and was pleased to see that the gangway was not being used. He went ashore quickly, shivering when the cool wind cut through his perspiration-dampened shirt. He started in the direction of the King's Arms, a tavern he had frequently visited in his uncle's company, but halted, grinning, when he realized that someone who looked like a dockhand would not be admitted to the dining room where shipowners and wealthy merchants convened.

John chuckled as he walked down the waterfront in the opposite direction. He not only resembled a cargo handler, but had become one.

The Pequot was one of the roughest inns in Boston, and it was rumored that Dutch, French, and even English seamen unfamiliar with its reputation were sometimes robbed and murdered there. Crown bailiffs had never been able to verify the stories, but it was true that the bodies of unfortunate sailors were sometimes found floating in the harbor.

Ordinarily John would have been too fastidious to go into the Pequot, but there was no other eating place in the vicinity. He pushed open the heavy, iron-studded door, then stood uncertainly inside the entrance. A low, muffled roar of baritone voices washed over him, and as he peered through a blue-gray haze of tobacco smoke in an attempt to find an empty table, the stale, slightly rancid odor of unwashed bodies stung his nostrils.

He ventured a few feet farther into the taproom, noting that two of the bawds he had seen earlier on the wharf were now sitting with several drunken members of the *Lydia's* crew. It was odd, but in the half-light they actually looked attractive.

"You, there!" someone bellowed. "Yes, you!"

John saw a broad-shouldered giant coming toward him, and recognized Dan Fowler.

"Who in hell gave you permission to leave the ship?" the foreman demanded.

John refused to be bullied. "I have as much right to my food as anyone else!"

7

"You'll do what you're told when I tell you to do it." Fowler rocked on the balls of his feet.

John could feel a knot forming in his stomach. "I'll go back to the hold as soon as I've put some food in me."

"You'll go now."

Men in every part of the taproom sensed trouble and, jumping up from their benches, hurried toward the stubborn, glaring pair.

Fowler rubbed the knuckles of his right hand against the open palm of his left. "I'm paid my wages," he said gruffly, "to get ships unloaded on time. My men stay healthier when they don't sass me."

"I've been doing my share, and I'll do more." John's long jaw jutted forward. "But I'll do it a blamesight better after I put a veal and ham pie into my belly."

The foreman's right fist lashed out, catching John in the midriff and doubling him over. "This is all you'll get in your belly until I give you leave to eat," he said.

The crowd roared its approval of his witticism.

John straightened slowly, glared at his antagonist and attacked suddenly, both fists flailing.

Fowler blocked the punches with his elbows and arms, then struck again, putting so much force into the blow to the cheekbone that John staggered backward and sprawled on the floor.

"I run my crew the way I see fit," the foreman announced in clear tones. "Thomas Hancock pays me for results, but even he don't tell me what to do."

John dragged himself to his feet, unmindful of a bleeding gash on his cheekbone. He staggered as he tried to regain his balance, and shook his head repeatedly.

"You got courage, boy. I give you that much." Fowler looked at him in surprise. "But don't make me hit you again."

"Be good enough," John said, "to come outside with me."

The crowd cheered him ironically.

"Alone," John added.

Fowler studied his right fist for a moment, shrugged and then winked at the men who surrounded them. "If that's how you want it. Don't nobody drink my ale," he called over his shoulder as he followed the youth out to the dirt road.

John gulped cold, fresh air.

"If you think you can go crying to your uncle, you're wrong."
Fowler measured him for another punch. "Your trouble, boy, is
you got no sense. After I put you to sleep, I'll douse you with cold
water. Then you'll go back to the hold, like I told you in the first
place."

John held up a hand. "I'm not stupid," he said quietly. "You've
already proved you can whip me. I don't know why you're so hard
on me, but I'm not denying your authority. That isn't why I
wanted to have a few words with you." He raised a hand to his
cheekbone, then smiled wryly as he looked down at his sticky
fingers. "You see, I know my limitations. I'm as familiar with the
philosophy of Aristotle or Cotton Mather as any instructor at
Harvard College. I'm qualified to teach grammar and rhetoric,
and I'm as fluent in Greek or Latin as I am in English. And I
don't mind saying there are few swordsmen in New England who
are my equal—"

"Oh, no!" Fowler had been listening in growing bewilderment, but suddenly became grim. "I reckon I can slice the wing
off'n a gull with a knife throw, but I never held a sword in my
hand, not in all my life. That there's a sport for gentry. You and
me, we'll settle our differences with our fists."

"You gave me no chance to finish," John said with unexpected
dignity, again feeling his cheekbone. "I'm being paid an apprentice's starting wages of ten shillings per week. I'll gladly hand
every penny of it over to you if you'll give me lessons in how to
use my fists."

Fowler blinked at him. "Damn my soul."

"That," John replied crisply, "is the Lord's decision, not mine.
Will you accept my offer?"

"You're a real Hancock, all right!" The foreman laughed ex-
uberantly. "When I saw you in all that silver and lace, I thought
you was one of them fancy lads who wouldn't dirty his hands.
Buy me a pint of ale now and again, and I'll give you lessons
after work every day."

John was pleased, but his smile froze when a huge fist suddenly
shot out, caught him squarely between the eyes and flipped him
onto the dusty road.

"This here is the first lesson," Fowler said, standing over him.
"Never lower your guard. We'll go to it again on the wharf at

9

sundown, and maybe someday you can knock me into the harbor. But right now, get back to the hold of the *Lydia!*" He spat, hands on hips, and went back into the Pequot.

John felt like retching as he forced himself to stand. His head ached, but he told himself he was fortunate. Apparently he was being starved on his first day of duty as an apprentice cargo handler to teach him discipline, but he no longer had an appetite.

Regardless of how miserable he felt, he would work until the end of the day, and would then meet Fowler for instruction in fist-fighting. Wiping a smear of blood from the side of his face, he laughed hoarsely. "Pericles was right," he said aloud. "He who would rule must be strong as well as wise. I learned the words at Harvard, but not their true meaning."

3

Lydia Hancock sat before a blazing fire in her own private sitting room of the enormous white clapboard house that dominated Beacon Hill. Her padded rocking chair creaked beneath her great bulk, and she hummed softly under her breath as she read a book of poetry, occasionally reaching out for a glazed, brandied fruit. The dish that stood on a table beside her was almost empty, but she decided not to ring for more of the delicacies that her husband had imported for her special benefit from one of the German principalities. Now and again she glanced out into the gathering twilight of a raw December day, and sighed when she saw three ships tied to the Hancock Wharf.

She still didn't know whether Thomas would bring the masters of the newly arrived vessels to the house for dinner or, without notifying her of his plans, go to a tavern with them. It simply didn't cross his mind that she liked to make plans for dinner; he expected her to deal with any emergency. Looking once more past the white picket fence at the far end of the property for a sign of his carriage, she put away her book, toasted her tiny, slipper-clad feet before the fire and pulled an embroidered bell-rope.

"You rang, ma'am?" A uniformed maidservant in white stood in the entrance.

"Yes. Tell the cook to heat the mutton stew she made this

morning. I still don't know if Master Hancock and his captains will be coming here for dinner, but we must be ready." She tapped pudgy fingers on the arm of her chair when the young woman, an indentured servant from the north of England, hesitated. "What is it?"

"You wanted to be told when Master John came home, ma'am. He's just stopped at the stables to see that his horse and dogs are being fed proper."

Lydia was annoyed, and gestured in the direction of the fence. "I didn't see him walking up Beacon Hill!"

"No, ma'am." The girl smothered a giggle. "He came up the back side and used the tradesmen's entrance."

Lydia dismissed her with a curt nod. Then, when she was sure the maidservant had gone off to the kitchen outbuildings to deliver her order to the cook, Lydia gathered her silk shawl around her shoulders. Taffeta skirt and petticoats rustling, she walked with the extraordinary grace of the overweight to the landing and swiftly mounted the stairs.

She was out of breath when she reached the third floor, but did not pause until she reached a large chamber in which a fresh log fire was burning. Not bothering to light a candle or an oil lamp, she went to a chair in the shadows beyond a fourposter bed, sat down and waited.

A few moments later quick footsteps sounded, and John came into the room, singing as he lighted a straw spill, adjusted the wick of a lamp and applied the fire to it. "Oh, we'll go to hell together, lads—"

"John!"

He started, the spill dropped to the floor, and he stamped on it with the heel of a dirty, calf-high boot. "I didn't know you were here, Aunt Lydia," he said, trying to sound casual.

"That's obvious," she snapped. "I'm tired of telling you not to sing those vulgar seafront songs under this roof."

"I'm sorry, Aunt Lydia." He tried to sound regretful, but failed miserably.

"Bring that lamp over here and let me look at you. Now, sir."

John walked across the chamber, averting his face when he drew near.

"Have you been drinking at one of those low places again?"

11

"I had a pint of ale with Dan Fowler at the Pequot, but I don't call that drinking."

"What else might one call it? And the Pequot again! I don't for the life of me understand why your uncle permits you to go to that vile place. It isn't suitable for a young gentleman of your age."

John hoped that, if he remained silent, he might escape a long lecture.

"A step or two closer, please. And hold the lamp higher."

He obeyed, sighing.

"John, you've been brawling again!"

"No, Aunt Lydia, Dan was teaching me some new punches." He placed the lamp on a table and peeled off his short seaman's jacket of coarse, heavy wool.

"Call it what you will, your eye is blackened."

John grinned cheerfully.

"Your shirt is torn again. And your boots are filthy!"

"I knocked off the mud at the door, Aunt Lydia. I swear to you that there isn't a mark on your rugs."

"I'll inspect them in daylight tomorrow. And I'm told you've used the rear entrance again."

John moved to the fire and extended his grimy hands, warming them. "A cargo handler doesn't walk in the front door of the finest house in Boston."

"You're a Hancock by birth as well as adoption, sir," she replied severely.

"When I dress like a gentleman, I'll come in the front door, Aunt Lydia."

"You are a gentleman, no matter how disreputable you look. Even though you seem to delight in embarrassing me. The whole household has been laughing at me ever since you became a ruffian."

"At the moment I'm an apprentice cargo handler, and I dress accordingly. What's more, you're wrong, Aunt Lydia. The servants are laughing with me. They think of me as one of their own class now."

"But you're not! You're our sole heir!"

"Uncle Thomas is enjoying the best of health," he replied quietly.

"Where is he enjoying it, this evening? Tell me that! Surely you thought enough of me to take a few minutes from your drinking and brawling to—"

"Uncle Thomas doesn't tell me his plans. An apprentice doesn't walk into his office when he's entertaining three of his captains. Perhaps next year, if I'm moved to the office to learn correspondence and bookkeeping, I'll be better able to keep watch on him for you, Aunt Lydia."

She stood, hugging her silk shawl so tightly that it creased her plump arms. "Between the two of you, John, you and your uncle will be the death of me."

"You don't mean that, Aunt Lydia." He turned to her.

"Don't you dare come near me, young man, until you've had a bath and changed into respectable clothes."

"I can't do either until you leave and let me undress." He paused, hoping she would take the broad hint, but she made no move. "Lizzie has brought two buckets of hot water up to the tub room for me, and they're probably getting cold by now."

Lydia looked at him sharply. "Lizzie? Are you referring to Elizabeth, the new serving maid?"

John nodded guiltily, realizing he'd made a slip.

Dark brown ringlets danced around Lydia Hancock's face as she shook her head. "All my years of training have been wasted. So has your education at Harvard. You simply won't learn that you must keep a barrier between you and the servants if they're to respect and obey you."

It was a waste of breath to dispute the lifelong convictions of a woman whose mind was closed, but John could not let the statement stand unchallenged. He wanted to soak in a hot bath, remove the dirt accumulated through a long day and eat a hearty dinner, but he felt it was even more important to make his aunt understand his feelings.

"There are two differences between your coachman and me. I have a rich uncle, and he hasn't. I was awarded two degrees at the best college in the colonies, but he had to go to work so early in life that he had no chance to learn reading and writing."

Lydia was horrified. "Your father and grandfather were distinguished clergymen. Your great-grandfather was a deacon of the church and Chief Tax Collector for Boston and Cambridge."

"I suspect he was also a rogue," the boy replied with a broad smile. "He must have helped the taxpayers of Cambridge avoid their duties to the Crown. Why else would they have elected him First Selectman of the town?"

She ignored the question. "You trace your ancestry back to the earliest days of Massachusetts Bay," she said stubbornly. "Your great-great-grandfather—"

"Was an illiterate farmer who scratched a living from soil the Almighty never intended as farmland! I'm sorry, Aunt Lydia, but your coachman isn't my inferior. I've heard it claimed in sermons every Sabbath of my life that the Lord will judge all of us equally on the Day of Judgment. I think the same standards exist here on earth. I'm luckier than your coachman, and have more opportunities in life. But I've yet to prove myself a better man. If you'll just read some of those essays of John Locke's, as I've been begging you to do, you'll understand that every man is endowed with rights of personal liberty and is the equal of his neighbor."

"You should have gone to work at the wharf years ago." Lydia's lips were compressed. "I'm shocked at the sedition they teach at Harvard, and I don't know what will become of your whole generation. I wouldn't be surprised if all of you end your days on the gallows!" She gathered her skirts, started toward the door and then halted as a belated argument flashed through her mind. "I suppose you think your uncle is the equal of His Majesty!"

John's smile became uncertain. "I'm not certain that a commoner is the equal of royalty, but I think I'd be inclined to deny the contention that George II rules by Divine Right."

"You go too far, young man! You're advocating treason!"

He wanted to explain that he accepted the authority of the King, his ministers and lesser Crown officials. But Aunt Lydia would not listen, and if he continued to uphold the philosophy of Locke she might burst into tears. It was far better to accept the rebuke and drop the subject. "I'm sorry, Aunt Lydia," he said. "I'll try to conform to more—ah—respectable views in the future. What are we eating tonight?" he added as hunger pangs reminded him he'd had no food since noon.

Lydia paused at the door. "Mutton stew."

He despised the dish, which was invariably swimming in fat,

and made a face. "I saw a mighty fine side of beef out in the kitchen pantry just now. Couldn't I have a beefsteak instead?"

"You preach equality," she said, laughing at him, "but you have expensive tastes."

John refused to concede that his views were inconsistent. "If we had to eat that greasy stew, I'd do it without complaint. But it so happens we can afford beefsteak. Yes, and although I enjoy a pint of ale, I prefer a bottle of Madeira. Blame yourself if I've developed a palate that's sensitive to good food and wine."

Lydia's fleeting smile as she turned away and left the room indicated that she would indulge his whim, as she had done so often in the past.

John closed the door, hastily stripped off his coarse work clothes and donned a dressing gown of fine-woven wool broadcloth, a fabric so expensive that the great ladies of Boston, Philadelphia, and Charleston had some of their most elegant gowns fashioned of it. Only a Hancock would think of ordering a dressing gown made of the precious material.

He took a stiff scrubbing brush and a jar of soft, yellow soap from the top of a chest of drawers and walked out into the chilly corridor. The tub room, a small, bare chamber with hardwood floors, stood at the far end of the hall, and he made his way to it quickly. A basin four and one-half feet long and almost as wide, made of tightly seamed oak planking, stood on the floor in the center of the room, and a few wisps of steam were arising from it.

To John's surprise, the new serving maid from the north of England was still in the room, an empty bucket in each hand. "I brought more hot water, Master John," she said, her accent more Scottish than English. "I could hear Mistress Hancock bashing away in your room," she added with a giggle, "so I knowed the water I'd first fetched would be cold enough to put goose bumps on your skin."

"Thank you, Lizzie. Next time, though, don't you haul those pails up from the serving pantry. They're too heavy for you. Get one of the men to carry them. Or I'll come down for them myself."

"I don't deserve your kindness, sir." She dropped him a curtsy. Something in her tone caused John to look at her more closely, and he saw at once that she was flirting with him in a manner far more subtle than he had ever observed in the trollops of the waterfront.

Sudden desire came alive as he realized it would be easy enough to close the door and make love to the girl here and now. Yet, at almost the same instant, he knew it would be wrong to take advantage of someone in the employ of Aunt Lydia and Uncle Thomas. Certainly he found the girl attractive, and considered it possible, if not probable, that she was drawn to him, too. But there were principles at stake.

The girl might be flirting with him because he was the heir to a fortune and she wanted a fat purse. In that case, she was no better than the harbor bawds. There was another possibility that struck him, too. Perhaps she had set her cap for him, and hoped to inveigle him into marriage. He had no intention of taking a wife until he had earned a post of responsibility in the Hancock enterprises. And when that day came, in spite of his talk about equality, he intended to marry a lady, someone of breeding who would feel at home in a mansion.

Above all, he had to admit as he squelched the urge to take the girl in his arms, there was something positive to be said for the point of view that Aunt Lydia always preached. A gentleman would be unworthy of his heritage if he crossed invisible but sharply defined boundaries. He could take lessons in fist-fighting from Dan Fowler, exchange rough, good-natured insults with him and even drink ale with him everyday. But both of them knew there was a difference in their social standing, and that someday Dan would be in John's employ. The knowledge was implicit in their friendship.

It wasn't even remotely possible to establish a similar understanding with the girl. If he made her his mistress, she would expect privileges, even demand them. She would confide in some of the other servants, the word would spread and the discipline of the entire staff would be undermined. The authority of Aunt Lydia would be weakened, and Uncle Thomas might lose some measure of his standing, in the city as well as at home, if the story leaked out. Worst of all, John knew, the whole household would think of him as an easy mark and would snicker at him behind his back.

Regretfully, but with a firm hand, he waved the serving maid out of the tub room.

Her expression changed from one of coy expectancy to blazing hatred, and she glared hard at him as he closed and bolted the door behind her.

The world was full of people like Lizzie, John reflected as he climbed into the tub, soaped himself and then sat down in the steaming water to scrub and rinse. Nothing he had learned at Harvard had prepared him for the clever greed of those who wanted to slip their hands into his purse. For every honest Dan Fowler who lived according to his own concepts of right and wrong and preferred to earn a man's friendship by smashing him in the jaw, there were scores of sycophants who flattered, cajoled, and tried to insinuate themselves in the good graces of the wealthy.

John stepped out of the tub, shivering, and dried himself with a rough towel, rubbing his skin far more vigorously than necessary. He was beginning to understand at last why Uncle Thomas had chosen to send him onto the wharves to begin his apprenticeship. The rich had problems as pressing as those of the poor, and a knowledge of human nature could be gleaned only through experience.

Johnny Adams, his boyhood friend who was now spending his last year as a Harvard undergraduate, was wrong when he said that a man could master the accumulated wisdom of mankind if he read diligently enough.

Instinct, not the written word, had prompted John to suspect that Lizzie was a bawd. He would do well in the future to follow Dan Fowler's advice and keep his guard raised high at all times.

4

A white blanket of snow covered the rocky Massachusetts fields and the surf pounded against the shoreline of Boston Bay, sending showers of icy spray high in the air. The Post Road was glazed, making the footing treacherous, but John Hancock and Johnny Adams were at ease in their saddles as they rode south from Boston to Braintree. At the ages of seventeen and nineteen, respectively, they were long accustomed to New England winters, and the ice, cold, and snow held no terrors.

"In my last letter home," Adams said, holding the reins under an arm as he blew on his mitten-covered hands, "I dropped a few broad hints. I said I'd spent the whole autumn term at Harvard dreaming of blood pudding and wild turkey with sausage dressing for Christmas dinner. I reckon the family will oblige me, even though nobody else cares much for sausage dressing."

"If there's any left after dinner," John replied, ducking as a mound of wet snow dropped onto his shoulder from an overhanging tree branch, "I can always drop over and eat it before it spoils. I wouldn't want your mother's efforts to be wasted."

"I'd forgotten that you like it, too. Why didn't you write home, as I did? Not that the Hancock cooks in Boston can't prepare any dish you want, but country dishes taste best when they're cooked in country kitchens."

"My stepfather," John said, sounding a trifle strained, "suffers from indigestion. So my mother cooks very plain meals for our whole family. He preaches about hell-fire and damnation so often that he's swallowed too much brimstone by now. Take a word of advice, Johnny, and don't go to services on Christmas morning. The Reverend Daniel Perkins will be at his best. He'll deliver a sermon more lugubrious than you've ever heard preached at Harvard. And as he doesn't give a hang about food, he'll talk for at least two or three hours. I haven't decided in my own mind whether he doesn't know the congregation is hungry or whether he's punishing his parishioners for the sins he's sure they're going to commit someday."

Young Adams looked covertly at his friend, but said nothing. John became very busy brushing snow from his shoulder.

It was difficult to make light conversation, but Adams tried. "I suppose you'll take your sister and brother skating."

"Of course. And sledding. I'll teach them to cut an Indian hole in the ice of the West Pond so they can fish the way we did when we were younger. I expect to go for some walks in the woods, and although I've never cared much for hunting, I'll probably try my luck with the musket that my father left me in his will. 'I bequeath my Holy Bible, my gold watch and my musket to my beloved son, John Hancock, III.' That's what he wrote, and it's right there in black and white. You aim to be a lawyer, so you know they can't dispose of the property. They're keeping the things for me until I'm twenty-one, and I suppose they hope I'll forget. But there's nothing wrong with my memory."

Adams coughed discreetly and warmed his hands again.

"I guess my visit won't be too hard to swallow this time. I'll only be here for five days." John blurted out the words before he could stop himself.

"Hasn't your uncle closed down his business for two full weeks, the way every other merchant in Boston has done?"

"Officially, yes." John brightened. "But it so happens that the Royal Customs office will be closed, too. So it may be that some dark evening, early next week, a ship from the West Indies may tie up at the Hancock Wharf. Cargo handlers who know how to keep their mouths shut have been told to be ready for a night of hard work. The holds will have to be emptied before dawn."

Adams' solemn eyes widened. "Then the stories I've heard about Thomas Hancock are true. He's a smuggler."

"Everybody in Boston knows it, even the Royal Collector of the Port. Just don't quote me." John shrugged and grinned.

His friend was dumfounded. "But that's breaking the law!"

"Uncle Thomas objects to paying a heavier tax than Parliament levies on merchants in England. He says he intends to balance the scales of justice in his own way until the House of Commons comes to its senses."

"Under the terms of a statute passed in the reign of George I," Adams said, "he can be prosecuted under criminal as well as civil law. Only three years ago the Lord Chief Justice denied the appeal of a merchant down in Kingston, Jamaica, who was caught smuggling."

"Uncle Thomas doesn't get caught," John said cheerfully, increasing his horse's pace as they came to a dry stretch of road. "He's forgotten more tricks than the Royal Customs people will ever learn. Besides, he's on such friendly terms with everyone in authority—from the Governor down—that nobody tries very hard to catch him. Don't forget that we wouldn't have captured the citadel up at Louisburg up in French Canada or beaten the French fleet, either, during King George's War, if Uncle Thomas hadn't had plenty of provisions and gunpowder in his storehouses."

"I can't deny that he's a farsighted man with a knack for making money, and I certainly wouldn't expect you to be disloyal to him." Questions of principle and ethics excited Adams, and he leaned forward in his saddle. "But you can certainly see there's a legal and moral problem involved."

"Oh, Uncle Thomas goes to bed with a clear conscience. I can hear his snores all the way up in my room."

"All the same, the law is the law. The Commons has passed certain measures, and the Lord Chief Justice has confirmed their validity. If Master Hancock doesn't think the law is equitable, he should send a petition to Parliament, asking for a redress of his rightful grievances."

"He told me once that he tried petitioning the Commons through his London agents. He's going to give me the correspondence to read when I'm moved from the docks into the office next year. But I can tell you, even without reading the papers, that words do no good in a situation of this sort, Johnny. The Commons sits three thousand miles from Boston, and I doubt if as many as three members have ever visited the colonies." John pointed toward a patch of dark elms, pines, and cedar, and laughed. "Do you remember that instructor in rhetoric who came over to us from Oxford two years ago? He kept imagining there were savages lurking behind every tree. If you ask me, Parliament feels the same way, and so does the rest of England. They think we're all heathens who live in the wilderness."

"I remember Dr. Browning." Adams did not smile. "I also recall that he went back to England because your class made life miserable for him. There wasn't a day passed in peace. Your whole class was involved in finding new ways to torment the poor fellow."

"He deserved it," John said firmly. "You didn't attend any of his lectures."

"I had no chance. By the time the class of '54 finished with him, he'd resigned."

"He was patronizing. He looked down that thin nose of his, and I honestly believed he saw Indian feathers sticking up from the head of every student who recited for him. I'll admit we aren't as sophisticated or as polished as Englishmen who live in the Mother Country. But we're Englishmen, too, and anyone who laughs at us will get what's coming to him."

"No one denies us our basic rights," his friend said quietly. "You get yourself worked up over nothing."

"Maybe, maybe not," John replied grudgingly. "All I know is that Massachusetts and Virginia—and even Pennsylvania—are as good as Kent and Sussex and Cornwall. And I'll take on anybody who claims otherwise in a free-for-all, with no holds barred."

Adams diplomatically dropped the subject. He knew from experience that John invariably became belligerent on the ride to Braintree, and it was better by far to give him no excuse to lose his temper.

<h1 style="text-align:center">5</h1>

Mary Hawke Perkins sat close to the small fire that burned in the grate of the cramped chamber that had been her late, first husband's study and that she now used as a sewing room. She patted her limp, graying hair with a callused hand and reached for her tea. There was no sound in the room but the hissing of the fire as she studied her eldest child over the rim of her cup. "You look more like a Hancock every time I see you, John." She made the comment as an unadorned statement of fact, and obviously did not intend it as a compliment.

But John half-rose from his straight-backed chair and bowed. "I thank you, ma'am," he said stiffly.

"Thomas and Lydia still spoil you, I see." She made no attempt to conceal her avarice. "That suit must have cost five gold sovereigns if it cost a ha'penny. And the lace on your shirt is worth a guinea."

"We import it from a Flemish lacemaker in Brussels who charges us twenty-seven shillings per yard." His tone was impersonal, his manner stiff. Certainly he saw no reason to explain to his mother that his suit of gray broadcloth with green velvet revers and a matching waistcoat was the only good clothing he owned, and that he needed one gentleman's suit to wear when Aunt Lydia and Uncle Thomas entertained guests. Nor did he care to tell her that the shirt had been made for his uncle, who had taken a sudden aversion to lace, and that consequently it had been cut down for him.

Mrs. Perkins' sigh seemed to hang suspended in the air. "I don't dare hope you brought me a length."

He refrained from mentioning that he knew Aunt Lydia had sent her a generous gift of four yards when the shipment had arrived. "I'm paid wages of ten shillings per week, ma'am. If I'm lucky I'll be granted an increase of five shillings when I'm promoted to apprentice clerk this coming October."

Mrs. Perkins sniffed, and her nostrils looked pinched. "I'm sure you lack for nothing, John."

"I have no complaints." He paused and, unable to resist the temptation, said lightly, "Dick Perkins and Mary were telling me this morning, when I took them sledding, that Reverend Perkins gets an extra one hundred and fifty pounds a year from his congregation now." No matter how hard he tried, he couldn't force himself to call his stepfather Reverend Dan, as the family wanted.

"I do hope you weren't prying information from your sister and Richard!" Mrs. Perkins sounded defensive.

"They volunteered the information, ma'am. They're proud of Reverend Perkins." John sat erect, stung by the suggestion that he might have used children to spy out his stepfather's private business.

"They have every right to be proud. He does the Lord's work for a pittance."

"He earns half again as much as my father made," John said pointedly.

"Prices go higher every year." His mother immersed herself in a great sea of self-pity. "I sometimes wonder how wealthy parishioners like Edmund Quincy and old John Adams expect us to live decently."

"In Boston," John said quietly, "prices have dropped since the end of King George's War, and are still dropping. I thought the same was happening here. I stopped in at Master Quincy's store yesterday and I noticed that iron kettles are selling for two shills and sixpence lower than Uncle Thomas charges. A ball of wool yarn is a thruppence less here, and even strained whale oil for lamps is lower. As to meats and vegetables, I know Aunt Lydia often says she envies you the prices you pay at country markets."

"I'll thank you and Lydia to let me stretch our little income as best as I can, in my own way."

It was difficult for John to remain civil, but he reminded himself forcibly that this greedy woman was his mother and therefore deserved at least his token respect. "No offense meant, ma'am, and I assure you that Aunt Lydia has great admiration for you."

"As well she should." Mrs. Perkins realized her remark was cryptic, and amplified it. "If I had tens of thousands of pounds, I could afford to speak charitably of poor relations, too."

"She's a frugal housekeeper, ma'am." John's temper inched toward the bursting point. "And I needn't remind you that she and Uncle Thomas not only took me into their home but adopted me to help relieve you of your burden."

"You earn your keep, I'm sure. The very idea of the richest man in the New World paying you only ten shillings a week! Thomas is exploiting you!"

Her talent for twisting facts to fit her own warped outlook was unlimited, and John's anger vanished in a burst of laughter. "Apprentices' wages are set by law, ma'am. If I'm not mistaken, Reverend Perkins was a member of the Massachusetts General Assembly the year the fee was established."

For a moment his mother had no adequate reply, but rallied quickly. "Have I no right to protest in behalf of my own flesh and blood?"

John dug his fingernails into the palms of his hands and kept his jaws tightly closed. Time had not eased the sharpness of the pain he felt at having been abandoned by his mother to relatives within a few months of her remarriage. He had learned to love Aunt Lydia and Uncle Thomas deeply, but his affection for them in no way replaced the emptiness of his relationship with the woman who had brought him into the world.

He knew that nothing he could say or do would change Mary Hawke Perkins' outlook on life. He had to accept as final the ugly fact that she felt no maternal love for her firstborn, who had become a symbol of the Boston Hancocks in her eyes. She would use him, if she could, as she used Uncle Thomas and Aunt Lydia, and only a miracle would force her to open her heart to him. Someday, perhaps, if he became sufficiently powerful and wealthy in his own right, she might learn to respect his worth, and that respect might in turn lead to affection. His hopes weren't high, but he could cling to little else.

In the meantime, it was necessary that he accept the world as it was, and be grateful for his place in it. There were scores of ambitious young men in Massachusetts—and in every other colony—who would gladly give years of their lives to become the adopted son of Boston's great merchant prince.

"I've brought you a message," he said, changing the subject abruptly. "Uncle Thomas will write you confirmation when his letter clerk returns to work after the holidays." He paused dramatically, knowing he had her full attention. "Eb's education is assured. Uncle Thomas will pay for his tuition and board at Harvard." It was his private opinion that his young brother, Ebenezer, showed no aptitude for book learning, and that a college education would be wasted on him.

If Mrs. Perkins appreciated the generosity of her late husband's brother, she didn't show it. "Will he be taken into the company, too?" she asked.

Life in the Beacon Hill mansion had taught John his uncle's habit of raising a cautious barrier to ward off the outstretched hands of the grasping. "Eb might want to become a physician or a lawyer," he said. "It could be he'll find he has a leaning toward the clergy, like Pa." He could not bring himself to pay his stepfather an easy, obvious compliment. "Uncle Thomas is a prudent man. He'll want to discover Eb's talents before he commits himself beyond paying for his schooling."

His mother bit her lower lip, and seemed lost in thought.

"I'll take word back to Uncle Thomas that you're most thankful to him," John said with heavy irony.

Mrs. Perkins was unaware of it. She hitched her chair closer to her son's and lowered her voice. "Strictly between us, I want you to tell me how I can call Richard to Thomas' attention."

Never had John's vision been so adult, and never had he been made more uncomfortable by his mother's unsatiable appetites. "Master Hancock," he said formally, "likes to find things out for himself."

Mrs. Perkins sensed his rebuke, and swiftly withdrew before retaliating. "I never dreamed you'd be so selfish that you'd want to keep that fortune to yourself."

He was exasperated. "You must think Uncle Thomas keeps stacks of gold in an iron strongbox. Well, he doesn't. His money is tied up in merchandise stored in warehouses and in ships at sea. If France declared war on us and sank his ships, he'd have nothing left but his house and personal belongings. It's a damnsight harder to keep and build a fortune than it is to make one in the first place. And I don't mind telling you I dread the day when I'll take over the business."

"Your father never cursed in my presence, nor has your stepfather."

He didn't realize he had used offensive language, and was inclined to believe she was trying to put him on the defensive. But it was easier to apologize than haggle. "I beg your pardon. And don't you worry about Dick Perkins. He's a bright boy, and he'll make out fine in the world."

Afraid to make a permanent foe of the hard-eyed youth who had become a stranger to her, Mrs. Perkins changed her tactics. "I'm so pleased to hear that you appreciate Richard. With your help I'm sure he can go far."

John liked his stepbrother, but could not accept a debt that he would have to repay at some far-off time. "I'm not in a position to help anybody, and I won't be for years—if ever. After I finish my apprenticeship the directors will decide whether they want to elect me to the board. I'll have to prove my own worth before I do anything for Dick. Or Eb," he added as a quick afterthought.

"I'm sure Thomas denies you nothing." Mrs. Perkins' smile was deprecating, and she waved aside his explanation of his position.

John laughed and slapped his knee, almost upsetting his own, untouched cup of tea, which was too weak for his taste. His mother wouldn't believe that he neither asked nor received favors from Uncle Thomas, who lectured him every morning at breakfast and on the carriage ride to the waterfront on the intricacies of the business, but seldom addressed a word to him on any other subject. "I walk home from Hancock Wharf every night," he said, chuckling again, "because I'm so covered with dirt and dust that I'd soil the silk upholstery of the coach."

Mrs. Perkins looked him up and down slowly, taking in every elegant detail of his attire, and the expression in her eyes made it plain she thought he was lying.

Again he changed the subject. "I have another message for you. Aunt Lydia wants me to bring Mary back to Boston with me for a visit until she goes back to school after the holidays."

"She's too young to travel home alone."

"Of course, ma'am. You can rely on it that she'll be given a satisfactory escort." He had already told his sister, swearing her to secrecy, that she would return to Braintree on board a Hancock brig, spending a whole night on board. Mary loved the sea, and the prospect thrilled her. But, it suddenly occurred to John, he was like his mother in one respect: she, too, distrusted ships.

"I'm afraid the stepdaughter of a poor small-town minister doesn't have the clothes for such a visit. She'd disgrace Lydia on visits to the grand ladies of Boston."

It was too great an effort to keep holding his annoyance in check. "People in Boston wear the same kind of clothes that folks wear here," he said, cruelly provoking her disappointment so he could watch her face fall. But a sense of guilt overwhelmed him as soon as the words were out of his mouth. No matter how much his mother hurt him, she was the one person on earth he couldn't strike in return. "Aunt Lydia," he added quickly, "will buy Mary a complete new wardrobe."

Mrs. Perkins' face cleared at once. "I've prayed that Lydia and Thomas would take notice of her, and now the Almighty has heard me! By all means, take her with you on Thursday."

John's stomach turned over and he made a rapid decision. "There must be a slight misunderstanding, ma'am." He took a deep breath and shaved a day off his visit. "I'm expected in Boston in time for dinner on Wednesday."

His mother accepted the loss with an indifferent shrug. "Noon dinner or evening dinner?"

John hesitated, trying to remember what social events his aunt and uncle might have planned for Wednesday. It was possible they might not appreciate the premature arrival of a little niece who would require a great deal of attention. On the other hand, there were enough servants in the house to look after a whole army of relatives. "Noon dinner," he said.

Mrs. Perkins drained her cup, found that the kettle was empty and stood. "I'll brew some more in the kitchen," she said. "Wait for me here, and we'll continue our talk. We have so few chances to speak to each other any more." Her sigh, intended for his benefit, was cut off sharply. "John, you're wasting your tea. We can't afford extravagances in this house."

He took a deep breath, then gulped down the luke-warm brew that tasted like faintly flavored water.

His mother looked at him reproachfully as she went off to the kitchen.

John moved closer to the fire, but could scarcely feel its warmth. Perhaps it was true that years of living in a mansion had spoiled him, and he braced himself for an inevitable round of sermons at dinner tonight from his mother—and Reverend Perkins. But he couldn't believe he had become as sybaritic as they painted him. It was true that he loved the luxuries that were commonplace in the great house on Beacon Hill, but there was no valid reason for the self-induced penury that made day-to-day existence under the Perkins' roof so miserable.

The place was chilly from autumn until spring, and he felt certain the others were always hungry, as he was, when they arose from the dinner table. Their miserliness was absurd. Even paupers kept warm by carting home free firewood from the deep forest southwest of Braintree. The poorest families grew their own potatoes, onions, Indian *asqutasquash*, and corn in their back yards, and he remembered vividly that he himself had tended such a patch under his father's benevolent direction when he had been a small boy. There were lobsters for the taking in the sea, and the tides washed up clams and mussels and crabs onto the beaches of Braintree.

Wild plums and raspberries grew in the woods in summer, there were trout in the Neponset River and fresh-water mackerel in West Pond. No one in the New World ever went hungry, as even the most poverty-stricken, debt-riddled English townsmen and farm laborers knew. Each year larger waves of immigrants arrived in the colonies, and soon discovered for themselves that they were in a land of plenty.

But in this house there was never enough to eat. Crouching before the fire, John was tempted to empty the contents of the wood basket into it. But it was better to stay cold than endure still another lecture. What irritated him beyond measure was the realization that even if he went off into the forest, carted back the trunks of three dead oaks and chopped them into firewood, Daniel and Mary Hawke Perkins wouldn't be satisfied.

How they loved their "principles," John thought angrily. It accomplished no useful purpose to waste his energy feeling annoyed over circumstances he was powerless to change, however, and he tried to follow Uncle Thomas' often-repeated advice to direct his thinking into productive channels.

A feeling of pity for Mary and Dick—and even stupid Eb— gave him pause. Instead of feeling sorry for himself because his mother and stepfather had grasped an opportunity to get rid of him so they would have one less mouth to feed, he ought to thank the Almighty every day of his life that he had escaped into a world of opportunity that would be limited only by his own wisdom, foresight, and patience—or lack of them.

Yet it wasn't quite enough that he himself was free. Through no fault of his, he had moved on into a happier realm. His sister, brother, and stepbrother were still here, and he owed it to himself as well as to them to do everything in his power for them.

Mrs. Perkins returned, a steaming kettle in one hand, a cup and saucer in the other. "You won't believe this," she said, "but I'm still using the little box of tea that Lydia sent me last summer."

Looking at the almost colorless liquid pouring out of the spout, John could well believe it. "May I have another cup?" he asked politely.

Perhaps she didn't fill his cup grudgingly. It was possible that he was doing her an injustice, and that she was merely surprised.

If it accomplished nothing else, the hot water warmed him. "Delicious," he murmured, and believed he had cured himself of his hatred.

TWO

1760 — 1761

1

In 1755 the peace of Europe was destroyed when a savage new conflict, later to be called the Seven Years' War, erupted suddenly, and once again England and France became enemies. Hostilities were resumed in the New World, too, and the French and Indian War, as it was known, was the most vicious in the history of North America.

For the first time whole regiments and even brigades of colonial militia from Massachusetts in the north to Georgia in the south marched into battle side by side with scarlet-uniformed British regulars. And for the first time local leaders gained renown beyond the borders of their own home colonies. When General Edward Braddock, the English commander who knew nothing of wilderness warfare, led his troops into an enemy ambush and paid for his fault with his own life, a young militia colonel from Virginia reorganized the dispirited corps and miraculously led the Anglo-colonial forces to safety. Schoolboys in Boston and Trenton, Baltimore and Charleston sang the praises of Colonel George Washington. In Philadelphia a remarkably peripatetic intellectual, Benjamin Franklin, was gaining world renown as an author, editor and publisher, scientist, inventor and man of letters who inspired a new generation of college students to think of themselves as

Americans. Simultaneously, almost by accident, he created new respect for the colonies in English political circles.

For three years England and her colonies had little reason to cheer. The French captured one frontier fort after another, Indian raiders killed, burned, and looted almost at will, and terror was universal. Then, gradually, the tide turned. A column of redcoats and colonials took Fort Duquesne in the west and renamed it Pittsburgh. Montcalm, the ablest of the French generals in the New World, was killed in a bitter, futile defense of Quebec. Wolfe, the English victor, lost his life there, too, but the Anglo-colonial forces continued to gain momentum. General Jeffrey Amherst, the British commander-in-chief, forced the enemy to withdraw from Fort Ticonderoga in New York and then captured Montreal. Fort Detroit fell to a regiment of colonial irregulars. The Indian allies of the French deserted in large numbers, and for all practical purposes the war in the New World was won by 1760.

Men in the cities and hamlets tallied their achievements, proudly discovered a new identity and became restless under wartime restrictions imposed on them by administrators in London. Citizens whose taxes had paid for virtually all military operations in North America grumbled because Parliament insisted they support the continuing struggle in Europe.

A young Massachusetts radical, James Otis, created a sensation in a speech delivered before the Supreme Court of Massachusetts when he demanded that the colonies be allowed to govern themselves. If England refused, he declared, the colonies had the right to proclaim their independence. Responsible citizens considered Otis mad, and only a few visionaries like Sam Adams of Boston, an author of essays and political pamphlets who called himself "an ink-stained wretch" took Otis' wild proposals seriously and dared to support him.

Meanwhile John Hancock continued to serve his long apprenticeship in his uncle's mercantile empire, learning every phase of a business that was expanding at a fantastic rate. The far-sighted Thomas Hancock doubled his fortune, then doubled it again, and by 1760 had become so wealthy he confessed that he himself didn't know how much he was worth.

British and colonial troops ate food that their quartermasters bought at Hancock-owned granaries. Their uniforms were cut from bolts of cloth purchased at Hancock's warehouses. Their muskets came from Hancock arsenals, their gunpowder and ammunition from hastily erected Hancock factories. Thomas became so powerful that he was the only man in the colonies who blithely ignored Parliament's order prohibiting the manufacture of cannon in the New World; three of his foundries made brass guns that, more often than not, did not explode when fired.

Twenty-two merchant ships flying the house banner of two crossed keys on a field of pale blue sailed unceasingly between Boston, London, and the West Indies. Their missions were legitimate, and Thomas estimated that approximately half of the more than one and one-half million inhabitants of the colonies used goods that had been transported in the holds of his vessels.

He also engaged in unpublicized trade, the details of which he confided only to his chief clerk, Elias Wheaton, and his nephew, who had learned to keep his mouth shut. It was rumored that Thomas was the owner or part-owner of scores of rakish merchantmen that specialized in raiding French brigs and brigantines on the high seas. These ships then came to Boston, it was said, docking after dark. And in direct defiance of the law, which specified that the Crown should receive fifty percent of the booty, the cargo disappeared in the vast recesses of Hancock warehouses, and the Crown was left emptyhanded.

No one could prove that these stories were true, but it was generally believed that these clandestine operations were directed by John Hancock, who appeared to be a model of sober virtue. Hancock Wharf, which had been lengthened, and two smaller piers recently constructed to its north were busy places at least one or two nights each week. Small torches could be seen burning as far away as Beacon Hill, and shadowy figures moved between the decks of dark ships and the wharves. But the curious who wanted to learn more about these clandestine operations were not allowed to approach the area. Husky men armed with spars sent them on their way, and even the Royal Collector of the Port decided not to test his authority. A handsome new carriage, a gift from Thomas imported from England at great expense, made the Collector's life easier to bear, and if his conscience troubled him, that was his own concern.

Merchants who gathered at the Bunch of Grapes and other expensive taverns occasionally noted straws in the wind that made them reasonably certain the smuggling rumors were true. Dan Fowler, the Hancock dock foreman, who now supervised gangs several times the size of those who had worked for him during peacetime, bought himself a fine new house on Treamount Street, one of the most fashionable thoroughfares in the city. No other man of his class could afford to pay the price of such a home. Lydia Hancock appeared at a harpsichord recital in the Town Meeting House wearing a new gown of material that the discerning immediately recognized as French silk. Other bolts, it was whispered, had been sent to merchants in Philadelphia and New York Town under armed guard.

John inadvertently provided the gossips with their most important clue. He was now sufficiently advanced in his apprenticeship to eat in taverns and inns frequented by the gentry, but appeared in them rarely. Asked one day why he preferred the Pequot or the Golden Ball, which were popular with sailors and cargo handlers, he replied succinctly, "I've developed a taste for French wines."

He refused to elaborate, but the city's merchants and shipowners jumped to rapid conclusions. Quantities of contraband wine were kept at the waterfront establishments for his personal use, they told each other, and as neither the Collector nor his assistants ever visited these low-class places, his secret was safe. John, like his uncle, went quietly about his business, and no one dared to press him too closely for more information. No banker or merchant wanted to jeopardize his own financial security by making enemies of the wealthiest family in all North America.

Thomas and his principal partner, Charles Apthorp, continued to make all major decisions regarding the company's interests, but John was almost universally regarded as a man of considerable power, even though his apprenticeship had not yet ended. The mothers of eligible daughters greeted him warmly on the infrequent occasions when he accepted invitations to dinners and receptions, but their efforts were a waste of time. The more perspicacious noted that he invariably brightened in the presence of attractive young ladies, but he refused to call on any of them.

Some believed he thought himself too good for them, and

others said that Lydia Hancock held him on too tight a leash. Both groups were wrong. He worked a minimum of sixteen hours per day, and literally had no time to develop a social life.

Some of his personal habits seemed odd to the gentry, too, but he satisfied himself that his reasons for his behavior were valid, and didn't care what anyone else thought. His routine on the morning of March 20, 1760, was typical. He and Thomas ate breakfast together in their dressing gowns, and their conversation was devoted only to the company's immediate problems. No other subject was allowed to intervene.

After fortifying themselves with molasses-sweetened porridge, cold salt cod and broiled beefsteaks, which they washed down with ale and strong tea, they went their separate ways. A quarter of an hour later John emerged from the Hancock mansion, resplendent in a suit of ivory-colored silk and knee-high boots, a feathered hat and a long cloak of wool broadcloth trimmed with a beaver collar and lined in red silk. He knew that people gaped at him and placed wagers on the color of the suit he wore each day and, enjoying the stir he created, he walked briskly down Beacon Hill, one hand on the silver hilt of the smallsword of Spanish steel that Aunt Lydia and Uncle Thomas had given him in January on his twenty-fourth birthday.

He paused near the foot of Treamount Street to pick up Dan Fowler, who was waiting for him, and they walked together with long strides down King Street toward the waterfront. John knew that several English members of the Governor's staff and visitors from other colonies thought it odd that a magnificently attired dandy and a burly ruffian in shabby work clothes should appear to be such close friends, but their opinions were of no interest to him.

This was the best time of day for him to discuss the unloading of illegal freebooters' cargo with Dan. And, as he was putting a little too much flesh on his bony frame, he enjoyed the exercise. Once he reached his desk, he would be chained to his stool for the better part of the day.

Promptly at seven-thirty he reached the office, waved goodbye to Dan and looked at his gold pocket watch. As always, he was so punctual that a young apprentice watching for him from a second-story window set the office clock. At that moment Thomas' carriage rolled up to the entrance, and the head of the house descended to the street that had been paved with cobblestones for his convenience. Both acted as though they had not seen each other earlier in the day.

John bowed low, removing his hat with a flourish and avoiding dragging its feathers on the mud-spattered cobblestones by no more than an inch or two. Thomas nodded pleasantly and walked into the building, his nephew deferentially standing aside. Then, while the older Hancock went straight to his second-floor office, John walked through the retail store to the warehouse at the rear. The company now owned eight newer, larger storage buildings, but this warehouse was still important.

French tapestries and pipes of wine, pickled beef and other foodstuffs that had been carried ashore the previous night from a buccaneer ship lucky enough to capture a French brig in mid-Atlantic were hidden beneath sheets of heavy canvas. John drew his sword and raised each piece of canvas with its point so he would not soil his clothes while he inspected the merchandise. A junior clerk who had silently joined him checked each item against a manifest, and when the inspection was completed John scribbled his signature at the bottom of the paper.

"Have the wagons arrived?" he asked.

"They're pulling up in the back alley now, Master Hancock," the clerk replied.

"Good. Have them loaded immediately, and remind the caravan master that I want a signed receipt when he delivers the cargo to our friends in New Haven." John walked quickly to the staircase, climbed to the second floor and exchanged greetings with Elias Wheaton, who was just taking off his greatcoat.

They sat down side by side at high, adjoining desks and climbed onto identical stools. The efficient Wheaton reached for a pile of correspondence which he intended to study, but looked up when he realized that John, who never squandered time, was staring out of the window in the direction of the harbor. Wheaton cleared his throat, John inclined his head in the direction of the window and they climbed down from their stools to walk to it, out of earshot of the junior clerks and apprentices.

"It was so dark and cloudy last night," John said in a troubled voice, "that I couldn't really see the French merchantman that a

34

prize crew from the buccaneer brought in last night. Look at her out there, tied up just beyond the freebooter. See what I mean?"

"She stands out like a boil on a dwarf's nose." Wheaton ran a hand through his thinning hair.

"Her stern is rounded instead of square, which immediately identifies her as foreign, and her foremast is as tall as her mainmast, which is even worse. And that gilded female figure on her prow. Only the French would carve an almost-nude woman, and then paint her gold in the bargain to make certain everyone sees her!"

"Maybe she's one of King Louis' mistresses, John." Wheaton laughed grimly.

John squinted and shaded his eyes. "I don't admire his taste. She's too plump. And we may be pickled in brine before the day ends. There are fifty men in this town—maybe more—who'd like to see us trapped on a smuggling charge, and there's the evidence." He began to pace up and down, the high heels of his boots clicking on the hardwood floor.

Wheaton fell in beside him. "We'll have to round up a crew and send her out to sea."

John nodded in the direction of three large ships at anchor in the deeper waters of the outer harbor, all of them flying the Union Jack. "They'd be the first to challenge her. No, Eli. That would be asking for a summons to appear before the Admiralty Court."

"My trouble is that I lack the imagination to handle this sort of situation."

"I have too much for my own good." John grimaced and increased his pace. "Well, we've got to do something," he said at last. "Ask Dan to block off the wharf while I see my uncle, will you, Eli? And you might send a boy on the run to fetch ten of our best men from the south yard." Not waiting for a reply, he hurried to Thomas' office and tapped on the door.

The Croesus of the American colonies did not look up from a document he was reading.

John explained the problem, wasting no words. "Our usual procedure in a situation of this sort is to sail the foreigner out to sea. But Admiral Lord Howard's ship-of-the-line and two frigate escorts are anchored in the bay."

Thomas remained unruffled. "I'm glad you reminded me. His Excellency is holding a reception for Lord Howard at sundown today. Your aunt and I will expect you to go with us."

John realized he would have to find time to go home in order to change into a darker suit. Only an ignoramus who knew nothing of London fashions would appear at such an event in ivory satin. "The Admiral," he said, "may have us in irons by this evening."

"I'm afraid you haven't learned to curb your tendency to exaggerate in moments of minor crisis, lad."

John stiffened. "Let me remind you, sir, that Parliament's Maritime Act of '58 not only directs that all vessels captured from the enemy be given over to the Crown, but that individuals found guilty of evading this law shall be punished with one hundred strokes of the lash and life imprisonment."

"My memory seems in need of considerable jogging this morning." Thomas stroked his jowls with a plump hand. "How much is the Frenchie worth?"

"We couldn't duplicate her for two thousand pounds, sir."

"Mmm. We'd have to hand over half her cargo, as well."

"It's too late for that. The caravan is already on its way to New Haven." John lied deliberately, knowing full well that the wagons wouldn't be loaded for another hour. Perhaps success had made him callous to danger, but he hated to give up a valuable property without a struggle. He had yet to meet a Crown official he feared, and although Lord Howard was reputedly a martinet, it was unlikely that he could match wits with clever colonials.

"What's your solution, John?" It was Thomas' inflexible rule that employees should be prepared to suggest methods of handling every problem they brought to him.

"I've already taken ten carpenters from the coastal brig that Master Apthorp is building in the south yard. I'll think of some excuse to give him so he doesn't demand that the board convene to hear his grievances."

Thomas chuckled but did not interrupt.

"We'll saw off that gilded nude, give the ship a false stern and cut down her foremast by several feet so it has British lines. With luck they should be done by early this afternoon. In the meantime, I'll put a painter to work on a new nameplate. With your

36

permission, sir, I'd like to call her the *Mary Hancock,* as a birthday surprise for my sister."

"You're a sentimental rascal." Thomas nodded approvingly. "What will you do with the prize crew who sailed her here?" Sailors who talked too much in waterfront taverns after downing a few drinks had been responsible for a half-dozen arrests in the past year, and it was rumored that the Governor had hired several secret informers to keep their ears open at all times.

"Her captain is traveling to New Haven with the cargo caravan. He's carrying a coded letter I wrote last night to Colonel Parker, who owns a one-third interest in a brigantine we control that happens to be unloading at New Haven this week. The colonel will send him aboard immediately as second mate, and he won't be allowed on shore again. The brigantine," John added innocently, "will put into eight West Indian ports, so we have nothing to fear from the French ship's master."

"What about her crew?"

John fingered his silk stock and ruffled shirt front. "There was a mild flurry on the wharf last night, sir. I told Dan to send the sailors up to our sawmill in the Maine District for a few days, until one of our ships heading out to sea could pick them up. Buccaneers are a suspicious, ugly lot, so Dan and I had to convince them we meant what we said."

"Is that how you acquired the cut over your left eye?"

"What cut, sir?" John asked.

Thomas dismissed him with a genial wave. "I'll leave this entire matter in your hands," he said, and could have paid his nephew no higher compliment.

2

John's paperwork was necessarily neglected through the day. He spent the better part of the morning on the deck of the captured French ship, supervising the labor of the carpenters, and did not return to his desk until the task was finished. He was so far behind in making out bills of lading, writing to his uncle's London partner, Christopher Kilby, and double-checking the inventory of the company's arsenal at the frontier town of Springfield that he was afraid he would have no chance to change his clothes. In six and one-half years he had never left his post before the end of a work day, but had legitimate cause this afternoon. He couldn't shame himself and degrade the family name by appearing at an evening reception in clothes appropriate only for daytime wear.

Concentrating furiously, John completed his duplicate inventory and didn't bother to wash his hands before snatching his hat and cloak from a peg. He dashed down the stairs two at a time, buckling on his sword, and was so intent on hurrying home that he almost collided with Dan Fowler at the front door of the building.

Dan grasped his arm, and John tried to shake off the huge fist. "I'm on urgent business, Dan, so we'll talk tomorrow morning."

"This won't wait," Dan said harshly, propelling him into the street and pointing toward the north.

John gasped as he saw a solid sheet of flame rising high into the air about one hundred yards to the north on the waterfront.

"Skinner's warehouses are on fire," Dan shouted as an excited crowd began to gather.

John recovered quickly from his initial shock. A stiff wind was blowing down from the north, and he realized that Hancock properties would be endangered unless something was done at once to protect them. "Take all your men—and everybody else you can find—to our wool warehouse," he said to Dan. "Form a bucket brigade, send a gang up onto the roof and keep the whole building doused. If it's wet enough, the fire will stop there. I'll join you shortly."

Dan obeyed instantly, and began to bawl orders in a voice that could be heard above the uneasy murmurs of the crowd.

John raced out onto Hancock Wharf and, cupping his hands, called to the skeleton crews on guard duty aboard the merchantman docking there. "Cut your hawsers, cast off and put out into the harbor," he shouted, and when the startled seamen failed to respond fast enough, he began hacking at the cables with his smallsword.

Soon the sailors understood that the vessels would be far safer at a distance from flying sparks. There was no time to hoist sail, but the wind was strong enough to drive the brigs and brigantines from north to south when the lines were severed and the anchors weighed. The guards on the ships tied to the smaller Hancock piers followed the example of their colleagues, and in a short time every vessel flying the blue pennant was drifting out into the bay.

John stood for a few moments at the end of the long wharf, awed by the ferocity of the fire, which was leaping still higher. As soon as he had assured himself that all the company's ships were safe, he ran back to the street and pushed open the door of the Pequot, whose ale and rum-tippling patrons were unaware of the emergency.

"I'll pay a guinea in silver to every man who'll follow me!" he called.

Many of the merchant seamen and cargo handlers would have been happy to commit murder for that sum, and a mob raced behind John toward the wool warehouse, the Hancock building that stood closest to the conflagration.

Fowler and his gang were working diligently to halt the fire. Two lines had been formed, and water scooped from the harbor was passed from hand to hand and hoisted onto the roof, where Dan, aided by two others, dumped the contents of buckets onto the shingled roof and northern wall of the building.

John realized that many more containers were needed. "I'll pay another guinea in silver for every bucket you bring me," he shouted, then directed the bo's'n of a Hancock brig to form the newcomers into another double line.

Buckets and small barrels began to materialize, almost by magic, and three volunteers climbed onto the roof to join Fowler and his companions. John was so eager to speed the operation that he seized a small but heavy barrel and dipped it into the cold salt water. As he straightened he spilled half of the contents onto his handsome cloak, and ripped off the offending garment, throwing it onto the cobblestones.

He realized that more than five years had passed since he had last worked as a cargo handler and that his muscles had grown softer. Physical labor was best accomplished by men accustomed to it, so he made his way down the new lines to the building, shouting encouragement, and then, on sudden impulse, began to scale the wall so he could judge the speed of the approaching fire.

He was breathless by the time he scrambled onto the roof, and smoke made his eyes smart. He began to cough, too, and when he saw that the others had tied cloths over their faces, he ripped off his neckcloth, dipped it into a bucket that was being handed up to one of the cargo handlers and spread it over the lower portion of his face.

Tying the strip of silk at the back of his head, he started to make his way toward the north side of the roof. The shingles were slippery, his fashionable, absurdly high heels made it difficult for him to keep his balance, and twice he sprawled on the roof, ripping his suit. But at last he reached the edge and peered at the fire through narrowed, watering eyes.

The spectacle was terrifying. All three of the Skinner warehouses were being consumed, and a small brig tied to a pier was ablaze, too. Sparks driven by the wind stung John's flesh and burned his coat, but he felt no sense of personal danger. The almost vain hope of trying to save Hancock property worth at least twenty-five thousand pounds filled his mind.

"John, get to hell down to the ground," Fowler roared, his voice muffled by his mask. "Master Hancock will flay me alive if anything happens to you." The giant tirelessly emptied bucket after bucket onto the roof. "Get down there, or I'll heave you down!"

"Damn you, Fowler, don't give me orders!" John's voice was high, almost shrill, but his almost startling tone of authority silenced the foreman.

The fire was no more than fifty feet away now. The nearest of the Skinner warehouses was an inferno, and waves of blistering heat rolled across the men on the Hancock roof. The smoke was so thick that John could no longer see clearly, but he knew that in a few moments the flames would leap across the alleyway that separated the burning building from his uncle's property.

He conquered a rush of panic, pressed his hands against his temples and forced himself to think calmly. He believed it unlikely that the frantic effort being made by scores of men would save the wool warehouse, and if it went, the fire would engulf the entire waterfront.

More than Hancock property was threatened. The fire had to be halted at once, or the whole city of more than twenty thousand persons might go up in flames.

John made his way back to the far lip of the roof, stumbling and falling repeatedly, but at last he reached the edge and looked down. Hundreds of men were milling around on the cobblestones below. Clerks and ships' officers, dock workers and seamen, and dignified gentlemen stared helplessly at the approaching fire, simultaneously fascinated and appalled.

A British officer in scarlet caught John's eye, and he ripped off his mask. "You, there! Captain!" he shouted.

The men wrenched their attention from the fire to stare up at the figure on the roof.

"Break into the warehouse," John called. "Divert one of the bucket brigades and soak every bolt of cloth on the north side of the building." Even in this moment of crisis he could not allow himself to forget his uncle's property. "I'll rely on you to see there's no looting. And for the Almighty's sake, hurry!"

The British captain understood what was required of him, and with the aid of a lieutenant and two sergeants who came forward out of the crowd he worked with cool efficiency to reorganize the efforts of the fire fighters. Glass tinkled as windows were smashed, the door of the building was thrown open and scores of fresh volunteers joined the bucket brigade line. The two redcoat officers stood at the entrance with drawn swords to prevent anyone from stealing bolts of expensive cloth and the sergeants quietly loaded their muskets, then stood with their feet apart, ready to act instantly if the crowd turned into a greedy mob.

John, still lying on his stomach as he looked down over the edge of the roof, was proud of the redcoats, proud that he, too, was a British subject.

Suddenly the contents of a barrel were poured over him, and he was soaked to the skin. He hauled himself to his knees, shivering, and when he saw Dan towering above him, started to protest, but quickly changed his mind. The waves of heat were becoming still more intense, and when he saw that icy salt water was dripping from Dan, too, he realized that his friend's foresight might save him from serious injury.

One of the brigades continued to send water to the roof, while the other, following John's demand, moved buckets and barrels into the interior of the warehouse. The fire fighters were working with frenzied speed now, as the nearest of the Skinner warehouses had become an inferno. Casks of rum were stored there, and when they caught fire, great yellow tongues darted in every direction.

The men on the roof of the Hancock building poured more water on themselves and John, and although they were bone-tired, they could not pause for breath. Clouds of sooty smoke enveloped them, and they groped blindly for the buckets that were passed from hand to hand.

The Skinner building collapsed with a deafening roar. John tried to suck precious air into his lungs behind the sopping piece of silk cloth that he had retied over his face, but he could not get enough of it, and was afraid he might faint. Wet shingles on the roof sizzled like drops of water in a hot frying pan, and here and there pieces of the thick wood began to smoke ominously.

Fowler changed the tactics he had been employing, and the men now devoted themselves exclusively to the task of emptying their barrels and buckets of salt water onto spots that appeared on the verge of bursting into flames. One shingle caught fire a few feet from John, and he tried to stamp it out. But the fire grew and began to spread, so he ripped off his sopping coat, threw it down and managed to smother the flames.

The next quarter of an hour was an agony of suspense. Someone in the street below organized a third bucket brigade, and a half-dozen volunteers came onto the roof to help the weary men who doggedly, almost mechanically, continued to battle the fire. John, who had no specific responsibility, roamed from one side of the roof to the other, still using his wet coat as a blanket whenever he saw a shingle about to catch fire. At one point it occurred to him that if the north wall of the warehouse collapsed, he and his companions would plunge to a fiery death. But he refused to let himself dwell on the possibility. He needed his wits and his remaining strength to perform his self-appointed duty, and he knew this was a time for action, not contemplation.

The Skinner building was reduced to a glowing skeleton, but no one on the Hancock roof realized that the worst was over until they heard hoarse cheering from the street below. The heat had not yet subsided, however, so John dragged himself back to the ledge.

"Don't stop," he shouted, and was surprised to hear that the sound was a husky croak. "We still need water!"

The brigades functioned smoothly for another quarter of an hour or more. Then the officials who were now directing the operation in the street sent one brigade to throw water on the gutted remains of the Skinner building. Clouds of steam rose high in the air, a shower of wet cinders descended on the exhausted men still working on the Hancock roof and then, finally, the fire was brought under control.

One of the cargo handlers buried his face in his hands and wept. Another laughed, but the majority stood limp and silent, too dazed to move. Fowler was the first to speak.

"I reckon we aren't needed here any more," he said in a rasping voice. "Let's go below."

The men moved to the edge, and John insisted that the others precede him to the ground. Someone in the street raised a ladder, and the fire fighters made their way down one at a time, very slowly. When it was John's turn, he discovered that his hands were trembling and his knees so weak that they scarcely supported his weight. Then hands reached up and lifted him to the ground, someone handed him a glass of raw brandywine and he downed it in a single gulp.

Elias Wheaton, clutching a heavy burlap bag, was handing out silver coins to a jostling throng, keeping the promises John had made to the men who had joined him at the beginning of the fight. The entire constabulary force of the city was on hand, holding back a mammoth throng, and streams of fresh volunteers were coming forward to join the brigades working to extinguish the last of the fire on the Skinner property. The brig that had been unable to escape was still burning at her berth, and had been reduced to a glowing, smoking hulk. A dozen sailors were heaving buckets of water onto her smoldering deck so a stray spark wouldn't start a new outburst.

John recovered his breath, found Dan Fowler and solemnly shook the foreman's hand. Fowler's eyebrows had vanished, and most of his hair was gone, too. John raised a hand to his own face, and was surprised to discover that his skin was painfully tender. His eyebrows were badly singed, too, and when he looked down at himself he began to laugh. His clothes were a soggy, blackened mess, the sole of his right boot was burned so badly that it cracked when he bent down to examine it and there were more holes and rips in his shirt and breeches than he could count.

Thomas Hancock came up to them, so overcome by emotion that he could scarcely speak. "I don't know how to thank either of you," he said, his eyes suspiciously moist.

John had rarely seen his uncle so overwrought. "Don't try, sir," he replied, managing a weak grin. "You'll be less happy when you see the bolts of wool that have been ruined in there."

"I'm fortunate," Thomas said. "A loss of merchandise worth a few hundred pounds is negligible. If the fire hadn't been stopped, I'd be bankrupt, like David Skinner, the poor fellow." Something intangible in his manner indicated that he intended to make an offer for the two Skinner ships that were at sea, and for the gutted waterfront property. Even in a time of tragedy his business instincts were infallible.

John grinned more broadly.

"I'm afraid I'll be very late for the Governor's reception, but I'm sure that His Excellency and Lord Howard will forgive me. Are you coming with me, lad?"

John was surprised to discover that night had fallen. The very idea of going home to change his clothes for a formal function struck him as ludicrous under the circumstances, and he laughed. "If you will, sir, give them my regrets," he said, linking his arm through Dan's. "We're going to the Pequot for the biggest beefsteak pies in Boston." He turned and jabbed a smoke-blackened finger at the others who had worked with them on the roof. "Come along, boys," he shouted, his tone as jovial as his voice was hoarse. "Eat and drink as much as you want. The treat is on me!"

Thomas watched them as they moved off together to the tavern. His nephew was an astonishing young man. Certainly he didn't consider himself a hero, and apparently thought of his efforts as part of a day's work. Ordinarily so fastidious, he wasn't in the least bothered by his bedraggled appearance. And he was deliberately staying away from one of the season's most important social events to spend an evening with waterfront rowdies. To say the least, the heir to the most prosperous business in the British colonies was unpredictable.

3

A huge wave smashed over the prow of the packet brig, *Benjamin and Samuel*, and every timber in the ship's hull groaned in protest. She dipped into a trough, then rolled heavily to starboard as another wave struck her port side. The wind howled through her rigging, and heavy rain that mingled with salt spray made it impossible to see anything through the glass of the porthole.

John balanced himself as best he could in his chair and tried to concentrate on the letter he was writing. But the effort was too great. He was afraid his jar of ink would spill, and his table, which was just a board lowered from the bulkhead of his cabin, was so rickety he thought it would collapse at any moment. These, however, were just minor disturbances. What really mattered was that the heaving of the packet brig made him queasy, and he knew that, at any moment, he might become violently ill.

Captain Herbert, the master of the *Benjamin and Samuel*, had assured him when they had sailed from Boston that the Atlantic was always calm in June. But John hadn't believed a word. He had learned, long ago, that Hancock employees were anxious to tell Uncle Thomas' heir what they thought he wanted to hear.

Dipping his quill into the ink jar again, John stared down at the paper, but his mind refused to function. What could a man write to a young brother who would be dismissed from Harvard College if he failed to pass just one more course? For the past year he had lectured Ebenezer repeatedly, telling him he was lazy and careless, that it was wrong to stake his entire future on the hope that he would be remembered generously in Uncle Thomas' will and that his own attitude would determine his success or failure in life.

Ebenezer was a fool, but the knowledge didn't help settle John's insides, which seemed to rise and fall with the erratic motion of the ship. The letter would have to wait until the weather cleared.

John stood, fell against the bulkhead as the ship lurched and became angry with himself. His letters of introduction to Uncle Thomas' associates in London would be worthless and he would be the laughingstock of the whole business community there if he failed to appear at Captain Herbert's cabin for dinner tonight. A man who was expected to become the second-in-command of the Hancock enterprises—which were based on shipping interests—could not afford to become seasick.

Nor could the future owner of a large fleet rely on the discretion of Captain Herbert, his mates and his crew. If a Hancock became ill in a storm, the joke would be too good for them to keep after they arrived in London. John had heard too many tales about the condescension of Englishmen to colonials and had himself seen too many instances of English haughty superiority in Boston to lay himself open to ridicule—if he could help it.

He took his hat and light wool cloak from a peg, donned them and forced himself to walk out into the passageway. The motion of the ship seemed even more intense here, so he ran to the nearest hatch and climbed to the open deck above. The wind was raw, as sharp and cold as weather on a March day at home, and the rain fell steadily, soaking his hat and cloak. But the air was fresh, and he made his way to the rail, then leaned against it gratefully when his knees almost gave way beneath him.

The sea was an ugly gray-green, the briny foam that capped the towering waves looked dirty, almost muddy, and John knew he was not cut out for a sailor's life. In fact, as he quickly discovered, it was a mistake to watch the waves, as he became more conscious than ever of the packet brig's rocking and pitching. He gazed up at the leaden sky, unmindful of the rain beating on his face, and forced himself to watch huge, black clouds that moved eastward overhead at a faster pace than the ship was sailing.

He refused to let himself become ill, and continued to look up at the sky for a long time as he breathed deeply. One of the ancient Greek philosophers—it was difficult to identify him at the moment—had written that a man's mind was stronger than his body, and John believed it when his queasiness began to dissipate. Eventually, to his surprise, he felt well enough to walk around, and actually enjoyed himself as he made his way aft. Gusts of wind forced him to cling to the railing, but he found the experience exhilarating, and was able to wave casually with his free hand when Captain Herbert hailed him from the quarterdeck.

John remained on the deck until his teeth began to chatter, and then common sense told him to go below. He hummed a militia marching song under his breath as he changed into dry clothing. Miraculously refreshed, he returned to the desk, and knew now what to tell Ebenezer.

His quill flew as he wrote in his large, bold hand: *Only you can decide your future. Remember, Eb, that a man's mind is the strongest force on earth, even stronger than Nature herself.*

4

George William Frederick, Prince of Wales, Duke of Cornwall, Hereditary First Baron of Ireland and Lord Protector of Scotland, had the loudest laugh in all London. At the age of twenty-two he still whooped like a schoolboy, and the sound made the rafters ring at the Theatre Royal in the Haymarket. Tears were still streaming down his face as the curtain fell at the end of the first act of Henry Fielding's satirical drama, *Tom Thumb*. His Highness, the undisputed heir to the throne of his grandfather, George II, slapped his knee, struck a companion in the royal box such a hearty blow on the back that the man almost fell out of his chair, and then vigorously wiped his face with the sleeve of his brocaded satin suit.

John watched him covertly from the front box at the opposite side of the theatre and hastily revised his concepts of royalty. The Prince of Wales was as exuberant and uninhibited as any Harvard freshman. In fact, he looked so young that, if he weren't wearing the blue ribbon of the Order of the Garter across his chest, he could easily pass himself off as a newcomer to Harvard Yard.

Jonathan Barnard and Christopher Kilby, Thomas Hancock's English agents and trading partners, exchanged significant glances. Their young visitor had taken such pains to conceal his reactions to the sights of London that they were at their wits' ends, but perhaps they had finally found a way to please him.

Barnard touched him on the shoulder. "Would you like to meet the Prince?"

John blinked at him. "Do you know him, sir?" Uncle Thomas made it his business to be on friendly terms with the Governor of Massachusetts and other leading Crown authorities in Boston, but it seemed inconceivable that a middle-class merchant, no matter how wealthy, might be on speaking terms with the young man who stood nearest to the throne which would someday be his.

Barnard nudged Kilby, smiled and stood. "Come along."

John followed him, nervously adjusting his stock and smoothing his ruffled shirt front as they made their way around the rear of the theatre to the royal box. Had he known he would meet the Prince of Wales he would have insisted the Barnard and Kilby tailor finish making at least one of the six new suits he had ordered last week. Fortunately he was wearing one of the more splendid items in his Boston wardrobe, a suit of pearl-gray silk threaded with genuine silver that had been part of the booty taken in a raid on a French merchantman. He was lucky, too, that one of Boston's better artisans had refitted it for him in time for his visit to London.

Adjusting his hat to a more rakish angle, John walked with his left hand resting on the hilt of his smallsword, after the manner of stylish gentlemen he had seen strolling in the Mall. Suddenly he halted and froze, his temples pounding. The Prince was directly ahead of him, only a few paces away, standing outside his box. Then Barnard's informality made him even more confused.

"George, you rogue!" the merchant called jovially.

The Prince showed his large, yellow teeth when he smiled. "Barnard, you rascal! How are you, sir, and how is your lovely niece?"

"She returns from her sojourn in Amsterdam next week, sir." Barnard dragged the perspiring John forward. "Permit me to present Master John Hancock, sir."

John bowed very low, sweeping the floor with his hat. "This is a great honor, Your Highness." The tremor in his voice annoyed him.

George, Prince of Wales, scarcely bothered to recognize his existence. "You know, Barnard," he said, "I was just commenting to Lord Roberts here that the wench who came on stage at the end of the act has as neat an ankle as I've seen in years." He fished in a waistcoat pocket for his snuffbox.

John had noted the actress, too, and privately disagreed with the Prince. A girl with ankles that heavy would be considered gross in Boston.

The Prince opened his enameled snuffbox, discovered it was empty and petulantly snapped it shut.

John immediately produced a handsome box of chased silver he had purchased for the enormous sum of three guineas the previous day. He hadn't yet learned to take snuff, which Aunt Lydia considered a vile habit, but was intending to experiment in the immediate future. "Allow me, Your Highness," he said, flipping open the lid and spilling tobacco on the floor.

George William Frederick took two generous pinches. "A damned handsome box."

Few men were given such a wonderful opportunity, and John replied instantly. "I'd be very proud if you'd accept it as a gift, Your Highness."

The Prince of Wales was surprised, but gladly took the box. "Here," he replied, "take mine in return."

Two of his gentlemen-in-waiting laughed, and John wondered if they were laughing at him because the Prince's snuffbox could have cost no more than ten shillings.

The scion of the royal House of Hanover puffed out his fleshy cheeks. "A dazzling cloth, Master Hopkins," he said, inspecting his benefactor more closely.

The scion of the less than royal house of Hancock stiffened. "Hancock, Your Highness. John Hancock."

"Ah, yes." The Prince of Wales nodded vaguely. "You aren't an admirer of William Pitt, by chance?"

John shook his head, ashamed to admit that he had no interest in politics. All he knew about Pitt was that he was First Lord of the Treasury and, therefore, the King's principal minister.

Barnard was conscious of the young visitor's embarrassment. "Master Hancock," he explained, "has few chances to watch debates in the Commons. He lives in Massachusetts."

Prince George's sudden whoop of laughter was startling. "No wonder he wears old-fashioned clothes cut like Pitt's! He's a colonial!" Still laughing, he strolled back into his box.

John could feel his ears and cheeks burning, and he hated himself for giving his handsome silver snuffbox to a boor.

5

Susan Barnard snapped her ivory fan shut, opened it again and struck a pretty pose as she sat back against the cushions of the coach that crept slowly down Fleet Street toward the Strand. It was almost midnight, but all London seemed to be awake. Peddlers wove in and out of traffic, blithely impeding carriage drivers, gentlemen on horseback, and the liveried bearers of sedan chairs. Pedestrians of every class were crowded against the buildings on both sides of the narrow street, but no one seemed to mind. Chestnut vendors were doing a brisk trade, as were the sellers of dried herring, and the shouts of a party of young men emerging from a tavern momentarily drowned the curses of exasperated coachmen.

"London can be so dull," Susan said with a light sigh as she fanned herself lazily.

John completely disagreed with her. There were more people in the streets of London on an ordinary night than he had ever seen in Boston. Not even the news that the French had lost Quebec had brought out such a crowd.

But he really didn't care what Susan said or thought. She was the most fascinating, sophisticated girl he had ever encountered, and tonight, after spending his third evening in her company, he was bewitched. A towering, powdered wig that covered her own blond hair was incredibly intricate, she wore a diamond-shaped patch of black velvet on her smooth cheekbone, her lips were delicately rouged and the subtle scent that she dabbed on herself so liberally was intoxicating.

Aunt Lydia certainly wouldn't approve of Susan's square-cut neckline, which dipped so low that it revealed the deep cleavage between her breasts. Nor would she think highly of another velvet patch, cunningly placed to call still more attention to a perfect bosom. But Aunt Lydia, with all her sterling qualities, was a provincial who would be utterly bewildered by London and its dazzling people.

Scarcely aware of what Susan was saying in her delicious drawl, John leaned toward her, watching her lips move and studying the saucy tilt of her nose.

"Amsterdam is small and rather quiet, I'll admit," she said, "but it has an air—a quaintness—that's lacking here." She broke off suddenly and let the ardent young man feel the full effect of her black antimony-fringed lashes and blue eyes. "I believe you want to kiss me," she said.

John swallowed hard, uncertain whether she was encouraging or reprimanding him.

"You may, if you insist." Susan leaned toward him.

He swept her into his arms, almost crushing her as their lips met.

Susan disengaged herself, took a small silver-backed mirror from a pouch that dangled from one wrist and dabbed expertly at her lips with rouge from a tiny pot.

Never had John felt so lighthearted and dashing. He was in love with the most glorious creature in the world.

Susan completed her cosmetic repairs, fanned herself again and yawned audibly.

John caught his breath.

"I was curious to see if you colonials had learned any new techniques from your savage Indian friends," she said, looking past him now to see if she recognized the livery of four sedan-chair bearers. "What a pity that you're rather crude."

John sank back into his corner of the coach, his face red and his fists clenched.

"Never mind, my dear." Susan tapped him lightly on the arm with her fan. "Think of the tales about the debauchery of civilized people that you can take back to your little friends in the forests."

Had she been a man, John would have struck her.

6

The Pipe and Leaf lived up to its name. The air was so thick with smoke that the red-faced, paunchy merchants who dined at the tavern just off Fleet Street had to wipe away tears when they first walked into the crowded establishment from the street. A film of tobacco residue coated the leaded window panes, earthenware bowls filled with four different kinds of tobacco were strategically located for the convenience of patrons, and the pipes smoked by habitués rested in wall containers, each tagged with its owner's name.

John, feeling slightly ill at ease in the presence of Christopher Kilby and two of London's biggest buyers, knew it was no accident that the Englishmen had chosen this tavern to discuss a revision of tobacco prices with him. Symbols, he gathered, were as important as facts to London's commercial leaders.

"Our situation is clear," Kilby said as he speared a slice of tripe on his knife. "The demand for colonial tobacco continues to rise, prices increase at the same rate and our margin of profit falls. Something must be done to insure us a larger share."

All three merchants looked at John. This was his first experience in conducting negotiations on his own authority, but he displayed none of his nervousness. He carefully cut a piece of meat in his steaming veal and kidney pie, ate it and sipped his bittersweet mead. "I wish we could help you," he said, "but our own profits are diminishing. As my uncle has written to Master Kilby, we're keeping only sixpence in every pound's worth of sales, the same profit he shows. What's more, we take all the risks."

"In what way?" Kilby challenged, stuffing another chunk of tripe into his mouth.

"We buy direct from the farmers," John said. "Tobacco is perishable, and inept handlers may ruin it when they store it. Our warehouses sometimes suffer from fire, and we run the danger of losses at sea. You assume no responsibilities until our ships put into English ports, but your earnings are as great as ours."

Kilby shrugged off the explanation. "I'm not dissatisfied with sixpence per pound, but these gentlemen run risks, too. After they buy the tobacco from me, they store it in their own warehouses here—where the fire hazard is as great as it is in the colonies. And they never know what price the retail merchants will pay in the day's market."

Allan Hubbard, London's most prominent buyer of tobacco, drained his mug of ale mixed with sack and belched politely. "I take a bloody gamble every morning of my life at the market," he grumbled.

"All of us gamble," John replied. "We pay the farmers a predetermined price—"

"Aye!" Martin Dinwiddie, who monopolized the Scottish tobacco trade, slapped his hand on the charred oak table. "Right there we find the key that will open the golden door. Pay them less, Master Hancock. Squeeze them dry. Give them half of what you offer now, and they'll never know the difference."

John was no longer surprised when the English showed how

little they knew of colonials. "Tobacco growers in the Carolinas and Virginia aren't fools, Master Dinwiddie. As for the Connecticut growers, they keep a hired representative in Boston to keep watch on price fluctuations."

"Then stop dealing with highwaymen!" Hubbard signaled to a barmaid, who brought him another brimming mug of ale and sack. "Spend a few pounds to buy the freedom of some of those miserable wretches in Newgate Prison, take them with you to the colonies and put them to work on tobacco farms of your own. Land costs next to nothing—"

"I'm afraid you don't understand, sir." The suggestions were unrealistic, but John spoke politely. "For one thing, land values are expensive. Only if you travel hundreds of miles into the interior can you buy property cheaply, and then you're faced with the problem of transporting your produce to the seaports, where our coastal brigs load."

His auditors exchanged blank looks, unable to visualize the vast domain of the New World.

"Furthermore, tobacco growing is a skill. I've heard it said that it takes two generations to train a farmer who can grow a prime crop year after year."

Hubbard grimaced. "From all I've ever read, your savage Indians grow the leaf, Master Hancock. And you can't tell me they're skilled workers."

John concealed his irritation. "To the best of my knowledge, sir, the Indians rely on wild tobacco, all of it inferior. Our best growers are intelligent, educated men who spend their entire lives studying ways to improve their yield per acre. Speaking for myself, I've never seen an Indian."

Kilby raised an eyebrow, and the other two made it equally plain they thought the young colonial was lying.

"Twenty years ago, I made a profit of eight shillings per pound's sale," Hubbard said forcefully. "Today I'm reduced to a mere thruppence, and I find the situation intolerable!"

John privately thought the margin of profit was more than adequate for a middleman who bought tobacco from Kilby, held it in his warehouses for a short period and then resold it to retail merchants. The volume of trade was so great that, he knew, he himself could acquire a large fortune within a few years if he stood in Hubbard's shoes.

Hubbard gulped his drink. "If Hancock and Company refuses to sell at a lower price—"

"We can't," John declared flatly.

"—we shall be forced to ask Parliament for help. If you won't give us our fair share, the Commons will set a ceiling on your selling price."

John laughed. "I can't imagine the House of Commons deliberately interfering by discriminating against a British seller in favor of a British buyer."

There was a tense silence. Dinwiddie stared down at his plate, then pushed it away in a sudden gesture. "You seem to forget, young man, that you aren't really British. You're just colonials."

Frustrations that had simmered in John for weeks finally came to the surface. "The North American colonies don't exist solely for the convenience of merchants in England, sir! Our loyalty to the Crown is as great as yours, and our achievements are greater. We've won the war against the French, but you're still fighting them over here!"

Hubband loftily dismissed the argument. "Your war was nothing but a few minor squabbles between savages."

John could not control his temper. "We've won hundreds of thousands of square miles of rich territory for the King! Surely the Crown and government recognize our contribution!"

"It remains to be seen whether there's any worth in the new lands, or whether they're worthless swamps fit only for Newgate scum." Kilby dismissed Quebec, Montreal, and the fur trade with a contemptuous wave. "Master Hancock, take your uncle a message from all of us who deal in tobacco, lumber and all the other produce we buy from the colonies. Tell him we insist on larger profits. If they aren't granted voluntarily, the Commons will force you to remember that we're still the masters in our own house."

"Don't try to scare us," John said, looking at each of the three in turn. "We won't be bluffed, and we're willing to put our faith in the King, his ministers, and Parliament. We'd rather deal with you because we think of you as kin, but we'll take our trade elsewhere if you get too greedy."

"You're naïve," Hubbard told him. "And vulnerable. The Commons has the power to insist that you trade only with England."

The idea was so ludicrous that John laughed. "The longer I stay in England, the more I realize how little you know of us in the colonies. Prod us with Parliament's bayonets, gentlemen, and you'll turn us into smugglers. But I can't imagine any of these things coming to pass. Let's work together, as we've done in the past, and all of us will live comfortably. We aren't trying to cheat you, and we'll continue to think of you as our friends, provided you don't try to scalp us."

He realized instantly that his choice of words had been unfortunate. He had merely confirmed the merchants' deep-rooted belief that American colonials were savages, and nothing he could say now would convince these Englishmen that colonials were unwilling to accept colored beads and other trinkets in return for valuable goods.

7

George II, head of the House of Hanover, died at the age of seventy-seven on October 25, 1760, after making several long, gratuitously unpleasant deathbed speeches that bruised the feelings of the few relatives still on friendly terms with him. The rest of his large brood enjoyed a sensation of relief, and so did his subjects.

A new era began, and George William Frederick, the old man's eldest grandson, became George III, King of Great Britain, Ireland, and the Crown Colonies the world over. The nation had no chance to rejoice, however, for the first act of the King was to dismiss his First Minister, William Pitt, the most conscientious, able, and popular public servant in the realm.

"George, be a king!" Princess Augusta had told her son repeatedly, and the young monarch was determined to follow her advice, but no one else's. He dutifully buried his grandfather with great pomp. Then, consulting only his own conscience, he rashly announced his intention of bringing the war against France to an end, thereby alarming Frederick the Great of Prussia and his other allies.

"I glory in the name of Briton," the King declared in a boastful speech, and forcibly reminded his subjects that he was the first of his line to speak English without a Hanoverian accent. Unfortunately, however, he lapsed into German whenever he became upset, and he was often disturbed. The people snickered, then laughed aloud when, with almost indecent haste after his grandfather's funeral, he announced his betrothal to a drab German princess, Charlotte Sophia of Mecklenburg-Strelitz.

One sensation followed another in such rapid succession that John Hancock postponed his return to Boston. "I shall stay to see the King crowned at Westminster in February," he wrote to Uncle Thomas, "as I think it likely that never again in my lifetime will I have the chance to witness such a spectacle. Master Barnard has obtained seats for us in a pew at the rear of the Abbey. More such seats are available than you might imagine, for the King has angered the Whigs so severely that most members of the Commons will not attend his coronation. He has dared to take all patronage rights from the Whig ministers, and swears he will appoint Crown officers himself. I believe he means to rule rather than reign.

"I have a reason stronger than curiosity, also, for prolonging my visit here. Recently I met Dr. Franklin of Philadelphia, who has an appointment to call on the King soon after the coronation, and has asked me to accompany him, having learned I am your Nephew. Dr. Franklin is afraid that the King sweeps with too stiff a broom, and will make changes in the affairs of the Colonies. But I believe his fears are exaggerated, and remain sanguine. Our prosperity brings gold into the Treasury, and no prince will bite the hand that feeds him.

"Nevertheless, I will go with Dr. Franklin. Should I some day marry and rear a family, a prospect I regard as dubious because of the fickle and abandoned nature of all ladies, dear Aunt Lydia excepted, I would be able to tell my children I had once been received by His Majesty in private audience. It is the Crown itself I respect. From what I have heard and myself seen of the man who will wear it after the ceremonies at Westminster, I do not hold him in too high regard."

8

John studied himself in the huge oval mirror at the far end of the drawing room of Sir John Pringle's fashionable house a stone's throw from Whitehall, and felt certain he would not disgrace himself at the audience. His powdered wig, which had cost a staggering eighty guineas, was set in the style that the King himself wore. His suit of cream-colored velvet was even more extravagant, but worth every farthing. The braid that bound his swallowtailed coat was genuine gold, and so were the buttons. His waistcoat was of French silk that sold at exorbitant prices because of the war, his stock and shirt were of the finest lawn, and his new walking stick, with a head of pure ivory from Africa, was worth a fortune. Not even George III would criticize his appearance today.

"I'm sorry to have kept you waiting, Mr. Hancock." Benjamin Franklin came slowly down the stairs.

John was unaccustomed to the form of address, which he considered affected. Franklin called no one Master, declaring he was his own. But if he put on airs in little things, his dress was so simple that John wondered if he had forgotten their appointment. His gray hair was his own, tied at the nape of his neck with an eelskin, like that of a poor Boston shopkeeper. He wore a suit of somber wool, and hadn't even deigned to put buckles on his plain black shoes. Of course he was so wealthy, almost as rich as Uncle Thomas, that he could do as he pleased. And he had won such renown as an author and editor, scholar and statesman and philosopher that it was possible no one cared how he looked.

All the same, John couldn't help feeling his own attire might be a trifle gaudy now that the coronation had been postponed. But he dismissed the thought as he bowed to the older man. Not being a famous, middle-aged eccentric who was on familiar terms with great lords, leaders of the Commons and Oxford dons, it was mandatory that he observe the amenities.

"Pringle was just questioning me about my experiments in smallpox inoculation, and you know how curious these physicians

57

can be," Franklin said cheerfully, removing his spectacles and dropping them into a pocket.

John knew nothing about smallpox, had only heard vaguely of the principles of inoculation and cared nothing about the interests of physicians. But he nodded, not wanting to reveal his ignorance, and hastily threw his new cloak of quilted silk over his shoulders. "I hope we won't keep His Majesty waiting."

Franklin took his time pulling heavy mittens of homespun wool onto his pudgy hands. "So many people are clamoring to see him that he's late for all his appointments, and I hate chilling my bones in drafty anterooms. Shall we walk to Whitehall? It's only a few steps, and I need to stretch my legs."

"Of course, sir." John hid his disappointment, having assumed they would ride to the palace in the glittering coach that had been put at Sir John Pringle's disposal when he had been appointed royal physician.

Franklin settled a bicorn squarely on his head, wound a long, shabby scarf around his neck and started out briskly. "I wonder if you're old enough to have learned the great disadvantage of being a colonial in London. No? It's this confoundedly damp weather. One needs to be born here not to suffer from it."

John held his breath as Franklin scurried across a street with his head lowered, paying no attention to the traffic streaming in both directions. It seemed miraculous that he wasn't struck down.

"Are there any subjects you want to discuss with the King?" Franklin glanced myopically at his companion.

"It would be helpful to learn something of his taxation policy on colonial imports and exports."

"Spoken like a true merchant, Mr. Hancock. I shall see that you're given your chance." Franklin waved affably to the redcoat sentries who stood at rigid attention outside the palace entrance, and apparently they recognized him, for he was neither halted nor challenged. "Poor lads. They must be vulnerable to the ague after standing out in the cold for hours. But we can be proud of them, Mr. Hancock. They're the best-disciplined troops on earth, the finest since Caesar's legions, and it's good to know that if there must be wars, they're on our side."

Several major domos were on duty just inside the entrance to Whitehall, but John noted that Franklin was in no need of their services, and made his way unaided through a maze of corridors. They came at last to a chamber in which several conservatively dressed gentlemen were standing, conversing in low tones, and Franklin greeted each by name as he went immediately to a coal fire and warmed his hands.

One of the group, apparently a gentleman-in-waiting, approached him at once. "I'll tell His Majesty you're here, Doctor."

John was surprised when the aide returned after a wait of only a few moments to conduct them into a large, ornately furnished bedchamber. His Britannic Majesty, wearing a dressing gown of padded silk and a tasseled nightcap, was sitting at a table, eating. "Come in and join me," he called jovially.

John swept the floor with his feathered hat, observing that the King was puffy-eyed, but otherwise looked much as he had at the theatre.

Franklin's bow was perfunctory. "The air in here is stale," he said reprovingly. "You should build the fire higher in your hearth and open some windows for a time, or you'll suffer an impairment of the lungs."

George III turned to a footman hovering behind him, and the advice was followed at once. "I remember your fondness for mulled brandywine and dried herring fillets, Dr. Franklin." He waved his guests to chairs. "You'll have some, too, Master Hopkins?"

The combination made John shudder. "I'll be honored, Your Majesty," he said, deciding the moment was not opportune to correct the King's impression of his name.

Franklin ate and drank with gusto. "I'm told you've read my pamphlet on the peace terms we should demand from France, Your Majesty."

"With great interest, Doctor, and as usual your suggestions are sound. I had always assumed the West Indian Islands were the most important properties in the New World, but your discourse on the economic potential of Canada is so impressive that I'll demand it instead."

John was staggered by the colossal royal ignorance, and wondered how any man, much less a monarch, would prefer to own some tiny islands rather than a vast domain rich in furs, lumber, and other wilderness resources. Hoping his expression didn't reveal his feelings, he lowered his head and forced himself to eat some salty chunks of herring, which he washed down with hot, spiced brandywine so powerful it scalded his throat. His mind wandered as the King and Franklin chatted about people he didn't know. Then he couldn't help feeling that he and the royal host were students in a classroom when Franklin launched into a long, involved dissertation on the enormous strides in scientific achievement the Prussians were making under Frederick the Great.

George fidgeted, too. "More to the point, Doctor," he said, breaking in when the learned man paused for breath, "are your opinions of the principles I should follow in governing the North American colonies."

Franklin had anticipated just such a solicitation of his views, and answered without hesitation. "As one who has been active for many years in the Pennsylvania Assembly, I find a growing desire for greater freedom in the conduct of our own internal affairs."

"Now you sound like a politician, Doctor." The King became patronizing. "The members of your little colonial legislatures ape the Commons. All politicians want more power."

"I suggest you read Locke and Rousseau, Your Majesty," Franklin replied, coughing gently behind his linen napkin. "All men, regardless of profession or station, yearn for the liberty that will enable them to govern their own lives."

"You're not suggesting that the colonial parliaments are disloyal to me?" George bridled.

The idea was so absurd that Franklin laughed heartily. "They're devoted to the Crown, Your Majesty."

The King relaxed and ordered his wine glass refilled.

"On the other hand, they feel they know more about their own local, immediate problems than administrators here. Mr. Hancock is a merchant, and I believe you'll find his thoughts illuminating." Franklin smiled at John, encouraging him to speak freely.

"Our taxes are too high, Your Majesty," John said bluntly.

The King's roar of laughter interrupted him. "There, Doctor, you hear the eternal complaint of the middle class!"

John tried to keep both his temper and dignity. "The Commons imposes tax penalties on the colonies, Your Majesty. You'll find no people more devoted to you than the citizens of Massachusetts.

But we resent being taxed on English-made goods. We bear the burden of shipping prices, and when taxes are doubled, merely because we're colonials, we must pay twice as much as Englishmen in England for our broadcloth and ironware—and even the spirits we drink."

George sipped his wine, and his air was infuriatingly condescending. "You look at the problem through the eyes of a colonial, which is natural, Mr. Hopkins—"

"Hancock, John Hancock."

"—but I must see my realm as a whole. A colony, by its very nature, exists to enrich and strengthen the motherland of which it is a small part."

John wanted to retort that the North American colonies were many times the size of the British Isles, but knew it would be shockingly rude to argue with a monarch. Besides, Franklin didn't appear disturbed, so he became somewhat calmer. "The present policy, if you'll forgive the bluntness, Your Majesty, is shortsighted. Heavy taxation slows our natural growth, and keeps money out of your Treasury."

George had made his own point, and lost interest in the subject.

"What Mr. Hancock means," Franklin said gently, "is that the men who live on our side of the ocean are very much like Englishmen on this side. They want security for themselves and their families, enough food to eat and a chance to improve their lot in the world. There has been a growing feeling in recent years that the Commons has discriminated against us for the benefit of London merchants."

The King tapped a finger on the table. "I was warned by my tutors to find ingratitude on every side, yet I'm constantly surprised to find their predictions coming true. Don't the colonials realize that the strongest army and navy in the world protect them from our enemies, that they enjoy the protection of British courts and British justice? Magistrates and colonels and commodores must be paid wages, too, you know."

Franklin sensed his growing irritation. "On another occasion, Your Majesty, I hope we can discuss the proposition that the free and unhampered economic growth of the colonies will strengthen the whole empire and enrich the Crown. But I know how busy you are, and I don't want to impose on you any longer this morning." He stood quickly.

John rose, too, and his annoyance increased when the King reached into a dressing-gown pocket and took out a familiar, silver snuffbox. By now he undoubtedly had forgotten how he had acquired it. And, unfortunately, there wasn't another in London like it.

The King's good humor was restored. "I hope you'll come to see me again before you visit the German states, Doctor—"

"Holland, Your Majesty."

George shrugged, and with the simple rise and fall of his shoulders lumped the small European nations together. As the ruler of the most powerful nation on earth, it wasn't necessary for him to know or care about the individual identities of his little neighbors. "Tell me how to increase Treasury revenues from the colonies, Doctor, and you shall have a peerage. Master Hopkins, good day."

John fumed as they walked down the corridor, still regretting his gift of the snuffbox. Perhaps he shouldn't let his vanity interfere with his judgment, either, but it was typical that the King could not remember his name. George III didn't listen to any voice but his own.

Franklin paused to converse briefly with several gentlemen they encountered in the corridors, but John remained silent until they had left the palace.

"By God, sir, he's an ignoramus!"

Franklin laughed tolerantly. "You find his parochial opinions of colonies and colonials too hard to digest, eh? Never fear, Mr. Hancock, the King will change as he matures. Remember he's young—even younger than you—and has received training for his post far less thorough than the education your uncle gave you. His grandfather had a closed mind, but the new King will learn. Pitt will teach him, and so will Newcastle—"

"They're both out of office, Dr. Franklin!"

"For the moment. But I have great faith in the English system of government, and I can't believe the Hanoverians are going to reverse the trend of history. The days when Stuarts believed they ruled by Divine right are ended."

John was still upset. "So help me, sir, he sounded like a Stuart."

A mittened hand patted John's shoulders. "It's the prerogative of youth to be dogmatic, Mr. Hancock. You think of taxes on imports, the King thinks of the glory his army and navy will win him—and you're more alike than you realize. I contend that freedom is contagious. We've tasted it in Pennsylvania, as you have in Massachusetts, just as people have breathed its clean air here. The House of Commons will reassert its authority after the coronation. And in time the King will realize that the more of a voice we're given in our own affairs, the more the whole empire will prosper."

John couldn't dispute the man who was recognized as the leading political authority in North America, but it was still his private opinion that George III was too pig-headed to change his mind once he formed an opinion.

Franklin saw his set expression and chuckled. "Your generation —and his—has just come of age. So take no offense, please, when I tell you I feel certain you'll both mellow with responsibility. Rejoice that you live in the era of enlightenment, Mr. Hancock. Reasonable men will work out compromises that will satisfy everyone."

The older man's serenity finally soothed John's fears.

"Do you recall your Latin from your college days?"

"Certainly, sir!"

"*Cujusvis hominis est errare, nullius nisi insipientis in errore perseverare.*"

"Horace, is it not?" It pleased John to think he could discuss learned matters with a great scholar. " 'Every man is liable to err, but only a fool perseveres in his error.' "

"Quite so. The King has a warped view of our situation because he knows so little about us. He may make a few mistakes, but the Crown will survive, and so shall we. Eventually all of us will achieve a far greater mutual understanding."

The thought was worthy of Dr. Franklin, and was probably an accurate forecast. But merchants had to live in the meantime, and a fortune could be lost overnight if the King requested Parliament to raise taxes on goods ordered but not yet delivered. John shook hands with the distinguished Philadelphian, but regretfully declined an invitation to have a cup of East Indian coffee in the Pringle drawing room.

Business came before pleasure—or anything else. A Hancock ship was sailing for Boston on the afternoon tide, and John felt it imperative that he write a full account of the audience with the King to Uncle Thomas. On his own authority he would cancel all orders he had placed for manufactured goods that could not be delivered in the immediate future, and would urge Uncle Thomas to fall back on warehouse stocks.

He'd have to word the letter carefully, of course, as French warships occasionally caught merchantmen on the high seas. But Uncle Thomas would know what he meant. Until King George demonstrated his willingness to behave like an enlightened monarch in a reasonable age, the house of Hancock would subsist on smuggling.

THREE

1764 — 1766

1

John Hancock mounted the throne of his own empire on August 1, 1764, when his uncle died of apoplexy. No one was surprised to learn the terms of Thomas' will, in which he left his entire business and the better part of his personal fortune to his adopted son. John's cash assets amounted to more than one hundred thousand pounds, a greater sum than any other man in the colonies could boast. Only he knew the worth of his other property, which consisted of ships, crammed warehouses, and vast real estate holdings in Boston and elsewhere in Massachusetts.

The funeral was a solemn event, attended by every man of consequence in the colony. And the following day the new monarch was not only elected to membership in the exclusive Merchants Club, but was simultaneously offered the presidency of the organization. He accepted, and his throne, like that of Uncle Thomas before him, was a chair of padded leather at the head of the table in the private dining room at the rear of the Bunch of Grapes, a tavern that had become the meeting place of the commercial elite.

Two days after the funeral John resumed his normal daily routine, and walked into the dining room of the Hancock mansion for breakfast just as dawn was breaking. He attacked his food with his usual gusto, and occupied himself by finishing the reading of his uncle's private file that he had started the previous day.

"John." Aunt Lydia stood in the entrance, haggard but erect. He jumped to his feet. "Dr. Warren told you to stay in bed."

"Joseph Warren is a well-mannered young man," she said tartly, "but I've yet to hear of anyone being cured of melancholy by feeling sorry for herself." She took her usual place at the table, rang a bell for a servant and asked for a pot of tea, broiled flounder and several of her favorite minced beef and pork patties in pastry shells. "I've arranged to meet with the trustees of Harvard College this morning to give them the books Thomas left to the school. This afternoon I want your brother to call on me. He needs someone to tell him not to squander his bequest, and I trust he'll listen to me. You'll give him an hour or two free from work for the purpose?"

"If you wish, Aunt." She needed something to occupy her mind, so her meeting with Ebenezer wouldn't be a complete waste of time, although nothing could curb his spendthrift tendencies.

Her tea was placed before her, she sniffed appreciatively and poured a steaming cup. "You aren't wearing the watch fob that Thomas left you." She sounded accusing.

"No, ma'am, I've put it in my strongbox. This one, that you and Uncle Thomas gave me on my twenty-first birthday, suits my purposes."

Lydia sipped her tea. "I trust you'll carry his walking stick."

"My hand has become accustomed to the feel of my old one." John ate rapidly.

"You're as bad as Thomas, gulping your meals."

"Dan Fowler will be expecting me in five minutes for our walk to the office."

Lydia was shocked. "Surely you're going to take your uncle's coach, as he did every morning of his life!"

John had hoped to avoid a direct confrontation, but realized that for the sake of his own tranquillity he could not remain silent. "I loved Uncle Thomas as a man and respected him as a merchant. But I must live my own life. I've spent ten years at Hancock and Company, and I must use my own judgment in my dealings. You and I revere Uncle Thomas' memory, but sentiment can't be allowed to interfere with profits." He emptied his plate and finished the last of his tea.

The old lady was stunned. "A Hancock is expected to live and act in certain ways. You're wasting the carriage and matched team."

"I place the coach completely at your disposal." He glanced at his watch and stood.

Lydia rose, too, and followed him to the entrance hall. "What will people say when they see the head of the most prosperous company in the New World walking to his office?"

"If they ask me, I'll tell them I like to stretch my legs. I have too few chances to leave my desk all day."

"Thomas always said his carriage was a sign to the citizens that he was still solvent!"

He tried to divert her. "I hope we'll stay solvent. Business has fallen off badly everywhere since the end of the war in Europe. We're the only city in the colonies that hasn't suffered much, but our turn will come." He saw no reason to mention that smuggling had helped sustain the merchants of Boston. He couldn't be sure how much she knew of Uncle Thomas' illegal activities, and there was nothing to be gained by talking about them. But the subject was one that troubled him incessantly. Now that the Royal Navy was no longer blockading France, scores of ships were patrolling the American coastline, and smuggling was becoming increasingly hazardous. Uncle Thomas had been deeply concerned, and now John was beginning to feel the weight of ultimate responsibility.

Lydia watched him as he settled a gold-braided tricorn on his powdered wig and took his walking stick from a front-hall rack. "If the company stands to lose money," she said, her expression and tone indicating that the thought had not occurred to her on the spur of the moment, "wouldn't it be wise to put some of our funds into strongboxes for safekeeping?"

John knew she was afraid he would bankrupt the business and squander her own fortune. "I've already put aside the money that Uncle Thomas left you. It will remain intact, no matter what may happen. If I'm able to keep the company solvent, you'll share in the profits, but if I blunder and lose my inheritance, you won't suffer."

He kissed her on the cheek and quickly left the house. Everyone, even Aunt Lydia, seemed to think that Hancock and Company would collapse. Clerks and dock workers who had been in his uncle's employ for years were already seeking other posts, warehouse handlers and wagon drivers were seeking assurances that he didn't intend to liquidate the business. Obviously he had not inspired enthusiasm in the years he had served as Uncle Thomas' deputy, so he'd have to prove Boston wrong.

That meant expanding at a time when other merchants, both in the colonies and England, were retrenching. John grinned at the prospect as he approached the foot of Beacon Street and raised his stick in a cheerful salute to Dan Fowler. What virtually no one realized was that Uncle Thomas had accumulated his fortune by taking calculated risks, and there was no reason his successor and disciple couldn't do the same. It was exciting to pit one's wits against the world—and win.

"Dan," he said as Fowler fell in beside him, "I want you to double our work gangs. Offer the men an extra shilling per day, and tell them I'll guarantee them steady employment for the next year."

Fowler cast a startled glance at him and rubbed the stubble on his chin.

"We can't afford to stand still," John said, his spirits rising as he faced the challenge. "The colonies are growing, and we must grow with them."

2

Attorney James Otis sipped his spiced rum and sat forward uneasily in his chair. "I don't often come to the Bunch of Grapes. It's too rich for my taste."

"I'm expected to eat here. And they prepare food to my liking." John disliked small talk. "Jim, I have a problem, and you're the best lawyer in Boston to help me solve it."

"I expected you to say something like that when I received your note inviting me to meet you here today." Otis lowered his voice so they wouldn't be overheard at the adjoining tables. "You're having difficulties with either the Governor or the Collector of the Port."

"Not yet, and if I do, I'm lost. You've made a good record defending our citizens against Crown tax claims, and I want you to take my case." John carefully diluted his own drink with water. "It's understood that anything I say to you is confidential."

"Of course. I'm just a little surprised you didn't go to John Adams."

"Johnny is a little too respectable."

Otis took no offense, and his leathery face became creased when he smiled. "His loyalty to the Crown in all things is too blind and stubborn."

"I wouldn't have put it that way, but no matter." John's sole concern was his specific problem. "I've just cornered the whale-oil market. Every last drop of it in the New World is mine, and is locked in my warehouses. I spent seventeen thousand pounds in cash to get it."

The sum was so staggering that Otis choked on his drink.

John waited patiently until he stopped coughing. "I smuggled it into town, and I intend to smuggle it out again."

"Naturally."

"As there's no other New World source, London will have to pay my price, and I can make a profit of one hundred percent." John relished the idea of forcing patronizing English merchants to accept his terms. "But these new Writs of Assistance the King persuaded Parliament to make into law can ruin me."

Otis saw his point at once. Crown officials were authorized under the Writs to search any dwelling, warehouse, or other private property in the colonies to seek and confiscate smuggled goods.

"It's my understanding of English common law that a man's home is his castle and may not be searched without a warrant issued by a magistrate for due cause."

"That's correct, and therefore the Writs are unconstitutional."

"They're also discriminatory. Our homes can be entered, because we're colonials. But the new law specifically exempts men living in the British Isles."

"True," Otis replied, "but Parliament has passed the law, so the Governor has been given adequate authority to make a search of any premises he believes might be harboring smuggled goods."

"Tom Hutchinson is a good fellow, and he's been sympathetic to our problems. But he's ambitious and isn't satisfied to remain Lieutenant Governor. Nothing would give him a bigger boost at the Colonial Office in London than to find my whale oil. You realize, I'm sure, that I can't afford to pay the new tax on it, either. The tax rate that the House of Commons has levied against us in its present session would bankrupt me."

Otis took a long spill of straw from a pitcher, turned to the small fire of oak logs burning in the hearth behind him, and seemed absorbed in lighting his pipe. "I wish," he said, when the pipe was finally drawing to his satisfaction, "that you'd join the Long Room Club."

"I've heard of it," John made no attempt to hide his distaste. "Frankly, men like Sam Adams and Jim Warren are radicals. I can't imagine what a respectable craftsman like Paul Revere is doing there. He should be concentrating on making pieces like the lovely silver bowl I bought from him last month."

"What makes you call the Long Room boys radical?" Otis asked softly.

The distraction was irritating. "Damnation, Jim! Look at the articles that appear in the *Gazette* every week. They actually urge people to resist the Crown with force!"

"When there's no other way to resist injustice, it's necessary to use force." Otis puffed calmly on his pipe. "Let's examine your situation. If the Governor—or Tom Hutchinson—should seize your whale oil, I could claim in the courts that the Writs of Assistance are illegal. But I'd lose the case. Eventually the Writs will be repealed, but that wouldn't do you any good. And even if I were to make a series of appeals to higher courts, the best I could do for you would be to postpone the inevitable for two or three years."

Color drained from John's face. "Every penny I own in hard cash is tied up in that whale oil. I've got to begin shipping it to England within the next month, or I'll have no money to pay wages and a thousand other bills."

"Then your choice is a simple one."

"The devil you say. Hutchinson is beginning a systematic search of the waterfront."

"Precisely. So you'll either have to submit to the Crown—or bar your warehouse doors and hope the troops won't shoot their way in."

John stared at the tranquil lawyer. Smuggling was a universal colonial pastime, but open defiance of Crown authority was treason.

3

"I wish you'd let me hire some bullies," Dan Fowler said, pacing up and down with John outside the Hancock waterfront warehouses. "At least let me bring some of our own boys off the wharves to protect you if trouble develops."

"I want no violence." John's walking stick tapped sharply on the cobblestones.

Fowler shook his grizzled head. "My cousin, the one you're sending through Harvard, read me the *Gazette* last night. And it said—"

"I can imagine. Sam Adams—or whoever is writing the *Gazette* —comes closer to preaching armed rebellion every week. The Lord only knows where it will end." John saw a squad of redcoats approaching behind Lieutenant Governor Hutchinson, and forced himself to halt. The inside of his mouth felt dry, but he could not afford to lose his dignity. "I'll say whatever is needful," he told Fowler, "and no matter what happens, don't start a fight."

The foreman cursed under his breath.

The square-jawed Hutchinson bowed informally. "Your servant, John. You've come out to meet me, I see."

"I have, Thomas." John thought it better, under the circumstances, not to offer his hand.

"We'll make only a routine examination of your storage houses." Hutchinson smiled broadly. "You own so many of them that I'm not sure I'd know which items were passed through the office of the Collector of the Port and which are contraband."

"All my goods have entered the port legally," John replied with a straight face.

"To be sure," Hutchinson said, politely maintaining the same fiction.

John removed a bunch of keys from his pocket. "Sir," he said, raising his voice, "here you see the keys to my warehouses. Acting on the advice of my legal counsel, I am compelled to inform you that I cannot open the doors for purposes of search. These keys can be taken from me only at bayonet-point, or your soldiers will have to batter down the doors with their musket butts."

Hutchinson was embarrassed, well aware that he was dealing with a gentleman of his own class, a wealthy and influential citizen who was held up to ridicule in the columns of the *Gazette* and the other radical publications that were advocating open resistance to the new tax laws.

"I cannot allow my fundamental rights as a subject of the Crown to be violated." Out of the corner of his eye John caught a glimpse of James Otis in the shadow of the nearest warehouse. It was good to know that the attorney was ready to join in the argument if needed.

Hutchinson shifted his weight from one foot to the other. "You place me in a difficult position, John."

"I realize it, Thomas, and I offer you my personal apologies. At the same time I must remind you that the King and the House of Commons have placed me in an even more awkward position."

Hutchinson continued to stand indecisively for a moment before turning to the young officer in charge of the military detail. "You may march your men back to their barracks, Captain," he said.

John dropped his keys into a pocket. "That was unpleasant for both of us, and now I hope we can adjourn to the Bunch of Grapes for some beefsteak pies and a few pints of ale." Linking his arm through that of the Lieutenant Governor, he grinned at the dumfounded Dan Fowler and winked in the direction of James Otis. It was disconcerting to realize he had taken a stand that placed him on the side of the rabble-rousers who were demanding opposition to the Crown, but he had saved his precious cargo of whale oil. His financial gamble for high stakes had succeeded, and that was what really mattered.

4

It was small wonder that Elias Wheaton raised an eyebrow as he ushered the visitor into the inner sanctum of the head of the house of Hancock.

Sam Adams was the most slovenly man in Boston, and probably the ugliest. His shoulders were hunched in a permanent slouch, he looked down at the ground when he walked and his gait was

a shuffling amble. Many of the more respectable citizens concluded that he drank sack to excess from morning until night, but
they exaggerated; his friends had never seen him drunk. His
clothes were shabby, his stock soiled and his waistcoat spotted.
His watery eyes were red-rimmed, his thinning hair was held
loosely at the nape of his neck with a tattered eelskin and he
carried neither a smallsword nor a walking stick, either of which
was considered mandatory for a gentleman.

John, reluctantly coming from behind his desk and holding out
his hand, thought it astonishing that this incredibly sloppy fellow
could be the cousin of John Adams, whose physical appearance
was as meticulous as his mind was orderly.

"Mr. Hancock, I've been waiting a long time for this day." Sam
Adams' voice was harsh and unattractively rasping.

"Your servant, Master Adams."

"Not Master! Ben Franklin may have made a fool of himself
with his announcements that the King and Commons would have
a change of heart over colonial taxation, but he was right in saying
we should call each other Mister!"

The stunned Wheaton was still standing on the threshold, but
John waved him away and coldly offered his guest a chair. He
needed no help in handling a boor or putting the fellow in his
right place.

"I've been looking forward to this meeting, too," he said. "You
did me no favor by trying to associate my name with your dubious
cause, and I don't appreciate the warped and melodramatic version
of my encounter with Thomas Hutchinson that appeared some
months ago in the *Gazette*. The position I took at that time was
my private affair."

Sam Adams remained calm in the face of his host's withering
scorn. "The *Gazette's* editors publish the news of the day as they
see it," he said mildly.

John pointed an accusing quill pen at him. "The editors, sir?
You!"

Adams shrugged his rounded shoulders.

"As to that farcical ceremony you held at the base of the old
elm tree on King Street last week—"

"The Liberty Tree." A hint of a smile appeared on Adams'
face, and he sounded pleased with himself.

"Call it what you will. There was no justification for a mob ransacking Hutchinson's house after the meeting. That was an outrage!"

"The crowd got a mite out of hand." Adams didn't look in the least apologetic.

"I deplore mob violence, sir. I'm not sure of your motives, but if you persist in inciting mob violence, you'll simply force the Crown to send additional troops to keep the King's peace in Massachusetts." It made John feel a trifle better to speak his mind to the instigator of the shameful riot rather than fume impotently at the Bunch of Grapes.

"King George," Adams declared quietly, "doesn't have that many regiments."

John looked at him in horror. "Are you actually advocating armed insurrection?"

Adams preferred to reply indirectly. "You fellows who rely on Crown justice keep stubbing your toes until you permanently cripple yourselves. Maybe you've heard that Ben Franklin has been discharged from his post as Deputy Postmaster General for the colonies and is in danger of being arrested if he doesn't leave England at once."

"You lie!" John was so shocked he spoke before he could bite back the words.

"Yes, I do. When I must. But I'd be stupid to tell a man of your standing an untruth, Mr. Hancock. Don't believe me, if it will give you temporary peace of mind. I hear you have a ship due from London in the next day or two, so talk to her master yourself, and ask him the news of Franklin in London."

John calmed himself with a great effort. Certainly Franklin wasn't infallible, he thought, remembering their conversation after their audience with King George. But it seemed inconceivable that the greatest and most respected of colonials should be in disgrace and threatened with imprisonment. The world was changing so swiftly that it was becoming difficult to retain normal perspectives. "On what grounds would he be taken into royal custody?" he asked wearily.

"My informants tell me he's been exceedingly outspoken in his opposition to the new Stamp Act."

"May the Lord bless Dr. Franklin!" John sat back in his chair, laughed and slapped his desk.

"Do I glean from your attitude that you're also opposed to the Stamp Act, Mr. Hancock?" Adams' tired eyes were shining.

"There's no need for you to glean it, sir! I'm willing to shout my opinion to the whole world. Do you realize that under the terms of this abomination I shall be required to purchase Crown stamps every time I buy or sell even the most insignificant item of merchandise? My imports will need stamps. My exports will need stamps. My local sales and purchases will need stamps. Even my correspondence with my London agents will have to be written on stamped stationery. I regard this new act of Parliament as an attempt to drive me out of business—and send scores of others to debtors' prison with me!"

"I'm pleased and relieved to hear your views, Mr. Hancock. That's why I'm here." Adams continued to speak softly. "You say you're willing to tell the world your stand on the Stamp Act. Is that a rhetorical phrase?"

"I mean it literally, sir." John regained his self-control, and was surprised to see that the quill in his right hand had snapped.

"Then you shall have your opportunity. A meeting is being held at Faneuil Hall on Tuesday to protest against the Stamp Act, and the committee in charge of arrangements will be pleased to list you as one of the principal speakers."

John was afraid his anger at the King and Commons over the passage of the new discriminatory bill had carried him farther than he was willing to go. "I'm a merchant, sir, not a politician." He shook his head. "It wouldn't do for me to make an address at Faneuil Hall."

Adams was unruffled by his abrupt change of mind. "Ah, then you intend to buy the stamps for your business transactions, even though you dislike the Act."

"I can't buy them. I'd be destroying my margin of profit and driving myself out of business."

"If Hancock and Company fails, what will happen to smaller merchants?"

"Their business will die, too."

Adams hitched forward in his chair. "My friends at the Long Room Club and I have been discussing the potential impact of

75

the Stamp Act for many evenings. We've known that lawyers and artisan-craftsmen—like Revere—would be forced into bankruptcy if they paid the tax. We've been assured that small shopkeepers would become penniless. Farmers would go home with empty purses after selling their produce at the markets. And now you tell me that even the wealthy merchants who are the spine of our colonial society would collapse. What remedy do you have in mind?"

"I can speak only for myself. I have no intention of paying the tax!" John stood and went to a sideboard. "I need some spirits to soothe my stomach. Will you join me?"

Adams beamed. "If you insist, Mr. Hancock, I'll have a drop of sack."

John filled two glasses. "I've been given the choice of living or dying, and I prefer to live."

"You and Ben Franklin and all the other men of reason find you've been backed against a wall. You stand with bayonets at your throats." Adams sounded solicitous as he raised his glass in a silent toast, then quickly drained the contents. "You're afraid of the bayonets, no doubt."

"Wouldn't you be fearful if you wore my shoes?"

Adams smiled again as he glanced at his host's gold-buckled shoes. "It's my contention, Mr. Hancock, that if the taxpayers of every colony unite, if we stand firm in our refusal to obey the Stamp Act, the Crown won't be able to retaliate."

John was forced to concede that the idea sounded logical.

"There aren't enough prisons in Boston and Charleston and Philadelphia and New York Town to hold all of us. I've been exchanging letters with men in other colonies who feel as we do, and we're all agreed that no individual will be made to suffer if hundreds of us—thousands, if you will—are guilty of the same offense."

John nodded thoughtfully.

"That's why we thought it would be helpful—to all of our people, everywhere—if you'd consent to speak at our Faneuil Hall meeting. Surely you realize, far better than I do, that you're no ordinary merchant, Mr. Hancock. Why, I've heard it said that you've doubled the size of your business in the year since you've been in charge here."

The rumor was exaggerated, although it was true that the company had expanded. "It's precisely because I am something of a —a symbol, as you call it—that I can't afford to become associated with rowdies who have no respect for other people's property."

"I assure you the meeting will be orderly, and no violence will follow in its wake. The poor riot only when they feel isolated. The sooner that men of your stature have the courage to express their views of unfair taxation, the sooner stability with honor will be restored."

"No one has ever accused me of lacking courage!"

"I make no such accusation now, Mr. Hancock. I merely urge you to reconsider your decision. And please don't misunderstand me. I know you're a student of Locke's philosophy—"

"You know a great deal about me, it seems."

"—but I wouldn't presume to suggest that you incorporate his views of freedom in your speech." Adams blithely ignored the interruption. "The committee on arrangements offers you a platform to express any views of the Stamp Act you care to make public. Jim Otis will introduce the speakers, and he's asked me to give you his pledge that he'll make it clear you don't necessarily agree with any other speaker. Jim is a man of honor, so you can be certain he'll keep his word."

"I wouldn't doubt him for a moment." John was still grateful to Otis, not only for the advice that had saved his precious whale oil, but for sending him a surprisingly small bill for his services.

"Say what you please, Mr. Hancock. My friends and I don't expect you to hold our opinion that the Crown must either stop taking advantage of us or face the consequences."

John thought it politic not to inquire into those consequences. It was enough that circumstances were forcing him to make common cause, for the moment, with insurrectionists. "I'll accept the invitation," he said, feeling trapped because he had no real alternative.

5

A huge crowd filled every seat in Faneuil Hall, and men were crouching in the aisles, standing four and five deep at the rear of the auditorium and clustering around the exits. Thomas Hutchinson, now Acting Governor of Massachusetts, had wisely pretended to be unaware of the purpose of the gathering, and there were no troops or official town constables anywhere in the vicinity. Order was maintained by several small groups of burly dockworkers, wearing white rag bands on their left arms, who roamed through the hall in response to unobtrusive signals from Sam Adams, who sat inconspicuously in a corner of the farthest row from the stage.

Outdoors a blazing sun beat down from a cloudless August sky, and inside the Hall there was no hint of a breeze. The odor of unwashed bodies hung in the stale air, which became increasingly suffocating, but no one seemed to mind. Men applauded and shouted as speaker after speaker exhorted them, and everyone seemed to be enjoying himself.

John, mounting the platform after a brief introduction by James Otis, was somewhat surprised by the mood. His fellow Bostonians were unusually cheerful, and he certainly sensed nothing ominous in the spirit of the gathering. Perhaps most of the brawny men packed together on benches before him were members of the mob that had ransacked Hutchinson's house, but he was surprised at how many he recognized, and guessed that at least a quarter were in his own employ.

There were men of standing in the perspiring throng, too. Nearly everyone who ate his noon-day dinner at the Bunch of Grapes sweltered in the front rows, as did a number of clergymen, physicians, and other citizens of repute, including several Harvard graduates he hadn't seen in years. Waiting for the applause to die down, John couldn't help wondering whether his own presence on the podium might be making insurrection a little more respectable. He wouldn't put it past Sam Adams to have invited him here for that very purpose.

At last the applause died away, there was an expectant rustle and stir, and John took a small, neatly folded sheet of paper from his inner coat pocket. "Friends, let me read to you a letter of instructions that I sent by packet ship to my business associates and agents in London. 'We, here in the North American colonies, are doing everything within our limited powers to convince His Majesty's government that the Stamp Act is an onerous and short-sighted blow that undermines the liberties of free-born Englishmen. I write to you now, as I have done so often in the past, to urge you to use your own influence to persuade the Commons to change its course. I now add another step to my previous instructions. In case the Stamp Act is not repealed, I order you to ship me no English merchandise, not one article. I intend to persuade others to follow my lead. I am certain they will do so. The principal merchants of this town and of the other trading towns of this province are united in their resolve, and we will gladly starve before we will lower our principles.'"

A roar made the wooden walls of Faneuil Hall quiver. Sam Adams, who hadn't known what to expect, was delighted, and exchanged a broad grin with James Otis, who twisted around in his front-row seat to peer toward the rear of the auditorium. Not only was Hancock taking a firmer stand than anyone had dared to hope, but he was a remarkably good speaker, with a mellow, liquid voice, a sense of the dramatic that enabled him to take full advantage of pauses and, if his beginning was any criterion, a natural-born orator.

John was pleased at the effect of his words, and tugged modestly at his lace cuffs before raising a hand for silence. "I am no hero, friends. I am only a merchant who has acquired a taste for beefsteak pies and port wine, and I am reluctant to change my diet."

The audience responded with a shout of laughter. No one had expected him to allude so openly and casually to his wealth.

"Each of us has his own reasons for opposing this shameful Act of Parliament, inspired by misguided leaders." It would be going too far to mention King George by name, but the murmur that swept through the auditorium indicated that the audience was in no doubt of the "leaders" he meant.

"I myself am opposed to the Act because it will entirely stagnate trade here. We who are citizens of Massachusetts Bay are determined never—I repeat, never—to submit to it!"

He was astonished to see men leaping to their feet, cheering. Public speaking was far easier than he had imagined, and the knowledge that he had the power to sway a crowd was very gratifying. Again he held up a hand for quiet, and waited until the men obeyed.

"I tell you, friends, that we in Massachusetts don't stand alone in our resolve. In the past few days I've had letters from fellow merchants in Pennsylvania and New York and Connecticut. They feel as I do—and as you do."

Sam Adams looked down at his ink-stained hands. It was no one's business but his own that letters from other colonies had poured in on Hancock.

"The people of this entire country will never suffer themselves to be made slaves by this foul Act that violates the English constitution, the spirit of liberty, and the principle of fairness. A gift of one thousand guineas in gold—nay, a much larger fortune—would not tempt me to apply for a stamp.

"Friends, I have inherited a comfortable sum and through good fortune have managed to increase my holdings. If I wished, I could retire to a life of ease. I could sit in my big house and spend the rest of my days reading. But what would I read? The works of great men who preach that all Englishmen are equal? What a mockery! The sight of those words on the printed page would blind me.

"No, I must fight for the cause I believe to be right, the cause that my heart and mind and soul insist is right and just!"

He was becoming accustomed to the pleasing roars of approval now, but did not smile. He meant what he was saying.

"I believe," he declared solemnly, "that not a man in England pays the tax that I do, in proportion to the size of his estate. If I were to pay the revenues demanded of me under the Stamp Act —and a score of lesser Acts designed to milk colonial merchants for the benefit of the government in London—I would be giving the Crown tax collectors a sum more than three times as large as that which my late uncle paid only thirteen months ago.

"Why? Are we still at war with France? We are not. England is at peace with the whole world. Have additional troops been sent to guard our wilderness towns against raids by savage tribesmen? They have not. Only last week an Algonkin raid near Springfield in the west of the province was repulsed by militiamen—colonials, like you and me. Yes, and their paltry wages are paid in local taxes—paid by you and me—and by the militiamen themselves as private citizens.

"I am no politician, so I have no notion of how often our General Court, our provincial assembly, has asked the government in London for help. I know only that repeated requests have been made. How does London answer these pleas? It sends no troops to our wilderness towns and villages. Oh, no. It contents itself with patrolling our coastal waters, sending frigates and sloops-of-war to harass and search honest merchant vessels carrying our produce to England.

"Speaking of our produce, friends, let me tell you a merchant's secret." John wondered if he might be saying too much, but couldn't resist. The continuing applause had warmed him, and his audience was listening intently, a sea of faces lifted to his. "We aren't as helpless as we may seem. England needs our lumber and farm products and salt—all the hundreds of things we ship across the sea. She needs them as badly as we need her ironware and bolts of cloth.

"And therein lies our hope for the future, our hope that reason will prevail, or hope that enlightened understanding will enable men in the mother country and her colonies to live together in peace and prosperity. But that tolerance, that understanding must be earned.

"England must be made to realize that you and I will not be slaves. We will not bow our heads meekly, accepting rash and unconsidered acts of a Parliament in which we have no voice. Farmers in Wales and townsmen in Yorkshire have a method of redressing their grievances. They send their elected representatives to the Commons. When those rogues disappoint them and vote against the best interests of their districts, the voters—in their mighty wrath—cast them out.

"We have no such voice. We have no representatives in the Commons. Why not? I ask. And you ask it with me!"

The question was rhetorical, and John was startled when his audience thundered, "Why not?"

"Give us representation in the Commons," he cried, "and abominations like the Stamp Act will never again be passed. Our own Members of Parliament will crush the heads of these vipers and kill them before their poison befouls our blood! Give us, I say, legal voices so that we may be heard!"

Men stamped their feet in unison, threatening the collapse of the hall. Sam Adams, abandoning his policy of self-effacement, hurried down to the front and conferred with James Otis in urgent whispers. The tumult was so great that both men were forced to cup their hands and speak close to each other's ears.

But John was unaware of their tensions. Carried away by his own enthusiasm and the approval of the crowd, he knew only that he had the miraculous ability to arouse an audience by expressing his own feelings and opinions. The men who shouted, applauded, and stamped weren't fawning on him because he was the wealthiest man in Massachusetts, but were carried away because his ideas and the force of his delivery struck a responsive chord in all of them.

"You have a right to the liberties and privileges of the English Constitution," he declared, his voice soaring. "I, too, have that right. Together we will enjoy those freedoms—no matter how great the cost, short of shedding blood. We, like our brethren across the sea, love justice and honor. They shall prevail! Then, united under the Crown, we shall go forward together toward a future bright with promise, a future that, with the help of Almighty God, we shall share in freedom and dignity!"

The audience gave him a standing ovation as he stepped down from the podium. James Otis went up to the platform to introduce the next speaker, and John crowded onto the bench beside Sam Adams.

"They loved it," Sam Adams told him above the uproar. "Listen."

John was forced to stand, wave, and smile repeatedly before order was restored.

"A man with your talent as an orator is needed in the General Court," Adams told him.

John still suspected the editor's motives. "My talent—or my money?"

"May the devil take and keep your damned money." Adams looked like a monkey when he became scornful. "You've done more to unite the men of this town than I've been able to do in a year of writing on the self-same subject in the *Gazette*. Look at them!"

John followed the direction of his gaze, and was surprised to see that the conservative merchants were glowing. The clergymen, physicians, and other professional men had awakened from their

82

lethargy, and the Harvard alumni looked as pleased as the dock-hands.

"Don't do anything that goes against your nature," Adams said. "But you owe it to Massachusetts as well as yourself to weigh the idea of taking a seat in the General Court."

John would have found the suggestion ludicrous when he had entered Faneuil Hall, but the experience he had enjoyed on the podium had changed his sense of values. "I'll think about it," he said.

6

The Stamp Act became effective on November 1, 1765, and chance thrust John into the limelight again. Through sheer ac-cident a Hancock ship, the *Boston Packet*, was scheduled to sail for London the following day. Her hold was crammed with cargo being sent to the English market, and under the law her owner was required to purchase tax stamps worth approximately one hun-dred and seventeen pounds.

John had no intention of paying a penny.

Both Governor Francis Bernard, who had recovered from a de-bilitating illness, and Hutchinson, his deputy, privately sympa-thized with the colonists in their struggle against the legislation that many farsighted men on both sides of the Atlantic considered unfair. Nevertheless it was the Governor's duty to enforce the law, and he sent to the waterfront for a direct confrontation with the owner of the brig in this initial test of the Stamp Act's effec-tiveness.

John had anticipated an official reaction of some sort, and shortly before the *Boston Packet* was scheduled to weigh anchor, he walked down to the Hancock Wharf from his office. To his surprise a large crowd had gathered, and he felt uneasy when he saw that many of the men who poured out of waterfront taverns were carrying barrel staves and spars. Sam Adams, who had a knack for turning up whenever trouble was brewing, stood at the far edge of the crowd with several cronies, and John frowned. Violence solved no problems, and he believed with all his heart that reason would prevail when questions of policy were settled on a high plane.

A few moments later an official carriage with the royal seal on its doors pulled up at the foot of the pier, and Thomas Hutchinson descended. He was accompanied by only one aide, a dragoon officer in full-dress scarlet tunic and brass helmet.

The crowd immediately converged on the pair, and John became angry when he saw merchant sailors, cargo handlers, and bullies who had no known means of support lock arms. Hutchinson halted, the aide put a hand to the hilt of his sword and they said something to each other in low tones.

John acted quickly, before a spark could set off an explosion. "Make way for the representative of the King!" he called sharply.

Men turned, identified the speaker and reluctantly allowed the pair to pass.

Both of the principals realized this was an occasion that would be recorded for posterity, and although they exchanged the smiles of friends, their bows were stiff.

"It has come to the attention of His Majesty's government for Massachusetts Bay," Hutchinson said in a voice loud enough for the whole crowd to hear, "that a merchant vessel flying the pennant of Hancock and Company sets sail today for England."

"Your Excellency's information is correct," John replied, speaking with equal clarity.

"You are the principal owner, sir?"

"I am, sir."

"Do you have a copy of her manifest?"

Elias Wheaton, who stood behind John, produced one.

Hutchinson studied it in silence for so long that the crowd became restless.

John was afraid that boredom might produce the violence he wanted to avert. "Under the terms of the Stamp Act passed by the Parliament," he said, "I am required to purchase tax stamps in the amount of one hundred seventeen pounds, eleven shillings and thruppence."

Hutchinson stopped doing mental arithmetic and smothered a relieved smile. "In the King's name, I call on you to pay your rightful tax."

The crowd became tense.

"In the name of justice, Your Excellency, I must refuse." It occurred to John that a riot would almost certainly break out if he was placed under arrest, unless he himself ordered the throng to disperse.

Hutchinson had known his reply in advance, and was not surprised. "Technically, sir, you are in direct contempt of a legal act of the British Parliament."

"In my opinion and that of my countrymen, the law itself is illegal and therefore invalid." Some of the rowdies were edging closer, and John hoped the verbal minuet could be brought to a swift end.

But the Lieutenant Governor had his intructions, and intended to obey them to the letter. If he was aware of the mob's menace, he gave no sign of it. "Do you realize, sir that you place yourself in jeopardy of a civil suit in the King's courts for recovery of the tax moneys, compounded at an interest rate of twelve percent?"

"I do, sir." John admired his courage, and kept a wary eye on three bullies armed with spars.

"Do you also realize, sir, that your refusal to obey the law places you in criminal contempt, and that you stand in jeopardy of prosecution in the King's courts?"

"I do, sir." The day was raw, with a chilly wind blowing across the harbor from the west, but John began to perspire.

"Let all present take due note of the warning given in the King's name to a Crown subject." Hutchinson paused, and his tone was informal when he raised his voice again. "Fortunately for you, sir, you err only on technical grounds. As it happens, no stamps printed under the authority of Parliament's Act are as yet available. Therefore I give you a certificate to that effect, in duplicate, signed by me and countersigned by His Excellency, Governor Bernard."

John accepted the two sheets of parchment with a solemn face, even though the crowd was now cheering lustily. Reason had indeed prevailed: Bernard and Hutchinson had chosen a graceful, civilized way to escape from the cruel dilemma imposed on them by London. He raised his hand for silence, and was surprised when the mob obeyed him instantly.

"Mr. Wheaton," he said to his chief clerk, not realizing he was using the form of address preferred by colonials instead of the long-familiar Master, "give one copy to the captain of the *Boston Packet*, so he may show it to the Collector of the Port when he reaches London. Place the other copy in our public records." There were no such records at Hancock and Company, but the phrase sounded authoritative.

Hutchinson's task was finished, and he bowed. "Your servant, sir."

John impulsively extended his hand.

The Lieutenant Governor shook it warmly, then turned toward the foot of the wharf.

The crowd fell back to give him passage, but several of the rowdies began to jeer, and in a moment the whole mob picked up the refrain.

John was outraged. "Quiet!" he called. "You men stand on private property—my property. And I'll permit no one to show disrespect to the Crown on my land!"

The jeers died away, and some of the roughly clad men looked at him in bewilderment.

Still not satisfied, John escorted the Lieutenant Governor to his carriage, and made a point of removing his hat as he bowed low before closing the door. It was enough, he thought angrily, that the Crown officials had no intention of trying to enforce the unpopular law. Even though the victory had been won by unorthodox means, it was still a triumph. Now it was important that men be taught to regain the respect for the Crown that had been lost during the bitter dispute.

7

Lydia Hancock had gained so much additional weight since her husband's death that she had been forced to have a whole new wardrobe made. But she cheerfully helped herself to a second, steaming portion of oyster stew, and liberally sprinkled it with squares of toasted wheat bread that had been soaked in butter and herbs. "This is the first night in three weeks that you and I have had dinner alone," she said, her manner mildly reproving.

John helped himself to another glass of Madeira, and was pleased that one of his ships had captured a Spanish merchantman off the northern coast of Jamaica. Spanish Madeira was far superior to its English imitation. "I find that the General Court takes up more of my time than I thought it would. Between meetings and dinners and my work at the office, I have very little time to myself these days."

His aunt glanced up from her bowl. "Your uncle wouldn't have approved of your political career."

"Times change, ma'am," he said politely.

"And I'd hate to think of what he'd have said if he had seen men like Revere and that dreadful Adams person sitting at this table!"

John laughed, then sipped his wine. "Paul Revere is a remarkable fellow."

"He makes exquisite silver." Lydia's tone put the craftsman in his place.

"Quite right. He also has read extensively. He knows more of the writings of Rousseau than I do, and he holds no degree from Harvard."

She ate her stew without comment.

"I can't blame you for disliking Sam, of course. Even his cousin has no great love for him."

Her sniff was eloquent. "I should think not. John Adams is a gentleman."

"But he respects Sam, as I do. As everyone does. There isn't a man in the colonies as energetic. And he has the quickest, most agile mind I've ever encountered. I don't believe that Dr. Franklin himself is as clever."

"How can you speak of that wretch in the same breath with Benjamin Franklin?"

John grinned at her over the rim of his glass. "There's the great paradox, Aunt Lydia. Sam is corresponding regularly with Dr. Franklin these days. And with Colonel Washington of Virginia, who is quite a gentleman, too, from all I hear. Sam is setting up a whole spider's network of correspondents in every colony, so we can keep in touch with each other for our mutual good."

"If you're not careful, Sam Adams will have you hanged, young man."

"I'll admit that some of his ideas are too radical. I can't agree

87

with him when he says we must be granted our representational rights in Parliament or declare our independence from England—"

"Don't even speak such treason under this roof!" Lydia forgot her stew for the moment and glared across the candlelighted table.

"Please don't become upset. It's just his form of daydreaming, Aunt Lydia. He's a practical man who seeks realistic results, and he has a genius for organizing and exciting crowds. He can make even the illiterates understand the basic principles of political issues, and he manipulates them for the good of the colonies."

"In my opinion," she retorted, "he manipulates you."

"Oh, he tries from time to time," John admitted. "But I think I exert a modifying influence on him. I see myself as a bridge between the Governor's Mansion and the *Gazette* office."

"I've yet to hear of a physician curing a case of the great pox, but a great many have become infected while treating their patients."

"If Sam hadn't aroused public opinion against the Stamp Act, I'd either be in prison today—or out of business. But I'm still prospering, in spite of a drop in prices both here and in England, so what more can I ask?"

"You're as bad as your uncle," Lydia replied with a deep sigh as she rang for a servingmaid and requested another platter of butter-soaked toast. "You think of nothing but your work."

John nibbled complacently on a sweet Danish biscuit, which he took from a box that a merchant in Copenhagen had sent him as a gift.

"I'm accustomed to neglect, but others are less likely to be forgiving. You haven't seen your mother in many months."

"I've had no chance to visit Braintree, and when I wrote to offer her a trip here, her only answer was that it would be inconvenient." Old hurts could still rankle.

"You must accept people as they are," she said gently.

"They must accept me, too."

Lydia wasn't quite ready to reveal her point, preferring to lead up to it indirectly. "You didn't go to your sister's wedding to Richard Perkins, either."

"I sent Mary and Dick a handsome gift of five hundred pounds and furnished their house. They'll come to Boston one of these days, you know. We're quite fond of each other. Besides," John added dryly, "I discharge my family obligations by employing Ebenezer. He believes that the Hancock name entitles him to a post of responsibility, and Eli Wheaton has had to hire a special clerk to check on everything that Eb does so his mistakes won't cost us dearly."

"I wonder if you realize you've become very waspish for a man just turned thirty."

"My foster parents," he replied half-seriously, "taught me that false sentiment would addle my wits."

"I also tried to teach you the difference between false sentiment and real." Lydia put down her spoon and faced him across the table. "You need a wife."

John groaned.

"You do. You've formed too many selfish habits, and you'll be transformed into a crusty old man before your time."

"The ladies of Boston make my life a nightmare, Aunt Lydia. Not a day passes without an invitation to dinner or tea or a salon visit, at the very least. It's astonishing how many women in this town have unmarried daughters and granddaughters. My home is my only safe refuge from them, so I beg you not to start conniving against me, too."

She found his bantering tone offensive. "Most of the ladies who have invited you to their homes are my good friends. You forget that you're the most eligible bachelor in Massachusetts."

"You're wrong, ma'am. They give me no chance to forget it. I'm sure some of them pace the floors of their bedchambers trying to think of schemes that will part me from my money." The Danish biscuits were tasteless now, and John pushed away the box.

"No man can be truly happy without a wife," the old lady said stubbornly.

"I'm sorry to contradict you, Aunt Lydia, but I'm living proof that a bachelor can be contented with his lot. My mind is free for business, my own and that of the General Court."

"Politics are no substitute for a woman."

He thought it unwise to tell her that he occasionally spent an hour or two in the company of one of the most attractive of the waterfront jades, who had moved into a small house on Hancock property not far from the wharves. Aunt Lydia, who knew nothing of such creatures, much less of a man's sudden cravings, would be sure to disapprove.

"Stop smirking. The head of Hancock and Company needs a son to succeed him."

John's smugness vanished. "When Parliament comes to its senses and prices rise enough to give us the profit margin I want, I'll have more time to myself. Then I'll have the chance to rearrange my private life and think more seriously of marriage."

"I hope you'll arrange to keep your evenings free next week," Lydia replied sweetly. "We're going to have a visitor from Braintree."

He peered at her suspiciously.

"Dorothy Quincy."

The Hancocks were distantly related to the Quincy family, but there were too many of them in Braintree for him to keep them straight in his mind, and he shrugged.

"She is Colonel Edmund's daughter, and a great beauty at seventeen."

John blinked. "A girl of seventeen is a child, Aunt Lydia."

"A young woman of seventeen is old enough for marriage!"

"I've been appointed to three General Court committees and will spend very few evenings at home." Refusing to let her meddle, he hurled the challenge at her.

"At seventeen," Lydia said gently, "a girl is also young enough to wait until a stubborn, selfish man comes to his senses. Roister with Sam Adams at that frightful Long Room Club, drink flip with him and fill the air with pipe smoke. You'll grow tired of those empty pastimes soon enough. In the meantime you'll have met Dolly. In fact, you'll be seeing a great deal of her, as I've decided to make her my protégé. Her parents are pleased—"

"As well they should be. Not every girl in Massachusetts is taken under the wing of the wealthiest dowager in the colonies!"

"—and have agreed to let her spend at least a part of every winter season here with me. She's the most handsome and witty young woman in all of the New World, and when she's been polished by Boston she'll be a rare gem. So you needn't look down your nose, John. If you don't want her, someone else will.

And that would be a pity, because I know of no one better suited to become the mother of your children."

He remembered hearing, on his visit to England, that Princess Augusta had been influential in choosing Charlotte of Mecklenburg as her son's wife. John had little sympathy for George III these days, but could understand how the King must have felt when he had been informed that a wife had been chosen for him.

8

Dolly Quincy sat beneath the crystal chandelier in the main parlor of the Hancock mansion, the light of the smokeless French tapers playing on her red-blond hair and bringing out the deep green of her eyes. Her bare shoulders were exposed prettily, the skirt of her green taffeta gown was draped at one side of her chair and, even though the snow was thick on the ground outside, she toyed with an ivory and lace fan. She and Aunt Lydia were deep in conversation, seemingly unaware that anyone had come into the room, but John was not fooled.

Pausing on the threshold, he wondered how long the girl had been posing, waiting for him to arrive. "Good evening, ladies," he said, bending to kiss Aunt Lydia's cheek.

They simulated surprise. "You're so late that we didn't know whether to keep dinner until you arrived." Lydia spoke calmly, but was furious because he was neglecting her guest.

John was too tired for verbal fencing. "I hope you received the note I sent you late this afternoon, Aunt. I told you I couldn't get home in time."

She nodded stiffly, glowering at him.

"I had some chops at the Long Room Club."

Dorothy flirted with him over the top of her fan, proving herself unusually adept for a girl of only seventeen. "We had a delicious dinner from a French recipe. It was ham cooked in a red wine—"

"Strips of ham sautéed with Burgundy, mushrooms, and onions," John said brusquely. "It's a Belgian dish Dr. Franklin ate in Holland some years ago. He was kind enough to send me the recipe."

The girl's enormous eyes widened.

He became conscious of a light dusting of freckles across the bridge of her nose, and grudgingly admitted to himself that she was even more attractive than Aunt Lydia had predicted. But the constant fluttering of her eyelashes whenever he had been near her in the past seventy-two hours was irritating. She was too wise, too knowing for someone of her tender years.

Lydia stood, determined to make up for lost time. "You must be chilled, John. Shall I have a rum toddy sent in to you?"

He was so tired after a long day at the office and a brisk discussion at the Long Room Club of the next step to be taken in the campaign against the Stamp Act that he knew a glass of strong rum would put him to sleep. "I believe I'll have a cup of tea, but please sit down, Aunt Lydia. I'll ring for it."

"Never mind, dear." Her bulk was no impediment when she wanted to move quickly. "I must check with the cook about tomorrow's dinner."

John found himself alone with Dolly Quincy, and literally didn't know what to say to her. "I trust you're enjoying your visit to Boston?"

She surprised him by giggling.

"I didn't know I had said something amusing."

"You ask the same question, in the same tone, every time we meet. So—let me remind you, once again—I'm no stranger to Boston, John. I spent six weeks here, two years ago, when Cousin Abby married John Adams."

He had forgotten she was related to Abigail Adams. "You don't resemble her physically, but are you alike in other ways?" Abigail's keen intellect had made him uncomfortable whenever they had met.

Dolly drew an intricate pattern in the air with her fan. "Don't tell her I said so, but I don't understand a word she says. She speaks of excise taxes and the development of personal freedoms under English common law. Gracious!"

John was relieved, although there was nothing so complicated about either subject that they were beyond the grasp of an ordinary intelligence. Knowing the views of Edmund Quincy, he suspected that Dolly had received a thorough education. "You were tutored in Braintree?"

"Your sister and I went to the same tutor for eleven years."
She had told him precisely the same thing only twenty-four hours
earlier, and it was difficult to keep an edge from her voice.

"I see." He saw far more than she realized. Mary Hancock
Perkins had received an excellent education, thanks to Uncle
Thomas' generosity, so Dolly obviously knew far more about
taxes and English common law than she was telling him. Apparently she belonged to the breed who concealed their intellect from
men prior to marriage.

It was Dolly's turn to ask questions. "What do you do for entertainment? Aunt Lydia tells me you have very few pleasures."

He wished, fervently, that Aunt Lydia would keep her mouth
shut. "I find it unexpectedly satisfying to hold a seat in the General Court."

Dolly laughed at him. "But that's work, like Papa's service as a
colonel of militia in the war against the French and Indians."

"A man finds his greatest pleasure in work." John was bored,
and wondered angrily why Aunt Lydia hadn't found someone
older and more stable to foist off on him.

"Many men don't share your views."

He wondered how a girl of seventeen was in a position to speak
with authority about "many men."

"Do you never dance the quadrille, John?"

He wanted to take off his wig, rub his scalp and go off to bed.
"I've never heard of the quadrille." He made no attempt to hide
his annoyance.

A servingmaid came in with his tea, and he tried in vain to
think of an excuse to detain her.

"Let me," Dolly said, pouring a cup deftly. "There."

He was forced to admit that her movements were exceptionally
dainty. "Won't you have some?"

"Oh, no. I've already been far too greedy this evening. If I
lived in a magnificent house like this, with a dozen servants to
wait on me, I'd never want to eat anywhere else."

"I dine with friends when the business of Hancock and Company or that of Massachusetts makes it necessary." He realized he
sounded pompous, and decided it was her fault.

Dolly was conscious of his sudden stiffness, and was afraid she
had gone too far in revealing her hopes. "It's a problem I shall

never have to face," she announced gaily. "None of my suitors are wealthy."

The tea was making John sleepy, and he stifled a yawn.

Dolly was stung, and flirted with him still more blatantly.

He watched the way she used her fan, and suddenly was reminded of Susan Barnard.

"I hope you'll let me teach you the quadrille and some of the other new dances."

"Not tonight!" He revealed his alarm more than he intended.

Dolly was on her own ground now, and smiled gently. "I doubt that even the Hancocks of Beacon Hill keep a company of musicians at hand to play at a moment's notice. We'll wait until you have an opportunity to relax. Next summer, perhaps, if you come to Braintree then. If not, you may have a little more time for frivolity when I visit Boston next winter than you have at your disposal now."

John was immeasurably relieved that she seemed no more anxious than he to pursue the romance that Aunt Lydia seemed so determined to arrange. "By all means," he said genially, "we shall dance together next year."

Dolly's green eyes narrowed. "I regard that as a promise, and I'll remember it."

9

On the morning of May 16, 1766, John sat at his desk in his shirt-sleeves, working furiously. The affairs of the colonies were taking up so much of his time that he had to attend to some of them in his office, and compensated for the lost time by delaying his evening dinner for an hour or two every night, but it couldn't be helped. Sam Adams was responsible for the formation of a new organization devoted to the cause of furthering colonial interests, the Sons of Liberty, and it was John's task to write the wealthy merchant members of the Committees of Correspondence in Philadelphia, New York Town, and other major communities.

He scribbled rapidly, and didn't bother to look up when Thomas Cushing, the first assistant to the aging Elias Wheaton and himself an active member of the Long Room Club, came into the office.

"The new brig has returned from London, John. She'll be casting anchor at Hancock's Wharf in a few minutes."

"Mmm?"

"The *Harrison* is putting into port after her round-trip maiden voyage," Cushing repeated patiently. "And I wish you'd let me send some of those letters for you."

"Jim Otis feels they'll carry more weight if I write them in my own hand, and I agree. Besides, you have a speech to deliver at Friday night's session of the General Court." John glanced out of the window at the brig nosing alongside the pier. "Go down and meet the *Harrison* for me, will you? And tell Captain Wright I'll take him to the Bunch of Grapes for noon dinner and hear his report then."

Cushing closed the door behind him.

John had learned that Committee of Correspondence letters were the most effective when they were a trifle informal, but he found it difficult to unbend, even on paper, and labored hard to achieve the right tone.

There was a loud knock at the door, and he looked up in annoyance as Cushing appeared again on the threshold. "Captain Wright wants to see you at once, John. He says his news is too important to keep."

Elias Wheaton stood in the background, shaking his head at the accessibility of the young Company head. In Thomas' day, no such breeziness would have been tolerated.

Captain Mark Wright, heavily suntanned, bounded up the stairs, pushed through the clerks' room and raced into the inner sanctum. "Mr. Hancock," he shouted in his quarterdeck voice, "the Stamp Act has been repealed by Parliament."

John was too stunned to move.

Eli was the first to react, and his high-pitched cackle echoed through the office.

"It's true, Mr. Hancock, so help me!" Wright declared. "William Pitt, Edmund Burke—all our friends in the Commons—worked like demons on our behalf. The repeal bill was passed on March seventeenth, and I delayed my sailing for two days while the papers waited at Whitehall for the signature of the King, damn his hide. He signed, all right, because he had no choice."

John's mind was whirling so rapidly that he didn't rebuke his ship's master for speaking disrespectfully of the King. Still trying to catch his breath, he pumped Captain Wright's hand. "Eli," he said at last, "close down the Company for the day. Give every man a holiday with full pay. Tom, take the news to Sam Adams and Jim Otis. Captain, I want you to come with me."

Tom Cushing was whooping with glee, but managed to stop capering around the room. "Where are you going, John?"

"To the Governor's Mansion. Bernard and Hutchinson were on our side from the start, and I want them to share this great day with us."

Cushing sobered, stared at him and shook his head. No other member of the General Court or the Sons of Liberty would have thought in terms of reconciliation with the Crown authorities.

Governor Bernard immediately issued a proclamation making May 19 an official holiday, and Boston went wild with joy. Church bells pealed at one minute past midnight on the nineteenth, and rang through the rest of the night and day. Militia units of war veterans paraded, hundreds of candles were lighted on the Liberty Tree, scorching the old elm's leaves, and eight bands of fife players and drummers provided enthusiastic, semimusical entertainment for the edification of the citizens.

The Sons of Liberty paid the bills of all who were being held at the debtors' prison, with John privately providing the funds. That afternoon he and a select company joined Governor Bernard in the Council chamber at Province House, the government seat, to drink the King's health in honor of the occasion. Most members of the General Court were conspicuous by their absence, and none of those who attended seemed to think that it was ironic, under the circumstances, to pay token honor to the monarch who had inspired the Stamp Act and then had been forced to back down in the face of united colonial opposition.

At sundown the Common was lighted by hundreds of oil lamps, some of them piled in a column more than one hundred and fifty feet high. Sam Adams had intended to present a number of speakers, but John dissuaded him, saying, "This is no time to gloat."

The Sons of Liberty put on a mammoth fireworks display attended by every man, woman, and child in town who wasn't ailing, and the unusual sobriety of the crowd was the most impressive feature of the festivities. Then John surprised the throng by inviting everyone to an even more spectacular fireworks show on the grounds of his Beacon Hill mansion. Barmaids and waiters from a score of inns, whom he had hired for the evening, circulated with trays of wine and beer and ale for the adults, glasses of melon juice for the children, and token gifts for the women. Thousands of small mirrors and strings of beads which had been purchased from English manufacturers for the use of frontier Indian traders were carted up to the house for the novel purpose, and were distributed with abandon.

The mansion itself was opened for the first time to the local aristocracy, merchants, and a small group of English officials. Governor Bernard thought his appearance might be misinterpreted in London, and sent his regrets, but Lieutenant Governor Hutchinson was in attendance. He and several members of his staff ate quantities of the most delicious of local delicacies, turtle meat poached in dry sack, and declared they had never tasted better.

The kitchen staff, working frantically under Aunt Lydia's direction, also prepared platters of cold salmon, venison steaks, and sides of beef, smoking joints of roast ox and superbly carved wildfowl. The best of English, French, and Spanish wine flowed freely, and the party was a smashing success.

Only Aunt Lydia disapproved, but did her duty bravely and forced herself to speak politely to her nephew's political associates. Her friends called her gallant, and Hutchinson paid her the supreme compliment of telling her, in the hearing of at least fifty guests, that she was a great lady.

John enjoyed himself. He promised four clergymen that he would import new bells at his own expense to replace instruments that had been cracked by enthusiastic sextons during the day. Carried away by his own enthusiasm, he also offered impressive donations to the ministers of seven houses of worship. Now that the Stamp Act had been repealed, he could afford to be generous, for Tom Cushing estimated that Hancock and Company would save a minimum of three thousand pounds per year that would have had to be paid into the royal coffers had the Act been rigorously enforced by the Crown.

Sam Adams, bored and ill at ease in the presence of ladies and gentlemen, retired to the corner of the dining room nearest the pantry entrance, and made no attempt to mix with the throng. He ate sparingly, and belied his reputation by drinking very little, which surprised those of the gentry who believed him to be a gross, rabble-rousing lout. Although he said very little, he missed no detail, carefully noting the attitudes of everyone present and storing away his observations.

It was midnight when John, flushed with wine and success, joined his political mentor and threw an arm around his stooped shoulders. "You haven't tried the roast goose or the venison-liver dumplings," he said accusingly. "This is the greatest celebration in the history of Massachusetts, Sam, so stop moping."

"Rich foods give me indigestion," Adams replied with a faint smile. "Even that turtle steak, which I love, is bad for my spleen. Besides," he added quietly, "this is only the first of our celebrations. There will be many more."

John's conviviality became somewhat uncertain. "But our dispute with the Crown and Commons has been ended. We've won the day, and good relations will be restored now."

"Are you saying you think there's no more need for our Committees of Correspondence or the Sons of Liberty?"

John considered the question. "Well, no. I wouldn't go that far. The Committees exchange useful information, and the Sons are a reminder to London that we're ready to take a firm stand again—in the unlikely event that the Crown and Parliament make unfair demands on us in the future."

"I wish," Adams said quietly, "that you'd apply your business acumen and the judgment of human nature you show in your trading operations to the realm of politics. The King and his supporters in the Commons have suffered a humiliating defeat. You've met George of England—and Hanover. Did he strike you as the type of man who will be genuinely humbled by this experience—and learn from it?"

John laughed. "He's far too arrogant to learn from anything. He's an opinionated boor with a closed mind."

"So I believe, too. That means he'll take the first opportunity

—even make one, if he must—to teach his disrespectful colonials a lesson. Every public statement he makes strengthens my conviction that he forgets he's a semi-impotent Hanoverian hampered by the English Constitution. Someone, I don't care who it may have been, persuaded him to believe he's a Stuart who rules by Divine right. So he'll try again and still again, like a parent disciplining a wayward child."

John was afraid he was right.

"Now, look at the situation as our people see it. The colonies took a united stand, and held firm. We've tasted liberty, and it's sweet. We're going to want still more freedom in the management of our own affairs, and we've learned how to win it. When two cavalrymen ride straight at each other at a breakneck gallop, and neither is willing to turn away, they collide."

The logic was so sound, so inevitable, that John could find no counterargument.

FOUR

1768 — 1773

1

"Even George III," Sam Adams told his friends at a dinner
meeting of the Long Room Club early in 1768, "has discovered
there's more than one way to skin a deer."

He was right. The Crown had suffered a severe loss of prestige
when the Stamp Act had been repealed, but the King and Commons found another way to increase revenues from the North
American colonies. Several new bills were passed by Parliament
which accomplished the same purpose. Called the Townshend
Acts, they imposed stiff duties on tea, glass, paper, and a number
of other consumer goods which the colonies had to import from
England.

Merchants in the colonial cities were undisturbed, and blithely
planned to smuggle goods past the overworked and understaffed
Collectors of the Ports, as they and their predecessors had done
with such success for a full half century. But the government in
London was prepared for just such evasive tactics, and large numbers of newly appointed customs commissioners crossed the Atlantic, accompanied by a small army of clerks and inspectors.

"The law," Thomas Hutchinson grimly announced in Boston,
"will be obeyed. Officers holding royal warrants will inspect every
ship that docks here before cargoes will be unloaded."

John had already told his friends and associates that he would permit no inspectors to board Hancock ships, but he decided a private stand was inadequate to meet the challenge when Hutchinson's ultimatum was printed and posted in dozens of public places in the city. Ignoring the advice of his more conservative colleagues who dined him at the Bunch of Grapes, he decided to express his own views in the General Court, to which he had just been re-elected.

"Colonials," he cried in an impassioned speech, "are not milk cows who graze in wilderness pastures for the purpose of providing pails of liquid gold for the nourishment of the Treasury. The King and Commons have forgotten the lessons of '65. We will not be taxed without due representation in the Commons. Nor will we submit to the shame, the ultimate shame, of permitting spies who carry the King's seal to board our ships.

"Under the English Constitution, a man's home may not be invaded without a search warrant that shows just cause for this breach of privacy. We in Massachusetts are a maritime people, and our ships are as inviolate as our homes. To many of us, they are our second homes.

"Therefore I give solemn warning to the Crown, and to all who hold royal authority here. Come what may, I will not suffer any King's officer to board any ship that flies my ensign!"

The speech created a sensation in Massachusetts, and was received with the same breathless interest elsewhere when the local Committee of Correspondence reported it verbatim to the other colonies. Sensible men agreed he might be going too far, but in the next breath admitted that they believed he had no honorable alternative. A principle was at stake—and so was the solvency of his commercial empire.

The new customs commissioners and their staffs arrived in Boston late in March 1768, and ten days later, on April 8, the flagship of the house of Hancock, the huge 580-ton *Lydia*, reached her home port with a cargo from London. Later that same day two customs inspectors, Owen Richards and Robert Jackson, went on board. John, who had been waiting in his office for just such a development, immediately went to the ship and, in the presence of numerous witnesses, instructed her master, Captain James Scott, not to permit the officials to go below.

The burly Scott relished his assignment, and gladly would have had both the officers thrown from the main deck onto Hancock's Wharf. But John specifically directed him not to use violence, which was unnecessary, as the frightened inspectors were glad to go ashore. The incident seemed to be at an end, neither the Governor nor Lieutenant Governor reacted and peace-loving householders breathed a collective sigh of relief.

The following evening, however, a messenger came to the Hancock mansion while John and his aunt were sitting down to a late dinner. "Mr. Hancock needs a little time to himself," Aunt Lydia told the servingmaid, unconsciously using the new form of address that had become almost universal throughout the colonies. "Tell the man to come back later. Or to see Mr. Hancock at his office tomorrow morning."

"Wait," John said. "Who is the fellow?"

"A sailor from the *Lydia*, sir."

John bolted from the table.

"Cap'n Scott's compliments," the seaman told him. "One o' them rascals who came on board yesterday has just sneaked into the hold."

"I'll be with you in a moment." John dashed to his own bedchamber, buckled on his smallsword and jammed two loaded dueling pistols into his belt.

Aunt Lydia nervously awaited him in the corridor. "I've just heard," she said, shrinking against the far wall when she saw his weapons. "What's going to happen?"

"I don't know." He wished he could comfort her, but there was nothing he could say or do to relieve her mind.

"Will there be a fight?" Plump fingers closed over his sleeve.

He shrugged. "If need be, I suppose."

"I—I realize you can't tolerate this sort of interference, John. But, please, let others go down to the ship for you. Don't become mixed up in this yourself."

He gently disengaged her hold. "I can't, Aunt Lydia. She's my ship. I couldn't live with myself if I sent other men to take risks while I cower and quake behind these respectable walls." He realized he sounded pompous, but didn't know how else to express himself.

"If you're there, and a fight breaks out with a Crown officer, you'll be responsible."

"It's my duty to bear the full responsibility." He smiled, trying feebly to ease her worry. "Even if there were no other reason, I'd lose my personal sense of honor. The *Lydia* was the last ship Uncle Thomas built."

The old lady burst into tears.

John patted her awkwardly on the shoulder, helplessly incapable of stemming her emotional outburst.

"You could be charged with treason," she wailed. "You, the most upstanding and loyal man in Boston!"

"I'll be home soon." Hurrying down the stairs two at a time, it occurred to him that after tonight no one would be able to take his loyalty to the Crown for granted again.

Accompanied by the sailor, he hurried down Beacon Hill and rapped on the door of Dan Fowler's house. The Hancock foreman listened without comment to an explanation of the situation, went off for the musket he used when he went deer hunting in the western part of the province and joined them. They paused at several waterfront taverns to augment their ranks with Company cargo handlers and seamen, and in the process picked up more than fifty idlers, who happily trailed after them as they walked rapidly to Hancock's Wharf, where the *Lydia* was tied.

Captain Scott met the ship's owner and his companions as they trooped onto the main deck. "I've let him scurry and scrape around below, Mr. Hancock, like a rat. He's still down there, but he can't see anything in the dark, so I don't reckon he's doing too much harm. The boys and I have been tempted to tie his hands and feet and throw him into the harbor, but I thought I'd better wait for your permission."

"There's no need for murder, Captain." John thought it strange that he felt as calm as he did when handling routine matters behind his desk. "Send a couple of sailors below to fetch the fellow. And post a guard at the gangway so no one except Company employees will come on board." He looked at the crowd of gesticulating men milling around on the pier and felt apprehensive.

"Aye aye, sir." Scott would have preferred a more vigorous solution, but obeyed orders.

John paced up and down the deck as he waited. He had reached a major turning point in his life, and knew that the colonies' problems with the Crown could no longer be solved by reason and good will alone. In brief, he was wrong and Sam Adams was right. The King and his supporters in Parliament wouldn't be satisfied until the spirit of independent, fair-minded men in Boston and Philadelphia and other towns was broken and their pride destroyed. The royal policy was mad, defying all logic, and England would suffer as much as the colonies. But fire had to be met with fire if traders and merchants in the New World hoped to survive and keep open the commercial channels on which the comfort of all colonials relied so heavily.

It was a nightmare suddenly come true that someone who loved the freedoms guaranteed by English common law and respected the institution of the monarchy should be placed in the awkward position of being the first colonial to defy the Crown forcibly, thus becoming a traitor. But there was no choice, no other way to protect his own liberties and those of fellow Americans. Perhaps, when the news reached England, the fact that a respectable man of substance had thumbed his nose at the King and Commons would rally the friends of the colonies to take matters into their own hands and restore the amity so desperately needed to prevent a still more drastic deterioration of a situation that had become intolerable.

Two broad-shouldered seamen pushed a middle-aged man in black up onto the deck through a hatch, caught hold of his arms and dragged him toward the owner and master of the *Lydia*.

Scott promptly lost his temper. "You dirty, snooping swine—"

John silenced him with his most imperious wave. "Who are you?" he asked the badly frightened man.

"Owen Richards, your worship. A royal customs inspector holding a warrant signed and sealed by His Majesty himself."

"Show me your credentials. Captain, I need a lantern." John waited until someone brought him a small lamp, then studied the man's commission. There could be no doubt that it was legitimate, and only the fact that it bore no date offered a small legal loophole to excuse what had to be done.

"Mr. Richards," John thundered, speaking in the slow, loud voice he used when making public addresses, "as the owner of this vessel I demand to know what you're doing here." The legal grounds for claiming that the inspector's presence was unauthorized were so flimsy that he decided to ignore the point.

"I'm doing my duty, Master Hancock." The Englishman, still held in the firm grip of the two sailors, was conscious of the giants who surrounded him.

"You trespass on private property, sir!" John knew the charge was absurd, but it would have a clear ring when repeated at Sons of Liberty meetings.

"Acts of Parliament grant me the right to inspect any vessel that puts into this port, Master Hancock." Richards' voice trembled, but he managed to defend himself. "The full power of the Crown is behind me."

John continued to play-act, aware that the men gathered on the pier would repeat every word he said. "I find it difficult to believe that either His Majesty or his distinguished ministers would send a spy sneaking onto an honest merchant's ship at this time of night." Suddenly he tired of the game. He was taking a stand for the sake of principle, as well as his own financial protection, and it irritated him to pretend.

"However," he continued, "even if the King and Commons had given you specific orders to board my ship and search her tonight, I would not permit you to do so. I know my rights as an Englishman, and must insist that you leave the *Lydia* at once."

Richards wanted to do his sworn duty, and shivered. "What will you do if I refuse, Master Hancock?"

John felt sorry for the man, and wanted to assure him he would suffer no personal harm. "You'll be escorted ashore. I'm taking note of the fact that you're leaving under protest," he added quickly, making certain that the man would not get into trouble with his own superiors.

Richards was aware of the favor, and smiled weakly.

"Dan, see that he's deposited ashore. Gently." John peered at the crowd of cargo handlers and seamen, and had second thoughts. "Hold on. Where are you living, Richards?"

"At an inn called the Bible and Three Crowns, Master Hancock."

"See that he gets there with no broken bones, Dan. I'll hold you personally responsible for his safety."

Fowler grimaced, but the thought of disobedience didn't cross his mind.

John watched as Richards was hustled ashore and led off past the waterfront toward the town.

"You were too damned kind to him," Captain Scott growled.

John disliked arguments with bloodthirsty men. It was enough, more than enough, that the circumstances had forced him to make a token show of force.

Sighing deeply, he walked ashore, and was startled when the crowd began to cheer. Several men hoisted him to their shoulders, and someone called, "Get some torches, lads! We'll parade past the Governor's Mansion!"

"I won't have it, boys. Put me down!" John struggled to the ground and faced the surprised throng. "I've made my point tonight, and I see nothing to be gained by rubbing salt into the Governor's wounds."

Turning away abruptly, he walked alone down the pier and started across the silent, dark town. He had accomplished his mission and supposed he should feel satisfied, but his heart was heavy. He, more than any other man in the colonies, had taken a huge stride in the direction of open rebellion against the Crown. And he knew there was no turning back.

2

The Crown Attorney General for Massachusetts, Jonathan Sewell, who happened to be Dolly Quincy's brother-in-law, investigated the ejection of the customs inspector from the *Lydia* and interrogated everyone who had played a role in the affair. Captain Scott and Dan Fowler suffered severe, convenient losses of memory, and none of the sailors or dock hands could recall the incident.

Richards, who should have been the chief prosecution witness, was so grateful for the consideration John had shown him that he refused to testify against his benefactor. Lieutenant Governor Hutchinson, who had been appointed special magistrate of the court of inquiry, was forced to rule that John had broken no laws. Boston laughed, the Sons of Liberty congratulated the hero behind closed doors—and Hutchinson wrote in his official report to London that he considered John Hancock as dangerous an agitator as Sam Adams.

Precisely one month after the affair of the *Lydia*, a still more serious incident flouted royal authority. Another inspector boarded a second Hancock ship, the *Liberty*, as she was about to unload a cargo of contraband Madeira wine. The master of the ship, James Marshall, immediately locked the royal officer in a cabin, took the precaution of boarding the portholes so the inspector could see nothing taking place outside and hurriedly unloaded the cargo before releasing the man.

The official was afraid to tell his superiors the truth, and for a time it appeared that John would again escape unscathed. Then a powerful British frigate, the *Romney*, sailed into Boston harbor for the express purpose of helping the Collector of the Port enforce the law. Captain Marshall died of a sudden heart attack, and that fact, combined with the arrival of the *Romney*, gave the inspector the courage to tell his story.

The *Liberty* was seized, towed out to the frigate and an order was issued under Hutchinson's authority proclaiming her government property. A large mob gathered soon after a meeting of the members of the Long Room Club in Sam Adams' office at the *Gazette*, and made such fierce demonstrations outside the Bible and Three Crowns and other taverns where the customs officials were living that the commissioners, inspectors, and clerks fled to the *Romney* and stayed there.

The patience of the King's ministers was exhausted, and a Principal Collector of Customs in London ordered John Hancock placed under arrest and fined one hundred thousand pounds, a penalty so staggering that most men could not grasp its enormity.

When the order reached Boston, John was released on bail and immediately hired John Adams as his counsel. The case dragged on for several weary months, but the evidence was so flimsy and Adams was so adroit that the charges were dismissed. But the *Liberty* remained in Crown hands and Hutchinson, again acting as presiding magistrate, ordered it permanently confiscated.

John went to the Bunch of Grapes for a celebratory dinner with his attorney, but sat gloomily in his chair, scarcely touching either his roasted salmon steak or his glass of German Rhineland wine, which had found its way into the tavern's cellars by mysterious means.

"Cheer up," John Adams told him, speaking in his prim, schoolmaster's voice. "We've won a great victory."

John rubbed his long jaw and said nothing.

"Do you realize you'd be penniless if you'd been found guilty?"

"Oh, I'm very grateful to you, Johnny. There isn't another lawyer in America who could have done as much for me. But, damn the souls of those royalist scoundrels, they still hold my ship!"

"If I were you, I'd forget the *Liberty*. Her loss is a small price to pay." John Adams carefully lowered his voice. "I can't say I approve of the open flouting of acts of Parliament. You and Cousin Sam and the rest of you would do far better, in my opinion, if you fought these unjust measures in the courts. But I don't see where you have any personal cause for complaint. The customs men are still living in seclusion on board the *Romney*, and not one merchant ship arriving here in the past eight months or more has been inspected. You haven't paid a farthing in customs duties."

A fleeting smile crossed John's lugubrious face. "No thanks to the Crown. How do I regain possession of my brig?"

The attorney carefully added some water to his wine. "A lawsuit would be a waste of time. Bernard and Hutchinson would refer it to London, and I'm afraid that feelings are running too high for you to get a fair hearing there these days. I can't help wishing we were still living uncomplicated lives in Braintree."

"We aren't," John replied succinctly.

His testiness left John Adams unmoved. "Now that you've been cleared of the major charges and can't be tried on the same counts again, you might submit a plea to the Governor. You could claim you're being unduly punished for acts not of your own doing."

"You mean I'd shift the blame to Captain Marshall, who is no longer here to defend himself?"

"Yes, something like that. Coupled with an apology to the Crown, it could embarrass the government. Whether they'd be sufficiently disturbed to return the *Liberty* to you is questionable, but you have nothing to lose by trying."

"I have a great deal to lose, and I won't do it." John realized that men at other tables were looking at him, but was too angry to speak more quietly. "Marshall acted on my orders when he forcibly prevented an inspector from examining his cargo. I'd be a hypocrite if I denied my responsibility."

"In that case, you have virtually no chance of recovering your brig."

"I hate to write off a ship that cost more than two thousand pounds to build. But I'd hate still more to lose my honor. Sam says that every man who sees the *Liberty* tied up alongside the frigate becomes a patriot. Even her name has become a significant symbol."

"I'm not sure I know what Sam means when he speaks of a patriot. Do you, John?"

"Of course. A patriot is a man who loves freedom and is willing to make sacrifices in order to achieve his birthright!"

"Do you still believe we should use peaceful means to halt the Crown's policy of harassment?"

"I prefer reason, provided the other side uses it, too. If they don't, we must turn to other weapons. The goal remains the same, but we must alter our tactics when we're threatened. Force is the only answer to force."

"You've changed," John Adams said gravely.

"Wouldn't you, if you were in my place? The Crown discriminated against me. This lawsuit was a monstrous miscarriage of justice, and I doubt if any other Englishman has ever been sued by the Crown for such a sum. They've hounded and humiliated me, they've tried to break and bankrupt me. And for what reason? Because I've refused to submit meekly when I'm treated as an inferior. If the King and his ministers recognize me as the equal of shipowners in London and merchants in Edinburgh and Manchester, I'll have no quarrel with them. But when they try to penalize me because I live in the colonies rather than in the British Isles, they'll find they've chosen the wrong victim. When someone hits me, I strike back."

"I can't blame you for feeling as you do, but I wish you hadn't become so partisan. I don't know where all this will end if the responsible men on both sides lose their tempers."

"I don't know, either. But I won't be tyrannized, and if I have any voice or influence, neither will anyone else in Massachusetts."

3

"If Dolly will forgive me for talking of business matters at the dinner table," John said to Aunt Lydia and her young guest, "I want you to hear the news from me before your friends give you distorted versions of the truth."

Dolly Quincy's smile was demure. "Please don't mind me. I spend so much time here that I feel like a member of the family."

The significance of her comment was lost on John. "The Crown," he said, "has finally gone too far."

Lydia momentarily lost interest in her minced beef and oyster pudding. "You aren't being sued again?" she asked fearfully.

"That would be very mild. Parliament has passed a new rash of laws, placing an export duty on everything manufactured in England for sale in the colonies. But the makers of the various goods won't pay the tax. We're ordered to pay at this end. Shipowners must pay a part, retail merchants another—and the man or woman who goes into a shop for a yard or two of cloth or a new kettle must pay the rest."

"Why do they hate us?" The old lady dabbed at her eyes with a linen napkin of double damask.

"There are sensible men in Commons, but they've been outmaneuvered by the royal party that believes we've been disrespectful to the Crown. As if anyone can admire that blundering oaf who disgraces the most glorious throne in Christendom!" John didn't let his deep-rooted anger interfere with his appetite, and helped himself to a bun stuffed with nuts, currants, and blueberries.

Dolly felt sufficiently at ease to enter the conversation. "Will you set an example again for the merchants of the colony?"

He continued to address himself to his aunt. "This time there will be no chance to smuggle goods off the wharves. I learned today that two regiments of infantry—the Twenty-ninth and the Fifty-ninth—are being transferred here from Halifax, and a full battery of artillery is being sent to Boston from England."

Lydia gasped, and Dolly replied first. "They dare to send soldiers to occupy the town—like a conquered French city?"

"It's the Crown's privilege to send British troops anywhere in the empire," he replied dryly. "Soldiers armed with loaded muskets and bayonets will protect the customs inspectors in the performance of their duties."

The old lady recovered sufficiently from her shock to ask, "How will you be able to operate the business at a profit, John?"

"I'm putting the whole fleet of merchantmen in drydock," he replied quietly. "I'm sending my last cargo to London tomorrow on the *Lydia,* and her master is carrying letters to all of my London agents, directing them to ship no more goods to me until the King and Commons recover their senses. May we have some tea, please?"

His aunt was in such a daze that Dolly picked up the bell and rang for a servingmaid.

Lydia folded her hands tightly in her lap. "Our income will be reduced."

"We'll have no income," John told her. "When the warehouses are emptied of merchandise, they'll be closed. I'll keep the office open only to pay wages to people like Eli and Dan, who have been with us for so many years, and to newer men like Tom Cushing, who are useful."

Both women knew be meant that he regarded Cushing as a valued political associate, even though he didn't elaborate.

It went against the grain to discuss personal affairs in the presence of an outsider, but John was afraid his aunt would burst into tears. "Don't worry," he said. "We can live for many years on what we've accumulated, without retrenching."

She nodded miserably and turned back to her plate, eating rapidly.

"What will you do, John?" Dolly asked.

He felt her green eyes studying him, and was irritated. If she thought the closing of his business enterprises would enable her to spend more time in his company, he would enlighten her without delay. "I've been elected leader of the Whig party in the General Court—"

"The majority party."

The girl's knowledge of politics surprised him. Few Boston women knew or cared what the provincial assembly did. "Yes. This evening Sam Adams and Joe Warren, the new Speaker, are coming here to discuss plans with me. We'll undoubtedly pass a resolution in the General Court, condemning the invasion."

"What will that accomplish?" Dolly wanted to know.

Her pragmatism pleased him, and the thought flickered through his mind that perhaps she wasn't as emptyheaded a little flirt as he had assumed. "The vote will do very little—except to put us on record." He spoke more to her now than to his aunt. "There are other, better things to do. For the past three or four years I've owned the meeting hall on King Street, near the corner of Brattle Street. I'm going to present it to the citizens of Boston as a gift, along with a fund to pay for concerts, pantomimes, lectures, and the like. I'll make the announcement next week."

Lydia found it difficult to speak with her mouth full of food. "Is this a time for philanthropy?"

"There's none better. Other merchants who don't have our resources are sure to fail, and men who own only one or two merchant ships will become bankrupt. Then there's the question of finding work for seamen and cargo handlers and warehouse men. I'm hoping the General Court will recommend the strengthening of the sea wall in the outer harbor and the draining of the swamps at the north side of Mill Pond. We have no funds of our own for the purpose, and I can only hope the Governor will allocate some. If not, we may have to take up a private subscription. But, to answer you, there's no better time for philanthropy. Our people are going to need entertainment to take their mind off our troubles."

Lydia nodded happily. "You're as generous as your uncle."

"I also have an ulterior purpose." John smiled coldly. "In making over the deed for the hall to the citizens of Boston, I'm stipulating that no British military or naval officers be admitted there, regardless of whether they're wearing uniforms or civilian clothes. Nor are common soldiers or sailors to be admitted."

His daring intrigued Dolly, and she clapped her hands together.

But the old lady frowned. "Won't that make bad feelings even worse?"

"Of course." John sniffed his tea, sipped it and sat back comfortably in his chair. "We want the troops to know they aren't welcome here. We hope they'll feel so ill at ease that General Gage will request the War Office to send them back to Halifax. I hope to visit all of our influential men in the next week or two and get signed pledges from them, promising they won't invite any officers from the garrison to their homes."

Lydia refused to retreat. "Sam Adams' schemes always cause friction, and everything keeps going from bad to worse. I still don't like that man."

"I've learned a great deal from Sam, but these ideas happen to be my own." Again John inhaled the fragrance of his tea.

Dolly brushed a reddish-brown curl away from her bare throat and shoulder. "Would it be helpful," she asked thoughtfully, "if the young ladies of Boston refused all social engagements with the officers of the garrison?"

John forgot his manners and brought his open hand down on the table. "It would be wonderful—if they'd agree!"

"It won't be easy, I know. Some girls are always impressed by uniforms, and the prospect of meeting a new group of handsome young men is exciting. But—if you like—I'll form a committee and see what we can accomplish."

"You'll be doing Massachusetts—and the other colonies—a great service." John grinned at her.

"That's why I'd like to do what I can." Dolly returned his smile.

Lydia glanced at her nephew, then at the girl she wanted him to marry. The familiar, safe world she had known all her life was disappearing, but for the first time these two were really sparking to each other. Perhaps something good would come out of the increasingly bitter quarrel with the Crown.

4

Six ships that made up part of the Hancock fleet did not go into drydock in the winter of 1769–70, after all. John's London agents couldn't believe he meant his instructions to them, and sent him a large consignment of manufactured goods. The officers of the newly arrived regiments braced for trouble, but he confounded them by announcing he had no intention of unloading them. Instead, he announced, he would send the merchandise back to England as soon as the vessels could be made ready for another voyage.

Adding insult to injury, he called a meeting of all the town's merchants and offered to return their cargo to London at his own expense, too. Then, to make sure that no one in Boston would fail to learn of the arrangement, he purchased space in the newspapers and gave the citizens the full details.

A huge crowd gathered at Hancock's Wharf to watch the six merchantmen sail past the long line of British warships now anchored in the harbor. A company of troops appeared, presumably to keep order, but the throng jeered so loudly that the commander of the redcoats wisely withdrew his men. Thomas Hutchinson, who had just succeeded Bernard as Governor, knew the government had been made to appear foolish again, but he could do nothing to prevent the ships from sailing.

Even the wealthy colonials were proud to wear out-of-style clothing. Cooking utensils and other ironware reached Boston in mysterious ways from illegal foundries operating deep in the interior, near the wilderness. Two redcoat lieutenants who tried to attend a concert at the hall that John Hancock had given the people were politely but firmly turned away at the door. And the day after three sisters, the daughters of a physician, had entertained a major and two captains at dinner, the unfortunate family's house, barn, and carriage were found smeared with red paint. It was assumed that the Sons of Liberty were responsible for the outrage, but it was impossible to accuse their leaders of participating in the affair. All of them spent the evening at John Hancock's mansion on Beacon Hill, attending a reception given in honor of the new Governor.

Dockworkers and other unemployed men blamed the regiments for their plight, and began to insult off-duty troops they encountered in the streets. Small boys aped their elders, and the regimental officers, themselves smarting because they were social pariahs, found it increasingly difficult to curb the tempers of their men. Minor brawls in waterfront taverns were indications that there might be worse to come.

John shared the apprehension of the town's substantial citizens, and expressed his views firmly at a meeting of the Long Room Club. "Either the Sons of Liberty will have to establish street patrols to stop the people from cursing at the soldiers," he said, "or we'll have to petition Governor Hutchinson to confine the troops to their barracks when they're off duty."

Sam Adams grinned at him from the far end of the supper table. "Why?"

"Anybody who rubs two sticks of dry kindling against each other long enough and hard enough starts a fire. There's going to be bloodshed."

Less than a week later his fears materialized. On the night of March 5, 1770, a barber and a British officer who owed him money became involved in an argument. A young boy called the officer foul names, a nearby British sentry lost his head and slapped the child, a crowd quickly gathered and the panicky sentry called out the guard. Tempers soared, and no one on either side was able to remember, later, whether the civilians or the soldiers were the first to attack. The only facts that stood out in bold relief were that a fight did occur, and the troops opened fire. When the smoke cleared away, eleven civilians were sprawled on the ground, five of them dead and the others wounded. The sentries quickly withdrew, afraid they had exceeded their authority, and the men who had taunted them fled to their homes. Neither side had intended to spill blood.

Sam Adams immediately gave the tragic incident a name, and by dawn, letters were dispatched to the Committees of Correspondence in other colonies, telling them the news of the "Boston Massacre."

At noon John Hancock led a delegation of citizens to the Governor's Mansion and formally requested that all troops be withdrawn to a fort outside the city.

Hutchinson felt the honor of the Crown was at stake, and sought a compromise.

But John remained firm. "Your Excellency," he said earnestly, "I'm afraid you underestimate the temper of the people. Men are pouring into Boston from Lexington, Cambridge, Braintree, Concord—every town and village in the area. All of them are carrying firearms. If you don't act quickly to separate the troops and civilians, hundreds will die before nightfall."

Hutchinson made a last effort to preserve his dignity. "In my opinion Sam Adams provoked the incident for this very purpose!"

"You may be right," John replied with unexpected candor. "But that's irrelevant at the moment. If you don't want a revolt in the streets, withdraw the redcoats!"

In the absence of instructions from London ordering him to take a firm stand, Hutchinson agreed.

John went at once to the Old South Meetinghouse on Cornhill Street, where a huge throng had gathered to await the Governor's response. Men cheered the announcement, church bells pealed and, to John's intense embarrassment, he was hoisted onto the shoulders of two cargo handlers and carried through the city in an impromptu parade that thousands joined.

"We're going too far," he told Sam Adams that evening. "It doesn't matter whether the civilians or the soldiers were to blame. We want peace, not an insurrection!"

Sam glanced at the front page of a special edition of the *Gazette* he had just printed, and pointed at the article in which he had demanded that the members of the redcoat guard who had participated in the "Massacre" be tried for murder. "I'm in favor of peace, but we can't have it without justice."

John gestured impatiently. "Don't talk piously to me. You know damned well you won't be satisfied until we've had a full-scale revolution!"

"If you know a better way to attain the peace you want—with honor—tell me about it, and I'll be glad to listen."

"There will be no other way if there are more shootings."

"Why are you so upset?" Sam cleaned printers' ink from his fingernails with a letter-opener.

"I've been maneuvered into a false position. I went to Hutchinson today because I'm honestly concerned and don't want Boston ruled either by bayonets or a civilian mob. But I was carried in triumph through the city—"

"No false modesty, John." Sam chuckled complacently. "Every man enjoys being a hero."

"I don't! Not when I'm hailed for winning a victory—when there has been no victory."

"It's true that the dead who were killed last night won't rise again, and the wounded will carry the scars of British bullets to their graves. But our purpose has been accomplished. The troops have been withdrawn from Boston, so you can take your ships out of drydock and sail them again."

"Impossible!" John pounded the table so hard that his wig slipped, and he had to straighten it. "I'd be accused—along with you—of creating the Massacre for the sake of my own financial interests."

"London will say all of that and much more, besides, before this affair is ended. You're like all good, noble men, John. You speak of principles—you even make considerable sacrifices for those principles—but you become frightened and run away when the issues for which you've fought cause violence."

"Those men died needlessly last night!"

"Who is to judge? Were you brought to trial needlessly? Was your brig confiscated without reason? Or do all the things that have been happening in these past five years and more fit into a pattern?"

John sank into a rickety chair and buried his face in his hands. "The vindictiveness I saw in the faces of the men who paraded through town today made me heartsick. And that's only one side of the ugly coin. I showed you the letter I received from London the other day saying that the new First Minister, the Earl of Guilford—Lord North, he calls himself—is a vain, petty fellow who fancies insults where there are none. Can you imagine what he'll do to salvage the honor of the Crown when he hears this news?"

Sam's eyes softened, and a fleeting expression of tenderness crossed his face. "You were reared and educated for a life as a gentleman merchant, but you were born into the wrong age. The world has become vicious, you see. It isn't the fault of that dolt, King George, any more than it's mine. We're symbols, all of us. Men in this country have tasted liberty, and want more of it. England feels us slipping away. And like any mother, she tries to bind us more tightly to her side. If troops hadn't come to Boston this winter, they'd have been sent to Philadelphia in the spring or Charleston in summer. We've been more outspoken than other towns, so it's probably no accident that our streets are the first to be stained by blood. But they won't be the last."

John felt ashamed of his rare display of weakness. "You make me feel like a pawn who has no control over his own destiny."

Sam smiled wearily. "I called you a symbol, not a pawn, and there's a great difference. But your destiny was decided for you long ago. It was decided by a wealthy uncle who adopted you. It was shaped when you and Johnny ran in the woods near Braintree as children and you learned to love the feeling of being free, your own master. You were nudged still farther when you studied philosophy. Descartes taught you that you had an independent intellect. Rousseau convinced you that you had a free and independent soul. Locke defined liberty for you."

"And now I've become a puppet who dances when Sam Adams pulls the strings."

"No, you became your own puppet-master long ago. I'd be foolish to deny I wanted your support for our cause because of your name and position—"

"—and my money."

"—and your money, of course. But you struck out for liberty yourself, in your own way. You accepted responsibility—and leadership. The portrait of you that the people have painted—with some help from me, I'll grant—doubled overnight when your own stand caused your arrest, the lawsuit and confiscation of the *Liberty*. Since then you've been a marked man. The people wouldn't have cheered you today if you hadn't been the leader of the social boycott against the troops. The Governor wouldn't have accepted you as the spokesman for the citizens of Massachusetts if you weren't the majority leader in the General Court. But your problem now is that you feel degraded by accepting homage as the hero of a tragedy."

"An evil tragedy that I didn't create."

"Ah, but you did! Your own defiance of the Crown, your own insistence on freedom and justice did as much to bring the troops here as anything I've ever written in the *Gazette*."

John was silent for a long time. "I suppose you're right, Sam," he admitted at last. "I can accept much of what you say—everything, in fact, except your views of destiny. We aren't characters in a Greek tragedy by Euripides. Our futures haven't been foreordained by primitive gods." Suddenly he smiled. "I believe, though, that you enjoy play-acting as the oracle of Delphi."

Sam laughed. "A scribbler of words finds it hard to resist the temptation."

"That's where you have an advantage over me. I was trained as a merchant. I fought the encroachments on my liberties because they hurt my purse and my pride as a free man. I spoke of principles and rarely mentioned my purse, of course. But now I find the circumstances—the ancient Greeks would have called it Fate—prevent me from earning a living without abandoning principles. Those principles are all I have left."

Sudden alarm showed in Sam's eyes.

"You needn't fear that I'll barricade myself behind the locked doors of my house. I can't retire from public life until this argument with the Crown is settled, once and for all."

Sam slumped in his chair and breathed an inaudible sigh of relief.

"I don't like violence. I don't like arguments based on emotion rather than reason. I courted the people with fireworks shows and gifts to churches. Today they acclaimed me as their leader—and even Hutchinson accepted me in that role."

"If you think you can change the course of history to suit your own conscience, you're welcome to try. Lead in your own way."

"By God," John said quietly, "that's just what I intend to do."

5

"You've become a very important man, John." Dolly Quincy looked radiant in a gown of beige silk that gleamed in the light of the lanterns that glowed from the branches of the trees on the grounds of the Governor's Mansion.

"Well, I've been unusually busy." Modesty had never been one of John's stronger attributes, but he tried to look humble as he adjusted the sash across the front of his new, scarlet uniform tunic.

"Everyone in Braintree knows that whenever there's an election, you win it. Gracious, you're Moderator of the Boston Town Meeting, Speaker of the General Court, President of the Commerce and Agriculture Commission—"

"Chairman of the Commission for the Promotion of Agriculture,

Manufacture, Commerce and the Arts in Massachusetts Bay," he interrupted, correcting her gently.

"And now Governor Hutchinson has made you Colonel of the Independent Corps of Cadets. Your uniform is very handsome, although I must confess I find it strange to see you dressed as a redcoat."

"I find it a natural consequence of all that's happened in the past year. I've always believed men of good will could restore peace between England and the colonies." He didn't want her to think he was trying to take all the credit for the improved atmosphere. "Johnny Adams' work as defense counsel for the soldiers accused of murder in the Massacre trial was brilliant. No one could have been more prudent or fair."

"So I've been told. Friends in Philadelphia and Virginia spoke of little else for many weeks."

"You've been traveling, Dolly?"

"Extensively." Apparently he hadn't realized that almost eighteen months had passed since her last visit to Boston, and she bridled.

She was more attractive than John had remembered her and, aware of her ruffled feelings, he tried to make amends. "I've always been grateful to you for arranging the ladies' boycott of the officers stationed here."

"Thank you." Her fan fluttered vigorously, concealing her face as they continued to stroll through the garden.

John bowed to several acquaintances. "Those days seem very distant now that we're reconciled. In fact, Colonel Dalrymple of the Twenty-ninth and I dine together occasionally."

Dolly made no reply.

He realized a fuller apology was needed. "Colonial affairs of state have taken up only a portion of my time. I've been working day and night on the operations of Hancock and Company since we've returned to business." It was odd that he could be so glib in conversations with men and invariably found the right phrase or word in his public addresses, but became tongue-tied in the company of a young lady. "I hope you'll forgive me for neglecting you."

"I haven't been aware of your neglect, sir." The fan snapped shut.

John didn't know what to say.

Suddenly Dolly turned away and brightened as an officer wearing the regimental insignia of the Fifty-ninth Infantry on his dress tunic approached them.

"I've been looking for you, Mistress Dolly!" Tall, blond, and rugged, he bent to kiss her hand.

John felt an unexpected stab of annoyance.

"Have you, sir?" Dolly's trilling laugh was a minor triumph of coquetry.

"Colonel Hancock, your servant, sir." The officer bowed politely.

"Good evening, Major." John's nod was stiff.

Dolly slipped her hand through the Englishman's arm. "I'm sure Colonel Hancock will forgive us for deserting him, but we have so many things to discuss."

Before John could reply, she led the officer away.

He watched them, tugging at the gold cord tied to the hilt of the ceremonial dress sword he had bought to wear with his uniform. All at once the confidence, bordering on arrogance, that the redcoat escorting Dolly was displaying created an unexpected sense of uneasiness in John. The man was a professional soldier, and no matter how much reading on military subjects he himself had done in recent months, he was still an amateur. He felt out of place in his bright red tunic, white breeches, and knee-high boots, and wished he hadn't ordered as bushy a plume for the silver helmet he carried in the crook of his left arm. It was an honor to be the commander of the most distinguished ceremonial corps in the colonies, but he was a merchant, and would feel more comfortable in civilian clothes.

"Ah, Colonel Hancock." Governor Hutchinson approached, smiling amiably.

"A splendid party, Your Excellency." John was still keeping an eye on Dolly and the officer.

"I had hoped," the Governor said with a faint smile, "that you colonials would drink the excellent tea that the Colonial Office sent to me in a diplomatic pouch. You do drink it in your own homes, you know."

The gulf between the thinking of Englishmen and colonials suddenly became greater than John liked to believe. "Our own tea," he said politely, "comes from Holland—I'm told." He couldn't admit openly to the King's personal representative in Massachusetts that his ships were once again engaged in smuggling operations.

Hutchinson's smile became knowing. "The difference is technical, you know. The English and Dutch East India Companies import their tea from the same places, sometimes from the same plantations."

"I must disagree, sir," John replied, sounding respectful. "When Parliament rescinded the discriminatory taxes imposed on us, nothing was done to remove the tax on tea."

"That was a matter of principle. His Majesty wanted to prove his right to tax his colonies as he sees fit."

"It's because of that very principle that we won't import or sell English tea, Your Excellency."

"Thruppence per pound is a very small tax."

"So small that it would scarcely prevent our poorest citizens from buying it. But even a penny tax would be more than we'd pay."

Hutchinson seemed sympathetic, but his words indicated a complete lack of understanding. "So many causes of unpleasantness have been removed," he said, "that I've been hoping to see a changed attitude in this one minor area of dispute."

"We've had the same hope, sir."

"His Majesty and Lord North have shown themselves amenable to compromise, you must admit."

John believed that the intransigence of the colonies had been responsible for the weakening of the royal position, but he didn't want to become involved in a long political discussion that would prove fruitless. The Governor could not admit in so many words that his master had been wrong, or that the strength of the opposition to his policies had forced him to capitulate. Dolly and the officer had disappeared, and John was anxious to find them and make some excuse to join them.

"We rely on men of your caliber and standing to persuade the Sons of Liberty to adopt a more reasonable and malleable attitude, Colonel."

Sam Adams had claimed from the day that John had been offered the command of the Independent Corps of Cadets that the commission was an attempt to bribe him. He had disagreed vehemently, preferring to believe that his own rise to leadership in provincial affairs had won him the honor. But Hutchinson's manner made him uneasy.

"I'm not sure," he said, "that my friends would listen to me if I urged them to abandon all they hold dear."

The Governor looked smug. "I have reason to believe that the citizens of Pennsylvania and New York have given up their boycott, and the East India Company's sales are improving in New Jersey and North Carolina every month."

The Committees of Correspondence in those colonies were reporting a gradual erosion of opposition to the ban on tea, and were unhappy about it, but John gave no indication that he was thoroughly familiar with the situation. The Crown authorities were unaware that the Committees existed, and even such moderates as Dr. Franklin, with whom he agreed, felt that the Committees should be maintained. The one lesson that the members in all thirteen colonies had learned when the Crown had tried to usurp their prerogatives was that they could impress London only when they stood together in times of stress.

"I'm in no position to speak for people elsewhere, Your Excellency, but Massachusetts is unique." It was difficult to conceal his pride in the citizens of the province.

Hutchinson's good humor evaporated. "His Majesty has listened to the Pitt factions pleas for tolerance, but his patience is limited."

The warning was too obvious to be ignored, and John became taut. "I hope, sir, that nothing will disturb our new prosperity and growth."

"For the sake of everyone in the colony, I share that hope, Colonel Hancock. I'm particularly sensible to your own situation. The economy of Massachusetts depends a great deal on your own success or failure, and I rejoice to see you earning handsome profits. Not that I know too much about your actual operations," he added as he saw the guarded look on John's face, "but I rejoiced—as did everyone in Boston—when you built another brig this winter and added a new warehouse to your properties." Nodding pleasantly, he went off to greet some late arrivals.

John stared after him for a moment. The hint was direct enough. If he persuaded his friends to give up the boycott on English tea, his own prosperity would not be threatened. But if the citizens of Massachusetts refused to accept the token tax, the King and Commons might take a stiffer stand.

No man more enjoyed earning a good income than John, but the Governor's suggestion was totally unacceptable. A few years ago he might have hesitated and tried to find some way to satisfy both sides, but he could no longer straddle the fence. The people of the colony had elected him to every high office at their command. They trusted him, and he was responsible to them.

He had curbed the rowdies in the Sons of Liberty, and Sam had toned down his belligerent articles in the *Gazette*. The Crown had as much reason to be grateful to him as he was thankful for the restoration of normal trade. But if policies in London changed again, it was his place to lead the opposition to fresh attempts to subjugate the colonists and deprive them of their liberties.

However, there was no sense in borrowing trouble. He had learned that, in politics as in business, the most prudent course was to take one step at a time while carefully studying the ground underfoot. It was possible that Hutchinson was bluffing, hoping to win a cheap and easy concession by appealing to his cupidity.

Meanwhile a more immediate challenge confronted him. Dorothy Quincy had snubbed him, directly and bluntly. No one in government, the commercial world or any other circle in which he traveled dared to treat him so outrageously, and he was furious. Moving to a vantage point on a slight rise of ground at one side of the garden, he began a systematic search of the crowd for her and her husky companion.

Aunt Lydia left a group of her friends who were clustered near a huge cut-glass bowl of raspberry water ice flavored with white wine, and came to him. "You've needed a slap across the face for a long time," she said calmly.

John felt like a schoolboy, and straightened his sword belt.

"I've wondered when Dolly would show some spirit, and I'm just surprised she didn't do it to you sooner. I suppose her father urged her to be patient, but you'd try the patience of a *Mayflower* settler."

He looked around to make certain no one else could hear her, but it was small comfort to realize they were alone.

"You've taken Dolly for granted," she said. "Two years ago, I think it was, I felt sure you were striking sparks. So did she. But when you continued to ignore her, she stopped coming to Boston. Do you know what she's been doing in her visits to other colonies? Husband-hunting! And I hope she finds someone wonderful. You don't deserve her, you—you oaf!"

"How have I offended her, Aunt Lydia? What have I done?"

"Nothing! That's the whole point. You've been so busy making love to the citizens of Massachusetts that you've paid no attention to a lovely, charming young woman." The old lady could scarcely control her indignation. "You may be the wealthiest man in America, and you may have more positions and more titles than anyone else in the colonies, but you've lost your chance with Dolly. You've hurt her pride, which is something no woman can tolerate."

"I haven't been intentionally rude. I've been busy—"

"Doubling a fortune—without providing for heirs. Gathering titles as president of this and speaker of that, with no family of your own to admire your diligence. You assumed that Dolly would wait for you forever simply because she was so inexperienced when she met you that she couldn't hide her eagerness to marry you. You had other things to do first, and no doubt you assumed she'd still be waiting whenever you'd condescend to propose marriage to her."

John was afraid his aunt would become still angrier if he admitted he had been too preoccupied to think in terms of marriage at all.

"You've robbed Dolly of her greatest asset, her youth, by keeping her dangling all these years."

He felt the charge was unjust. "I made no commitment to her, Aunt Lydia. I certainly didn't ask her to wait for me."

The old lady's gaze was withering. "You have no understanding of women."

That much of the charge was true.

"And it will soon be too late for you to learn. In another three years you'll be forty, and when I'm gone there will be no one to look after you." She gathered her skirts before firing a last salvo. "You'll become a lonely old miser, counting your gold and your titles."

John retained the presence of mind to bow politely before going off through the gardens to find Dorothy. She meant no more to him now than she had an hour earlier, but it was intolerable that she should reject him. If the British government took care not to antagonize him unduly, he had a right to expect at least as much from a young lady who had nothing in particular to commend her except a pretty face and a flirtatious manner.

His search was hampered by other guests, anxious to improve their own social standing by stopping him for a chat, and it took him a long time to go from one end of the extensive grounds to the other. Dolly and the British officer were nowhere in sight, and he could only conclude that they had left the party. Common sense urged him to forget her, but he refused. Dorothy Quincy had challenged him, and he wouldn't be satisfied until he forced her to capitulate.

6

"The East India Company employs agents so persuasive that the Commons has been charmed. And the Crown is even more short-sighted than ever, even though His Majesty now uses spectacles." John handed a packet of letters from London across his desk to Thomas Cushing. "Give me your opinion of these, Tom."

The junior partner of Hancock and Company read them carefully. "Well, the rumors that the East India people have more tea on hand than they can handle must be true. But it's astonishing that Parliament would grant them the exclusive right to the colonial market."

"There's a copy of the new Tea Act in those papers."

"Yes, I have it."

John had just learned that the British officer who was seeing so much of Dorothy Quincy smoked incessantly, so he himself was learning to use a pipe. He took one from a rack on a table behind his desk and stuffed it, making certain he spilled no tobacco crumbs. "The monopoly is bad enough. The new tax of twelve-pence per pound is insane. I can only assume that Lord North is not only trying to satisfy his friends on the East India directorate, but bleed us at the same time."

Suddenly Tom laughed. "Surely Barnard isn't serious when he

says we can acquire the exclusive rights to act as the East India Company's agents in the New England colonies!"

John remained sober-faced as he lighted his pipe with a flint and tinderbox. "He means it, unfortunately."

"You and I would be tarred, feathered, and hanged from the top branches of the Liberty Tree."

"The idea is absurd, of course. But what bothers me is that Barnard, who has spent a lifetime dealing with us and earns his living in the colonial trade should have so little understanding of our point of view. What makes him think we'll pay a twelvepenny tax when we've balked at thruppence?"

"Someone can make a very tidy profit as the exclusive agent here." Tom waved away a cloud of smoke blown at him from the opposite side of the desk.

"No one in Boston or New Haven or anywhere else will earn a penny from this arrangement," John said. "Apparently the government believes our will to resist has ebbed away because these past few years have been quiet." He swallowed some smoke and coughed, but doggedly continued to puff on the pipe. "We'll have to tighten our boycott and warn the Committees of Correspondence in the other colonies. Fortunately there's nothing new in this sort of situation, and I'm certain London will back down when we put up a firm, united front."

7

John looked resplendent in his uniform as Colonel of the Independent Corps, and his silver field spurs clattered and crashed as he paced up and down the modest drawing room of Abigail and John Adams' house. His mood was anything but martial, however, and he looked at his watch for the fifth time in as many minutes. "Damnation, Johnny, I specifically told Dorothy in the note I wrote to her this morning that my time would be limited when I came calling today!"

John Adams concealed a smile. "All I can tell you—again—is that Dolly insisted on going shopping with Abigail."

"I'm mounting guard duty with my troops at the wharves in

another half hour. I think she's avoiding me, just as she's done ever since she started this new visit to you and Abigail."

"Perhaps she's forgotten you intended to call."

"I say it's deliberate!"

"Why is it so necessary that you patrol the waterfront?"

"The *Dartmouth* has docked with one hundred and fourteen chests of tea on board. The *Eleanor* arrived yesterday with an identical cargo, and two other ships are due with more of the East India Company's smallpox. The people of this town are incensed, and I can only thank the Lord that my fleet isn't involved." John paced still more rapidly.

"You and Cousin Sam can blame yourselves for the excitement. Your mass meetings at the Old South and your rallies at the Liberty Tree have been creating hysteria. I fail to see why we aren't satisfied to follow the example of Pennsylvania. People there have simply renewed their pledge to buy no tea, and that's the end of the matter."

"The abuses here are far more flagrant," John said angrily. "Hutchinson's sons and nephew are the agents for New England!"

"Maybe they accepted because no colonials would act for the East India Company." Adams spoke quietly, shaking his head. "There's no need to stir up still more trouble."

"We didn't start this new argument. London is solely responsible." John tugged at his watch fob again. "Dorothy knows the Independent Corps is standing watch to prevent disorders. The Sons of Liberty have posted notices all over town. She's staying away until she can be sure she won't see me!"

Adams looked at him sympathetically. "Does she mean that much to you?"

"She gives me so few chances to spend time with her that I don't know what I feel!" He picked up his helmet and gauntlet gloves.

"Forget Dolly Quincy for a moment, and listen to me, John. It can't be a surprise to you that you aren't popular with the government in London. And you must know Hutchinson is sorely disappointed in you. He believed he tamed you when you accepted his commission. For the past few days there have been rumors that violence will be committed at the wharves, and if anything unlawful happens while you're on duty, you'll be playing into the

Governor's hands. He and Lord North would like nothing better than to arrest you on charges of treason. As your friend, I advise you to protect that tea with your life. As your attorney, I urge you to let nothing happen to that property while your Corps stands guard. You may be unpaid volunteers, but you wear the King's uniform."

John reddened. "The Pennsylvanians can afford to be orderly and meek. No one has landed any tea in Philadelphia, but there will be at least three hundred and forty chests of the poisonous stuff on our wharves by the end of the week. We've got to get rid of it! Three times I've called on Hutchinson as the head of a committee to ask that the ships return to England, and three times he's refused!"

"By going to see him yourself, you've made it very clear that you're in charge of the boycott movement. You're giving him a perfect excuse to have you hanged."

"He wouldn't dare. The Sons of Liberty would tear down the walls of every prison in New England to set me free."

Adams sighed. "Of all men in Massachusetts, you should understand the British mind, but you don't. The Governor would have you taken on board a frigate. You'd be sailed to England and tried there. Cousin Sam might be pleased. He could write pamphlets describing you as a martyr to the cause of liberty. But I don't think you'd enjoy going to the gallows for treason."

John rubbed his throat before fastening the strap of his helmet beneath his chin. "Our sentry duty won't extend beyond midnight for the rest of the week. The Sixty-fourth Regiment is responsible from dawn until sundown, but no one has been assigned the early morning hours." He brightened. "The Governor must think that cargo is going to be safe between midnight and daybreak."

"I don't know what you're talking about, and I refuse to listen to any details. But I do insist that you send your men straight to their homes when they're relieved. If you're wise, you'll change into civilian clothes yourself, and then you'll go to some place where you'll be seen by reliable witnesses, preferably members of the Governor's staff."

John nodded and smiled. "Hutchinson himself has been in the habit of stopping in at the Bible and Three Crowns late in the evening with some of the warship and regimental commanders."

"The very place for you, then. You've been there often, so no one will think you're trying to establish a legal excuse. One thing more. Anyone who accompanies you should be able to afford the high Bible and Three Crown prices."

"You don't think I should be seen with Sam."

"Not under the circumstances, and not at a tavern that's too expensive for his purse. You might tell him, quietly, that I suggest he be seen elsewhere, and that above all he must make certain his witnesses are respectable men who are loyal to the Crown in all things."

"There aren't many of that breed in Boston."

"If he values his neck, he must find them."

John peered out of the window into the gathering dusk for the last time to see if Dorothy and her hostess might be returning. "I'm grateful to you, Johnny, and I'll follow your advice. I can also promise you I won't drink a drop of tea at the Bible and Three Crowns. If the proprietor is wise, he'll conserve his supply, because it will soon be the rarest commodity in Massachusetts."

8

Dorothy Quincy paid a surprise visit to the Hancock mansion shortly before noon on December 17, 1773, and John made no attempt to hide his delight as he led her into the library. "I'm afraid Aunt Lydia has gone to the meat and poultry markets," he said, not sounding in the least regretful.

"I'm here to see you," the young woman replied bluntly.

He could scarcely believe his good fortune, but remained warily silent as he helped her remove her long wool cape with a thick beaver collar.

"There are redcoats patrolling the waterfront this morning." She sounded accusing. "I know, because I've been there."

"Yes, the port has been closed for the day, perhaps longer, which is why I've stayed at home. What took you into that part of town?" He waved her closer to a crackling fire in the hearth.

"Cousin Abigail woke me up this morning to tell me you had

been arrested after some acts of terrible violence took place on the piers last night."

"Oh, that." He offered her a glass of sack, but she refused. "The Governor sent two of his deputies to question me, but as they well knew, I was at the Crown and Three Bibles last night. The reports are very confused, but I understand that a band of several hundred Narragansett Indians boarded three merchantmen and dumped chests of tea into the harbor. As I told Governor Hutchinson's deputies, I deplore all attacks on private property, and I commiserate with the directors of the East India Company. If the stories are true—and I have no way of confirming them, of course— three hundred and forty chests of tea were destroyed. That's a loss of four to five thousand pounds in gold."

She smiled nervously. "I hope you sounded more convincing when you spoke to the Governor's men. No one believes the attackers were Indians, and the whole town is certain that you and Sam were responsible."

"Perhaps you'd like a drop of Madeira if sack isn't to your fancy," he said blandly.

"I'm not fond of spirits except for a glass with my meals."

"Some coffee, then, or a cup of West Indian chocolate? We have no tea in the house."

"You're incorrigible!" She laughed, then became annoyed with herself. "It was a waste of effort to feel alarmed about you this morning."

"Ah, did you?" He hooked his thumbs in the pockets of his silver-embroidered waistcoat. "I'm flattered."

"You needn't be, sir. I—I was concerned for Aunt Lydia's sake."

"If I were you, I wouldn't criticize others for being poor liars."

"May I have my cloak, please?"

"Not just yet. There are one or two things I want to say to you."

"Will you hold me here by force, Mr. Hancock?"

John grinned at her. "Your talents for play-acting are wasted, Mistress Quincy. There are no theatres in Boston, and I'm certain your father would disapprove if you wanted a career on the London stage. So would I."

Her temper flared again. "You, sir? You have no voice in the management of my affairs."

"You're mistaken, Dorothy." He spoke quietly now. "I intend

to have a final voice. In these past weeks since you've returned to Boston, I've tried dozens of times to see you, even though it's been the most hectic period of my life. No matter. You punished me for my previous neglect, and no doubt I deserved all that you've made me suffer. But that's in the past now. The months ahead are going to be troublesome. The Governor will try to prove I organized last night's Tea Party, and I'll be alert. London is sure to be unhappy, and we may have still more difficulties before the King and Lord North realize the colonies don't exist for the convenience of the East India Company. You and I have waited long enough, Dorothy. It's time we're married."

She was annoyed because he used her formal Christian name instead of calling her Dolly. "Is this a proposal of marriage?" she demanded, raising her eyebrows in mock amazement.

"Of course!" He could see a pair of redcoat sentries pacing up and down outside the fence, and the Governor's attempt to intimidate him was irritating. Certainly he had no patience with a feminine display of coyness.

"I am not a consignment of merchandise to be stuffed into the hold of a Hancock ship." Dolly deliberately turned her back on him, faced the fire and made a show of warming her hands. "I'm not a bolt of Midlands wool or a cask of French wine."

"You're a confounded woman!" John shouted. He was being subjected to all the strains he could tolerate, but she was amusing herself by making him feel still worse.

"There's no need to raise your voice, sir." Her tone indicated satisfaction, almost smugness, in the knowledge that she had acquired power over him.

"Will you or will you not marry me?" He curbed the strong desire to strike her.

"You're not engaged in a business transaction, Mr. Hancock. Perhaps you can get almost anything you want by ringing a little bell, but you can't get me that way. A girl infinitely prefers sentiment to a strongbox filled with gold sovereigns."

His exasperation rendered him inarticulate.

"I'll also have you know I'm not so desperate that I'll leap to accept. I blame myself for waiting so many years for you, but other men still find me attractive, and I have a number of serious suitors."

"I forbid you to see any of them again. Damnation, I love you!" He caught hold of her shoulders, turned her around and began to shake her vigorously.

For a moment Dolly was frightened, but her sense of humor came to her rescue, and she laughed.

John was so startled that he stopped shaking her.

"That, sir," she said demurely as she fought for breath, "is what I was waiting to hear. I'm pleased to accept your proposal of marriage."

Her sudden change made him still more bewildered.

Dolly moved closer to him and lifted her face. "I believe it's customary on occasions like this," she murmured, "for a man to kiss his future bride."

FIVE

1774—1775

1

The Crown and Parliament could allow Boston's defiant challenge to go unpunished, but in their zealousness King and Commons went too far. A new series of bills, soon to be known in the colonies as the Coercive Acts, were rushed through the Commons and the House of Lords.

The most drastic was the Boston Port Bill, which placed the city in a virtual state of quarantine by forbidding the import or export of any merchandise. The Royal Navy was instructed to enforce the act with due vigor, and all shipping ceased abruptly. Even more serious from the point of view of those who held individual liberties dear was the Massachusetts Government Act, which converted the province into a Crown colony, gave the Governor the right to appoint all local officials, and specifically prohibited town meetings without the Governor's specific approval.

The Quartering Act permitted all royal officials to be tried in England for charges brought against them in the colonies, and stipulated that colonials were required to open their homes for the billeting of troops, on demand. The so-called Quebec Act infuriated Virginia and Connecticut as well as Massachusetts by extending the boundaries of the province of Quebec, thereby ignoring the western wilderness claims of the other colonies.

Hutchinson was accused of being too soft, and the Colonial

Office relieved him, replacing him with Lieutenant General Thomas Gage, a veteran of the French and Indian War and a military martinet. Finally, royal warrants were issued for the arrest of John Hancock and Sam Adams, who were believed to have been the instigators of the Boston Tea Party. However, Hutchinson had already departed, Gage had not yet arrived from England and, as no other Crown official was willing to spark riots that might erupt into open insurrection, both men continued to walk the streets in freedom.

John was busier than ever before in his life. Belatedly realizing that the government reaction was far more vehement than he had anticipated, he began to sell the ships of his merchant fleet, disposing of them to Dutch, French, and West Indian buyers, but refusing to entertain bids from English merchants.

On the night of March 5, 1774, he went even farther. The Sons of Liberty ignored the law preventing town meetings, and posted circulars by the hundreds, advertising a rally at the Old South to commemorate the fourth anniversary of the Boston Massacre. *John Hancock, Speaker of the General Court and Moderator of the Boston Town Meeting, will deliver the address, albeit the Crown has put a price on his head,* the posters declared.

More than twenty-five hundred people had jammed themselves into the hall an hour before the start of the rally, and the overflow crowd outside was so enormous that, even though the March night was raw, the windows and doors were opened wide so the people in the street and on the lawn could hear the oration.

John put aside the transactions in which he was methodically disposing of his commercial empire, and spent the entire day writing his speech. The size of the crowd surprised him, so he cast aside his carefully measured remarks and, following Sam Adams' advice, deliberately played on the emotions of his audience. For a quarter of an hour he used all his skill to build to a peak, and then exploded in a torrent of oratorical wrath.

"I come reluctantly to the transactions of that dismal night four years ago," he said heatedly, "when Heaven, in a dreadful moment, suffered Hell to take the reins; when Satan, with his chosen band, opened the sluices of New England's blood and sacrilegiously polluted our land with the dead bodies of her guiltless sons. Let all America join in one common prayer to Heaven that the inhuman, unprovoked murders of March 5, 1770, may stand forever in history as symbols of cruelty and treachery without parallel."

The crowd roared, and John glanced for a moment at Dorothy and Aunt Lydia, who stared up at him in dazed disbelief from seats of honor in the second row. It was difficult for women to realize that in times of crisis the calumnies of the opposition had to be painted in broad strokes in order to solidify the opposition to tyranny. It would be wise not to look at his betrothed or his aunt again.

"You dark, designing knaves," he shouted, his fervor rising as he tried to conquer the fear that Dorothy would think his performance ludicrous. "You murderers, you parricides! How dare you tread on the earth which has drunk in the blood of slaughtered innocence shed by your wicked hands? How dare you breathe that air which wafted to the ear of Heaven the groans of those who fell a sacrifice to your accursed ambition? But if the laboring earth does not expand her jaws, if the air you breathe is not commissioned to be the minister of death, yet hear it and tremble! You must be arraigned, must lift your hands, red with the blood of those whose death you have procured, at the tremendous bar of God."

Dorothy appeared impressed, in spite of herself, and no longer looked as though she would burst into loud laughter.

John hoped she didn't think he had won his audience because of his unique position in the community. He had won the respect of his fellow citizens because he had made their cause his own, without fear of possible consequences, and he wanted her to know it.

"Despite the glare of wealth," he said, and for an instant met the steady gaze of her blue-green eyes. "The people who pay greater respect to a wealthy villain than to an honest, upright man in poverty almost deserve to be enslaved. They plainly show that wealth, however it may be acquired, is, in their esteem, to be preferred to virtue. How foolish they are, how misguided and wrong!"

The warmth of the crowd's reaction warmed him, and he was delighted to see Dorothy join in the applause. Only Aunt Lydia still looked as though she didn't believe he meant a word of what he was saying.

"I thank God," he cried, "that America abounds in men who are superior to all temptation. As my beloved uncle told me so often when I was young, love your country. Love America if you would cherish liberty."

The reference to Uncle Thomas cracked the wall of Aunt Lydia's reserve, and John felt completely free at last. Now he could say what he pleased without fear of sounding absurd.

"The King and his venal ministers have tried to isolate Boston, like a victim of the Great Pox being locked in a dark room. I cannot blame them, friends, for our disease spreads more swiftly than the deadliest plague. That disease is human freedom, for which every soul on this tortured earth yearns. We are free men who will not be denied! We will maintain our liberties, no matter what the cost! The King cannot rob us of our freedom, nor can his Houses of Parliament, nor can his scarlet regiments with their muskets and bayonets.

"We ask only that Americans be granted the privileges that are our rightful heritage. Hear me, George of England, and heed my words. Justice and freedom are more precious to us by far than our loyalty to you. Deny us at your peril. Americans love liberty more than life itself, and come what may, we shall remain free!"

There was bedlam in the hall, in the street beyond it and in the grounds outside the open windows.

John mopped his forehead with a silk handkerchief and knew that, carried away by his own fervor, he had gone further than he had intended. The Crown might well interpret what he said as an invitation to open rebellion. Yet he realized at almost the same instant that every word, every syllable had been sincere. Even if the Tea Party had been too violent a response to commercial exploitation, the incident did not warrant the severity of the Crown's reprisals.

The colonies were willing to live in peace with England if they were treated as the mother country's equals. He himself would continue to accept the King as his liege lord if George III respected his inviolable rights as a subject. But neither he nor any other American would bow to tyranny.

If his speech had been treasonable, let the Crown institute proceedings against him. He was prepared to use every means at his disposal to fight dishonor. It was far more important that his address had helped to stiffen the resolve of his fellow citizens.

And it was sweet beyond measure to see tears of pride in Dorothy's eyes as she stood with the rest to cheer him. Certainly she had been drawn to him because of his wealth and position, but she was learning to admire him because he placed principle above money or standing. He couldn't ask for more, and bowed his head in reply to the prolonged cheers of the throng.

2

John glanced at his reflection in the pier glass set in the door of his dressing room and straightened his epaulets. Smoothing his tunic beneath his sword belt, he settled his burnished helmet on his head, drew on his gauntlet gloves and walked downstairs, humming under his breath. There wasn't a cloud in the sky, the June weather was balmy and the day was one that Boston would long remember.

"He's going ahead with this madness. Stop him, Dolly." Aunt Lydia appeared from her first-floor sewing room, followed by Dolly.

"Your servant, ladies." John raised his hand to the visor of his helmet in a reasonable approximation of what he believed to be a smart military salute.

The old lady was in no mood for his pleasantries. "Can't you let the commanders of the British regiments meet General Gage when he comes ashore?" she demanded.

"Oh, I'm sure they'll be on hand, too." He smiled at Dorothy.

She remained solemn. "I much prefer a living husband to a martyred betrothed, John."

"My dear, the primary function of the Independent Corps is to act as a guard of honor for the Governor. We'd be delinquent in our duty if we failed to meet Gage on his arrival from England and escort him to the Governor's Mansion."

The girl exchanged a glance with Aunt Lydia. "We know the London newspapers reprinted excerpts of your Massacre anniversary speech. Some of them exaggerated—"

"They lied!" Aunt Lydia declared.

"—and there's no way of knowing what the new Governor may

believe about you. For all you know, he may order you seized and hauled off to prison."

John grinned at her. "I'm confident that the Cadets of the Independent Corps will defend their Colonel to the death."

"I'm not joking!"

"Neither am I, my dear. Would you have me ride west to Springfield and hide in the wilderness until I learn whether the Privy Council has decided to rescind the order for my arrest?"

"I know as well as you that you'd never run away, but you could behave sensibly by sitting here quietly until you discover what General Gage will do."

"I've never been one to twiddle my thumbs while others take the initiative."

"He's impossible," Aunt Lydia muttered.

Dolly's warning look begged the old lady not to interrupt. "John, wearing that uniform to meet the new Governor is a deliberately insolent gesture. Everyone else in Boston is aware of it, too. You're daring the Governor to take action against you."

John smiled amiably. "You might say we want to test his resolve."

"Why must it be you who tests him?"

His smile faded. "Because the Crown has chosen me as the symbol of Boston opposition, Massachusetts opposition—even American opposition, if you will. No man in the colonies is in a better position than I am to determine how far Lord North's government is prepared to go in its determination to crush us. We have a few plans of our own," he added cryptically as he walked to the window, "and we want to test the wind before we set sail." The Corps, two hundred strong, awaited him on the gravel driveway, and he had to hurry. Saluting the ladies, he left the house.

A groom helped him mount a magnificent, pure white gelding that stood eighteen hands high, and John rode at the head of his company toward the harbor. The Sons of Liberty had made certain that everyone in the city knew of the Corps' intention, and thousands of citizens were gathered on Treamount Street and King Street to cheer. John bowed graciously but gravely, barely resisting the temptation to draw his sword and wave it. Only once did he smile. Sam Adams and several other members of the Long

Room Club were gathered at the open window of the chamber directly above the *Gazette* offices, and grinned at him.

There was no need for conversation between them. He had met with them until dawn deciding what would be done to meet every possible contingency. No matter what the new Governor had in mind, the colonial leaders were ready.

The Crown embargo was so effective that not one merchantman was tied up at the docks. A dozen frigates and two huge ships-of-the-line rode at anchor in the outer harbor, however, their gun ports lowered and the muzzles of their huge cannon gleaming in the spring sunlight. John tensed when he saw the warships, and was pleased to note that the whole waterfront was deserted. Cargo handlers, merchant sailors and other members of the Sons of Liberty had made certain that no colonials would be on hand to greet the new representative of the King.

The commanders of the four redcoat regiments now stationed in Boston stood at the far end of the Long Wharf, chatting with the senior Royal Navy representatives and a handful of British civilians who worked in the secretariat of the Governor's office. If the military and naval men were surprised by the unexpected appearance of the Independent Corps, they concealed their feelings admirably and displayed no emotion as they returned John's salute. But the civilian deputies were far less urbane, and whispered fiercely to each other, scowling and shaking their heads.

The colonels and captains had been John's guests at various social functions, but they held themselves aloof, and pointedly refrained from asking him to join them. Even though he had more or less expected the snub, it stung, and he stood alone at the far side of the Long Wharf, looking out at the water.

After an interminable wait, a gig and several longboats were lowered from the main deck of a frigate, and began to move toward the shore. The new Governor had actually arrived the preceding evening, but had chosen to make a ceremonial entrance into his capital. John saw him sitting in the stern of the gig, and felt a trifle sorry for him. The Governor was only human, and would be disappointed by the chilly welcome that awaited him.

Lieutenant General Thomas Gage stood as the boat drew nearer to the Long Wharf, and a quick scrutiny told him all he needed to know. A grizzled veteran who had served under Lord Amherst at Montreal and subsequently had been in command of the Boston garrison, he was well acquainted with every man present—as well as with the colonial leaders who were distinguished by their absence. A tight, hard smile indicated that no subtlety of the cool reception was lost on him.

The Cadets of the Independent Corps stood at attention, presenting arms with their muskets as the new Governor came ashore, and John drew his sword, saluting with an extravagant flourish. Gage greeted each member of the secretariat by name, spoke briefly to the regimental commandants and the Navy captains, and then turned to the long figure at the far side of the wharf.

John went to him quickly and, saluting again, noted that the Governor had chosen to wear military rather than civilian garb. "Welcome to Boston, General," he said, deciding on the spur of the moment that the Sons of Liberty would address the colony's new chief executive as "Your Excellency" only when he appeared in less martial attire.

"To what do I owe this unexpected honor, Hancock?" Gage pointedly refrained from shaking hands.

"For the past fifty years the Corps has had the honor to escort the Governors of Massachusetts Bay on formal occasions."

"Let me not be the first to break precedent," Gage replied dryly, and turned to a Royal Marine officer supervising the debarkation of his men from the longboats. "Major Williams, you'll fall in behind us. Gentlemen," he added to the colonels and captains, "I trust you'll come with me?"

John intervened quickly. "I've brought you a horse, General."

Gage was surprised by the unexpected civility. "Thank you," he said, and not until the procession started off in the direction of King Street, with the Cadets of the Independent Corps in the lead, did he realize he had been outmaneuvered. He and John, who rode on his left, were the only mounted men in the company, and the new Governor was placed in the embarrassing position of appearing on seemingly friendly terms with a colonial who was regarded by the government as a dangerous radical.

But Gage made no attempt to change the line of march, and chuckled quietly. "I told the King and Lord North they underestimate your intelligence, Hancock."

"His Majesty knows me by now." John was grimly amused.

The Governor coughed behind a gauntlet glove. "In a manner of speaking."

John's fleeting sensation of triumph vanished.

"But there are others well acquainted with you and your various activities. For myself, I deplore your judgment, but I'm forced to admire your courage." Gage looked up King Street, which was now deserted. "A clever manipulation, making sure there would be no crowds on hand to greet me."

It was difficult to look innocent.

"No doubt your dock bullies drove the people to their homes."

"Had you come back to Boston in any other capacity, General, a great many of your friends would have been on hand to see you. But our citizens needed no urging to make their feelings clear today."

"Have you stopped to think where this idiocy will end, Hancock?"

"That decision is in the hands of the Crown and Lord North. When will they realize we can't be treated like children?"

"Boston has committed flagrant offenses."

"We were denied our liberties as free-born Englishmen."

Gage sighed. "We get nowhere in this discussion. I trust you realize my own hands are tied, and that I don't formulate policy. I carry it out."

"I'd enjoy renewing our personal friendship, but I can't let down the people who have elected me to various posts."

"Those offices no longer exist, Hancock."

"Disband our legislatures, sir, and others which are far stronger and far more demanding will spring up to replace them. There aren't enough troops at your disposal to prevent us from administering our affairs."

"I believe the Attorney General would call that observation treasonable."

"It's a fact, General."

"For your own safety, Hancock, be careful of what you say and where you say it. I carry the Privy Council's order for your arrest as a traitor, but it's been left to my discretion to take you into custody, if and when I think your conduct and the occasion warrant it."

"Arrest me, General, and you'll have to arrest one and a half million other Americans."

Gage turned in his saddle. "Are you so enamored of popular acclaim that you seriously believe the colonies would support you in preference to the Crown?"

"Not me, General. I mean very little as an individual. What matters is that men in every colony feel as I do."

"Are you telling me that you've been conspiring with other rebels?" Gage's voice became metallic.

"Does it matter? Isn't it far more important that there is the same reaction everywhere to the Coercive Acts? Isn't it far more significant that men in other towns aren't awed by the Navy's embargo here? Can't you see that New Haven and Baltimore and Wilmington are saying that what has happened here may happen next to them?"

"So it will if they don't obey the law!"

"The time to reach an understanding is growing short, General. London takes the loyalty of the colonies for granted, and the government makes a grave error. Americans don't feel indebted to England. We built our own cities in the wilderness, we cut down our own trees, uprooted the stumps and planted crops where none had ever grown. We've fought floods and droughts and famines and savages. We've made our own place in the world, often in spite of England rather than because of any help we've received. Even so, we have no real desire to break away from the mother country, but I don't know how to make you see it." They were approaching the Governor's Mansion, and he began to speak more rapidly. "We share the same language, the same heritage, the same love of personal liberty. We won't take the initiative into our own hands unless you give us no choice."

"If you radical Whigs take up arms against us, I'll use all of the very considerable means at my command to crush the insurrection and bring the ring leaders to justice."

The new Governor's inability—or unwillingness—to understand the colonial position was maddening, and John made a last effort. "General," he said earnestly, "you've called me a traitor and you threaten to arrest me. What do I stand to gain? It will do me no good to lose my life, I assure you. I enjoy this world far too much. I have a handsome home, I intend to marry a charming lady and I want to rear sons who will carry on my business after me. Doesn't it stand to reason that I prefer to reach an accommodation with the Crown than to encourage violence?"

"If those are your true feelings, use your influence with your friends here. Persuade them to accept royal authority, repay the East India Company for the destruction of its property and make your peace with the government."

"Will we be given a guarantee of representation in Parliament if we tug our forelocks? Will our right to govern ourselves in local affairs be restored to us?" John's voice boomed through the empty streets. "We've already been told, all too clearly, that we must grovel in the dust, and only if we humble ourselves enough will we be thrown a few crumbs of mercy. That isn't good enough for free men."

"The Crown is more important than any of its parts," Gage replied stubbornly.

John could not accept the fallacy. "The Crown will fall and shatter if the columns of the building that support it are removed."

They glowered at each other, neither willing to compromise, as the Independent Corps drew to a halt in front of the Governor's Mansion. General Gage dismounted, inclined his head slightly in a token farewell and walked quickly into the house.

Too late John realized that he had forgotten he was commanding a military unit, and that he should have ordered a salute. But his mind was too full of more significant matters. Gage intended to enforce the harsh laws passed by Parliament to humiliate the colonies, and the outlook was bleak.

3

"His Excellency Thomas Gage, Vice-Admiral, Captain-General and Governor-in-Chief of Massachusetts Bay, hereby revokes the commission of Colonel granted to Master John Hancock of Boston, who will not serve henceforth in any capacity as a member of His Excellency's Independent Corps of Cadets.

"The failure of the Corps to tender His Excellency the salute due his rank upon his arrival at his official Mansion was a slight deliberately conceived and executed by the said Hancock in an attempt to cast ridicule on the Crown and the principal Crown official in this colony."

4

"The Independent Corps of Cadets hereby announce to the citizens of Massachusetts Bay, whom they represent, that they are disbanding. The decision to take this step was made by unanimous vote after the abrupt dismissal from command of Colonel John Hancock, who was removed from his post of high trust without just cause.

"The flags, banners, uniforms and equipment of the Corps, having been purchased at the personal expense of its members, will be retained by the former Cadets in the hopes that, at a more propitious time, the Corps will again be activated.

"The members thereof are also unanimous in their intention to serve under no Officer-in-Command except their beloved Colonel John Hancock, whom they admire as a leader and man."

5

"Are you quite sure," Dolly asked, "that the new wallpaper for the parlor and the tapestries for our bedroom will arrive by Christmas?"

John paced up and down the length of his library. "The tapestries have already been smuggled into the country, and the wallpaper will be landed at any day. I'm positive the house will be ready to receive you by the end of the year. But we may be forced to postpone the wedding."

"Not again!" She began to twist the long curl that hung prettily over her shoulder, a sure sign that she was angry.

He rubbed his haggard face. "With Sam and the others attending the First Continental Congress in Philadelphia, I have more to do here than can reasonably be expected of one man. As

President of the new Massachusetts Congress and Chairman of the Committee of Safety, I have no time to myself."

"That's because you insist on holding each of your meetings in a different town, like a pack of schoolboys playing pranks!"

"It's no prank. Our meetings are illegal, and Gage could jail the lot of us—if he caught us at a meeting." He smiled wearily. "So far we've outsmarted him, but it isn't easy."

"If you didn't insist on breaking the law, you wouldn't have to scurry from one little town to another."

"Would you have me fail the people of Massachusetts when the threat of martial law hangs over our heads?"

Dolly was a shade less sure of herself. "I'm tired of waiting for our wedding! Just yesterday Sally Church and Betsy Bowdoin were teasing me, and I was mortified when they kept saying they don't think we'll ever be married."

"Bowdoin and Dr. Church are involved in all this as deeply as I am."

"Sally is sure you sit around drinking flip together."

"There's no harm in sharing a cup after a long night's meeting." He hated being placed on the defensive.

"If you can drink with your friends, you can take the time to marry me."

"I'll gladly arrange to have the ceremony performed tomorrow. Or tonight, if you wish—after my meeting in Cambridge. But I can't afford to take a ten-day trip after the wedding. I'm needed here."

She thought it absurd that the wealthiest man in North America couldn't take a week and a half from his work and, all other means of persuasion having failed, she resorted to tears.

John was unmoved. "Come over here," he said, taking her hand and leading her to the windows. "Look down at the Common."

Dolly hastily dabbed at her eyes. "I know. The tents of the troops who just arrived from Halifax were raised there yesterday."

"Gage is building a large corps of infantry and artillery here. Why? The War Office has sent Lord Percy to Boston as the Governor's military deputy. Why? The Crown intends to force us to our knees, and it's my duty to make sure our legs are so strong they won't bend."

She watched the redcoats from Halifax marching up and down the snow-flecked Common under the command of stiff-backed drill sergeants, and her pouting, peevish manner gave way to genuine fright. Slipping her hand into John's again, she clung to him. "Where will it end?"

"Sam writes me from Philadelphia that the other colonies feel as we do. Compromise with freedom is impossible."

"But I read in the London newspapers you gave me the other day that Pitt and Burke and other reasonable men are demanding that the government act reasonably."

"Our friends in Parliament are in the minority." John released her hand, walked to his desk and removed a cumbersome silver locket and thin chain from a drawer. "Here, my dear. I want you to wear this at all times. Don't ever be without it."

The gift was anything but attractive, and Dolly found it difficult to sound enthusiastic or grateful. "Thank you, dear." His taste in jewelry was usually good, but it was painfully evident to her that he had other things on his mind.

John grinned at her. "Watch," he said, and pried open the back of the locket with an embossed Spanish poniard that had been part of the loot taken by one of his remaining ships in a recent mid-Atlantic raid.

Dolly saw a carefully folded sheet of wafer-thin paper inside the locket.

"I've taken the precaution of moving my cash funds out of Boston," he told her. "If anything should happen to me, this is a complete list of where you'll find my strongboxes, together with instructions ordering them surrendered to you."

His confidence was the highest form of trust, the ultimate proof that he wanted to marry her in spite of the many delays. But she was too shocked to feel any sense of pleasure. "Are conditions that bad?"

He shrugged. "We can no longer take unnecessary risks. England is preparing for the worst, and we must do the same."

In spite of the rouge on her cheeks, Dolly paled. "There will be war?"

"I no longer believe it can be avoided. They've gone too far to back down gracefully, with honor, and so have we."

6

Yankee Doodle came to town,
For to buy a firelock;
We will tar and feather him,
And so we will John Hancock!

The regimental trumpeters played lustily, the drummers struck their instruments in unison and the redcoats of the two companies behind them sang at the top of their young voices as they paraded past the mansion at the crest of Beacon Hill. Bringing up the rear was an artillery cart, pulled by two horses, and on it a scarecrow in tattered finery and a Cavalier hat with a drooping feather was dangling from a makeshift gallows. Obviously the demonstration was not spontaneous, but the British troops, tired of the hostility shown by the citizens who now lined the streets to watch their parade, demonstrated an enthusiasm that more than compensated for their lack of originality.

John adjusted his bicorn hat, wishing he had worn something more ornate, with a feather, and smiled tolerantly as he stood in his driveway and watched the troops pass. In his pocket was a polite but urgent note, summoning him to a conference with the Governor, and he wondered whether the troops had been ordered to put on their exhibition in the hope of intimidating him. He would find out when he learned why Gage wanted to see him.

His carriage awaited him at the front entrance, but he didn't want the British to think he was afraid of them. "Take the coach back to the stables," he told the liveried groom who stood beside him. "The winter air will be good for me."

He walked briskly out the main gate and started down Beacon Hill, but slowed his pace when he saw several redcoats armed with axes committing a deliberate act of vandalism. While a red-cheeked young lieutenant, apparently the commander of the detachment, watched approvingly, a sergeant and four soldiers hacked off a length of fence ten feet long and smashed it to kindling. A group of civilians was gathering on the opposite side of the street, but the troops paid no attention to their angry muttering.

John took a firm grip on his walking stick, approached the officer and pointed the cane at him. "By what right do you desecrate my property?"

The lieutenant was unabashed. "It's a cold day, and my men were in need of exercise."

John was struck more by the officer's extreme youth than by his insolence. He could not have been more than eighteen or nineteen years old. "Do you hold an official warrant for this act of destruction?"

"We don't need permission to wreck the property of traitors." The lieutenant emphasized his words by placing one end of a picket under his boot and cracking it.

The crowd was growing and began to inch closer, but John waved the citizens back. Tempers on both sides were so raw that even the best-disciplined redcoats needed only the flimsiest excuse to open fire, and the civilians, many of whom now openly carried pistols in their belts, would be sure to retaliate at once. He didn't want an assault on his property, even though unprovoked, to be the cause of a blood bath.

"Your name and regiment, young man," he managed to speak quietly.

"Sir Philip Dawes, Sixty-fourth Infantry."

The youth's patronizing air reminded John of the attitude he had encountered so frequently during his own visit to England, and he had to curb his own irritation. "You shall hear further in this matter."

The officer struck a belligerent pose for the benefit of his own men. "Do you intend to fight us?"

"If I must, I shall choose my own time and circumstances."

The crowd cheered, and Sir Philip became flushed. "You won't feel like fighting after you've spent a month in the iron brig of the frigate that will take you to England. By then, all of this will belong to us. We'll take your grounds, your house and everything in it. Would you like to know how we spend our time at the Sixty-fourth's mess? We throw dice to see who'll get your plate, linen and silver."

"Very interesting, I'm sure." John turned to the crowd behind him. "I'll take care of this matter in my own way friends. Trust me."

The sergeant hacked off the last cross-bar still protruding from the ruined portion of the fence. "We're much warmer now, sir," he said with a coarse laugh.

"Good, then we'll be on our way." The lieutenant gave an order, the men fell in behind him and they marched off down the hill.

Several civilians stooped to pick up stones, and a boy in his teens began to pack snow into a hard ball. John quickly restrained them. "They're trying to goad us into attacking first. But there are more appropriate methods of handling this incident. I'm on my way to a meeting with the Governor, and I can promise you I'll call this to his attention."

"Be careful he don't lock you up!" a man with a deep voice called.

Only John smiled. "Never fear, I can look after myself." Raising his walking stick in a jaunty farewell gesture, he walked down Beacon Street, crossed Treamount and made his way to Province House, which now looked more like a military headquarters than a seat of government.

Four sentries armed with loaded muskets and bayonets stood at the entrance, and John had to show the Governor's letter to the corporal of the guard before he was admitted to the building and put into the keeping of a captain wearing the gold braid of an aide-de-camp on his left sleeve. They walked down troop-lined corridors in silence, and John began to feel uneasy. Perhaps the advice of the man in the crowd had not been as far-fetched as it had sounded. If the Governor was intending to make a sudden arrest, his victim could be made to disappear without a trace.

A lieutenant colonel sat behind the desk in the waiting room of the gubernatorial suite that had always been occupied previously by a member of the civilian secretariat. His heavy suntan indicated that he had probably been stationed at Port Royal, in Jamaica, and John made a mental note to mention the possibility to Paul Revere, who was coordinating information for the Committee of Safety. Perhaps the troops landed after dark under Royal Navy escort two nights earlier had come from the West Indian Islands rather than Halifax, as the Committee of Safety had assumed. The possibility required a thorough investigation.

The lieutenant colonel glanced at the letter John handed him, then stood languidly. "I'll find out when His Excellency will be free to receive you."

John had no intention of swallowing the calculated insult, and took his watch from his pocket. "I was asked to be here at three o'clock, and it's now two minutes before the hour. I'll wait a reasonable time, five minutes—until three minutes past the hour, but not one second longer. My time is as valuable as his."

Apparently he spoke more loudly than he realized, for Thomas Gage appeared in the entrance to the inner office. Wearing the full uniform of his high rank, he smiled with unexpected cordiality. "Come in, Master Hancock. I've been expecting you."

"Your servant, General." John didn't glance again in the direction of the aide as he preceded the Governor into the office he had known so well during the administrations of Bernard and Hutchinson. Refusing a chair, he took the initiative by launching into a rapid but precise account of the incident at his fence.

"Regrettable," the Governor murmured. "The tempers of the young are always dangerous."

"Very," John replied acidly. "It would be a pity if the windows of the Governor's Mansion were broken—or the house set on fire during the early morning hours when even sentries grow sleepy."

Gage stiffened.

"I make no threats, General. I'm merely trying to point out to you that two sides can play this unfortunate game. However, you have nothing to fear from me. As a gentleman I deplore all thoughtless acts of vandalism."

The Governor refused to be outdone in gallantry. "Sir Philip Dawes will receive an official reprimand, and the men who tore down your fence will replace it for you before tomorrow noon."

John was slightly mollified. "It was coated with heavy paint rather than whitewash."

"The new section of fence will be painted, too."

John finally consented to take the chair opposite the Governor's desk, and their eyes met. "What a pity, General, that we can agree only in these little things that are second nature to the gentry."

Gage ran a finger under the high collar of his tunic. "My troops would be less on edge if the citizens of Boston treated them with greater respect, and if they didn't hear rumors that native irregulars are drilling in the country towns."

"The people would be far more generously disposed to a small garrison than to an army. They feel the city has become an armed camp, occupied by foreigners. As to the stories of militia mobilizing and training, I'm afraid I can't confirm them."

"Militia, eh? A clever name to make rebels believe they have official sanction of some sort."

John contrived to look blank.

"I suppose you haven't any information, either, on the collection and storage of arms and ammunition in farmers' barns and other hiding places? I've even been told you devils are gathering artillery pieces, though I can't imagine where you'd find them."

John laughed deprecatingly. Unless Gage was a superb play-actor, he didn't know that cannon had been stripped from enemy warships captured in the French and Indian War, and were now being converted into land-based weapons.

The Governor joined in the laugh. "We understand each other."

"We do, General, but whether for good or bad I don't know."

"I didn't ask you here for a verbal duel, Master Hancock, nor for an exchange of our philosophies of government. I need your help."

"I'll be glad to give it, if I can."

"The troops that joined the Boston garrison were ordered here by the War Office at the request of the Colonial Office, both of them acting under Crown authority. Regardless of whether you and I approve or deplore their presence, they're here to stay."

John's shrug was noncommittal.

"I tried quartering the first two thousand newcomers in private homes, but the experiment was a miserable failure. You colonials found scores of ways—hundreds, really—to make the men feel they were contaminated with smallpox. I had to move the battalions out into the open to prevent them from mutinying."

"I defer to your greater knowledge of military affairs, of course. But I've heard it said that troops stationed far from their homes are particularly sensitive to rebuffs and slights."

"I've often wished we had you on our side in this unfortunate controversy. However, you've made your position clear, and I can only appeal to you now on humanitarian grounds. More than four thousand soldiers are sleeping in flimsy canvas tents in the Common and cooking their meals in the open. They're suffering great physical hardship, and I'm afraid illness might sweep through their ranks at any time."

"What a shame," John murmured, "that they had to leave their comfortable quarters in Halifax."

"Less than forty-eight hours after I announced that barracks would be constructed for them here, a lumber shortage developed in Boston. There isn't a single plank of wood to be found in the whole town."

John nodded thoughtfully.

"Master Hancock, you yourself shipped countless tons of lumber to England!" The Governor lost his composure.

"So I did, General, but the embargo of Boston forced me to give up my business. There's no lumber in my warehouses."

"Oh, I'm sure there isn't. But there are millions of trees—tens of millions—in Massachusetts!"

"Our farmers can no longer export tobacco and other crops to England," John replied pointedly. "They must work harder to support their families, and they're so busy raising enough food for themselves and the townspeople in the colony that they have no time any more to cut down trees and bring them to Boston."

"Are the carpenters busy, too? The Navy will go to Quebec for logs, and I've told the commodores to have their own men cut down trees for me. But I need carpenters to fashion planks and put up the buildings. I've offered to pay double wages, thirty-eight shillings per week instead of nineteen, but I haven't been able to hire even one carpenter!" Gage was red-faced.

"The embargo stopped the growth of the city and took hard money out of circulation, General. Men who were planning to put up new offices changed their minds and decided to retrench instead. I myself know a man who had been hoping to put up a new tavern, but he's decided the gamble is too great, and he's going to wait until the embargo is lifted. Then there are the young people who are planning to be married. Not many of them are in my fortunate position. For that matter, they aren't my age." John smiled at his own feeble witticism. "They can't afford to spend much, with funds not plentiful, so they're moving in with their parents."

"What does all this have to do with carpenters?" Gage was becoming increasingly annoyed by his blandness.

"There has been no work for carpenters, General, so the men who earned their living with hammers and saws have turned to other trades."

"Does that explain why we can't buy a keg of nails in the shops?"

"I hope you haven't forgotten that we're forbidden by law to operate our own foundries. Our nails must be brought in from England, and as you know better than anyone, no merchant ships have entered or left Boston harbor."

"You refuse to help, sir?"

John raised his hands, palms upward, and let them fall to his sides again.

The Governor stood, indicating that the interview had come to an end. "If I were in your boots, I'd probably refuse, too—if I didn't know I'd need a friend at court when I was brought to trial."

"I've lived under the threat of arrest for a long time, General. And I've learned something that the people of Boston have been learning, too, since your redcoats have been pouring into the city. Americans can't be bluffed and won't be frightened."

7

John sat with Sam Adams before a small fire in the cramped living room of the Reverend Jonas Clark, and the two guests looked out at the quiet street in the little town of Lexington, northwest of Boston. Both were restless, but their host pretended to be unaware of their distress as he poured them glasses of cider from an earthenware mug.

"I made this myself from last October's apple crop. I reckon it's a mite strong by now."

John's palate was accustomed to smoother and more mellow beverages, but he sipped politely and concealed a shudder.

"You're very kind to put us up here, Reverend Clark, but we must get back to Boston."

"Cap'n Johnny Parker of the Lexington militia said you're not to leave, so you'll stay here," the clergyman replied cheerfully.

Sam quietly drained his glass and refilled it. "We can't go anywhere until we get fresh horses. In the meantime, I want to know this man Parker's authority for keeping us here."

Reverend Clark was neither awed nor cowed. "He organized the local militia when your Committee of Safety sent out a call for volunteers, and he's been training the boys for three or four months."

John looked at his watch and sighed. "I promised Dorothy and Aunt Lydia I'd be home in time to make specific plans for the wedding, but even if someone brings us horses I can't possibly arrive in time for dinner."

"If what I suspect is true," Sam replied, one corner of his mouth twisting upward in the wry smile that many people regarded as a sneer, "the anger of Dolly Quincy is the least of your worries at the moment."

John looked at him inquiringly, but Sam shook his head.

"I can't say as I blame you for being careful," the clergyman declared. "Those British down in Boston would pay a fortune in gold to know what's in your minds." He took a stocking cap and long muffler from a wall peg, donned them and went to the door. "Ever since my son joined the militia, I've been pumping water from the well myself around this time of day. It's good for me to stretch my muscles." He left, closing the door behind him.

John watched him cross the side yard, then went to the door on the opposite side of the room and peered into the dining room. "We're alone, Sam." They had been taking such precautions for so long now that neither thought his actions strange.

"I have an idea word has been passed through the militia from Boston that it isn't safe for us to go back."

"Why would Gage act now after being afraid to set off a spark all these months? Even if he's heard that the Committee of Safety has asked for six more batteries of artillery, he won't believe we'll be able to provide the men with guns. Besides, our meeting in Concord was secret, and we know we can trust everyone who was there."

"It's a waste of time to speculate." Sam helped himself to more cider. "We'll have to wait until someone brings us word."

The advice was sound, but John couldn't follow it. In moments of crisis he demanded immediate action, and it was torture to exercise patience, to let others take the initiative.

In this situation, however, he had no alternative, and spent a miserable day as the hours dragged. The Reverend Clark kept busy with chores, and twice, when parishioners called on him, the visitors were forced to conceal themselves in a tiny bedchamber on the second floor of the clapboard house.

Not until an hour or two after sundown did a pair of riders draw to a halt outside. One, Captain Parker, stationed himself at the door as a sentry while the other halted at the entrance to wipe his dusty boots on a rag mat. John and Sam, listening from the second floor landing, recognized the voice of a fellow member of the Long Room Club and hurried down to the living room, where silversmith Paul Revere greeted them somberly.

"It's happened at last," he said. "General Gage is searching for you, and has offered rewards of one thousand pounds for each of you."

Sam Adams chuckled. "I'm worth a blamesight more as a prisoner than I am as a free man."

The reasons for the arrest order were far more important than the long-anticipated warrant itself. "Why?" John demanded.

"One of my most reliable boys, who works at the Governor's Mansion as a coachman, says Gage has heard we've stored large supplies of arms and ammunition in Concord village. He also discovered you were there for a Committee of Safety meeting, and he put two and two together."

The information the Governor had gleaned was accurate, and John was dismayed. "How did he find out?"

Revere ran long, slender fingers through his graying hair. "The same way we learn things, I reckon. Through spies. Some men talked big about standing up for their rights, but now that there may be a real fight, they're backing down. I'll find out who gave us away—that's my worry."

"Yes, we've got to think of the munitions at Concord. I hate to move them still farther west unless we have no choice."

Sam agreed. "Every mile we take them from Boston makes it that much easier for Gage to hold the city."

"If he sends troops to seize the stores, I'll know it in time," Revere said. "What concerns me is you two."

"We'll have to take our chances," John declared.

The silversmith shook his head. "The Committee forbids you to go near Boston. The vote was unanimous." He held up his hand when both began to protest. "You're needed too badly. For a spell you'll have to stay in these villages northwest of the city. We're arranging to have you sheltered at a different place every night. So far we've made arrangements in Concord, Billerica, and Bedford as well as here at Reverend Clark's. You'll move every night and stay hidden by day."

"That's a damned nuisance," John said.

Sam accepted his fate more calmly. "A reward of one thousand pounds, just for me. Gage has paid me a high compliment."

"I have personal responsibilities to discharge," John said angrily. "I can't leave my fiancée and my aunt stranded in that big house."

"I went to see them day before yesterday," Revere replied quietly. "I went there openly, without arousing redcoat suspicions, by pretending to discuss the pattern of some pewter mugs with Dolly." He laughed unexpectedly. "I took some samples with me, and she loved one of them. When this fuss is ended, I'll expect you to order a dozen from me."

"I'll give you the order for two dozen right now. What plans are the ladies making?"

"They've already left Boston. Dolly hired ten or twelve carts to take some furniture and drapes and paintings to her father's house in Braintree. The boys would protect your mansion if they could, but I reckon Gage will take possession of it now that you're a fugitive."

John vividly recalled the boast of the British officer whose messmates had thrown dice for the Hancock plate and silver. But he couldn't dwell on the potential loss of mere physical property. "The Governor allowed Dolly and my aunt to leave?"

"Not even Gage has sunk so low that he'll make war on women, and Dolly would be too much for even a British general to handle." Revere peered at John to see if he overstepped the bounds of propriety, then grinned. "She and Mrs. Hancock will be here in the next few days, as soon as we make sure Gage isn't having them followed."

John blinked, but was speechless.

"Dolly made up her mind she wants to be near you in a time of danger, and nobody could put her off. Reverend Clark's daughter, Elizabeth, will bring her here."

John had no desire to be encumbered by an attractive young woman who regarded the current difficulties as an exciting adventure, or by an elderly lady long accustomed to a gracious mode of living. "Will you see Dolly again, Paul?"

"No, but I can get word to her."

"Tell her I want her to go with Aunt Lydia to her father at Braintree—and stay there until we know how this business will be resolved."

Revere smiled sourly. "She knew that's what you'd say. She told it to me in almost the same words you've just now used. But she'll be here, all the same."

8

Dolly Quincy and Lydia Hancock arrived at the Lexington parsonage of the Reverend Jonas Clark on April 12, and when John joined them the following evening to spend twenty-four hours under the same roof, their attitude astonished him. They made beds, helped Elizabeth Clark with the housework and cheerfully put up with countless inconveniences in the cramped house. Dolly further surprised her future husband by doing all of the cooking, and prepared a beef and vegetable stew so succulent that even Sam Adams asked for a second helping.

The interlude was the only bright spot for John in an increasingly grim and anxious week. A steady flow of reports from Revere and Dr. Warren in Boston convinced the Committee of Safety that the patience of General Gage was exhausted and that he was finally preparing to take action against the colonials. The Forty-seventh infantry regiment was placed on combat status, and messengers from both Warren and Revere said that combat veterans were cleaning their muskets, sharpening their bayonets, and oiling their field boots.

Militiamen in every village and town were put on the alert, and those who lived on remote and inaccessible farms left their fields and moved temporarily into the houses of others who lived closer to Boston.

The Committee of Safety held daily meetings, each in a different place, and scores of agents were assigned to watch every move the British made. On April 17 a large shipment of arms just smuggled into Boston arrived at Concord, and Sam Adams went there to supervise its distribution to hiding places the Committee considered relatively safe. He completed his mission without difficulty, and rejoined his colleagues the next day for a meeting at Wetherby's Tavern in the tiny village of Menotomy, six miles from Lexington.

"I believe we can expect trouble in the next day or two," John announced. "Just this morning Gage sent out patrols to stop anyone from taking the roads to Lexington and Concord from Boston. Most of the troops left the city without their arms, but other men brought their muskets to them later, in wagons."

There was an immediate clamor, and several members suggested that the munitions secreted at Concord be moved.

Elbridge Gerry, a fiery young merchant who was one of John's closest associates, demurred. "We can't," he said flatly. "We have enough weapons and bullets and bags of powder there to fill the holds of ten ships. We'd need a hundred and fifty carts and a thousand cargo handlers to transfer the stores."

"Even if we moved them, where would we take them?" John added. "No, gentlemen, our arms will stay at Concord."

The others became silent as the enormity of his decision struck them.

"I see no real choice," he continued. "If Gage is determined to seize the weapons we've acquired to defend our liberties, he'll have to use force. We must stop him somewhere short of Concord."

The Committee members exchanged worried glances, as it was evident to everyone that a pitched battle might have far-reaching consequences.

"The Virginians faced a somewhat similar situation recently,"

Sam Adams declared. "But you'll recall that Governor Dinwiddie backed down when he realized he'd have to shed colonial blood to carry out his purpose."

"We can only hope that Gage will prove as sensible in a crisis." John rapped the table with his empty flip mug. "The chair will entertain a resolution dealing with this matter."

"I move," Gerry said, "that the stores be kept at Concord."

"All in favor will so signify."

There were no negative votes.

"The chair will entertain a resolution pertaining to our defenses. I suggest that all militia units be ordered to take a stand south and east of Concord, but that we leave the tactical decisions to the field commanders."

"I so move," Sam said gravely.

"All in favor will so signify."

The chorus of "Ayes" was soft-spoken. The men who were determining the future of Massachusetts were fully aware of the responsibility they were assuming.

"We'll meet tomorrow noon at this same place," John said. "It's close enough to Boston for those of you who are staying in Cambridge or Charlestown, and Sam and I won't have too far to travel." He glanced out of the window and saw that dusk was falling. "If there's no further business before the Committee, we stand adjourned."

He and Sam were silent as they rode borrowed farm horses to the Clark parsonage in Lexington. Dolly had prepared an excellent cod and oyster pie, there were ears of fresh spring roasting corn on the table and John was given two enormous halves of buttered *asqutasquash*, but he ate glumly, scarcely aware of what he was tasting. Sam drank only one small glass of mead brewed by one of Reverend Clark's parishioners, and the dour tension of both men communicated itself to the others.

For a time Dolly tried to chat with Elizabeth Clark about a dress in a new French style that one of her sisters in Braintree had recently acquired, but she gradually became aware of her flippant tone and fell silent, too.

Reverend Clark gave a quiet benediction, and then Aung Lydia's voice cut through the air. "We've spent years preparing for this emergency, haven't we?" she demanded of no one in particular. "If they want a fight, we'll give it to them!"

John grinned at her as they left the table. He and Sam went off to a corner of the living room, and for two or three hours they went over every detail of the already familiar situation, but neither was able to contribute fresh or constructive thoughts.

Suddenly a loud rap sounded at the door, and Captain Parker admitted a breathless messenger. "Gage is on the march!" he said loudly as he came into the room.

John gripped the back of a chair so hard that his fingers ached. "Are you sure?"

"Positive, Mr. Hancock! Revere brought the word from Boston, and a dozen of us are spreading the news. I was told to warn you and Mr. Adams without fail. Gage wants to capture you as bad as he wants our muskets and powder."

John felt calmer than he would have believed possible. The long years of conflict with the Crown could have led to no other conclusion. "Thank you for the information," he said, and turned to Parker, who still stood at the door. "You've heard, Captain?"

"Yes, sir. My sergeants are alerting the company, and we'll be assembling on the Green."

"I'll join you there when the time comes," John said, and was surprised when everyone gaped at him.

"Don't be a fool!" Aunt Lydia snapped. "You're needed for more valuable duty."

"I'm not afraid to fight for my country." He turned to the messenger. "Mr. Adams and I are grateful to you."

The man hurried away, and John went up to the loft he and Sam shared, returning a few moments later with a long wilderness rifle he had purchased through an intermediary from a Springfield trapper. Sitting down before the hearth, he began to clean the weapon, his jaw set as the others stared at him.

Aunt Lydia and Reverend Clark looked at Sam, who shrugged, knowing it was useless to waste his breath. Then they appealed to Dolly, who went quickly to the fireside and sat down beside her future husband.

"You've proved your courage for six months and more by staying in Boston and continuing to lead the opposition to the Crown," she said. "You could have been arrested at any time, but you refused to dissemble or run away. No one can accuse you of cowardice—or a refusal to expose yourself to the risks that others take."

John inserted a ramrod into the barrel of the rifle and moved it back and forth vigorously.

Dolly tried again. "You've spent your life behind a desk for many years. Let younger men who have worked on farms and at artisans' tasks in the towns run across fields and climb hills. Such labor would exhaust you."

He glared at her. "I'm not yet decrepit," he said icily.

She changed her tactics. "If you and Cousin Sam should be killed or captured, Massachusetts would become a body severed from its head."

He was inclined to agree, but couldn't admit it without running the risk of offending his colleagues if his remarks should be repeated. "Johnny Adams has the best mind in New England."

"Cousin John isn't serving on the Committee of Safety." Dolly could be maddeningly logical.

"Gerry could take my place, and so could Dick Devens or Abe Watson."

She stared at him for a long time without speaking. Then, gathering her skirts, she quickly left the house, not bothering to take a cloak.

John methodically continued to clean and oil the rifle.

A quarter of an hour later Dolly returned, accompanied by Captain Parker, and the militia officer spoke his mind bluntly. "Mr. Hancock," he said, "I mean you no disrespect, but we've got to understand each other. If British troops come to Lexington, you won't be here. You and Mr. Adams aren't going to be taken prisoner in my sector."

"I appreciate the motives that inspire your concern, Captain," John replied courteously, "but I must remind you that you're responsible to the Committee of Safety."

Parker remained at ease. "I guess you don't know much about armies," he declared, unwittingly adding insult to injury. "I take orders from Colonel Myers, my regimental commander in Concord—and nobody else. Mr. Adams, you'll be sensible, I hope?"

"I never quarrel with armed men, unless they're redcoats," Sam replied mildly.

"Thank you, sir. Now, Mr. Hancock, I hope you aren't going to make problems for me. Most of my boys have never fired a musket at anything deadlier than a goose or a partridge flying south in the autumn, and I'm not sure how they'll behave when they face real troops. I'd hate to distract them. But if you won't leave peaceably, I'll have you trussed and carted away in a wagon." He smiled, saluted, and left the house.

John was furious, and glowered at Dolly. "I hope you're well pleased with yourself!"

She pretended not to hear him as she rummaged in an embroidered bag for a shawl she was knitting. Thereafter the room was silent except for the steady clicking of her wooden needles.

Sleep was out of the question for anyone at the parsonage, but there was no further word until two o'clock in the morning. Parker, haggard but calm, returned with news that a strong column of British regulars was marching toward the northwest on the road from Boston. "They know they won't take us by surprise," he said. "They caught some of our lads, but two of them slipped away."

"How large is the column?" Sam Adams wanted to know.

"They outnumber us by about three to one, sir." The captain appeared undisturbed.

The tension became still greater, but Sam Adams dozed for a time in a chair near the hearth. John found this period of waiting intolerable, and started to pace, ignoring silent pleas from Dolly to sit down again. The long months of meetings and maneuvers, of pitting wits against the King's ministers and Parliament were at an end, and the issue would be decided by trained troops in uniform and freedom-loving Massachusetts citizens in homespun. If one side or the other gave in to a threat of force, complex questions of Constitutional law and trade, guarantees of personal liberty and taxation—all beyond the scope of semi-literate young fighting men—would be quickly determined.

It was insane to gamble, to pit the courage of raw colonial irregulars against the skill of impersonal, professional soldiers, but there was no choice. If the militia fled, opposition to Gage would crumble everywhere, and the Crown would win a tremendous, bloodless victory. But if the citizens held their ground, as the Virginians had done, Gage would be compelled to notify his superiors in London that Massachusetts would not yield its rights, even when a bluff was carried to extreme limits.

"We need something to eat," Dolly said, breaking the silence. "Liz, let's roast the salmon your cousin brought us yesterday afternoon." When she saw John brighten she knew she had found the right way to divert him. "Shall I coat it with that dressing of butter and chopped onions you like so much, dear?"

John was surprised that she knew one of his favorite recipes. "There's no better way to cook salmon." He hadn't realized it, but the long vigil had made him hungry.

The two young women retired to the kitchen, an outbuilding adjoining the house, and for a lack of anything better to do, John accompanied them. Elizabeth laughingly refused to let him build the fire for her, and he watched in wonder as Dolly expertly slit open a large salmon, removed a sac of roe and crushed the red globules in a skillet with butter, white wine, and finely chopped onions. She would be a far better housekeeper than he had imagined, and it was comforting to know that she would demand maximum efficiency from their servants.

Dolly put the salmon on a thick, scarred wooden platter and slid it into the hearth, adjusting the dampers with infinite care to attain the precise heat she wanted. Then, while the fish was roasting, she slowly stirred the mixture in the skillet on the top of the stove.

John inhaled the fragrant aromas, smiling blissfully, and virtually forgot the crisis that had preoccupied him for so long. He was distracted for a moment by the sound of voices at the stable behind the house, but bent down with Dolly to peer into the hearth at the cooking fish. "Delicious!" he exclaimed. "It looks ready!"

Dolly couldn't help laughing at him. "It isn't. I must turn it over and cook the other side. You'll have to wait another twenty minutes."

They were interrupted by a youth of nineteen or twenty, who wore the sash of a sergeant over his rough-spun linsey-woolsey coat. "Cap'n Parker's compliments, Mr. Hancock, but that there Lobsterback battalion is just down the road. We've hitched the bay team to your carriage, sir, and you've got to get out of here quick. Isaac Willoughby will drive you. He's too old to fight, and he knows every road in the province like he knows the wrinkles on his face."

John jolted back to reality. "I'll have to wait longer than twenty minutes for that salmon, I fear," he said to Dolly as they raced back to the house.

"I'll save you the best part of the steak, and you can eat it later in the morning."

"You and Aunt Lydia must come with us, Dorothy."

"Nonsense. We'll be safe enough here, and you can travel much more quickly without us." Dolly threw his cloak over his shoulders and took his bicorn from a peg while he buckled on his sword.

They went to the door together, and although neither believed in demonstrating affection in the presence of others, they kissed quickly.

Then John climbed into the carriage, sat down beside Sam and barely managed to close the door before Willoughby cracked his whip and the team of horses started off down the road.

The first, dirty streaks of dawn were showing in the sky, and in the murky light the two men peered out at the company of militia assembled at the Green. Husky young farmers and a few townsmen stood in a ragged, double line, most of them leaning on rifle and musket butts as they talked quietly. Captain Parker, the only member of the unit who was mounted, drew his sword and saluted as the carriage swept past.

"I'm afraid they don't look very impressive," John said, "but appearances can be deceptive, particularly at this time of day."

Sam was too weary to answer.

Suddenly a single musket shot rang out and echoed through the quiet village.

"My God!" John twisted to peer out of the small window behind him, but the Green was far behind and he could see nothing.

A volley of musket fire crackled, then another.

"This is open war," John said in a hoarse whisper.

9

The rain was gentle but persistent, and the two men crouching under the budding willow at the edge of the swamp shivered. Neither could see more than a few feet ahead, and after wandering aimlessly in the marsh for the better part of a day and a night they were exhausted, bone-weary. An owl hooted nearby, making Sam jump, and in the distance a dog howled. The area was so deserted, so primitive and lonely that it was difficult to believe the village of Billerica was less than two miles away.

"The British will never find us here," Sam muttered. "Neither will that fellow, Wyman, who brought us here. I think we're doomed to stay in this infernal damp until we rot."

"No matter how many patrols may be searching for us," John replied hoarsely, "we can't stay here beyond mid-day. We're expected at Worcester by sundown, and if we aren't there, Tom Cushing and Johnny and Bob Paine will leave for Philadelphia without us." Suddenly he began to laugh. "I doubt if any two wretches have ever looked less like delegates to the Second Continental Congress. Do you have any more of that bread and cheese Wyman left us?"

"Not a crumb." Sam rubbed his face with a grimy hand. "I don't suppose there's any more whiskey."

"We finished it at midnight." John felt a bug crawl across the back of his neck and slapped himself hard. "My cook bakes a wonderful breakfast cake of minced beef and whipped eggs."

"I don't want to hear another word about your damned cook." Sam's laugh sounded more like a cackle.

"If the other delegates don't wait for us at Worcester, I hope they leave our clothing boxes for us."

"Cousin John will wait. Wyman promised to send word, if he could."

"If—if—if. Damnation, when are we going to learn something definite? We can't find out what happened at Lexington, we don't know if the British found our munitions store at Concord—everything is still in an infernal, confused muddle. And we stay here in this swamp, hiding like a pair of escaped criminals."

"Patience, John. The news of the world will catch up with us. Until then we'd best keep walking so our blood doesn't freeze."

They continued to circle the edge of the swamp until long after daybreak, plodding wearily, too tired to exchange more than an occasional word. Finally, off to their left, they heard the distinctive, mellow call of an oriole, which was repeated twice.

Remembering their instructions, they halted and waited for their rescuers to come to them. Eventually three young men appeared, all in homespun and all carrying muskets.

"Morning, Mr. Adams, Mr. Hancock," one of them called. "We've been searching for you an hour or more. You've come to the farthest side of the swamp from Billerica."

"But you're safe now," one of his companions added. "There isn't a Lobsterback in the area—not a live one, anyways."

"Do you know what's happened since the morning of the nineteenth, boys?" John demanded. Information was infinitely more important then food.

"Yes, sir. There was a fight at Lexington, and maybe a dozen of our lads was killed. The company scattered, and the Lobsters went on to Concord. There was another skirmish there, but the redcoats didn't have their heart in more fighting, I can tell you. Our lads had been picking them off from behind trees and stone fences, so they headed back for Boston as fast as they could."

The party climbed out of the marsh and started toward higher ground.

"Did they find our munitions?"

"No, Mr. Hancock. They were hurting too bad to tarry in Concord. We hear tell that not one Lobster in three reached Boston alive."

"You have no exact figures on our losses?"

"No, sir. But they were pretty bad. Not as bad as we gave it to them, though."

John thought of the young sergeant who had come to the Clark kitchen to tell him of the British approach, and his throat felt dry.

One of the trio handed them small loaves of freshly baked bread as they walked toward some horses tethered at the edge of a patch of woods.

The positive knowledge that a battle had been fought, with losses on both sides, made it impossible for John to eat. It no longer mattered to him, either, that his clothes were soiled and torn, his stockings and breeches ripped by brambles and his shoes soggy. His personal discomfort seemed trifling now.

"Wyman sent your carriage back to Lexington, like you told him, and the ladies went off in it."

It was a small note of cheer to realize that Dorothy and Aunt

Lydia were safe. By this time, he hoped, they had arrived safely at Edmund Quincy's Braintree house.

More bread, cheese, and small jugs of cider were taken from saddlebags when the group reached the horses. Sam ate quickly, taking frequent sips from his container of cider, and John forced himself to nibble a little food as the guides continued their recital.

"There ain't a Lobster who dares to show his face outside of Boston, not a damned one," one of the young men said. "Our company is going off to join the rest of the militia regiment at Cambridge today, and we'll meet the boys there after we take you to Worcester."

"We'll be obliged to you for the loan of the horses," John said, "but we have no need of an escort."

The youths laughed raucously. "To hell you don't!" the tallest of them exclaimed. "Old Gen'l Gage is offering five thousand pounds for your heads now, dead or alive!"

"Five thousand for each of you," another added.

John couldn't blame them for being impressed, as the sum was enormous. He found it difficult to believe that either of them was worth that much to the colonial cause, and he looked in amusement at his grubby companion.

But Sam, munching thoughtfully on bread and cheese, cared nothing now about his own situation. He had said nothing during the conversation, and his expression was remote.

The trio continued to supply details of the military engagements at Lexington and Concord, then boasted how the militia would lay siege to the British garrison at Boston. John listened attentively and, glancing now and again at his friend, hoped the enforced stay in the swamp hadn't injured his health.

"I want to know just one thing," Sam said at last. "Who fired the first shot at Lexington?"

"Nobody knows, Mr. Adams."

"Did we, or did they?" Sam gripped his arm.

The youth was surprised by his ferocity. "Cap'n Parker hisself don't know for sure, Mr. Adams. Sergeant Williams told me it was too dark to see. Somebody got excited, that's all. Maybe it was one of us, maybe it was one of them. But it don't matter. There was a fight."

"It matters more than anything that has happened in the past ten years," Sam declared. "We must tell the world the redcoats did it. In the eyes of our own people and of the nations from whom we want support, it must be clear that the British were the villains. How else can we win popular approval for our independence?"

John stared at his friend in undisguised horror. "Children fight with their parents, Sam, but if they're civilized, one doesn't disown the other. We must convince London we're strong and determined, and we'll be treated as an honored son, not a wayward one." Aware that Sam was looking at him in silent contempt, he swung into the saddle. A muddy field outside a remote Massachusetts village was not the place to decide the most far-reaching issue that Americans had ever faced.

10

The road from Worcester to Philadelphia was a triumphal route. Thousands turned out in Hartford to greet the two men who had become the symbols of America's refusal to be cowed, and John joined the meetings of Connecticut authorities who were planning to send an expedition under Benedict Arnold of New Haven and Ethan Allen to capture Fort Ticonderoga in New York, the gateway to Canada. Dolly and Aunt Lydia reappeared, and John left them in Fairfield, Connecticut, at the home of Thaddeus Burr, a close business associate, swearing he would return to be married as soon as his duties as a delegate to the Second Continental Congress permitted.

New York Town greeted the two fugitives from Massachusetts ecstatically, and so many dinners, meetings, and banquets in their honor were planned that John had to remind his hosts that he and Sam would be derelict in their duties if they remained for more than a few days.

William Alexander, a fiery patriot who disliked his inherited title of Lord Stirling, met the pair at the New Jersey border with an honor guard, Newark gave the heroes a wild welcome and the journey south through that colony was slowed by fetes and meetings, barbecues and rallies.

Philadelphia, the largest city in the New World, with a population of nearly fifty thousand, was sedate and sophisticated, but the doors of every red brick house were thrown open to the two most popular men in the colonies, and the warmth of their reception was overwhelming.

John was flattered by the adulation, but this was no time to bask in glory. He engaged a large suite of rooms in a private house off Market Street, and immediately made it his business to become acquainted with delegates from the other colonies, learn their views and analyze their character strengths and weaknesses.

On May 10, 1775, the Congress officially convened, temporary committees were established and the delegates soon split into two groups. The moderates, who were in the majority, favored restoration of amicable relations with England, and looked to John for leadership. Ironically, Sam became head of the small but vocal faction that wanted the colonies to sever all ties with the Crown. John was disturbed by the split, and did his best to reconcile the opposing points of view.

It was universally assumed that Dr. Franklin of Philadelphia would be elected President of the Congress, but he declined, saying he preferred to serve in a lesser capacity. Benjamin Harrison of Virginia promptly proposed the name of John Hancock, and at noon on May 24 he was elected by acclamation.

Surprised and pleased, John mounted the rostrum in the Statehouse and waited for the applause of the wealthy merchants and planters, lawyers and physicians and prosperous farmers to die down. This audience would not appreciate rabble-rousing rhetoric, and the occasion did not warrant a flowery speech, so he spoke in the crisp manner he used at business conferences.

"Gentlemen, friends, fellow Americans, I appreciate your trust and will try to be worthy of the honor you place in me.

"As our first order of business, I am pleased to inform you that dispatches have just been received by messenger confirming the capture of Fort Ticonderoga by troops under the command of Colonel Arnold and Colonel Allen."

The delegates cheered as wildly as a crowd of Boston cargo handlers.

"It will be our immediate duty to authorize, equip and maintain an army to capture Montreal and Quebec. It will also be necessary for us to authorize and form a corps that will lay siege to General Gage in Boston. Private letters reaching me from associates in Massachusetts indicate that although volunteers from many colonies are arriving at Cambridge to join in the effort to compel Governor Gage to negotiate with us on honorable terms, our efforts are hampered by a lack of unity and general confusion.

"Consequently it is incumbent upon us to establish a Continental Army, appoint a commander-in-chief responsible to this body, and provide him with the means to obtain a corps of officers, troops, training facilities, and all necessary supplies and munitions. I urge that we elect such a commander-in-chief today, and give him—at once—the authority he needs."

It was evident to every man present that the new President not only possessed talent as an executive, but had given much thought to the problems the colonies faced.

"I also believe it essential that we create a Navy as rapidly as possible. I myself hold the temporary chairmanship of the Maritime Committee, and unless the Congress deems it unwise for me to do so, I will continue in that capacity. Perhaps this is an appropriate time for me to announce that I shall contribute the sum of ten thousand pounds for the construction of two warships under the supervision of the Massachusetts Committee of Safety."

The cheers were a guarantee that the new President would serve in a dual capacity.

"But our martial efforts will be a vain mockery if we do not take immediate steps for the restoration of a just peace. Most of you know I favor a peace whereby we remain British, if it be possible to reach an honorable accommodation with the Crown. To you who disagree with me, let me stress that I share your fundamental conviction. A peace that fails to guarantee our liberties is no peace, and rather than submit to injustice, I would prefer a severance of ties to Great Britain.

"All of you are aware that negotiations are necessary for the achievement of a satisfactory accommodation with the Crown. Therefore, even while we maintain a strong military position, we must make our beliefs known to our friends in England, as well

as to those who oppose us." (He carefully refrained from referring to Lord North, his ministers and the majority in Parliament
as enemies.) "In order to clarify our stand, I direct that this Congress issue a declaration explaining our reason for taking up
arms. Mr. Jefferson of Virginia has volunteered to head a committee that will draw up such a declaration for the consideration
of the Congress, and I appoint him to the post, requesting that
he submit a draft of the declaration as soon as he and his colleagues can prepare one. I further urge him to include in the
membership of his committee men who represent all points of
view expressed by the delegates.

"Now, gentlemen, before we proceed to the election of a commander-in-chief, I beg your indulgence for a personal word. It is
no secret that I possess a not inconsiderable fortune, much of it
consisting of buildings, warehouses, and other property in the
town of Boston. That city is occupied by General Gage, who is
preparing for a siege. If we fail to obtain a victory over him by
force of arms, our cause will fail and the Crown will treat us with
the contempt due a subjugated and rebellious people.

"Lest anyone harbor the mistaken impression that I would protect my own property at the expense of our common cause, I
take an oath, with you as my witnesses. Burn Boston and make
John Hancock a beggar if the public good requires it!"

The dramatic declaration brought the delegates to their feet,
roaring, and John bowed his head. His vow was sincere, but at
the same time he realized he had been aware of the effect he
would create. Perhaps, under the circumstances, he would be given
the command of the Continental Army, a selection that seemed
to him a natural outgrowth of his service with the Massachusetts
Independent Corps. Now that he held the top civilian position
in the United Colonies he wouldn't want the military post, which
was subordinate, but would enjoy refusing the honor. It was vain
to expect so much, of course, but his long and arduous labor on
behalf of the colonial cause deserved such double recongnition.
Dorothy would be pleased, his stature would be enhanced in
England as well as in America, and he would be in a far stronger
position to negotiate with Lord North's government. In fact, the
Crown would be forced to recognize him on terms of equality
which would enable him to obtain the guarantees of rights which

men from New Hampshire and the Maine District of Massachusetts to Georgia were demanding with such unanimity.

When the cheers subsided and the delegates settled back in their seats, they broached the matter immediately. "The first order of business now before this Congress," he said, "is the selection of a general who will command a military force authorized by us and responsible to us."

Several delegates requested the floor, and John felt a warm glow when he saw that John Adams was one of them. "The chair recognizes the gentleman from Massachusetts."

The cautious attorney spoke with his usual brevity and care. "Mr. President, fellow delegates, no position is of greater importance than that of the leader of our joint military force. The man we select must have several unusual qualities of character. It is self-evident that he must be someone of proven experience as a soldier. It is also vital that he be a man of known moderation in order that the Crown will suffer no misunderstanding and will know at once that this Congress is eager to reach an accommodation that both England and America can accept without loss of honor. It seems to me that only one man in the colonies possesses all of these necessary attributes."

John tried hard to show no emotion, but thought it admirable that his childhood friend could describe him with such tact and accuracy.

"We who espouse the cause of moderation hope with all our hearts that the militia from all our colonies gathering at Cambridge will win concessions from General Gage without bloodshed. If there must be fighting, we pray it will be kept to a minimum in order that peace terms may be achieved with as little rancor on both sides as may be possible under these tragic circumstances. We desire nothing more than that our enemy of today will once again be our brother and comrade-in-arms tomorrow.

"The gentleman who comes to my mind—who is in all our minds—is extraordinary. His judgment is sound in all things. He has demonstrated his talent for reconciling quarreling factions in our own midst. He is highly regarded in England. He tamps the fires of the hot-headed, spurs the sluggard and inspires the militiaman. He has served the mother country and our own America with great distinction in the field with the rank of colonel. He has won the confidence of men in every colony, and can weld our militia into a striking force of Americans who speak with one voice and fight with one purpose.

"Gentlemen, I propose Mr. George Washington—Colonel Washington of Virginia—for the post of supreme command."

John was stunned, unable to conceal his dismay. In all fairness he had to admit that Washington, who had served so brilliantly in the French and Indian War, fitted the description well enough, but it was shocking that a lifelong friend should place the Virginian's name before the Congress. Never before had Johnny shown such blatant jealousy.

The delegates rose to their feet, applauding, and Washington rose from his seat beside Thomas Jefferson and the other Virginians. His face a fiery red, he fled modestly from the hall.

John made a belated attempt to hide his own feelings and gaveled for order. "The chair," he said, trying to speak calmly, "recognizes the gentleman from Maryland."

Thomas Johnson, who had been one of his strongest supporters for the Presidency, took the floor. "Gentlemen," he said, "Mr. Adams' remarks leave me with no alternative. I take pride in placing the name of Colonel Washington before this Congress, and hereby nominate him for the post of commander-in-chief of the Continental Army."

Again the applause was prolonged, and then Sam Adams struggled to his feet from his seat in the back row.

John hid his elation, as he knew what his closest associate for the past decade would do. "The chair recognizes the gentleman from Massachusetts."

"I second the nomination of Colonel Washington, and suggest that we show our confidence in him by making his election unanimous."

The blow was so staggering that John caught his breath. Sam was striking back at him, viciously, because he had refused to accept the radical position and support the minority demand for independence from England. Hancock pride demanded that the unavoidable be accepted with good grace, but John would never forgive the deliberate insults of the Adams family.

Smiling now with the aplomb of a man who agreed without reservation to the suggestion, John asked, "Is it the desire of the Congress that Colonel Washington be selected by acclamation?"

The shout that greeted his question was even louder than the response to his suggestion that, if necessary, Boston be burned to the ground.

On sober reflection, John knew Washington was an excellent choice, which he could support enthusiastically. Nevertheless, he could never forget the stabs in the back inflicted on him by men whose personal loyalty to him he had taken for granted.

11

Unable to forgive the slight, real or imagined, inflicted on him by John and Sam Adams, John scorned their personal assistance during the arduous weeks that the Continental Congress organized and oiled its machinery for the struggle against the Crown. Soon he and they were no longer on speaking terms, but all three enthusiastically supported the Declaration of the Causes and Necessity of Taking up Arms written by Thomas Jefferson.

That document, which won the approval of both moderates and radicals at the Congress, said, "We are reduced to the alternative of choosing an unconditional submission to the tyranny of irritated ministers, or resistance by force. The latter is our choice. We have counted the cost of this contest, and find nothing so dreadful as voluntary slavery."

The cost was far greater in financial terms than anyone attending the Congress had anticipated. Gunpowder was exorbitantly expensive, cannon had to be imported from France, and the total cost of the supplies requested by General Washington for the siege of Boston amounted to a mammoth five hundred thousand dollars in the new medium of exchange the delegates had adopted to replace the British pound. John quietly contributed half the total out of his own pocket, and worked with Jefferson on the last portion of the public statement.

The Declaration, so firm in its opening, ended on a conciliatory note that even the most conservative members of the Congress could accept. "We mean not to dissolve that union which has so long and so happily subsisted between us," Jefferson wrote, "and we pray that the Ruler of the Universe may dispose our adversaries to reconciliation on reasonable terms."

Pending the day when mutual good will would prevail, the colonies were required to devote their efforts to strengthening their position. John wrote personal letters to every member of each of the thirteen colonial assemblies, and threw himself into the organization of American resistance to the Crown with such fervor that he worked eighteen to twenty hours per day, taking only one hour for his evening dinner every night and sleeping for no more than three or four hours.

The Congress assumed control of the force gathered at Cambridge, issued commissions to officers and directed each of the colonial legislatures to raise money and provide Washington with men.

The American military position looked encouraging. Gage sent his new deputy, General William Howe, to capture and reduce American artillery set up on the heights of Charlestown, opposite Boston, and the Battle of Bunker Hill was fought before Washington reached his headquarters. The Americans lost the heights, but inflicted losses on the redcoats far heavier than they received, and the ring of Continentals around Boston became tighter. Two columns of American troops were marching north, and high hopes were entertained for both. Even the cautious Washington believed Richard Montgomery would capture Montreal, and Benedict Arnold's chances of taking Quebec appeared excellent. In the South, too, the colonies won victories. A force of Tories, men loyal to the Crown, were repulsed by the militia of North and South Carolina, and when the supposedly invincible British fleet tried to capture Charleston, its cannonballs lodged harmlessly in the soft wood of the shore-based palmetto-log forts, while the land batteries inflicted such heavy damage on the attackers that the fleet was compelled to withdraw.

John and most of his fellow delegates were convinced that the combination of the appeal to reason and the strong show of military solidity would create an atmosphere favorable to a conference that would iron out all difficulties. Late in August 1775, the Congress adjourned for five weeks, and John set out at once for Massachusetts, intending to join General Washington at Cambridge.

A matter of the utmost personal importance caused him to break his journey for twenty-four hours in Connecticut, however. He dispatched a messenger to Dorothy at Fairfield as soon as he was reasonably certain of the adjournment date, and in a brief letter asked her to make all necessary arrangements for their wedding as soon as he arrived. It would be unfair to her if there should be another delay, he wrote, and he was in constant torment because she was not at his side.

He arrived so soon on the heels of the messenger that Lydia Hancock and an aunt of Dolly's who lived in Fairfield were the only members of either family present when the Reverend Andrew Eliot performed the Anglican ceremony in his little church on August 28. The groom had arrived only an hour earlier, and although he had changed into a clean lawn shirt and silk stock, the dust of the road was still thick on his boots.

The wedding party adjourned to the house of Thaddeus Burr for a buffet supper of turkey, smoked eels, and boiled lobsters, and eleven members of the Connecticut legislature, which had also adjourned, took advantage of the occasion to become better acquainted with the man whom the Congress had elected the first citizen of the colonies.

The gentlemen gathered at the cut-glass punchbowl, where they drank a powerful concoction consisting of rum, sack, and hard apple cider. John, the center of attention, explained in detail the policies that the Congress was attempting to pursue. Scores of questions were asked, and he answered each at length. The punch helped him to dispel the fatigue of recent weeks and the exhaustion of the journey, which he had made on horseback. Rarely had he encountered an audience that listened more attentively to every word, and he scarcely realized that one or another of his admirers kept his cup filled to the brim with the potent but innocuous-tasting punch.

Dolly, who had not had time for the final fittings of her white bridal gown and consequently had been married in a dress of peach-colored silk, spent several hours in the company of the ladies in the auxiliary parlor adjoining the room in which the men were helping themselves to the punch. For a time she enjoyed the flattery of the Connecticut legislators' wives, the first tribute she had received in her new role as the first lady of the colonies, but eventually she became bored by the usual domestic chatter.

Ordinarily no woman dared to interrupt a serious political discussion, but a bride was privileged to do what she pleased on her wedding day. Dolly shut out the droning voices of Aunt Lydia and her own Aunt Dorothy Jackson, who were assuring each other they would find true comfort only when they were buried at the sides of their late husbands. Making certain that the velvet beauty patch glued to her left cheekbone hadn't come loose, she stood and walked boldly into the main parlor, her smile polite but frosty.

The courtly Thaddeus Burr saw her at once, as did two bachelors with whom she had flirted with concentrated innocence while waiting for the Continental Congress to end its deliberations. But John, who was explaining in detail to his listeners why the overwhelming desire of the British electorate for a just peace would compel Lord North to negotiate with the colonies, remained unaware of her proximity.

"Mr. Hancock!" she said, and her tone was so sharp that every man in the room turned to look at her.

John's smile was as bland as his habitual expression on the dais when he conducted a public meeting.

Dolly realized he had no idea why she had come into the room. The Connecticut legislators made way for her as she joined her bridegroom, and her eyes became a little softer as she slipped her arm through John's. "I'm sure," she said pointedly, "that many of you will want to chat with His Excellency again when we establish temporary residence in Cambridge."

It was the first time anyone had ever called John by the title usually reserved for colonial Governors, and he made no protest as Dolly led him into the dining room, where food was heaped high on two long tables.

"You're in need of food, sir," she murmured.

The baked hams, smoked oysters, and salad greens sprinkled with the juice of crushed Spanish olives made him feel a little queasy. "I'm not hungry, my dear," he protested.

"No one else can touch the food until we've eaten," she whispered.

He nodded, reflecting that he was fortunate to have a wife

aware of protocol. Servants standing on the far side of the tables filled a plate for him and carried it to the gardens, where it was placed before him under trees glowing with multi-colored lanterns. He gallantly held Dolly's chair for her, took his own and was not surprised to note that the other guests were streaming after them.

Dolly coaxed him to eat the better part of his meal, which he washed down with a strong ale made in a New Haven brewery owned by Colonel Benedict Arnold. Thaddeus Burr led the company in songs honoring the bride and groom, and then three young militia officers from Norwalk who were leaving in the morning to join General Washington's corps at Cambridge started to sing "Yankee Doodle."

John scowled, thinking it an inappropriate occasion for a redcoat song that mocked Americans, but he relaxed when he heard new lyrics that presented colonials in a favorable light.

Servants appeared with huge trays of brandywine, and Thaddeus Burr stood to propose a toast. "God bless the King!"

John was disturbed when he saw that at least half of the men present refrained from raising their glasses.

"To the bride and groom," the host declared. "May they live together in happiness and health."

The entire company drank.

John rose to reply. "Mrs. Hancock and I am grateful for your felicitations," he said, "and we hope you will stand with us for our anthem of loyalty." In a hoarse, off-key voice he started to sing the first stanza of "God Save the King."

It would have been rude for even the most radical not to follow the example of the President of the Continental Congress.

At the conclusion, glasses were refilled, and John drained his in a single swallow. Then everyone crowded forward to kiss Dolly on the cheek and shake his hand, and he astonished his bride by remembering the names of all the guests, even those whom he had met for the first time earlier in the day. He made a mental note to urge her to train her own memory so she could perform the same feat. It was essential that a man in public life recall the face and name of everyone presented to him, and people would be doubly flattered if the wife of the statesman knew him, too. Dolly had a great deal to learn.

Thaddeus Burr extricated the bridal couple from the throng,

and conducted them to a suite on the second floor of his house, which he had prepared for them. "I've instructed the staff to bring your breakfast to you at any hour you ring," he said.

"We hope to put in a full day of travel," John replied. "There's so much military traffic to Cambridge that we'll be obliged to leave very early."

Dolly could not hide her surprise, and her green eyes widened for a moment before she gained her composure.

Burr flourished a handkerchief before his face to muffle a grin as he closed the door behind him.

John locked the door and turned to embrace his bride.

For a few moments Dolly clung to him, then disengaged herself and averted her gaze with a disarming mixture of modesty and coyness. "If you'll give me leave," she said, "I'll rejoin you shortly."

"Of course, my dear." John watched her from the sitting room as she made her way through the adjoining bedchamber to a dressing room beyond it. It was strange to realize that she was his wife at last, but far stranger that their courtship had been so long. She was the loveliest and most charming of women, and years of their lives had been wasted. It was unfortunate, he thought with a sigh, that a man who had dedicated himself to the public good could not call his time his own.

Drifting into the bedroom, John wished he had not eaten such a large meal. Punch and brandywine didn't mix with rich food, particularly when a man had been subsisting on only a few short hours of sleep every night for many weeks. One of the servants had laid out John's nightclothes, so he removed his wig and put it on a stand, vaguely conscious of a mild but persistent headache. He undressed slowly, and twice caught himself starting to doze after he sat down to remove his boots.

Hauling himself to his feet, he slipped into his sleep-coat of French silk that had been smuggled into Philadelphia from Martinique, donned a dressing robe of matching, quilted silk and, focusing with some difficulty on the floor at his feet, stepped into satin slippers he had ordered from a New York Town bootmaker who had recently migrated to the New World from England.

Dolly seemed to be taking a long time, and John could hear no sound from the far side of the dressing-room door. He yawned, stretched and looked at the inviting four-poster bed with its three mattresses of down and plump pillows. Yawning again, he could not resist the temptation to rest while he waited for his bride.

He lowered himself to the bed, which felt even better than it looked, and a half-groan, half-sigh escaped from his lips. This was the first night in more than three and one-half months in which he had read no reports, dictated no letters and held no conferences. The sheets were cool, the mattresses supported his weight as though he were floating in the air like a seagull being carried by a breeze, and he closed his eyes.

Dolly opened the dressing-room door and paused to take a quick, last appraisal in the pier glass. Her hair, falling in curls below her shoulders, looked like newly minted sovereigns, she appeared far younger than her twenty-eight years in a peignoir of white silk with puffed sleeves and a huge collar framing a low-cut neckline. Even her high-heeled slippers of watered white silk were of the latest design, thanks to a cargo recently landed by one of Colonel Arnold's merchantmen which had slipped through the blockade of British warships off the American coast after a voyage from Brest. Her scent, a pungent but subtle West Indian fragrance, came from a new jar, and she knew she had never looked more enchanting.

Her smile froze when she heard John's deep, even breathing.

She went to him, touched his hand and then shook his arm, but he did not stir. Dolly's fury was so intense that she quivered, but suddenly, in spite of her anger, she began to laugh.

"Well, Mr. Hancock," she said aloud, "we've waited for so many years that another night and day won't really matter." Wiping the tears of laughter from her eyes, she blew out the oil lamps, removed her peignoir and, climbing onto the bed beside him, pulled the silk topsheet and blanket over them. Perhaps she should have inveigled him away from the punchbowl earlier, but it was too late now for regrets.

12

Dorothy and John Hancock enjoyed little privacy on their honeymoon. They went to Cambridge, and after the President held several meetings with General Washington and a number of his own

Massachusetts political associates, returned to Philadelphia for the opening of the new session of the Continental Congress. Everywhere on the road local patriot leaders rode with them to discuss affairs of state with the colonies' civilian leader, others dined with them at the inns where they spent their nights, and even when they retired to their own quarters they were frequently interrupted by Congressional messengers and military couriers.

"I didn't know," Dorothy said when they reached their rented rooms in Philadelphia, the same quarters John had occupied as a bachelor, "that I was marrying the United Colonies."

"You look ravishing, my dear," John told her fondly. "Do you suppose you can arrange a small dinner for tomorrow evening? I realize this is short notice, but I've appointed a representative from each colony to the Maritime Committee, and I'm anxious to begin building our Navy this year."

Dolly hadn't unpacked her belongings, she had come to Philadelphia with no silver, linen, or tableware and hadn't yet set eyes on the kitchen outbuilding they were to share with the other two tenants of the house. On her one previous visit to Philadelphia she had not gone near the meat, fish, or produce markets and had no idea which sellers the local ladies of quality patronized. For a moment a helpless feeling flooded her and she became panicky, but she knew by now what was required of a woman in her position. "Will seven o'clock be all right, dear?"

John took her calm for granted. "Eight will be safer. As the session is convening tomorrow morning, every delegate will want to make a speech, so we may not adjourn until rather late."

Dolly nodded, thinking the parlor would look sprightlier with new drapes. "Give Cousin John my love, please, and tell him we want him to dine with us before the end of the week."

John had already told her of the incident that had marred his relationship with his oldest associates, and he glared at her. "I don't intend to entertain John Adams under my roof."

She returned his gaze steadily. "Nonsense, Mr. Hancock!"

He was too startled to reply.

"You've acted like a spoiled child, and Cousin John's behavior hasn't been much better. I've exchanged several letters with Cousin Abigail, and neither of us will tolerate such conduct.

You're a responsible man, I expect you to act accordingly, sir. Tell Cousin John we shall expect him here on Thursday at seven. And while you're about it, invite Cousin Sam, too. If I can overlook his atrocious table manners, you can forget a fancied grievance."

"I assure you, Mrs. Hancock, that I was the victim of genuine slights."

Dolly did not relent. "I'm proud of your many admirable qualities, which all our countrymen recognize. But be good to realize that you lack General Washington's military experience and his flair for waging a campaign. If you won't extend the invitations, I shall come to the Congress myself for the purpose."

John's capitulation was complete. "That won't be necessary, ma'am," he said meekly. "I'll ask them here for dinner on Thursday."

13

The delegates to the Continental Congress recognized Dorothy Quincy Hancock's power over her proud husband when she quickly and efficiently forced his reconciliation with John and Sam Adams. Thereafter her parlor was crowded with gentlemen from every delegation who sought her support for private projects, and John protested in vain that he saw as much of his colleagues at home as he did on the floor of the Congress.

Dolly's interest in political affairs quickened, and when a messenger brought word to the lodging house that Montreal had fallen to an American corps, she took delight in carrying the news herself to the Congress.

The delegates had little to cheer them other than the fall of Montreal in the autumn of 1775, however. King George considered the Declaration an intolerable act of insolence, and although both the War Office and Colonial Office were eager to reach a mutually agreeable accommodation with the colonies, the monarch refused. The Battle of Bunker Hill, he said, was "the most shocking affront ever suffered by a King of England, and the rebels must be crushed."

Lord North pushed a bill through Parliament establishing a far more stringent blockade of American ports while simultaneously forbidding other nations to do business with the rebels. Army recruiting was increased, and top-ranking officers who opposed the dispatch of a strong punitive expedition to the New World were summarily retired.

A rumor reached Philadelphia that the Crown was not only planning to send a large English expedition to teach the Americans a lesson, but that a custom long established in European wars was also being followed and that German mercenary regiments of professional soldiers were being hired. Late in the year a brig arrived at Baltimore with positive confirmation of the story.

Hopes of reconciliation with the mother country were virtually abandoned, and members of the Congress who had planned to go home for Christmas responded to President Hancock's urgent request to wait until a question of the utmost importance had been settled.

Every delegate was present on the morning of December 14, and John came to the point quickly. "Gentlemen," he said, "we must act decisively before our territory is overrun with redcoats and Hessians. This may be our last chance to prevent a full-scale war. It is my personal belief—which I have discussed with many of you informally during the night and early hours of the morning—that we cannot compel His Majesty to listen to reason until we are the absolute masters of our own house.

"Gage still sits in Boston with his troops, and the Crown nourishes false hopes that Howe and Percy will bring the rest of Massachusetts to her knees. We no longer can afford the luxury of allowing General Washington to conduct a leisurely siege. The Continental Army grows stronger each month, and General Washington has assured me that he will soon have the men and munitions to drive Gage into the sea. I believe he must. The King will take a far different view of our situation when not one foot of our soil is held by his troops.

"Therefore I recommend that the Congress instruct the commander-in-chief to attack General Gage with all might, at his earliest convenience. Washington may choose to launch a surprise assault, and that decision must be his alone. But if he should believe that our interests wouldn't be compromised by a public declaration of his intentions, I hope the Congress will instruct him to issue a warning well in advance of the attack. Gage is a compassionate gentleman, and I feel certain he would permit the evacuation of civilians from the city so that noncombatants won't be killed and wounded in battle."

A delegate in the second row stood and raised a hand.

"The chair recognizes the gentleman from Pennsylvania."

Robert Morris, Philadelphia's most prosperous merchant, was one of the few men in the colonies whose fortune was almost as large as John's. "Mr. President," he said gravely, "I know very little about the detailed state of your finances. But your situation must be more or less similar to mine, here. If there should be a severe cannonading by one or both sides, and if street fighting should force either our own corps or the redcoats to build barricades of fire, you'll lose a major part of your personal property."

John was embarrassed by the introduction of his personal affairs into the discussion, and tried to silence the speaker.

But Morris continued to stand. "On the day you were elected to your present position, Mr. President, you stated in your acceptance address that you would welcome the burning of Boston if the public good required it. All of us remember your willingness to be beggared. We appreciated your sentiment as an expression of patriotism, sir, but this body cannot allow a colleague so devoted to our cause to lose all his worldly goods. The sacrifice is too much to ask of anyone."

The courtly Richard Henry Lee of Virginia jumped to his feet and spoke without waiting for recognition. "Mr. Morris is right. An attack on Boston would destroy one individual, no matter what the outcome of the battle. The Congress cannot be a party to such a flagrant miscarriage of justice."

The members applauded heartily.

John gaveled for silence. The concern for his welfare was flattering, but he was annoyed by the delegates' shortsighted inability or unwillingness to look beyond his own welfare. "If some of the houses and wharves I own should be ruined, would I suffer more than a young volunteer who loses his life in battle? Of course not. If my home should be looted and burned, would my sacrifice be greater than that of a patriotic infantryman who gives an arm or a leg for our cause? Hardly."

The applause began to swell again, and John became still angrier. "There are occasions when rhetoric and cheers are appropriate, gentlemen, but this isn't one of them."

Robert Livingston, a distinguished New York attorney and landowner, asked for the floor. "I submit to the Congress a resolution thanking the President for patriotism so selfless that he sets an example for all of us."

John felt that such a resolution would make him look foolish throughout the country. Citizens everywhere were being asked to give time and money for freedom's sake, thousands of young men were joining the Continental Army and people would resent what they would interpret as a wealthy man's attempt to win popularity. "You're out of order, Mr. Livingston," he said tartly. "The chair will accept no resolution except one empowering General Washington to drive the British from Boston before it becomes too late to negotiate an honorable peace."

Roger Sherman of Connecticut, a lawyer and treasurer of Yale College, came to his rescue. "I so move, Mr. President, and suggest that our instructions be worded with such care that General Washington will be left in no doubt regarding the wishes of the Congress."

In order to facilitate the discussion, the body formed into a committee of the whole, and the rest of the day was devoted to drafting the orders to the commander-in-chief. The document was ready at seven o'clock in the evening, and the Congress adjourned for the day.

A number of members came to John to congratulate him, but he withdrew quickly into a shell and cut short the conversation. In the past he had often used theatrical gestures to curry favor, and readily admitted to himself that he enjoyed praise. But the current situation was far too serious. Necessity forced him to take a tremendous gamble, and he refused to cheapen himself by using adulation to soften the impact of the blow. Even if he lost the better part of his fortune, he still had his health, his wits and enough strongboxes scattered throughout Massachusetts to make a fresh start and try to rebuild the Hancock empire if and when an accommodation was reached with the Crown.

A secretary brought him the letter to General Washington, and he sat down at a table behind the rostrum to read it, moving an oil lamp closer. When he could spare an hour, he thought, he would visit a physician and order himself a pair of eyeglasses.

He signed the document with his usual flourish, sanded it and then added a personal note on another sheet of paper: "This passed after a most serious debate in a committee of the whole House. As you see, the execution is referred to you. May God crown your attempt with success. I most heartily wish it, although I myself may suffer. I mention my own position in this matter only because I urge you to ignore it. I do this in my capacity as President of the Congress and as a private citizen. Liberty is sacred. The property of one man, or of many, is not. Do what you must to win a victory that will force the King to change the sour tune he sings, and let not one of our brave boys lose his life trying to protect my home or offices or warehouses. Liberty is our goal, and must be achieved, no matter what the cost. J.H."

He sealed both papers, using the official seal of the Congress on one and his own signet ring on the other. "Take these to General Washington in Massachusetts," he told the waiting courier, giving the man several gold coins from his own purse. "Change horses whenever your mounts tire, don't tarry on the road, and make certain that no man except the General himself receives these papers from you."

One of John's own servants handed him his bicorn and cloak, and told him his carriage was waiting. But he hadn't set foot outside the hall all day and, even though the night was bitterly cold and damp, he decided to walk the short distance to his lodgings. Chestnut Street was virtually deserted when he emerged into the open, and he stood for a few moments in front of the Statehouse, aware for the first time that his head was aching dully.

It was strange, he thought as he started off down Fifth Street, returning the salute of two constables in stocking caps and long capes, that he had taken pains to insure that every American knew of his lesser contributions to the cause of freedom. In fact, it was no exaggeration to admit that their admiration had always meant almost as much to him as the principles for which he had stood. Now, however, he wanted no discussion of a gesture that could deprive him of the better part of his fortune.

He found it difficult to understand his motives, but finally concluded that his reticence was caused by the realization that the dispute with England was entering a new phase. It was no longer possible to believe wholeheartedly that the King, his ministers, and the Tory majority in Parliament would agree to a reasonable settlement of the argument.

Sam Adams had been right from the start. A taste of freedom was not enough, and men who sipped it wouldn't be satisfied with less than the whole bottle. John sighed deeply as he skirted a patch of snow and knocked a chunk of ice from his path with his walking stick. If the capture of Boston from General Gage failed to convince the Crown that all Americans refused to be bullied, the colonies would be compelled to sever their ties with England and suffer the consequences of unrelenting, full-scale war.

Soon it would be too late to turn back, even though there were men in every colony who remained loyal to the Crown. There would be civil war as well as war against the mother country, and John's sense of bleak despair deepened. Colonies still trying to learn the art of working and living together would be pitted against the strongest power on earth, a nation that had humbled imperial Spain and brought France to her knees.

He tried to imagine the consequences, but the scope of the problem was too vast. All he knew for certain was that everyone in America would suffer. Countless thousands would lose their lives if fresh brigades of redcoats and regiments of hired Germans were sent to the New World. The colonies needed trade in order to survive, but the intensification of the Royal Navy blockade would choke off commerce, and even little children incapable of understanding the issues at stake would go hungry in scores of seaboard towns.

The possible loss of his own fortune seemed inconsequential under such circumstances, and he smiled grimly as he thought of a phrase that might prove useful in a speech: it was better to be a free pauper than a wealthy slave. Men whose pens were more subtle and subdued, like young Jefferson of Virginia, sometimes winced at his oratory, but the pomposity of the phrase made it no less true. He had committed himself to a cause, he believed in it without reservation and he would devote his talent, his energies, and his remaining fortune to its success.

A bright, warm fire burned in the parlor hearth a quarter of an hour later, Dorothy was wearing a low-cut gown of flimsy silk that helped to show off her beauty and John's spirits rose as he stood in front of the blazing logs, sipping a cup of flip. His mind continued to dwell on matters of state, however, and only when he heard a note of suppressed gaiety in his bride's voice did he study her, see a sheen in her eyes and realize belatedly that something out of the ordinary had excited her.

Dolly had planned to tell him her news at dinner, but couldn't wait. "We're going to give a ball before the Congress adjourns for Christmas! I think the Statehouse would be the best place for it."

John blinked, and refrained from saying he could think of no place less appropriate. "What's the occasion?"

"I had a letter from Mrs. Washington today. She's stopping here on her way to join the general in Massachusetts, so we'll hold it in her honor."

He continued to stare at her.

Dolly sensed his opposition. "Martha treated me royally when I visited Virginia."

"That's hardly sufficient cause for a ball at the Statehouse," John said dryly. He liked humoring her, but she was going too far.

Her joy was dampened and her eyes became cold, but her manner remained soft and feminine. "It's our duty, dear."

"How so?"

"Really, John. The President of the Congress and his wife are obligated to give a function for the lady of the Congress' military commander."

"What you're saying," he replied with the calm that had so often infuriated men trying to win an advantage over him at the conference table, "is that you're Mrs. Washington's friend, she was a person of consequence when you visited her in Virginia and you're anxious to show her that you've acquired a rather high place in the world since your marriage."

"I'm proud that you're the head of Congress, if that's what you mean." Her good humor was vanishing rapidly.

He shook his head. "That is not what I mean. You've missed balls and other such affairs since you came to Philadelphia with me. I've seen you yawning behind your fan when our guests have discussed state business. It was just last week that you and that

pretty Mrs. Jefferson were giggling for no reason at all after dinner while we were discussing the possible worth of a new appeal
to the Crown."

"Surely it's no crime to be bored by the lack of social life
here. Pennsylvanians are lacking in our graces, but if you and I
teach them there's more satisfaction to be proud at a reception
than at a solemn conference on their precious commerce, we'll
have done our share in civilizing them."

John didn't expect her to understand the complexity of the
colonies' problems, but her frivolity was outrageous. "A city can't
be properly judged by the charm of its hostesses," he said. "There
are so many parties in London every night of the week that no
one, not even a bachelor of means with an insatiable appetite
for the company of pretty ladies could attend more than a handful of them. But London is the most decadent town in the
world."

"I hope to form my own opinion of London when you take
me there, sir. For the moment I don't care if it is the equal of
Athens in its prime. We'll be disgraced if we don't present an
entertainment for Martha that Philadelphia will remember for
years."

"We'll suffer eternal disgrace if we do," he said, draining his
flip and resisting the temptation to drink more.

"I insist, Mr. Hancock!" Dolly stood with her feet apart, hands
on her hips.

He was too tired to handle her with discretion. "This is not a
subject open to argument," he said. "I've already given you my
final decision."

"I refuse to accept it!" Dolly retorted.

John was so tired he was afraid he might lose his temper, too.
Smoking gave him no pleasure, but he deliberately crossed the
room to a rack of pipes, filled one and then returned to the
hearth to light it with a spill. "I hold myself to blame for allowing
you to develop a false impression of our relationship," he said
at last. "I'll clarify it now, and that will be the end of the matter."

"I won't let you deprive me of the right to hold a ball in
Martha's honor." She dug her long fingernails into the palms of
her hands.

It occurred to John that she was anything but attractive when she lost her self-control. "General Washington," he said quietly, "will soon lead his men into battle. Hundreds from the Carolinas and New Hampshire and Connecticut will be killed or maimed. Will their grieving widows and mothers be pleased to hear that their commander's wife spent an evening gallivanting with the men who ordered that the battle be fought? I think not. And as I bear a greater responsibility than anyone else for the blood that will be shed, I carry a double burden of guilt. What's more," he added almost casually, "we couldn't afford the cost of such a ball, even if the occasion were more appropriate. We may have to curtail our expenses soon."

Dolly couldn't believe him. "If we're too poor to entertain a few guests, no one in America can afford to give a reception."

"Even the cheapest wine may soon be too dear for a Hancock. My property in Boston may soon be reduced to burning embers and rubble."

She had dreamed for years of becoming mistress of the great mansion on Beacon Hill, and looked at him in horror. "You're the President of the Congress!"

"Precisely. The protection of our liberties is more important than the preservation of my own property." He was too weary for a prolonged dispute, and sank into a chair near the fire.

"You're no longer a single man who can do what he pleases, when he pleases."

"And you accepted obligations to all our people when you married me." He gave in to his desire for more flip, and rang for a servant.

"You can't give me orders!"

The last threads of his patience snapped, and he jumped to his feet. "That's enough!"

Dolly retreated to the far side of the parlor, afraid he would strike her.

A servingmaid opened the door, saw the President of the Continental Congress shake a fist at his wife, and inadvertently slammed the door in her haste to depart.

John was unaware of the interruption. "Many years ago," he said harshly, "my Uncle Thomas once called me a jackass. I was very hurt at the time, but he was right. I've often been a jackass since that day. I was worse than that when I let myself imagine I had a legitimate grievance against Sam and Johnny Adams. You knew I was wrong, and that's why I gave in so quickly when you told me to behave myself. But I'm afraid that occasion may have given you a false impression of me. I have no intention of abdicating my role as master in my own house or letting you assume it for me."

She felt her shoulders touch the wall, and halted.

"You're in charge of our household, and I'll be happy never to plan another dinner as long as I live. The servants are responsible to you, and you may hire and discharge them at your pleasure —until we can no longer afford their services. But when I make a decision based on principles I believe right, my word is final. I'll do you the courtesy of explaining the reasons for my stand, as I just did regarding the ball you wanted to give. But I'll tolerate no insubordination. No one forced you to marry me, Dorothy. You became Mrs. John Hancock of your own free will, and now you'll act accordingly. I have too many worries on my mind to spend my evenings quarreling with a shrew."

She had never seen him show such firmness, and stood gaping at him, one hand at her bare throat.

"We'll give a small dinner for Mrs. Washington, provided it isn't elaborate. We'll invite the Virginia delegates and two or three others. I'll make out a list for you when I have the chance to think about the matter. Until then, the subject is closed. Do I make myself clear?"

She nodded, wishing he would stop crowding her into a corner.

John turned and walked to his seat near the fire. He still wanted his drink, and tugged hard at the bell rope.

The servingmaid, who had been listening outside the door, came into the room a little too quickly, but was relieved that both her master and mistress were too upset to notice her indiscretion.

John's anger began to dissipate when he sipped his fresh cup of flip and stretched his feet before the fire.

Dolly saw him relaxing, and came to him. "Did you really intend to slap me just now, dear?"

He felt embarrassed. "I thought of it," he admitted.

She bent down, curled her arms around his neck and kissed him fervently.

John looked up at her in astonishment when she finally released him and moved away again. He had found it distasteful to express himself so vehemently, and had assumed that a high-spirited young lady would hate the humiliation of bending to her husband's will, no matter what the reason.

Instead she was even happier than she had been when she had started to outline the plans that he had vetoed. It appeared that marriage compounded a man's inability to understand women.

"You'll want to invite the chairmen of the Congressional committees and their ladies to our little dinner for Martha," Dolly said, taking a chair opposite his.

"Yes, I suppose so. But it must be a simple dinner, mind you. An elaborate banquet would be in bad taste."

"Of course, dear." She was lost in thought for a moment. "Cousin Abigail will be here by then."

"You'll want her and Johnny here, naturally."

"Thank you, dear." She hesitated delicately. "Will the other members of the Massachusetts delegation feel slighted if they aren't asked?"

"They might, so invite them, by all means."

She was silent for a few moments. "We wouldn't dare leave out Dr. Franklin."

It went almost without saying that even a quiet, informal dinner would be incomplete without the colonies' most distinguished citizen, the one member of the Congress whom all other delegates respected. "I'd like to have Livingston of New York, too," he said.

"Mr. Morris' nose will be out of joint if you do."

"Oh, yes. I'd forgotten Morris for the moment." John decided that a small dinner party would provide the right atmosphere to talk with Morris about financing the building of American warships, a project that was proving difficult to launch.

"The Shermans were very kind to me in Connecticut during those lonely weeks before we were married, and so were the Wolcotts."

"Then we must have Roger and Oliver." He was feeling much better, and held his feet closer to the fire. "As there are only four delegates from Connecticut, we don't want to create hard feelings by excluding the other two."

"Whatever you say, dear." Dolly thought she had made enough progress for one evening, and decided to wait until breakfast before mentioning the Maryland and New Jersey delegations. "We do have one problem, I'm afraid. Our dining room here is so cramped."

"The taverns here aren't in a class with our Boston inns, but you might have a word with the proprietor of the Royal Sceptre tomorrow. Their banqueting room on the second floor would be more than adequate for our purposes, and we'd provide our own cook, of course." John yawned lazily as he looked into the fire. "Tell him we won't want his wines. I'll find an hour to buy four or five kinds between now and Mrs. Washington's arrival."

Dolly smiled. "Thank you, dear, but I can manage, if you'll tell me what to get."

"No, there's no need for you to bother. Wines are a man's responsibility, and we'll want something memorable for Mrs. Washington."

Dolly's expression did not change. It would be dangerous to urge her husband to give the ball, and she was forced to agree that a glittering affair would be in bad taste. But the banqueting room at the Royal Sceptre was large enough to accommodate all of the members of Congress and their ladies, and a small group of violinists would provide a festive air without offending anyone.

Far more important than the dinner, which would be the year's most exciting event, was the lesson she had learned this evening. Not only had she acquired respect for John, but she had made errors she would take care never to repeat.

SIX

1776

1

"His Excellency," Dolly said to the young officer-courier wearing the new blue and buff uniform of the Continental Army, "worked until two o'clock this morning and needs more than four hours of sleep."

"I was told to give my letter to no one except the President, Mrs. Hancock." The young man refused to be intimidated.

"Come back for breakfast, then, and His Excellency will see you at a more reasonable hour."

"His Excellency," John said sleepily from the doorway as he knotted the tie of his dressing gown, "refuses to keep a staff officer waiting. When a messenger arrives from Massachusetts at dawn, his news must be important."

The officer stood at attention and saluted. "I bring you a letter from General Washington, Mr. President."

John accepted the sealed document, taking care to observe the amenities. "My dear, see that this gentleman is given a broiled fish and a pint of ale. I'll join him for a more complete breakfast when I'm dressed."

The cook and other members of the household staff were not yet out of bed, so Dolly made the best of the situation. "Perhaps you'll come with me to the kitchen and help me light the fire," she told the officer.

The young man was embarrassed. "Please don't bother on my account."

John silenced him with an imperious wave. "Bother? Rubbish! You look as though you've been riding all night, boy, and you must be starved. Please attend to him, my dear."

Dolly hated being treated like a servant, but headed toward the dining-room doors that led to the kitchen outbuilding. She saw no reason why the courier couldn't wait an hour or two, but she knew that her husband, irritable after only a few hours of sleep, would make an unpleasant scene if she protested.

When John was alone he rubbed the stubble on his chin, turned the letter over and over and realized he was afraid to open it. So much of the news in the first eleven weeks of 1776 had been bad, worse than anyone had anticipated. The expedition to Canada had failed, in spite of the courage and devotion of General Arnold, who had been forced to evacuate Montreal after vicious winter weather had prevented him from taking Quebec. British shipowners were observing the embargo on shipping to the colonies so meticulously that the Continental Congress had just issued a desperate appeal to France for commercial help.

And Washington, still striving to build a competent striking force in Massachusetts, had not yet become strong enough to launch his expected attack on Boston. In the meantime the War Office had recalled Gage and replaced him with General William Howe, a far more energetic officer, so it was possible that the Continentals had been smashed. If so, the colonies' cause was hopeless.

John took a breath, broke the wax seal and opened the letter. He stared in disbelief at the words written in General Washington's neat hand: "It is with the greatest pleasure I inform you that, on Sunday last, the 17th of March, at about nine o'clock in the forenoon, the Ministerial army evacuated the town of Boston, leaving by sea. The forces of the United Colonies are now in actual possession of the town."

The news was almost too good to be true, and John discovered to his astonishment that there were tears in his eyes. Obviously Washington's siege had been more successful than anyone had dared to hope. The Congress would rejoice, but John knew, even in this moment of elation, that his first duty required him to send a word of warning to General William Alexander, who commanded a small force of Continentals, bolstered by militia units from New York, Connecticut, and New Jersey. Espionage agents in Boston had been sending out word for weeks that the redcoats were anxious to take New York Town, so Alexander would have to be doubly alert now.

There was a smaller sheet of paper inside the parchment, and John opened it, blinking away his tears. "The town of Boston," General Washington wrote in this personal communication, "although it has suffered greatly, is not in nearly so bad a state as I expected to find it. The citizens are in need of foodstuffs, which are being sent in to them from the country parts in generous quantities. Howe exercised better control over his troops than I anticipated, and the destruction of physical property has been negligible.

"I have a particular pleasure in being able to inform you, Sir, that your house has received no damage worth mentioning. Your furniture is in tolerable order, and the family pictures are all left entire and untouched."

The news was miraculous. John had never been particularly devout, paying only absent-minded lip service to religion, but now a line from the Book of Matthew struck him with great force. "For what is a man profited, if he shall gain the whole world, and lose his own soul?"

His willingness to sacrifice his earthly possessions for a cause more important by far than his own personal security and comfort had been rewarded by the return of his fortune. The colonies could benefit by his experience, and it was his supreme obligation to teach others what he himself had just learned. A willingness on the part of men in all thirteen colonies to take any steps necessary for the preservation of their liberties would result in the achievement of freedom, no matter how great the struggle.

2

Dr. Franklin made his guests comfortable, and John, as usual, accepted a cup of flip. General Washington, who had arrived in Philadelphia the previous evening for consultations with the Congressional leaders, wanted only a glass of mild wine, to which he added liberal quantities of water. Sipping it, he looked around the pleasantly furnished parlor of the Franklin house, and glanced briefly at the half-dozen men who had come for a private talk with him.

Everyone present realized that the future of the colonies would probably be decided by their discussions, and the mood was solemn, almost funereal.

John used his pipe as a gavel, and tapped it gently on the top of a table inlaid with rare wood that George II had given to Dr. Franklin in happier days. "We're anxious to learn your assessment of the military situation, General."

The commander-in-chief rubbed his long jaw. "Howe will try to take New York this summer," he said in his cool, unemotional voice. "There's no longer any doubt in my mind that he intends to launch a major campaign. If he succeeds, he can cut the colonies in two. I believe we can also expect an attack in the south, probably at Charleston, and the British would be very foolish if they didn't put pressure on us from the north, too."

John Adams absently opened and closed a small mother-of-pearl snuffbox he had picked up from the table beside him. "Will they use Regulars in all their campaigns?"

"They'll use all the forces they can muster," the general replied. "I have positive knowledge that they're recruiting battalions of volunteers in Canada, and if they obtain a foothold on our territory, you can be certain they'll also try to raise Loyalist battalions here." He hesitated briefly before continuing. "Much as I hate to make an accusation of crime before a deed is committed, I also have irrefutable evidence that the Iroquois nation, the Ottawa and other savage tribes are being given arms and money. I'm afraid our wilderness settlements will be in for trouble."

Robert Livingston tugged at his gold watch fob. "We can't defend ourselves everywhere."

"We must try," the General said.

The members of Congress looked at each other gloomily, and John asked the question everyone was thinking. "Do you have enough troops to prevent the capture of New York Town, General?"

"No, Mr. President. Our call for volunteers has brought an enthusiastic response, but it takes time to teach recruits discipline. I'll need more militia—all I can get—from every colony."

Franklin adjusted his spectacles. "Our citizens face an almost impossible choice. If our men leave their homes, their families will starve. But if they don't join the colors, we'll be overwhelmed and enslaved. It seems to me that we must make military service attractive enough to leave the families of volunteers financially secure."

"An admirable goal, but we can't achieve it." Robert Morris hunched forward on the window seat beneath leaded panes. "The Congress hasn't been authorized to levy or collect taxes, and the support of the Continentals is proving to be a great burden. Each of the colonies must support its own militia."

Several men started to speak simultaneously, and again John tapped for order. "We go too far, gentlemen, and too quickly. General, is it your opinion that the Crown intends to wage a full-scale military operation to force our surrender?"

"I'm convinced of it."

"My own analysis of the political situation in England forces me to the same conclusion." John turned to Franklin. "You know London better than any of us, Ben. What do you think?"

"The King and Lord North can't turn to conciliation now without seeming weak in the eyes of the Tory majority in the Commons. Our friends in both Houses of Parliament still beg for reason and decency, but their voices can't be heard in the wilderness. We shall have war, and must either win or perish."

"Does anyone dispute that view?" John asked.

There was a long silence.

"It seems to me," John said, "that we must alert the people of every colony to our danger. For too long now we've been hoping the Crown and Parliament would adopt an attitude that would prevent war. Certainly I clung to this delusion, so I may be guilty for fostering a sense of too much complacency in our citizens. General, how soon will Howe launch his attack on New York?"

"It's now May," Washington said carefully. "I expect to meet him in July or August."

"Then we have three to four months." John took a tattered pamphlet from his inside coat pocket, and put on his new spectacles to look at the smudged print. "We must mobilize Americans quickly, and I have here a remarkable little book that Mr. Jefferson has called to my attention. It's called *Common Sense* and was written by a man named Paine who recently migrated here from England." He handed it to Washington. "I call your attention to the marked passages."

The general studied the little pamphlet, reading aloud. "Reconciliation is a fallacious dream . . . Everything that is right or natural pleads for separation. The blood of the slain, the weeping voice of nature cries, ' 'Tis time to part.' Even the distance at which the Almighty hath placed England and America is a strong and natural proof that the authority of the one over the other was never the design of Heaven . . . Freedom hath been hunted round the globe. Asia and Africa have long expelled her. Europe regards her like a stranger, and England hath given her warning to depart. O! receive the fugitive and prepare in time an asylum for mankind."

"He uses strong language," John Adams said, "but I'm compelled to agree with him."

"I propose," John declared, taking the pamphlet from the general, "that we publish copies by the thousand, by the tens of thousand. I propose that we send them to every town, village, and farm in the United Colonies. Paine's words are certain to swell the ranks of the militia, if anything will."

Morris scowled. "The Congress will spend weeks debating the expense of this project, Mr. President."

"The same thought occurred to me," John replied, "so I shall pay the costs of publication myself."

Franklin, who was already familiar with the pamphlet, smiled cheerfully. "You won't be too much out of pocket, lad. I'll print the copies—at cost."

Everyone laughed, but sobered again when General Washington stood. "I hope no one is too optimistic, gentlemen. The whole prestige of Britain is at stake in this conflict, and David will be pitted against Goliath."

"We must be both prudent and daring," John replied, "but let no one forget that David won his fight with Goliath."

3

To the honorable members of the duly elected assemblies representing the people of these, our thirteen United Colonies, Greetings.

I feel it incumbent upon me to take you into my confidence and that of your Congress following our meetings with His Excellency, General Washington and your receipt of copies of *Common Sense*, by Mr. Thomas Paine.

I need not dwell overlong on the immediate need to disseminate Mr. Paine's little book, and I urge that it be read to those who cannot themselves read. Nor can I urge too strongly that all possible steps be taken at once to improve your defenses, increase your regiments of militia and place them at the disposal of the commander-in-chief. See to it, too, that your financial house is in order. I make these claims on you not as one who stands above you, but as one who stands at your side, working together with you for our mutual good and salvation.

Our affairs are hastening fast to a crisis, and the approaching campaign will, in all probability, determine forever the fate of America. Such is the unrelenting spirit which possesses the Tyrant of Britain and his Parliament that they have left no measure unessayed that had a tendency to accomplish our destruction.

Be not pleasurably deceived by Howe's evacuation of Boston. The real battles are yet to be waged, and not one colony will be spared Death, Devastation and Privation. I speak to you frankly, as comrades in arms, so that you may more fully appreciate the odds against which we fight to raise Freedom's banner. Headwinds are strong, the sea turbulent and the planks of our ship of state are unseasoned, so that we must pray our vessel does not spring leaks.

Should the Canadians and Indians take up arms against us, which there is much reason to fear, we shall then have the whole force of that country to contend with. No fewer than eight regiments of hired troops from the German Principalities have already been employed by the Tyrant, who will, it is to be feared, hire still more of these merciless men without souls who struck terror in the hearts of French brigades. Moreover, the ranks of the British Devils in Red are being augmented each week by new arrivals at Halifax of battalions that dare not mutiny against the brutal Caesar of Whitehall.

Our foes are formidable. What, then, of our defenses? Our

Continentals are brave lads and true, but they alone are unable to stem the torrent. Nor is it possible at this day to raise and discipline new battalions of Continentals ready to take the field by the time they are needed.

The militia of thirteen colonies will decide our fate. You will decide it, for these companies will be raised and trained by you, paid and supplied with victuals by you. The Congress is building three new forges and two powder mills, but you must find the arms for your militia until the day comes when the Congress will furnish your needs.

Should the United Colonies be able to keep their ground this campaign, I am under no apprehensions on account of any future one. We have many disadvantages at present to struggle with, which time and progress in the art of war will remove. But this circumstance should rouse us to superior exertions. The militia will fight as men inspired.

I am confident that the militia of the United Colonies may be depended upon. They are called upon to say whether they will live slaves or die free men. The cause, as you know, as I know and as they know, is a glorious one.

In short, on your exertions, together with those of the other colonies, the salvation of America now depends.

Quicken your preparations and stimulate the good people who rely on your wisdom and strength—and there is no danger, notwithstanding the mighty armament with which we are threatened. Stand firm, strong and ready, and you will lead them to victory, to liberty and to happiness.

I am, Sirs,

Your obdt. svt.,

John Hancock,

President, the Second Continental Congress and Delegate thereto from the Province of Massachusetts Bay.

4

On June 7, 1776, Richard Henry Lee presented to the Congress a resolution, promptly seconded by John Adams, demanding a dissolution of all bonds that tied the United Colonies to Great Britain. The subject was discussed almost endlessly in three days of heated debate, and even the most conservative of the delegates, who were reluctant to commit an overt act of treason against the Crown, knew the die was cast.

Finally, on Monday afternoon, the tenth, President Hancock decided there had been enough talk. It was urgently necessary that each of the colonies convert itself into a free and independent state, and that each of the thirteen legislatures grant their Congressional delegates the power to form a national confederation. He held a private conference with Dr. Franklin, whom he appointed as temporary head of a special committee empowered to prepare a Declaration of Independence. Others named were John Adams, Roger Sherman, Robert Livingston, and Thomas Jefferson, who was made permanent chairman of the group.

The Congress then adjourned for three weeks to enable the representatives to return to their homes and speed the transformation of colonies into states.

John felt it necessary for him to remain in Philadelphia, however, as did Secretary Charles Thomson of the Congress. Correspondence with legislators and other leaders was heavy, scores of decisions had to be made daily and aside from a few hired clerks, they were the only officials authorized to transact business on behalf of the nation-in-embryo that planned to call itself the United States of America.

There was no precedent to help John solve the problems that mounted on the desk at his headquarters in a small office building opposite the Statehouse, which was now being called Independence Hall. A government could not operate without money, and as gold and silver were in short supply, he authorized the printing of paper dollars pending Congress' approval. The drawing was ugly, and the engraving so primitive that it encouraged counterfeiting, but John had no choice. He dispatched a hasty letter to Paul Revere, asking for a more professional engraving, and in the meantime Franklin's presses printed tons of the new money.

The thirteen legislatures were so jealous of their prerogatives that they were reluctant to grant rights to the Congress, which could not function efficiently without authority of its own, and John dictated hundreds of letters to political leaders in each of the new states, sometimes pleading, sometimes storming. "We must stand united in fact as well as in name, or we shall surely perish," he said repeatedly.

The threat was not an idle one. Plans for the British attack on New York were progressing, and Washington had learned that Howe, supported by the Royal Navy, was also hoping to take Philadelphia. Funds to buy uniforms and arms, provisions and blankets and other essentials for the Continental Army were lacking, and John spent what time he could spare helping Robert Morris wheedle donations from the wealthy merchants and landowners with whom both had done business in previous years.

Each day there were new crises to overcome, fresh dilemmas to resolve, and John abandoned all attempts to live even a semblance of a normal life. He saw Dolly only at breakfast, ate his noon and evening dinners at his desk and rarely stumbled into bed at their lodgings until the early hours of the morning.

Dolly understood that an emergency unique in the experience of Americans required her husband's full attention, and she made no complaints, greeted him each morning with a loving smile and managed to keep herself occupied during her long and lonely days.

John was surprised one day in mid-June when his personal groom appeared at his office with a hastily scribbled note from Dolly, asking him to come to her as quickly as possible. "Is Mrs. Hancock ill?" he asked, his work forgotten.

"She didn't say, sir."

Rather than waste precious time trying to break through the man's phlegm, John hurried out to the coach and was driven to their nearby lodgings.

Dolly's eyes were red-rimmed, but she managed to speak calmly as she handed him a letter. "It's Aunt Lydia," she said.

He braced himself, and scanned the communication from

Thaddeus Burr. Thomas Hancock's widow had suffered an apoplectic stroke almost identical to her late husband's, and had died a few hours after losing consciousness. Two Fairfield physicians had attended her, but neither had been able to help.

John walked to the window and stared with unseeing eyes at the heavy, full branches of the elms in the yard. The excitement he had felt over the formation of a new nation had vanished, and a bleak, incredibly lonely sense of despair engulfed him.

Dolly joined him and put a hand on his arm.

His duty prevented him from leaving Philadelphia, no matter how great his desire to stand at his aunt's graveside when she was buried. "You'll have to represent both of us," he said thickly. "I'll arrange an escort at once so you can start out for Connecticut this afternoon."

She shook her head. "I can't go."

His sorrow turned to rage. "You must!" Only a few weeks earlier she had babbled incessantly about making a journey to Boston in order to put the Hancock mansion in order, and the thought that she was reluctant to pay her last respects to his beloved aunt infuriated him. "You'll leave this afternoon, Dorothy."

To his amazement she sank into a chair and burst into tears.

John handed her a large, lace-edged handkerchief and waited impatiently for her hysteria to subside.

"This is the worst of all times to tell you the news. I—I was waiting until Sunday, when we might have an hour or two together."

He was afraid he would beat her if she pleaded the excuse of a frivolous social engagement.

"I saw Dr. Rush yesterday, and he confirmed what I've suspected for two or three weeks. I—we—are going to have a child."

The shock swept away the last of his own self-control, and he wept, too.

"I'm not allowed to travel until the baby has come."

Unable to speak, he nodded, then went to her and took her in his arms. The knowledge that he would be a father, that Dorothy was giving him an heir was overwhelming. But the realization that Aunt Lydia would never see the baby was a sorrow too great to bear.

"I wrote her last week, so she knew." Dolly understood his need, and comforted him with a quick lie.

"The Lord gives," he said soberly, "and the Lord takes away. Blessed be the name of the Lord."

5

On Monday, July 1, the Congress reconvened, and the delegations representing nine of the new states voted in favor of Richard Henry Lee's resolution cutting America's ties to England. On the following day the other delegations added their vote, and the decision was unanimous.

The Declaration written, in the main, by Jefferson, was formally inscribed on parchment on July 3, while the Congress attended to business that had accumulated during its absence. The following day the Congress assembled promptly at nine o'clock in the morning, and spent several hours attending to routine business. Visitors holding special cards signed by Secretary Thomson were admitted to Independence Hall shortly before noon, and a large crowd that had gathered in Chestnut Street applauded when Dorothy Hancock stepped down from her carriage. She smiled shyly, unaccustomed to such demonstrations in her honor, and hurried inside to the section reserved for the wives of delegates and other guests.

A churchbell in the neighborhood chimed at noon, and John announced that he would accept a motion tabling the subject under discussion. Then, as a hush settled over the assemblage, he declared, "The chair recognizes the gentleman from Virginia, chairman of a committee that has drafted a document expressing the sentiments of this Congress, for the purpose of reading that document."

Everyone looked at Jefferson, who flushed as he rose. His lean frame straightened, however, and his voice was resonant and clear as he began to read, "A Declaration by the Representatives of the United States of America, in General Congress assembled.

"When in the course of human events, it becomes necessary for one People to dissolve the Political Bands which have connected them with another, and to assume among the Powers of the Earth, the separate and equal Station to which the laws of Nature and of Nature's God entitle them, a decent Respect to the Opinions of Mankind requires that they should declare the Causes which impel them to the Separation.

"We hold these Truths to be self-evident, that all Men are created equal, that they are endowed by their Creator with certain unalienable Rights, that among them are Life, Liberty and the Pursuit of Happiness. That to secure these Rights, Governments are instituted among Men, deriving their just Powers from the Consent of the Governed, that whenever any form of Government becomes destructive of these Ends, it is the Right of the People to alter or abolish it, and to institute new Government, laying its foundation on such Principles, and organizing its Powers in such form, as to them shall seem most likely to effect their Safety and Happiness. Prudence, indeed, will dictate that Governments long established should not be changed for light and transient Causes; and accordingly all Experience hath shown, that Mankind are more disposed to suffer, while Evils are sufferable, than to right themselves by abolishing the Forms to which they are accustomed. But when a long Train of Abuses and Usurpations, pursuing the same Object, evinces a Design to reduce them under absolute Despotism, it is their Right, it is their Duty, to throw off such Government, and to provide new Guards for their future Security. Such has been the patient Sufferance of these Colonies, and such is now the Necessity which constrains them to alter their former Systems of Government. The History of the present King of Great Britain is a History of repeated Injuries and Usurpations, all having in direct Object the Establishment of an absolute Tyranny over these States."

No one in Independence Hall moved or spoke as he went on from the preamble to read the grievances of the former colonies. The Crown, and the Crown alone, was held chiefly responsible for the violation of a contract or compact with the people of America. But the Declaration also charged that, in some instances, the King had conspired with others. It was obvious to everyone present that Jefferson referred to Lord North, other British ministers of state, and the Parliament.

The conclusion was succinct, and Jefferson's voice echoed against the walls of the chamber as he declared that "these united colonies are, and of right ought to be, free and independent states."

There was a deathly hush as he came forward to the rostrum and placed the Declaration of Independence before the President.

John took a quill pen from a clerk and dipped it into a jar of ink. "As President of this Congress, which represents all the people of the United States, I obey the instructions of the Congress and with my signature make our intentions known to the world as a valid, legal, and binding document."

He signed his name in his usual slashing hand, but made the characters even larger. The members of the committee that had drawn up the document stood to his right, and several of them smiled. The King, he remarked to them quietly, would be able to read his name without wearing spectacles. Then he caught Dr. Franklin's eye and his own grin broadened. It was unlikely that George III would ever again think of him as "Hopkins."

Secretary Thomson stepped forward and signed his name to the Declaration as a witness.

The document was now official, and someone standing at a window waved his hand as a signal. A new nation was born, and a great bell pealed, its clapper striking the side with such force that some thought the bell would surely crack.

The crowd gathered outside Independence Hall went wild. Men shouted, a fife and drum corps began to play and in spite of the acute shortage of gunpowder, muskets and pistols were fired into the air.

The members of the Congress did not rejoice, however, and the atmosphere inside the hall remained solemn. No other signatures were needed, but the delegates wanted to put their own sentiments on record. They knew that, by signing their names, they would be excluded from an amnesty in the event that Britain crushed the rebellion. If captured, they faced certain execution as traitors.

Nevertheless they came forward, one by one, and wrote their names below John's.

At last the ceremony was ended. John shook hands with Jefferson and the other members of the committee, and then accepted a motion that the Congress adjourn until the following day.

The President's work was not done, however. While a copy was read to the cheering crowd outside and thirteen cannon boomed, recklessly using still more powder, John went to his desk. He wrote a personal letter to the legislatures of each new state, enclosing copies of the Declaration, and sent still another to General Washington, requesting that the commander-in-chief proclaim the news to the armed forces of the new nation in any way he deemed appropriate.

The arrival of a courier further delayed the President, who had hoped to join some of his colleagues at a quiet celebratory dinner. There was good news from New Jersey: a British ship-of-the-line had run aground on a sand bar, and when her commander tried to prevent the approach of armed patriots by firing a broadside, several of his guns had exploded, killing a number of sailors and making his ship a useless hulk. The crew had been evacuated by longboat to other warships hovering offshore, and Americans had swarmed onto the disabled craft, which they had stripped. The cannon, iron balls, and powder they had captured would enable the New Jersey militia to form its first artillery units.

But the news from New York Town was somber. General Howe had captured Staten Island, only a short distance from Manhattan, and now had a base of operations for his first major campaign of the war.

The same letter, written by one of Washington's aides, warned that a powerful Royal Navy fleet was moving south from New York along the Jersey coast. Philadelphia was threatened, and so was Baltimore.

John quickly wrote letters to the Pennsylvania and Maryland Committees of Safety, telling them to be on the alert for an attack launched by men-of-war capable of hurling heated, twenty-four-pound cannonballs capable of wreaking havoc.

The infant nation had come into being, and her trials were about to begin.

6

The burdens of high office were heavy, the vexations infuriating, and the Congress soon discovered that the ratification of the Declaration of Independence by the thirteen states was no guarantee that the government of any one state was interested in the prosecution of the war beyond its own borders.

The wives of Congressmen became alarmed when their haggard husbands lost weight steadily, ate quick meals at irregular hours and subsisted on so little sleep that Dr. Benjamin Rush, Philadelphia's most eminent physician and himself a member of the Congress, told his colleagues in an address that they were killing themselves.

Abigail Adams was the first to deal with the situation, and enlisting the aid of five other women, gave a small dinner at the lodgings she and her husband had rented. The men were forced by the laws of etiquette to spend a reasonable time at the table as they ate fish, mutton, and cherry tarts. The ladies interrupted whenever affairs of state were mentioned, and for two hours light conversation predominated, the first time in months that the men had concentrated on anything but their official burdens.

Then the ladies left the table. John Adams, still observing the British custom of passing a decanter of port to the left, turned at once to the President and Gerry. "Massachusetts," he said, "is behaving in a shocking manner."

John nodded. "Ah, you've seen Washington's letter, then. He needs at least three more battalions from Boston, but the legislature has replied that the volunteers from the state who have joined him are all they can spare."

"I've been in correspondence with a half-dozen friends at home," Gerry declared, "and I can understand their feelings. They believe we need to hold back some of our own troops for duty in the Maine District, near the Canadian border."

"According to my information," John said as he splashed a little port into his glass, "they're sending very few companies to Maine."

Adams leaned his weight on his elbows. "I want to be fair about this. Our people are no less patriotic than those of any other state. But Boston is the only city that has been subjected to enemy occupation, and our legislators want to keep troops close to home for self-protection."

John gestured impatiently, sipped his wine and found it difficult not to make a wry face. Johnny Adams was probably the best lawyer in the country, but his taste in wines was atrocious. "I think your reasoning is false. Just last week I signed a commission appointing a naval officer, John Paul Jones, as commander of a new frigate, the *Providence*. The Rhode Island legislature refused to recognize my authority and gave him a commission of their own. I don't care who grants him the right to sail. He's a competent sailor, he's eager to fight the British and the important thing is that he puts to sea with an experienced crew and enough cannon to hurt Lord Howe's fleet."

Jefferson, who had been immersed in another conversation at the far end of the table, shook his head. "I must disagree with you, Mr. Hancock. Basic rights are vested in the states, and the Congress assumes only those which don't conflict with a state's prerogatives. We've had enough experience with a tyrant, and we don't want one here."

John had refused to take part in the discussions on the theories and philosophies of government which fascinated so many of his colleagues, but he refused to side-step a direct challenge. "We face a realistic situation, Mr. Jefferson. I've had three appeals for troops from General Washington in the past two weeks. He's in desperate need of men, and so many troops are being enlisted in state militias for short periods, usually no more than ninety days, that his recruiting sergeants can't build the ranks of the Continentals."

"Does it matter if he uses Continentals or militia?"

"Not in the least—provided he gets the militia. That's my whole point. You know that Virginia hasn't sent him nearly enough militia companies. Meanwhile General Howe lands more transports from Halifax every day." John saw the problem only in pragmatic terms. "If we have too small an army to face Howe's regulars and German mercenaries, we'll lose New York Town, and a combined land and sea attack can topple Philadelphia."

Adams smiled quietly. "Aren't you being pessimistic? Only a short time ago you wrote the legislatures assuring them of victory in New York."

"We'll win there," John replied doggedly, "if Washington has enough troops. My letter predicting victory was based on the assumption that the states would be wise enough to look beyond their own back fences. As Dr. Franklin said just the other day, we'll all hang together if we don't work together."

"Self-government is new to us," Jefferson said. "We must learn how to govern through experience. As the thirteen legislatures see the need to cooperate, they will. They're all men of good will working toward the same goal."

"While we're being educated," John replied bitterly, "England may win the war."

"Are you advocating a stronger central government? Would you give Congress the power to absorb militia into the Continental Army?"

"If necessary, I would!"

"Not one of our states will give up its own rights for such a purpose."

"If you were in my boots, Mr. Jefferson, how would you persuade the states that a failure to support Washington in New York may mean a permanent loss of our liberties? How would you persuade them to contribute funds to the building of our Navy? How would you establish a sound currency acceptable in every state? How would you convince them they must compromise their individual differences for the good of the whole country?"

"You're a student of Locke, as I am, so you certainly know the only weapon you can use is reason."

"I've written so many letters in my own hand that there are lumps on my fingers and aches in my joints!" John was becoming so angry that Gerry touched his arm.

"Increased danger," Jefferson replied thoughtfully, "will unite us more closely. Differences of opinion will disappear as the state leaders come to realize that we'll survive as a nation only if temporary powers are given to the Congress."

"But Washington has no left flank and a weak right flank." John was exasperated.

"I have every confidence in the General," Jefferson said, "and I pray he'll win."

"He needs men more than prayers." John no longer cared how rude he sounded. "I'd go to Boston myself to address the legislature, but I can't spare even a half-day from my work here. The only other man influential enough to sway the Massachusetts assembly," he added bitterly, "is Sam. And he agrees that the Massachusetts militia should stay at home."

"It seems to me," John Adams said, "that we're victims of our own enthusiasms and fears. We've promised the states final victory if they'll contribute militia companies to Washington in New

York, and we persuade ourselves that our cause is lost if Howe wins there. Let's examine the true state of affairs more closely. Howe has already landed too many men to drive him from the country, even if Washington beats him. Lord Burgoyne is building another powerful army in Canada, and more warships join Admiral Lord Howe's fleet every month. The British intend to fight a long campaign. They have the men and resources to wage war against us for a year, two years—even three.

"Now examine our side of the coin. Boston was occupied—but is free again. New York, Baltimore, Philadelphia—all may fall—temporarily. And I stress the time element. I don't believe that Lord North can muster enough British troops, or that King George can buy enough Germans—to inflict a permanent defeat on a nation of one and one-half million people who live in a territory of millions of square miles."

John became calmer, and once again realized that his old friend's analytical powers were superior to his own. He knew, too, that Jefferson was a young idealist almost without experience in the hard worlds of commerce and business. He accomplished nothing by arguing with someone so determined to defend principle that he lost sight of the practical means of conducting that defense.

He himself was guilty of exaggeration. In his eagerness to provide Washington with an overwhelmingly powerful field force, he had come to believe the case he had presented to the states in stark black and white terms. It was his primary duty as President to use persuasion rather than force, to reconcile conflicting viewpoints rather than take sides himself. "It strikes me," he said with a faint smile, "that I have as much to learn as the state legislatures. Sooner or later Washington will get his militia companies and the Congress will be granted the authority we need. My trouble is that I was responsible to no one but myself for so many years that I try to run the country like a shipping house. Mr. Jefferson here has spent all of his young life in Virginia and has seen too little of the world. And Johnny always understands all sides of every question, which can be a handicap in a street brawl.

"You're right when you say the state governments have a great deal to learn. So have we, and if we realize what's good for us, we won't forget it. I know only one thing for certain. As Ovid wrote hundreds of years ago, the acts of men are surveyed in Heaven with eyes of justice. Our cause is noble, and eventually we'll triumph. Gentlemen, I propose a toast all of us can drink with good hearts and clear consciences."

He stood, and the others rose with him. "May the Almighty watch over the United States of America, shield her from harm and lead her to liberty, no matter how thorny the path."

7

Later in August General Washington's raw battalions of citizen-soldiers finally met Howe's disciplined redcoats and veteran Germans on Long Island. Some units, like Dan Glover's Massachusetts fishermen and several squadrons of Virginia cavalry, fought courageously and more than held their own. Others were less fortunate, became panic-stricken and fled from the field in such wild disorder that the British horsemen who pursued them contemptuously ordered their buglers to play hunting calls.

Washington proved more adept than his conqueror, however, and miraculously extricated the bulk of his force, retreating to New York Town. Two weeks later Howe, who had been knighted by the King for his victory, followed the Americans. The sounds and terrors of battle were no longer a novelty to the Yankees, and although badly outnumbered, the whole Army fought with valor before being forced to evacuate the city. Once again Washington proved himself a superb tactician, and managed to escape from another trap into New Jersey. He had lost the third largest city in the United States, but wrote to President Hancock, "The Continentals are not dismayed, sir, but have found their collective soul."

The Congress was in a glum mood when it met to hear the official news of the losses, and John spared the feelings of no state delegation. "The commander-in-chief has informed me," he said, "that militia companies from every one of the New England states, from New York, New Jersey and Pennsylvania, from Delaware, Maryland and Virginia have left him without permission and gone home. He informed me that he had too few units from the Carolinas to desert, and none from Georgia. The members of the Congress may want to comment on the present situation, but the chair prefers not to waste the time or insult the intelligence of the Congress by subjecting the membership to speeches of justification, excuse or rationalization." He looked around the hall, then said quietly, "The chair recognizes the gentleman from Virginia."

Thomas Jefferson slowly pulled himself to his feet. "For the past hour and more," he said, "we have heard members commiserate with New York on her loss. Mere words will not recoup that loss, nor relieve the citizens of New York Town who live now under the heel of the tyrant, nor prevent future catastrophe elsewhere. Mr. President, the Virginia delegation has the honor to inform you that we have written a joint letter to our state assembly, urging that an immediate contribution be made to the Congress for the purpose of creating a new fund to be used for the recruitment and enlistment of Continental Army troops."

John Adams leaped up. "Will the member yield for the submission of a resolution?"

Jefferson nodded, remaining standing.

"I move," Adams said, "that all delegations follow the example of Virginia in this matter and send similar requests to their state legislatures."

The motion passed by an overwhelming vote, with only Sam Adams and a few others who were very jealous of the rights of individual states voting against the resolution.

Jefferson resumed his address. "This vote," he said, "expresses better than I can do here to stress the sentiments of the Congress. But it is not enough for us to beg money. Am I correct, Mr. President, in believing that recruiting sergeants sent by General Washington have been forbidden to enter towns in several states?"

"The gentleman's information is right," John replied, "and those misguided communities have disgraced their country."

Jefferson looked around the hall. "I place the following resolution before the Congress. Be it resolved that any person or persons residing in any state in the confederation of the United States of America who interferes with the recruitment of personnel, the purchase of provisions and supplies or with any other activity intended to promote the strength and welfare of the Continental Army of the United States places himself in jeopardy of contempt of the Continental Congress, and is liable to prosecution by the

Congress, which may levy a fine not to exceed the sum of five hundred dollars for each offense which the Congress judges to have been perpetrated."

The resolution was debated and refined, but its basic principle was unaltered, and it passed by a voice vote. John was pleased and thought it significant that Jefferson, the ardent advocate of allowing the states rather than the confederation to hold the reins of government, had proposed the first law that gave the Congress punitive powers. If the whole nation awakened to the need for concerted action, the temporary loss of New York Town might prove a partial blessing in disguise.

8

"Your stables have been repaired," Thomas Cushing said as he stood close to the hearth in the parlor of the Hancocks' rented quarters in Philadelphia, "and a new kitchen has been built."

"I can't understand why the kitchen should have been destroyed and the house itself left untouched." John poured his guest a glass of sack and took a platter of dried herring strips from Dolly. "It makes no sense."

"Vandalism never makes sense," Cushing replied.

"Well, you shall have a new kitchen when we go home, my dear." John smiled at his wife.

Dolly sighed and adjusted the folds of her loose-fitting maternity gown. "It's strange, you know. I've been married for almost fifteen months and I have yet to live as the mistress of my own house."

A warning look from his host told Cushing to change the subject; women in the last stages of pregnancy often became morose if allowed to feel sorry for themselves. "Your wines are intact, John. I checked your cellars myself against the inventory you sent me, and I'll be damned—begging your pardon, ma'am—if there are only two pipes of Madeira and one small keg of ale missing."

"If anyone but you brought me that news, Tom, I'd call him a liar."

"I don't blame you, but you must remember that Howe and his

deputy, Sir Henry Clinton, were living in the house—and they're gentlemen."

John laughed. "I'm not sure I'm capable of defining a gentleman these days. Sir William might sit down to dinner with me, and if he were the host I dare say it would be a good one, but it would also be my last before he had me hanged in the morning."

Dolly sighed again, more deeply.

It was impolite to discuss details of the war in the presence of ladies, but Cushing thought it better not to dwell any longer on personal subjects. "I was astonished to find how little of New Jersey the Lobsters are holding. I'd assumed that with Washington in Pennsylvania now, the enemy would be everywhere between here and New York, but our convoy commander used four or five New Jersey roads that were completely free."

"It's Howe's greatest error, but it may not be his fault," John replied. "If he wants to keep a town, he must establish a garrison there. If he wants to hold a road or a bridge, he must post sentries on it. He doesn't have that many troops. There's a bridge south of Indian Mills in Jersey, on the little Mullica River, that Howe wanted as a safeguard for his supply lines. Captain Hamilton, Washington's aide, was here a few days ago and told me the story of that bridge. One night the Lobster sentries there were shot, both of them. The next night Howe posted four men there, and all four were shot. He doubled the guard again, and forty-eight hours later all of them were killed before morning. This time our boys used bows and arrows—and knives, because the redcoats were expecting a musket attack."

There was little humor in Cushing's laugh. "I've heard that Lobster soldiers in New York Town don't dare go into the streets at night in groups of less than a dozen or so."

"It's no wonder Washington believes Sir William has little heart for his task."

Dorothy became petulant. "Is there nothing in the world these days but destruction and bloodshed?"

"Very little, my dear." John nibbled a herring strip and sipped his drink.

She turned her back to him. "What's the news from Boston, Tom?"

"Work on the *Hancock* is progressing nicely, and she'll be ready to put out to sea by early spring."

"A portrait of you will be placed in the great cabin," John added, but decided this wasn't the moment to explain that he was naming the frigate in memory of Uncle Thomas.

"Is Mrs. Bolton's dressmaking shop on Treamount Street still open?" she wanted to know, showing no interest in the warship that was costing her husband a fortune to build.

Cushing looked blank.

"All the ladies of your family went to her for years, sir!"

John went to his friend's rescue. "Tom has been busy trying to persuade the Massachusetts legislature to work in harmony with the Congress, Dorothy. I dare say he's had little chance to listen to talk of dressmakers."

For the guest's sake, Dolly tried to be gracious. "It wasn't so very long ago that you two could talk by the hour about the fabric in a new gown. You'd study it, feel it, nearly tear it off a lady's back if you thought it might sell in quantity."

Both men laughed a little sheepishly.

"I shall be relieved and very happy when the war ends and there's no more talk of battles and politics. John doesn't know how pleased I'll be when he spends his waking hours directing the affairs of Hancock and Company."

John glanced uneasily at his former partner, then cleared his throat. "For our son's sake I shall keep a few ships at sea and fill a half-dozen warehouses with merchandise. I won't deprive him of the opportunity to make a career for himself as a merchant, if that's what he wants to do with his life. As for me, I find it difficult to believe I shall ever be able to abandon public service."

Dolly stared at him in dismay.

"I feel the same way," Cushing told her, hoping that, by sharing the burden with his former partner, he would make her censure less severe.

John tried to explain. "Few men seek office, and fewer still are qualified, my dear. The need will be as great after our independence is won as it is now, perhaps even greater. I'd be shirking my duty if I failed to give my country the benefit of the experience I've been acquiring."

"Well said," Cushing murmured.

Dolly's contempt was directed only at her husband. "What you love," she said acidly, "is the pomp. You revel in the glory. The applause of an audience when you deliver a speech means more to you than a beefsteak pie or the Palatine wine Robert Morris drinks that you just heard about recently."

"It's called Riesling." There was just enough truth in her accusation to make John belligerently defensive. "I'll be grateful, madam, if you'll tell me what pomp you find in the Congress meetings at Independence Hall, or in the dark little office I've been given—with a hearth so small that I suffer a permanent chill and haven't been free of the ague in more weeks than I can remember. As to my public addresses, the people like what I say because the Almighty gave me a small talent for oratory. But I lack Jefferson's knack for words—or Dr. Franklin's—and I think it unlikely that even our own grandchildren will read records of what I've said." He laughed derisively. "And if you think there's glory in the Presidency, I tell you honestly that I'll gladly give up the post when we find someone else who can soothe our geniuses and persuade them to work together. I shall become immortal only if Howe catches me and has me hanged."

The domestic exchange embarrassed, and he tried to ease the tension. "Our people need the leadership of those able to provide it, but I must admit that the ladies of our leaders find time heavy on their hands. Loneliness is one of the sacrifices they make to the cause of liberty."

"Isn't it enough that I haven't yet opened the door of my own home, thanks to John's insistence on being a member of the Congress?" Dolly had conveniently forgotten that Dr. Rush had forbidden her to travel before her baby was born.

John had heard the complaint many times, and cut her short. "My dear," he said benignly, but with a hint of firmness in his voice, "Tom spent a long day on the road, much of it dodging Lobster patrols, and he must be even hungrier than I am."

Dolly didn't look in his direction as she hurried out through the dining room to the kitchen outbuilding.

"My apologies for subjecting you to connubial unpleasantness." John's smile was forced.

"It's a disease all of us seem to suffer these days. I think women are less able to tolerate the strains of war than men."

"No, there's another, deeper reason, although I wouldn't admit it to Dorothy. She spoke of pomp and glory and applause, but those aren't the real reasons we make sacrifices by working in the Congress or in state assemblies. I deny no man the motive of patriotism, Tom, so don't misunderstand me. We labor for the United States because the Crown will enslave us if we lose. So, in that sense, any man of principle and courage has no choice today. If we don't serve our country well, we'll have neither a country nor freedom. And we ourselves will surely perish. I'm told the price on my head has gone still higher. But that merely confirms what I suspect about all of us. We have selfish reasons, not just patriotic ones, for giving ourselves to the country."

"If you mean that we could have quietly accepted the taxes imposed on us, you're wrong. We'd have stayed in business, of course, but our pride would have been destroyed. We'd have been wealthy slaves."

"No, that isn't what I mean in the least." John refilled their glasses. "Haven't you found that you enjoy being the leader of the Massachusetts General Court?"

"Well, yes. Except when you send me directives from Congress and try to tell me where to assign our militia. Or virtually demand still another contribution of funds for the legislature's treasury."

"If you spent six months in the Congress, you'd sing a different tune," John said dryly, "but the point I'm trying to make is as valid for the Congress as it is for the General Court. I find that in spite of all the tribulations and worries, government work is more challenging than merchant shipping. To be truthful with you Tom, I like the feeling of influencing history. Our names will probably be forgotten in a hundred years—maybe in fifty—but people will be living in a free America. We'll be responsible for that, just as the confederated government we're forming and the laws we're passing will guide them."

"I think I know what you mean, but I'm not sure I agree with you, John. If I want to be remembered, I'll have my widow and children spend a thousand dollars on the biggest and most ornate tombstone ever built in the New World. But I don't quite know what that will prove."

"No, you don't understand. I'm not making my point very clearly, but it isn't the acclaim of posterity we're seeking. Not at all. We're pitting our minds against King George's feeble wits—and the strongest military and naval forces the world has ever seen. Our citizens have entrusted us with the task of leading America, and we're conscious of the role we're playing in shaping destiny."

"I hadn't thought about it in those terms," Cushing admitted, "but I suppose you're right."

"We're very much like the King and Lord North. And Parliament, for that matter." John extended a hand, palm upward, and slowly closed it into a fist. "Our reward for the inconveniences we suffer, the long hours, even the opposition and sometimes hatred of old friends and comrades—is the sensation of power, a genuine sentiment, you know, because we do exert real power."

"Are you claiming that each of us in government wants to be a tyrant?"

"Certainly not! There are members of the Congress who fool themselves, to be sure. Their aims are good, but if they acquired more power, they'd become benevolent tyrants. But their benevolence would diminish as they acquired more and more power. In spite of their good intentions they'd become tyrants in time."

"There are men in the Massachusetts General Court like that, too. You and I know them well."

"In all justice to them, Tom, who is to say I wouldn't become a despot if I mounted a throne? The more I see of the actions of those who govern, the more I study my own heart and curb my own impulses, the more convinced I become that we must establish a permanent form of government in the United States that will prevent any one man—or small group of men—from gaining a tight enough hold on the reins to become a tyrant.

"The King suffered the illness of despotism from the day he mounted the throne. I saw it in him myself, and with each passing year his ailment has become worse. In my opinion Lord North is just a toady, so we can dismiss him from consideration. But think of Pitt, our best friend in England, a man who treasures liberty. Had he remained First Minister for another ten years—twenty years—whatever—would he have gradually relished his power so much that, in spite of his good intentions, he'd have become a despot? I honestly don't know, and it's what frightens me."

"Is Philadelphia so different? I've found no cause for fear in Boston." Cushing was polite but incredulous.

"There you see men striving for control of Massachusetts. Here, with anglers from thirteen states throwing their lines over the side of the ship, we think more in terms of the whole country. The temptations are greater."

"All the more reason, then, for each state to be zealous in guarding its own sovereignty."

"That's no protection, as I see it, unless the states are familiar with the methods of power-seekers. At present the Congress has too little authority, and our need for a stronger central government to prosecute the war is urgent. Of course, if it should become too strong, I don't see how any one state—or any combination of states—could prevent the rise of a man determined to make himself a king. The problem is complicated, Tom, and can't be reduced to simple terms. Where do we draw the lines? How do we decide what powers will be given to the Congress and what powers will be reserved by the states? We need time to experiment, to achieve delicate balances between the government of the confederation and the governments of the states. But with Howe's army only fifty miles away, we may not be given the opportunity to experiment until we can find the right blend of power distribution.

"We want liberty, but men who work together for the common good must have the right to make decisions that will be binding on all the people. That means the individual must sacrifice a measure of his personal freedom for the common good. How much must he give up? If we knew, we'd be better able to organize our joint efforts against the British. We'd stop trying to snatch the tools of power from each other.

"Our greatest problem is that we're amateurs. Our soldiers are civilian volunteers, our statesmen have been politicians sitting in colonial legislatures that advised Crown governors but exerted no authority of their own. And our tax collectors are men who are opposed to the very principle of taxation.

"If we win the war it will be only because our love of liberty is great enough to overcome our lack of experience. I'll give up my life rather than surrender, but in these past weeks I've become frightened. I've admitted this to no one else, but unless our civilian leaders in the Congress and the states can hitch themselves to the same carriage and our soldiers start thinking of themselves as Americans rather than as Virginians and Pennsylvanians and Carolinians, we're doomed."

9

Most members of the Congress devoted their efforts exclusively to the affairs of the new nation, but so many physicians had remained loyal to the Crown and had fled to New York Town that there was a desperate shortage of medical practitioners in Philadelphia. Consequently Dr. Benjamin Rush was harried, overworked, and unable to snatch even a few hours for relaxation or the pursuit of the many scientific subjects that fascinated him.

Gaunt, irritable, and looking much older than his thirty-one years, the physician arrived at the lodgings of the President late on a gray, overcast afternoon, long after he had been summoned. He offered no apologies for his tardiness, and dropping the cloth case containing his instruments and elixirs onto a parlor chair, went straight to the fire. "What seems to be the matter?" he asked in his blandest professional manner.

John, who had been in a frenzy since noon, lost his temper. "Damnation, Doctor, I told you in my note! Mrs. Hancock is in childbirth!"

"Oh, yes. I remember now." Rush continued to stand calmly before the fire, smiling as he warmed his hands.

It was inconceivable to John that anyone—much less the physician attending Dolly—could forget she was giving birth to his son. "In the name of the Almighty, sir, go to her!"

Rush made no move. "When did her acute distress begin, Mr. President?"

"A little before noon, when I left the rostrum of the Congress."

"I wasn't able to attend today's session." The physician saw no reason to explain that since daybreak he had already performed four surgical operations and had visited eight other patients, all of them gravely ill. "She is being attended, no doubt?"

"Mrs. Adams is with her, as are two other ladies and one of her servingmaids." John was becoming still more frantic.

"Ah, then she's in good hands. You've been visiting her from time to time?"

"They won't allow me near the room." The stubborn attitude of the women was unbearable, and John made no attempt to hide his bitterness. "Every now and again they send me to the kitchen for buckets of hot water, but I'm damned if I know why."

Rush stifled a grin. "A shrewd midwife in ancient Greece discovered that the best way to keep the husband and father busy at a time like this is to send him for boiling water. The custom proved very effective, and no doubt that's why it persisted."

"Doctor, Mrs. Hancock and my son may die while you stand here chatting with me about the practices of antiquity!"

"Don't you believe it, Mr. President." The physician went to his case, opened it and made a leisurely check of its contents. "I've made a study of the Conestoga and Lenape tribes, and I've discovered their squaws are unattended at childbirth. They believe their independence makes their sons stronger and more courageous warriors."

"Mrs. Hancock is not a savage Indian, Dr. Rush!"

"Unfortunately for all of us, she isn't. I intend to write a paper someday on the softening influences of civilization on childbirth." Rush tucked his case under his arm and nodded in the direction of a closed door, behind which the steady murmur of feminine voices could be heard. "Is that the room?"

John nodded and swallowed hard.

"Try a few drops of brandywine, Mr. President. You'll find it very soothing, but don't try rum or gin. I've found they have calamitous effects on fathers in the last stages of childbirth." The bedroom door opened and closed.

John shivered and moved close to the fire, but his chill persisted and he followed Dr. Rush's advice, pouring himself a small, carefully measured drink of French brandywine, a recent gift from Robert Morris.

As he lifted his glass to his lips, Dolly screamed, and he spilled half the contents over his hand. Afraid she was being murdered, he started toward the bedroom, but his courage failed, so he halted, gulped down his drink and poured another. The second glass proved to be too much for him, however. He perspired, felt queasy and was afraid he might faint.

Dolly was older than most women having babies for the first time, and someone had told him that mature women found childbirth far more difficult than girls still in their teens. If anything happened to his wife, he would never be able to forgive himself for his refusal to consider marriage when she had been seventeen.

Again Dolly screamed, and John wrenched off the arm of a chair, not realizing what he had done until he found himself gazing stupidly at the piece of polished maple in his hand. His lawn shirt was soaked, and he moved closer to the fire once more, not daring to take another drink.

His feeling of hysteria gave way to a deep sense of foreboding, as he was unable to hear any sound now on the far side of the bedroom door. He braced himself, expecting Abigail Adams to appear at any moment with the news that Dolly had died.

The thin, piercing wail of an infant drifted into the parlor and rang in John's ears. His apprehensions vanished, he laughed foolishly and poured himself a still more generous drink. "To John Hancock the Fourth!"

He could not resist the temptation to smash the glass in the fireplace.

He was so pleased with himself that another quarter of an hour passed almost unnoticed. He would send immediate letters to his sister and brother, and grudgingly decided to write his mother, too. She wouldn't care, but he owed her the courtesy. And nothing would give him greater pleasure than to enter the boy at Harvard College. He would be ready in 1789, or in 1790 at the latest.

The bedroom door opened, and Abigail came into the parlor, carrying an infant wrapped in a soft linen sheet and white blanket.

John stumbled as he hastened to her, beaming, then tried to conquer a sense of dismay as he stared down at a baby with a red, wrinkled face. "Well," he said bravely, "he's very handsome, isn't he?"

"You have a daughter, John."

The news was so stunning he couldn't believe it, and for a moment thought she must be joking. Then the wild thought that Dolly had betrayed him passed through his mind, but he dismissed the notion quickly and struggled to regain his equilibrium. "Splendid," he said, trying unsuccessfully to sound enthusiastic. "Is Dorothy—all right?"

"She's fine. You may see her, but Dr. Rush doesn't want you to stay for more than a moment."

Dolly looked exceptionally pretty and at peace, with her head resting on two silk-covered pillows.

John bent down, kissed her and made a supreme effort. "I'm very pleased, we have a daughter." He seemed to mean it.

Dolly knew how much his attempted enthusiasm cost him, and felt closer to him than ever before. "So am I," she whispered, and hoped he would assume she was weeping tears of joy.

10

General Sir William Howe's redcoats and Germans occupied the town of Trenton, New Jersey, in December 1776. Washington was forced to retreat to the Pennsylvania side of the Delaware River and, his forces shrinking each day as discouraged militia companies ignored threats, pleas, and exhortations to remain with the dwindling band of Continentals.

With the enemy only twenty miles from Philadelphia, the Congress became panicky, and at least a dozen members who had boasted that they would resist the Crown to the end now spoke in terms of surrendering quickly in order to obtain favorable terms. A meeting was held behind closed doors, with no one but delegates present, and as soon as the session was adjourned, President Hancock set out for the commander-in-chief's headquarters in Newtown, accompanied by Captain Alexander Hamilton, Washington's aide-de-camp, who acted as his guide.

They arrived at the quiet Pennsylvania farmhouse at ten o'clock, and the general came out into the cold, coatless, to greet his guest.

Tired young officers scarcely bothered to look up from their work in the parlors of the old clapboard building, and Washington smiled sadly as he nodded in their direction. "Their devotion is greater than yours and mine, Mr. President. You and I fight on because we'll be executed if we're caught. Those lads would be granted amnesties, but their devotion hasn't wavered."

"I would to God I could say the same of the Congress," John replied bitterly.

"Or of the fair-weather militia." Washington led his guest into the dining room, where a platter of cold beef, a jar of soft cheese, and a pitcher of ale sat on a table set with two places. "I knew you'd be hungry after your long ride with no dinner," he said, closing the door, "so I've let my own meal wait, and I can only apologize for the meager fare."

John was touched by the Virginian's consideration. "This is a banquet, sir."

Gentlemen understood each other, and the commander-in-chief smiled wistfully as they took their places. "It may be a long time before either of us eats a real banquet again, Mr. President." He passed the platter of meat. "Is it agreed that everything we two say in this room must be kept confidential?"

"There's no choice, General, as you'll understand when I tell you the mood of the Congress."

"My news may be worse than yours, Mr. President." Washington broke off a chunk of dark wheat bread and spooned some butter onto his plate. "My staff out there is trying to keep count of the troops we have left, and it's a never-ending task. Militia units go home by day, Continentals desert after dark. I have less than six thousand men right now, and if the present rate of departures continues, I'll be fortunate to have five thousand by the end of the year."

"And the enemy?"

"They've had to establish a garrison in New York Town and station at least four battalions in New Jersey to protect their supply lines. I've heard various figures on the number of effectives Howe can throw into battle, but I believe that Captain Harry Lee has brought me the most accurate estimate. His scouts say the red-coats can put fifteen thousand infantry, nine squadrons of cavalry, and fourteen batteries of artillery in the field."

John was shaken. "Is Howe aware of your weakness?"

"Of course. His cavalry patrols make a close surveillance of us every morning and afternoon. He realizes we'd crumble if he attacked in strength."

John was surprised to see that Washington's appetite was hearty. "Then why doesn't he, General?"

"Sir William is a good soldier—and an equally good Whig, Mr. President. He feels a measure of sympathy for our cause, and he's indicated in two notes he's sent me when we've exchanged prisoners that he believes it will be easier and simpler to arrange peace terms if we hold fighting to a minimum. As a commander, he's doing just what I'd do if I were in his place. He's simply waiting for the rest of my army to disintegrate. I'm losing more men by desertion than he could kill in battle. So, if he waits for another month or two, he reasons that I'll have no one to send into the field against him, and he'll win a complete victory without bloodshed."

John smiled grimly. "You have five thousand courageous men who are determined to stay with you, General, so I must congratulate you. It's unfortunate their example does nothing to inspire the Congress."

"Your letter of yesterday merely said the members have become badly frightened."

"So frightened, General, that they voted this afternoon to flee from Philadelphia and retire to Baltimore, where they'll be farther from Lobsterback vengeance."

"Don't they realize the effect of such a flight on the entire country's spirits—not to mention my recruiting program?"

"The members of Congress are intelligent men, General, although they're behaving right now like children who run out into the woods to escape a spanking. I told them they could damned well go to Baltimore without me, and both Dr. Franklin and Robert Morris said that as Pennsylvanians they wouldn't leave Philadelphia. I'm sorry to admit that no one else supported me, and I avoided a decisive vote only by declaring the motion to transfer deliberations to Baltimore out of order. I doubt if the ruse will work again. Too many members are lawyers, and next time they'll be waiting for a trick."

"We seem to be champions of a lost cause, Mr. President."

John's fork clattered to his plate. "I refuse to accept defeat, General Washington. Lead a few companies across the mountains into the wilderness—I don't care how small the band—and I'll go with you. And I'm not the only one. If need be, we'll set up a rump Congress in the forests, and we won't be satisfied until you've recaptured every town, every inch of ground you've had to give up to the enemy."

Washington's long, solemn face broke into a broad smile, and he held out his hand. "Thank you for your confidence, sir. It's good to know you realize I have no intention of giving up the fight."

"Both of us recognize the odds against us on a short-term basis, but if we can hold out long enough, Howe and all the other commanders the War Office may send against us will be forced to see that no one can enslave a people determined to gain freedom." John sat back in his chair and sipped his ale. "That's a high-flown phrase, isn't it, General? I could bring a crowd to its feet with patriotic rhetoric, but words won't solve our joint problem. My task is to prevent the Congress and state legislatures from losing heart. Yours is to halt desertions and encourage fresh enlistments. So we're trying to do the same thing, really."

By now Washington, like his guest, had lost interest in food. "We must prove—to all our people—that we have both the capacity and the will to resist."

"I'm intending to increase our efforts to obtain an open treaty of alliance with France, General. Silas Deane is an able negotiator, but the letter I received from him the other day on a ship that slipped through the Royal Navy blockade indicates he faces a long and difficult task in Paris. The French are willing to increase their secret aid to us—and send us money and arms in our own ships. But we need more than token help."

"I can scarcely blame them for their reluctance to give it," Washington replied. "I can think of nothing better for our cause than the opening of a campaign in Europe that would force the British to keep their troops and warships on the other side of the Atlantic. But the French can't have forgotten their last beating only thirteen years ago."

"Our strategy, General, is to convince them they can recoup their losses, as I'm convinced they can. But Deane needs help from someone who is known and respected in Europe."

Washington's glacial blue eyes came alive. "Dr. Franklin?"

"He's the only American the French and every other European nation regard as a great man. John Adams and I have had several long talks with him, and he's willing to join Deane in Paris. We want to keep the whole matter quiet, obviously, as the Royal Navy would win a victory far greater than the taking of New York Town if it could capture Dr. Franklin on the high seas."

"You're giving him adequate protection, I'm sure."

"I'm admittedly an amateur as a head of state, General, but I spent my whole life in shipping, and I can assure you that Benjamin Franklin will reach France safely, no matter how many ships the Admiralty may have afloat between here and France." John lighted his pipe, having discovered recently that he found the taste soothing. "But it won't be enough to land him there. He'll need time to deal with the French government, charm King Louis and use his logic in his talks with their foreign ministry."

"How much time do you suppose he'll require, Mr. President?"

"I can only guess, General. Six months, a year—who can say? Diplomatic battles aren't won overnight."

"Nor are military."

The atmosphere had become cooler. "I realize your handicaps are staggering, General."

"Thank you, Mr. President. But you also know that the American people must have a solid demonstration of some sort if their hopes are to be kept alive. I've been well aware of the need for some time, and I plan to take positive action before the last of my regiments vanish."

John brightened and leaned forward, elbows on the table.

"I mean you no disrespect, sir, when I tell you I can give you no details—for the reason that I don't yet know what I'll do. I must improvise, just as you must handle the Congress from day to day."

John slumped back in his chair. "You know, General, we both take pride in being reasonable men. But I'm inclined to believe we're a little mad. Viewed sensibly, the cause of American liberty is hopelessly doomed, yet we refuse to surrender. If we win—as we shall—it's because we lack the intelligence to know when we're beaten."

11

Benjamin Harrison of Virginia looked abashed and tugged uncomfortably at his waistcoat. "A half-dozen of us asked that the vote be postponed until you returned from General Washington's headquarters, John, but the majority wouldn't hear of it. The Congress insisted on leaving Philadelphia for Baltimore today."

John pounded his desk in impotent rage. "What was the vote count?"

Roger Sherman looked sheepishly at the bare floor. "The issue was decided on a voice vote."

"A pack of damned cowards!" John's face was a dangerous shade of red.

The two men who had been appointed to break the news to him exchanged swift glances. "You're too hard on the members, John. They share your goals, but they've chosen a different means to achieve the same end."

Sherman gained the courage to brave the apoplectic Presidential wrath, too. "It's as unfair to call the members of Congress cowards as it would be to brand them as traitors. We'd be in no position to do the country any good if Howe throws a ring of troops around Philadelphia. We could neither caucus nor vote in a redcoat prison."

He had a valid point, but John was too angry for logic. "Damnation, what will the country think?"

"People would be a blamesight more upset," the urbane Harrison replied, "if you and Tom Jefferson were let down from tree branches with ropes around your necks."

"We haven't been caught yet. And Howe is a full day's march from the city."

"Lobster cavalry can travel fast," Sherman replied, "and from all we hear, Washington can't muster the strength to stop them."

John became calmer as he realized that nothing was more damaging to the American cause than the spread of stories that the Continental Army was falling apart. "I have sufficient faith in our battalions," he said, "that I shall remain here with my wife and daughter. I hope that within a few days the Congress will be sufficiently encouraged by my example to take heart—and return to our capital."

"You're running a terrible risk," Harrison told him.

"It may be that I'm taking a chance," John replied, "but I think it's necessary. If the leaders of Congress don't set an example, who will?"

12

On December 19, 1776, President John Hancock capitulated to the will of the Continental Congress and set out for Baltimore in a caravan consisting of two coaches and seven wagons, with a troop of Continental horsemen as his escort. His wife and infant daughter, Lydia, rode with him in the lead carriage, but neither the presence of Dolly nor of the baby, who had suddenly become quite pretty, relieved his gloom.

"This is a day I'll never forget," he said, staring out of the window. "When Sam Adams and I had to take to the swamps up home, I swore I'd never run from redcoats again. But here I am—running."

"I'm sure we'll be more comfortable in Baltimore, dear." Dolly was looking forward to the prospect of a rented house all to themselves.

"To blazes with comfort. I'm thinking of sending you and the baby home to Boston soon."

"Without you?"

"I'm chained to the Congress, and will have to go wherever it goes."

"Then," she said quietly, "I'll stay with you."

John stared at her in astonishment. "I thought you were anxious to reopen the house and set up a nursery."

"So I am, but I prefer to be with you. I don't want the people to think I'm shirking my duty."

Her awareness that she had an obligation to her fellow citizens was an unexpected ray of light in the darkness, and he reached out to pat her hand.

"Don't wake up the baby."

John snatched his hand away.

Dolly laughed. "You're more afraid of your own daughter than you are of the British."

"I've known redcoats for a long time, and I understand their ways." He studied the infant, thinking it strange that he had been disappointed at the birth of a daughter. In the most heavily guarded of the wagons, which contained the plates and presses that were used for the printing of Continental dollars, were his Christmas presents for his wife and daughter, a wide gold bracelet with the baby's name inscribed on the back for Dolly, a narrower band for Lydia.

"You know them so well, sir, that you were willing to chance letting your family fall into their hands by remaining in Philadelphia."

"Sir William Howe would no more harm you and a helpless child than General Washington would hang the ladies of Philadelphia who openly declare they can't wait to be rescued by the Lobsters." John opened his window and peered down the road. "It's chilly."

"Sorry, my dear." He closed the window again, ineffectually helping her wrap Lydia more securely in her blankets.

"You're worried about something, John."

"I suppose it's unfair not to tell you. In my opinion you'd have taken no risk at all by staying in Philadelphia. Washington has given me an escort today because it would be a feather in Howe's cap to capture me—and our presses." He saw no need to mention that his wine supplies and those of Robert Morris, which had been placed in his care for safekeeping, were a prize for which British cavalrymen would fight enthusiastically. "I'd have preferred to travel to Baltimore without a military escort. The presence of troops in our company gives the enemy the right to fire on us if we're overtaken."

Dolly was incapable of believing she could become involved in violence, and remained serene.

John gestured in the direction of a young officer, who rode beside the carriage, leading a saddled horse without a rider. "If there's trouble," he said, "the lieutenant out there and I will make a dash and try to escape."

His calm convinced her that he was serious, and jarred her, as a warning could not have done. "Are you so unafraid of death?" she asked, realizing she still didn't know the man she had married.

"I find my life very pleasant, and in this coach with me are two excellent reasons for wanting to prolong it. But I knew long ago, when I chose the path of direct, open opposition to the Crown, that in British eyes I would become an outlaw. That's what I am now, and I suppose the knowledge that a secret Loyalist sympathizer could put a bullet or a knife into my heart at any time has made me callous to personal danger. Odd, isn't it, how circumstances create conditions that force a man to adopt a heroic posture? I feel no more heroic now than I've ever felt. In fact, my only reaction to the possibility of losing my life in the immediate future is rather frivolous. I hope, very much, that I'll live long enough to drink at least one bottle of that superb Spanish Calavados brandywine that Robert Morris presented to me this morning as a parting gift."

13

The members of Congress were in a surly mood as they crowded into their temporary Baltimore meeting-place. It was bad enough that President Hancock had refused them the right to adjourn over the Christmas holiday season. He had claimed that the country would neither appreciate nor condone an adjournment at a time when the armed forces were fighting for survival, but many of the delegates were convinced he was punishing them for their flight from Philadelphia.

Certainly they thought it strange that he should summon them to a special session at ten o'clock at night, sending messengers to find them at their lodging houses and in Baltimore's inns. A few, who had left half-eaten dinners, were openly indignant, and the majority looked up at the rostrum in stony hostility as the President's gavel demanded silence.

"Some of you have been inconvenienced," John said, "but I can offer you neither apologies nor sympathy, gentlemen. A situation has developed that, in the opinion of the chair, warranted the calling of a meeting tonight rather than waiting until late tomorrow morning.

"I have just received an extraordinary communication from General Washington. A little less than forty-eight hours ago, on Christmas Night, he led his force of Continentals and a few militia units in a surprise assault on the enemy garrison at Trenton. In spite of the difficulties created by the crossing of the Delaware River long after nightfall, the raid was a complete success. Both redcoat and German units retreated in disorder, and General

Washington has had the honor to inform me that he has captured more than one thousand Hessian prisoners. He will exchange these captives for badly needed men of our own taken by the enemy on Long Island, at New York Town, and during the retreat through New Jersey.

"Here, gentlemen, is the answer to those who believed our cause was hopeless. The United States has not been crushed. We survive—as free men. Our Army has won its first great victory."

The roar of approval made the walls shake as the delegates rose to their feet.

John let them cheer themselves hoarse. The military significance of the victory at Trenton was questionable, but Washington had made a great contribution to the country's spirit, reviving hope when it had almost died. Now it was the turn of the Congress to provide America with the sinews of war, and John knew the principal burden fell on him. The Battle of Trenton was just the beginning.

SEVEN

1777 — 1781

1

"I won't and can't dispute Washington's military genius." John paced up and down the handsomely appointed library of Robert Morris' Philadelphia mansion. "His strike at Princeton after his victory at Trenton sent Howe and Clinton and Lord Cornwallis scurrying back to New York Town for the winter and gave us possession of New Jersey again. It even enabled me to bring the Congress back here from Baltimore. But our ailments aren't cured. The elixir has given the patient temporary relief, nothing more, Bob."

Morris spread several long sheets of paper covered with figures across the top of his mahogany desk. "It's not easy to convince the states they must increase their contributions to the confederation treasury when they've seen us win a major military campaign with such paltry funds."

"I've sent every last one of them copies of Washington's assessment of the situation. He believes Howe can strike again at any time."

"The legislatures know the new Continental Army recruiting campaign has been successful, particularly after Tom Jefferson persuaded that Paine fellow to write his new pamphlet that you had printed and distributed. The realization that Washington has eleven thousand men with him at Morristown gives them a feeling of much greater security."

John glowered. "They can't fight redcoats and Germans with their bare hands."

Morris smiled quietly.

"Forgive me, Bob. You've given more out of your own pocket than anyone else in the country."

"You're too modest. I believe you've matched me, penny for penny. And if it weren't for the gifts of a few private citizens like Chaym Solomon, we couldn't keep going."

"That's my whole argument." John felt a sudden wave of dizziness and stopped pacing as he waited for it to pass. "The loans you've been negotiating with those French and Dutch bankers will be a great help, of course. As a merchant I stand in awe of the terms you've arranged."

Morris' smile was self-deprecating.

"But we're still marching toward financial chaos." John took one of the papers from the desk. "This gives me the ague. We've issued over one and one half-million Continental dollars—and we have a treasury of less than two hundred thousand in specie to support our paper money. By all the rules of orthodox finance, we're a totally bankrupt nation!" He started to move again, but couldn't rid himself of a hazy feeling that clouded his vision.

"I've been using every means I know to persuade the states to increase their contributions, but they treat me as though I were King George's chief tax collector."

"That's the solution to the problem, Bob. The Congress must be granted the right to impose taxes!"

"No state will grant us the right."

"I'm afraid not, just as no state will voluntarily increase the sum it pays into the national treasury. I wrote my friends in Massachusetts, demanding more money for the Congress. The General Court's answer was to grant me a commission as Major General of Massachusetts militia. I was flattered, of course—that was last month, when I gave you the additional fifty thousand out of my own purse. I have a nagging suspicion there are men in Boston who know me well enough to realize that's what I'd do. But—damnation—the United States can't survive on gifts of charity from a few men who'll soon exhaust their own funds!"

"One of the faults with a democratic form of government—if

it is a fault—is that we move very slowly before accepting any new concepts or ideas. There are advantages to the system."

"Not when Washington has eleven thousand men to clothe and arm and feed!" John felt as though he was choking. Pulling his silk stock from his neck, he sank into a chair, but the condition didn't improve. He gasped for breath, one hand at his throat, and was afraid he would lose consciousness.

Morris bent over him anxiously. "What is it?"

John was unable to reply.

"I'll send a boy for Dr. Rush."

John shook his head and, clutching the other man's arm, held on to it until he was able to mutter a few words. "A drop—of brandywine."

Morris splashed some liquor into a glass and handed it to him.

Sipping very slowly, John finally managed to regain his equilibrium. Color returned to his face, the choking sensation vanished and he was able to focus clearly once again. "I'm so sorry. I had no intention of inconveniencing you."

Morris waved aside the apology. "Has this sort of thing happened before today?"

"Once or twice."

"Has Dr. Rush examined you?"

"I need no physician, Bob. This is a minor indisposition, and I'm sure it will soon heal itself."

Morris regarded him dubiously. "Rush may have novel theories, but he's a cautious physician. I'm inclined to suspect he'd put you to bed."

"That's why I'll be damned if I'll go to him, Bob—or to any other doctor. All of them like to build a little case of phlegm into a major disease. I've never missed a day of work in my life, and I don't intend to start now, when there's so much to be done and so few of us willing to do it!"

2

Sam Adams knew Dolly disapproved of him, and rarely visited the Hancock lodgings. But he would let nothing deter him from his duty, and presented himself there one Sunday afternoon in the spring of 1777, shabbier then ever in a suit that was rumpled and stained.

Dolly tried to hide her surprise when she herself answered his summons, the members of the household staff having been given an afternoon off. The first thought that crossed her mind was no man had ever been more in need of his wife's presence to help him improve his appearance. But Elizabeth Adams' influence on her husband had always been negligible.

They exchanged polite but guarded greetings, Sam inquired after the health of the baby and Dolly led the guest into the parlor. "If you'll sit down," she said, "I'll tell John you're here, and then I'll make us a pot of Dutch chocolate."

"There's no need to be sociable, Cousin Dorothy," Sam replied dryly. "I'm here on business. Is John at work?"

"He never does anything but work. I persuaded him to spend the day here instead of going to his office so he could see a little something of Lydia—who'll grow up to be a stranger to him. But he hasn't come out of that little study of his once all day, not once."

Sam remembered that a pantry behind the dining room had been converted into a small office. "I'll go to him there," he said, and didn't bother with the formality of a bow as he left her in the parlor.

John was working in his ruffled shirt and waistcoat, and Sam saw him for the first time in many months without his wig. His hair was becoming much grayer and, combined with the weight he had gained as a result of too little exercise, he bore a striking resemblance to his late Uncle Thomas.

Not bothering with customary greetings, he pointed a quill pen at his guest. "How can I persuade Rhode Island to hand over two counterfeiters to Connecticut for prosecution?"

Sam chuckled as he sank into the one comfortable chair in the room and, unbidden, helped himself to a glass of sack from a decanter on a table beside him. "Threaten to send them criminals from the jails of every other state if they won't cooperate. Rhode Islanders are the most ornery, independent-minded people on earth."

"I know. I deal with them every day of the week." John belatedly remembered his manners. "It's good to see you here, Sam."

"Your wife wasn't overjoyed, but we'll let that pass." He came to the point at once. "You're proud of those frigates."

"The *Hancock* and the *Boston* are going to prove themselves the best investment I've ever made."

"They've just fought an engagement with three ships of Lord Howe's fleet off Cape Cod." When circumstances warranted a blunt approach, Sam preferred it to a subtle one.

John's pride was hurt. "Why was the news sent to you rather than to me?"

Sam curbed his own annoyance, and refrained from saying that as both frigates had received commissions from the Commonwealth of Massachusetts, they could not be regarded as the property of any one man, not even the philanthropist who had built them. "You have more friends at home than you realize, John," he said quietly. "They thought it might be better for you to hear the story from someone who has known you well."

John's anxiety sharpened his realization that he and Sam had drifted apart in the past year or two, but it certainly wasn't his fault that Sam hadn't grown with the country and placed the interests of Massachusetts before those of the whole United States. "Don't keep me in suspense! They acquitted themselves ably in battle?"

"The *Boston's* crew was young and had never faced gunfire. We can't blame those boys for running, any more than we can point a finger of scorn at Washington's recruits who became panicky on Long Island." The task was more difficult than Sam had imagined. "The harbor batteries covered her retreat, and she was able to reach port without suffering damage."

John winced. "And the *Hancock?*"

"She took a beating before she struck her colors."

"She was sunk, then?"

"No," Sam replied, "captured."

It was inconceivable to John that a ship he named after Uncle Thomas could have suffered such an ignominious fate.

Sam was startled by the tears on his old friend's lashes. Many men relieved their emotions by weeping, but John had always been too proud of his strength. "The crew tried to scuttle her, but the British boarded her and kept her afloat. They call her the *Orion* now."

243

"By God, I'll build another *Hancock*. I'll test the oak timbers for her hull myself, to make sure they're tough. And I won't hand her over to Massachusetts until I've investigated every member of her crew and satisfied myself there isn't a coward in the lot."

Sam stood and put a hand on his shoulder. "How long has it been since you spent a full day with your family?"

John glared at him and blew his nose, using a huge handkerchief of raw silk with an embroidered hem. "I need hardly tell you, of all people," he said coldly, "that the Congress is badly understaffed. I can't afford to fritter away my time."

Sam had never seen him so taut. "You can't afford to ignore your health."

"Have you been talking with Dorothy? Or with Bob Morris?"

"No, is there reason I should?"

"I'm tired of being told I stand with one foot in the grave at the age of forty-one! Before you start lecturing me, let me remind you that you're a damnsight older than I am!"

His ferocity stunned Sam. "I believe in letting a man live his own life as he sees fit," he said mildly. "But from the looks of you, it wouldn't do you any harm to remember that King George and Lord North don't work seven days and seven nights a week."

"They can afford to take their ease. I can't—until the last redcoat has been driven from our soil and the last Royal Navy ship has evacuated American waters!"

3

Dolly concealed her annoyance until her husband's breakfast was interrupted for the third time by a courier. She clutched the frilly neckline of her dressing gown and tapped a slipper beneath the table as she watched his meal grow cold.

John read the papers in his hand with his usual thoroughness. "I'll send a reply to the South Carolina legislature after I've conferred with Carolina delegates," he told the messenger. "My secretaries will have my reply waiting for you at noon."

The young man was embarrassed. "If it's no imposition, Mr.

President, I could travel much farther today with an earlier start."

"I'll try to have it drafted by ten o'clock."

Dolly intervened before he could ask the courier to join them at the table. "If you'll stop at the kitchen," she said with a courteous but firm nod of dismissal, "you'll be given something to eat."

"Thank you, ma'am." The young man beat a hasty retreat.

"Why don't you insist that these people wait for you at your office?" she demanded as soon as she and John were alone.

"Every state thinks its problems are urgent—and so they are. Dealing with them requires the patience of the Archangel Gabriel."

"No, the President's wife must have that patience. Would you like some hot porridge?"

He shook his head and shuffled through the documents the messenger had left with him.

Dolly resisted the temptation to snatch them from his hands and throw them on the floor. "Then please try the veal and hard-boiled eggs. Veal is scarce these days."

"Thank you, my dear, but I'm not particularly hungry this morning."

Before she could reply with an angry retort that would be certain to precipitate another breakfast-table quarrel, the nursemaid she had brought to Philadelphia from Braintree appeared in the dining-room entrance, beckoning, and Dolly left the table. Glancing back over her shoulder, she saw that her husband was so deeply engrossed in his reading that he failed to realize he was now alone. Only the nursemaid's presence prevented her from making a scene.

A shrill scream of terror brought John to his feet.

Papers scattered on the floor as he raced to the nursery, where he found Dorothy weeping hysterically.

"I couldn't wake up the baby, Mr. Hancock," the nursemaid said in a broken voice. "She—she died in her sleep."

John reacted instantly, and took his wife in his arms. Words could not comfort her in this terrible moment, but he held her close, deftly pressing her face into his shoulder so she could not look at the still figure in the little bed.

Lydia looked so tiny, so fragile that he wanted to weep, too, but Dorothy's need for him was too great for him to give in to his own feelings.

"Find Dr. Rush," he told the nursemaid, and ignored Dorothy's protests. "No matter what he's doing, bring him here at once." It was too late to do anything for Lydia, but a dose of laudanum would soothe Dorothy and ease her shock in these first hours.

Gradually the weeping woman's hysteria subsided. John, still holding her, looked down at their daughter. Dorothy had been right when she had accused him, again and again, of treating the baby like a stranger because of his preoccupation with government business and the never-ending emergencies created by the war. A sense of impotence, of helpless guilt swept over him, yet he knew that, given the same circumstances again, his behavior would be no different. The demands of his beleaguered country were insatiable, and in his post of responsibility he could not shirk them.

Releasing Dorothy for an instant, John bent down and drew the sheet over Lydia's face. Then Dorothy clung to him again, comforted by a strength he was far from feeling. He stroked her, scarcely aware of what he was doing as he stared bleakly into space.

By now the anteroom of his office was filling, and people were besieging his harried secretaries for appointments. But this was one day when the business of the United States would have to wait.

4

"The next two or three months will decide our fate for all time, Mr. President." General Washington looked calm, as usual, despite the gravity of his pronouncement. "The reason I've come into the city to see you privately is because I didn't want to put any of my observations on paper."

"Surely you'll stay overnight with us, General." John spoke so warmly that it was obvious the invitation was sincere.

"Even if I dared to leave my troops for that long, sir, I wouldn't impose on Mrs. Hancock's grief."

"You made such a point of mentioning this visit to no one

that I've said nothing to her, General, but she'll feel far worse when she learns you couldn't avail yourself of her hospitality."

Washington returned his bow and, courtly gestures out of the way, got down to the business at hand. "The Congress has been concentrating on my defense of Philadelphia, and I've made no attempt to tell the members they're in error. I want Howe himself to think I consider Philadelphia of primary importance."

John was startled. "Don't you?"

"The campaign in the north is of far greater significance." Washington went to a map of the United States pinned to a wall and used a quill pen as a pointer. "Look here. Lord Burgoyne is moving south through New York through Lake Champlain. Another, smaller column of Loyalists and Indians under a rascal named St. Leger hopes to rendezvous with Burgoyne near Albany. If Lord Johnny succeeds, he'll cut off all of New York and New England. He can take the northern states at his leisure, digesting them one by one. Most of our industries are in those states—"

"I'm well aware, General, that the United States can't survive without New England. What are you doing to contain Burgoyne?"

"We'll have to smash him, not contain him, Mr. President. The frontier militia will have to look after St. Leger. Unfortunately, we just don't have enough men to use Continentals against him. You see, I've secretly sent off some of my divisions to join the Army of the North, and I have reason to suspect that Howe has reduced his own garrison in order to strengthen Burgoyne."

"One moment, General." John studied the map. "If the northern campaign is so important, shouldn't you be in command there yourself?"

The commander-in-chief allowed himself the rare luxury of a laugh. "I need hardly tell you that a general, like a head of state, can't be in two places simultaneously. It's unfortunate that General Schuyler had to retire because of his ill health and age, but I feel I have the best possible men in charge."

"I don't mind confessing to you, sir, that I'm not impressed by Horatio Gates."

"He's cautious, but Arnold will give the Army of the North all the fire it needs as his deputy."

"Shouldn't Arnold have been given the command, then?"

Had anyone else asked such a question, disputing the judgment of the commander, Washington's icy temper would have flared. But he returned the gaze of the haggard man to whom he was responsible, and replied gently. "Benedict Arnold is too impetuous. It's my hope that Gates will curb him, and that Arnold will inspire Gates. I've done all I can for them, and their campaign is now in their own hands. That brings me to the reason for this visit, sir. Howe believes he'll destroy the nation's will to fight if he takes our capital. He's beaten me twice on the approaches to the city, and he thinks I'll make a last stand to throw him back. I simply don't have the strength."

John was horrified. "He'll take Philadelphia, General?"

"I don't have the men or the artillery to stop him. What I'm trying to make you understand, Mr. President, is that it doesn't matter, basically. If Gates and Arnold can defeat Burgoyne, the British will have to pull back. They won't be able to hold Philadelphia for more than a few months."

"I see." John drew himself erect. "You're telling me to send Mrs. Hancock home to Boston—"

"Without delay!"

"—and to withdraw into the interior with the Congress."

"At once, Mr. President."

"I prefer a town in the interior to Baltimore." In spite of his fatigue, John was thinking clearly and rapidly. "It's a way of serving notice on the enemy—and making the whole country realize—that our evacuation of Philadelphia is only temporary."

Washington nodded solemnly.

"The people must be able to see for themselves that we're making a deliberate move far different from our disgraceful flight to Baltimore."

"It will be different," the commander-in-chief told him, "only if the Army of the North sends Burgoyne back to Canada in defeat."

"I won't allow myself to think of the alternative." John passed a hand across his face.

"Neither will I." They shook hands, and Washington hesitated for a moment. "Forgive my intrusion into your personal affairs, but are you in ill health, sir?"

"I've never felt better." John failed to realize that his protest was savage.

General Washington let the subject drop. America stood with her back to the wall, and in his own tired state he knew how John Hancock felt. A man so bone-weary could not admit his exhaustion for fear he might drop.

5

Huge bowls of oysters and clams in their shells filled the center of the round table, and the small group of Congressional leaders slit them open with sharp knives, ate them and washed them down with claret wine. But no one attending the gathering at Philadelphia's patrician Oyster Club was in a holiday mood, and the men listened silently as Robert Morris explained that the three million dollars in silver he had recently obtained in a loan from Spain was more than offset by the need to print another twenty-five million dollars in unbacked paper. Many of the states were now following the example of the Congress, he added, and the whole country was being flooded with paper that even the most patriotic merchants and farmers were reluctant to accept in return for shoes and breeches, flour and eggs and cheese.

John paused on the threshold of the private second-floor dining room, reluctant to interrupt, and did not join his colleagues until Morris had completed his recital of the nation's financial woes. Then, very quietly, he slipped into the vacant chair between Morris and John Adams. "Forgive my delay, gentlemen," he said in a voice hoarse with fatigue, "but I've just seen Mrs. Hancock and Mrs. Adams off to Boston."

The delegates had known nothing about the ladies' departure, and were startled.

"Luckily, only a few Congressional families are in the city at present, and I've already requested the heads of those households to send their wives and children home. You'll have to forgive my high-handed assumption of authority, but the present situation is too critical to waste time by submitting questions to Congressional committees."

Benjamin Harrison pushed a bowl of oysters toward the new-comer. "I can't remember a time when our situation wasn't critical." He sighed heavily.

John poured himself a little claret and opened an oyster, but was too tense to eat or drink. "This," he said, "is the ultimate crisis." He repeated his conversation with General Washington.

The Congressmen stirred, and Caesar Rodney of Delaware expressed the anguish of the entire group. "Are you suggesting that we take to our heels again?"

"I've already made the necessary arrangements, with the help of Mr. Morris," John said, seeing no need to dwell in detail on the frenzied activities of recent hours. "Couriers are rounding up the delegates for an emergency meeting at midnight tonight at Independence Hall. I shall demand a formal vote of approval, and at dawn we'll travel together to the town of Lancaster."

Some of the delegates looked blank, so Morris added, "It's sixty miles to the west, here in Pennsylvania. We'll pause there for a day or two, and then go on to the town of York, another twenty-four miles to the southwest."

"The reason we've selected these particular communities," John continued with a tired smile, "is because both have enough inns to feed and house us."

Henry Laurens of South Carolina, a wealthy retired planter, protested mildly. "The purses of some members may not be fat enough to stand the strain."

"I neglected to mention," John replied, "that Bob Morris and I have agreed to share the costs of transportation and of lodging those members who don't have funds of their own for the purpose."

Laurens, who had generously and repeatedly contributed to the American cause, looked hurt. "Why am I being excluded? It's my right to share these expenses with you."

John accepted graciously, as did Morris, and both bowed their thanks.

John Adams absently ate a clam. "Won't the citizens of Philadelphia believe—and with good reason—that we've deserted them?"

"I've prepared a statement under my signature," John said, "telling them the government can't and won't disband or allow itself to be captured. I made no mention of the military situation in the north, of course, as General Washington wouldn't appreciate our alerting Howe. I've hired seventy men to distribute copies to householders and post others in all prominent places. Philadelphia will be fully informed by breakfast time tomorrow morning. I'm also having some thousands of additional copies taken west with us so the members of Congress can send them to their state legislatures."

"Apparently you've thought of everything." Adams sipped the coffee he preferred to claret.

"I doubt it, Johnny, but I'm convinced there will be less panic throughout the country if the people understand our motives— at best I've been able to explain them without dwelling on the military problems." John shoved aside the bowl of oysters so he could gesture more broadly. "Let's proceed quickly, gentlemen. You form the Steering Committee, and I want to be able to inform the Congress tonight that our move has your unanimous consent."

Laurens, who was the chairman, restlessly swung an expensively booted foot and leg. "There are so many aspects to be considered that I'd like a little time to think about them."

"Sir William is giving us no time, Henry." John was so angered by the unexpected show of what he interpreted as opposition that his voice shook.

Morris put a restraining hand on his arm.

But his rage continued to mount. "You'll do your thinking in the brig of a man-of-war that will take you to England for trial. Damnation, Henry, you're not a fool, so use the wits that the good Lord gave you!"

Laurens' chair toppled over backward as he leaped to his feet.

John was too furious to realize he was insulting a valued and trusted colleague. "By this time tomorrow night, Lobsterback cavalry advance guards may be riding through the streets of Philadelphia. In the names of Satan and all his imps, what is there to think about?"

"You may be entirely correct in everything you say," Laurens replied in a cold, formal drawl, "but as a democratically elected delegate to a democratically representative government, I don't like being told what to do. It's my prerogative—and that of every other Congressman—to consider the merits of this situation and reach a sound conclusion."

"Do what you please, then, and be damned to you!" John knocked over his glass of claret as he, too, jumped to his feet. "Delay and argue and consider and debate all you please—if you think the Continentals will still fight after their government has been captured and cast into prison. Ponder to your heart's content in chains while whole battalions of militiamen desert. Force Ben Franklin and Silas Deane to ask for asylum from the French because the country they represent no longer exists. Yes, and watch Spain and Holland send in troops, too, to protect the loans they've given us." He tried to wrench free as John Adams gripped his arm.

Adams had never seen him in such a fury. Remembering a story John had told about his youth, he made a deliberate, desperate effort to prevent a fist fight. "John Hancock," he said, "you're a jackass!"

John wilted, color drained from his face and he would have fallen if Adams and Morris had not supported him. They lowered him to a chair, and Morris quickly handed him a glass of brandy-wine. He drank a little of it, then looked up in sheepish apology at the still indignant Laurens.

"I guess I really am a jackass. I—I don't know what came over me just now."

Laurens was quick to accept the gesture. "I'm as much to blame. You had the double advantage of talking with General Washington and then living with this crisis for hours, but the whole situation was new to me. I'll support your recommendations at the emergency meeting tonight." He held out his hand.

John still felt abashed as he shook it. He couldn't remember a previous occasion in his adult life when he had given in so completely to a wild and unreasonable temper. Even though the crisis was as grave as he had pictured it and he felt positive there was no solution other than that which he had already arranged, Laurens' position certainly was justified. Aware of the glances being exchanged by the men who were his closest associates, John couldn't help wondering whether, in this hour of supreme trial for the United States, he might be losing his mind.

6

Members of the Congress, some riding in carriages and others on horseback, with carts carrying the files and records of the government, reached the town of Lancaster in time to convene for a single meeting on October 27, 1777. Most of the delegates were tired after their long journey from Philadelphia, but good news awaited them. Colonel St. Leger's column of Loyalists, Indians, and Canadian volunteers had been soundly defeated by companies of frontier militiamen fighting for their lives. St. Leger's Indian allies had deserted him, and he had returned to Canada, harried on the trail by wilderness riflemen.

Burgoyne was still pushing in the direction of Albany, apparently unaware that St. Leger would not be able to rendezvous with him there. He, too, was encountering difficulties, and the members of the Congress cheered when John announced that troops sent into the Vermont District to obtain supplies for Lord Johnny had been mauled at the town of Bennington by the soft-spoken Colonel John Stark and his militiamen. State troops, it was now evident, could hold their own with Continentals.

The fall of Philadelphia to Sir William Howe's redcoats had been expected, and the news was received quietly.

On October 30 the Congress established itself at the town of York, convening at the Provincial Courthouse, which was barely large enough for the purpose. Accommodations were scarce, but John was able to engage a suite of two rooms at an inn on King Street that, ironically, was still called the George. He soon discovered, however, that conditions would not allow him to live in the style to which he had become accustomed since his adoption by Thomas Hancock, and he offered to share the rooms with the Adams cousins.

Food was plentiful in the hill country, and thrifty farmers of German descent came into the markets of York every morning with tubs of butter, round loaves of bread their wives had baked before dawn and baskets piled high with eggs, cheeses, and more fruits and vegetables than the delegates had seen in their long sojourn in Philadelphia. Trout and other fish ran in the hill rivers, deer and other game abounded in the nearby forests and even the most pessimistic of Congressmen became more cheerful when they traveled through the district and saw well-tended herds of cattle, fenced pigpens and extensive poultry yards.

Three enterprising young men started work at once on the construction of a large new inn on Queen Street, promising they would put in a taproom that would rival any in the United States. Local beer was brewed in the German fashion, and was much mellower than that which the seaboard residents had drunk all their lives. The ale was good, too, and although strong spirits were scarce, the beekeepers of York brewed a mead that was delicious.

The delegates settled down in contentment, Dr. Franklin's transplanted presses began to print huge new batches of Continental dollars and the members hailed the genius of President Hancock, who had brought them to this new Eden.

John did not share their joy. Food had lost its savor and, unable to sleep, he began to spend the better part of his nights as well as his days working at a desk in a tiny office behind the courtroom in which the Congress met. It was difficult to communicate with the state capitals from this little town, more than one hundred miles west of Philadelphia, and on several occasions he worked himself into rages while setting up efficient courier services, which he financed out of his own pocket.

He was not satisfied until he had hired enough messengers and bought enough horses to establish mail exchanges on a regular basis with the legislatures and General Washington's headquarters in the field near occupied Philadelphia.

The new nation had been in revolt for more than two and one-half years, but her problems were multiplying. Washington, calmer in adversity than in the rare moments of victory he had enjoyed, wrote that he needed food, clothing, and blankets; deserters were disappearing with sorely needed arms, and General Henry Knox, the Boston bookseller who had become his artillery chief, was embarrassed by a lack of cannon and shot. Benjamin Franklin sent the President a witty letter from Paris describing the splendors of the court and household of Louis XVI, the excellent Bordeaux wine available at eight cents per pint, the beauty of French girls and the stimulating atmosphere at the University of Paris, where he frequently lectured. He added in postscript, all the more significant because of its seemingly casual tone, that neither King Louis nor the Count de Vergennes, his Foreign Secretary, would give serious consideration to the recognition of the United States as a nation until American troops proved themselves capable of defeating the British in a major campaign.

The New England states were engaged in a bitter dispute, each claiming the right to charge the others' privateers for the right to harbor space. Maryland farmers refused to send their produce into Pennsylvania, and there was such chaos in Virginia that Thomas Jefferson resigned from the Congress in order to re-enter his state's legislature, where he hoped to reduce the confusion.

Only Henry Laurens, who had become John's ally since their brief quarrel at the Oyster Club in Philadelphia, shared the President's concern over what appeared to be a nation-wide deterioration of the ability to wage war effectively. Robert Morris worried because more than one hundred million dollars in unbacked paper money had now been issued by the Congress and the states. The problems of foreign relations and West Indian trade held John Adams' attention, Elbridge Gerry and a half-dozen others concentrated on the formation of a Navy that would break the British blockade, and Roger Sherman encouraged the individual states to enlarge and intensify the training of militia battalions. Sam Adams' preoccupation with liberty, as such, seemed somewhat old-fashioned now, everyone else taking it for granted that freedom of the individual would be assured if the Americans won. Only John and Laurens were concerned with the details of what would happen if the former colonies were vanquished.

Snow fell early, slowing communications between the York hills and the outside world, and in mid-November John started to write a proclamation that would extend the Massachusetts autumn holiday in remembrance of her first settlers, Thanksgiving, to the other states. He submitted his draft to his colleagues on a day when the Congress was meeting as a committee of the whole and, as he had anticipated, was almost overwhelmed when a bitter wrangle developed over the wording of the document.

The faces of the members blurred, their voices became indistinct and he had to grip the sides of the rostrum to keep his balance as the debate droned on. He found it difficult to concentrate, and wished that Jefferson were there to prepare a succinct Thanksgiving proclamation that everyone could accept without argument. What he had intended as a unifying gesture was being used to promote regional causes, the New Englanders supporting the publication of a proclamation, others claiming that a section of the country other than their own was being glorified at their expense.

John's attention was diverted when a booted and spurred courier came into the courthouse and brought him a letter. He broke the seal, which he recognized as Washington's and beads of cold perspiration broke out on his forehead as he read the letter.

Several delegates were on their feet, clamoring for recognition from the chair, but John summarily gaveled for silence. "Sit down!" he ordered brusquely.

Even friends who sympathized with him were startled by his lack of civility.

"Gentlemen," he said, speaking loudly to overcome the huskiness of his voice, "I have just received a communication that takes precedence over all other business before this body. General Washington informs me that General Gates' Army of the North has won a great victory. Lord Burgoyne was defeated in a fierce engagement at Saratoga, in New York. He and most of his army have been made prisoners of war. Our own casualties were low. General Arnold, who performed great feats of valor and whose conduct may have won the field for us, was wounded. He has survived, however, and is recuperating in Albany."

John paused for a moment, and his voice broke when he resumed. "A miracle has occurred, gentlemen, a miracle that answers all our prayers for the future of our nation. I feel confident that Dr. Franklin will now win the official recognition of the French monarchy, and that King Louis will give us the help we need. It is not rash of me to predict that we will soon have arms —including artillery. We will have all that we need in ammunition and powder. It is not too much to hope that the French fleet will come to the aid of our own infant Navy and the ships of our states' fleets.

"The recognition accorded us by France will be only the beginning. Great Britain has many enemies in Europe, and it is my conviction that all of them will come to our assistance.

"Far more important than the help from foreign lands is our gain in self-esteem. Now, at last, our people will know, for all time, that the British regiments of King George and his German mercenaries are not invincible. Americans from thirteen states have fought side by side, as brothers, and have vanquished a powerful, ruthless foe sent from across the sea to enslave them.

"Rejoice, gentlemen, as all Americans will rejoice. Mark well this victory, and learn from it. Just as troops from Georgia and New Hampshire buried their petty differences and stood together, so can you forget your quarrels to work side by side for that final victory which will and must be ours."

As the delegates cheered lustily, John looked out at the assemblage with glazed eyes. The courthouse seemed to spin before him, and before he could grasp the rostrum again, he slumped to the floor and lost consciousness.

7

Dr. Benjamin Rush planted his feet apart, clasped his hands behind his back and looked down at the pale man whose head was propped up by pillows. "Both of my colleagues agree with my diagnosis, Mr. President. You've driven yourself without mercy for years. You need a period of complete rest, for a minimum of two to four months, and I recommend that you go home, where your wife can look after you."

John shook his head, ignoring the ache in his temples when he moved. "I've told you, Doctor, the boiled trout I ate for my breakfast must have disagreed with me."

The physician's smile was firm. "You've been in a bad humor for months, as every member of the Congress can tell you. You've lost so much weight that your clothes no longer fit you."

"That, sir, is due to the fact that Pennsylvania water stretches them when they're washed."

"I'm sorry, Mr. President, but I've given you my opinion, and your arguments won't sway me. We're dealing with a medical subject now, not a political matter to be decided on the floor of the Congress." Dr. Rush moved a step closer to his patient. "A sentry of nineteen or twenty becomes weak and sickly if he's forced to remain on his feet too long without proper food and sleep. The same thing has happened to you, Mr. President, but I need hardly remind you that you aren't a boy of twenty. You're well advanced into your middle years."

John glared at him with more ferocity than dignity.

Dr. Rush averted his face for a moment to hide his smile, then sobered. "I can't compel you to follow my advice, Mr. President. I've written to Mrs. Hancock, hoping she'll exert her influence on you—"

"Neither she nor anyone else can force me to abandon work vital to the future of the United States."

The physician shrugged.

"What's more, Doctor, I'm disinclined to trust any member of your profession. You tell me I must rest for two to four months, but what guarantees can you give me that I won't be invalided for a year or even longer?"

"None, sir," Rush replied bluntly. "Your future will depend in part on the care you give your body, and in part on the way your body responds. No medical practitioner can predict how long that process will take. What I can and do say to you is that I won't be responsible for the consequences if you neglect your health."

"I'm needed here!"

"And I must visit two other delegates who are ailing before the start of today's session." Rush inclined his head and hurried out.

John could hear him conferring in low tones with someone in the adjoining room, and a moment later Sam Adams came into the bedroom, muffled in a shabby dressing gown.

"All I need," John told his friend in a sudden burst of indignation, "is a few bottles of good port to thicken my blood. I'll be myself again in a day or two."

Sam raised an eyebrow, returned to his own room and came back with a glass of port wine. "The English make a better port than the Spaniards, I must hand the devils their due. But you'll drink Spanish wine because there's nothing else in town."

John accepted the glass and raised it in a toast.

His friend sat down in a chair near the open hearth and regarded him morosely. "Doctors are cowards, you know. Rush is a member of the Congress in good standing, so he could have told you himself. But he insisted that I do it. Whenever there's something unpleasant to be done these days, I'm given the assignment."

"Damnation, what are you talking about?"

"Don't raise your voice, John, or that Mrs. Pfessinger we hired as your nurse will throw me out. This is harder than I thought. I believe I'll have a drop of wine myself." Sam went out again, returning with a brimming goblet.

"Now, sir, if you'll be good enough—"

"Easy, lad. Last night Dr. Rush held a meeting with the Steering Committee and the chairmen of all other committees. An informal meeting. He gave us a frank report on your health, and read us the letter he'd written to Cousin Dorothy."

"A minor case of indigestion caused by a spoiled fish is nobody's damned business but my own!"

"Two days and nights in bed haven't improved your disposition," Sam said mildly. "Well, lad, after Rush left us, we sat around together, talking. And we finally reached a consensus, you might call it. There was no vote, nothing as formal as that, but all of us were agreed on what must be done."

"You don't usually beat around the bush, Sam. What are you trying to say to me?"

"Let me do this in my own way. The United States still has a long climb, but Gates and Arnold cleared away the underbrush at Saratoga, and we can see the road ahead now. Your little speech before you fainted summed up the situation rather nicely, and the reports that have come in yesterday and early this morning confirm our victory. The real task now isn't going to be in the Congress. Young Jefferson was right to go back to Virginia. I'm thinking, myself, of giving up my seat here in January. I think I can do more good by making the General Court see that Massachusetts must learn to cooperate with the other states."

"I'm well aware of the need for the states to work together!"

Sam ignored the interruption. "Laurens has taken over as President *pro tempore*, and he's doing a fine and fair job. He lacks many of your good qualities, but the Congress doesn't require a man of your strength now."

John braced himself.

"Hellfire, lad, I'll tell you plain. Your friends—and by God, everyone here is your friend—know you won't spare yourself. They insist you take a leave of absence for an indefinite period of months."

"I won't! No one can force me—"

"If you refuse, it was the consensus of the Steering Committee and the chairmen that the Congress will be required to ask for your resignation. If there's a formal vote, it will be unanimous, because every last delegate is concerned about your health."

John stared at him in stunned silence. Dr. Rush had convinced the Congress he was a sick man, and the delegates didn't want to be burdened by an invalid President. Sam was telling him, gently but emphatically, that his life of public service had come to an end at the age of forty-one, and he had to accept the blow, hold his head high and put up as good a front as he could to conceal his pain.

8

My Dear General Washington, Sir:

It is now above two years since I have had the honor of presiding in the Congress, and I should esteem myself happy to render further service to my country in that department. But the decline of health occasioned by so long and unremitting an application to the duties of my office, both in the Congress and out of the Congress, joined to the situation of my own private affairs, has at length taught me to think of retiring to my home in Boston for two or three months.

You may hear that my retirement will be of longer duration, but I beg you, dear General, do not believe such calumnies. I shall return to the service of the country we both love at my earliest opportunity.

Whilst abed I had little to occupy my mind other than the reading of a long poem by John Milton, which I find exceedingly dull. It has therefore been my pleasure to dwell on our association and to review the intercourse between us.

I feel a great degree of pleasure in having endeavored to

execute the business committed to my care and, in a particular manner, with regard to the Army under your command. I flatter myself my conduct will meet with your approbation. The politeness and attention I have ever experienced from you will always be a source of the most pleasant satisfaction to me.

I am, sir, ever

Your humble svt.,

John Hancock

My Dear President Hancock, Sir:

It gives me real pain to learn that the declining state of your health obliges you to relinquish a station which you have so long filled with acknowledged propriety. Motives, as well of a personal as of a general concern, make me regret the necessity that compels you to retire and to wish your absence from office may be of as short a duration as possible. In the progress of that intercourse which has necessarily subsisted between us, the manner in which you have conducted it, accompanied with every expression of politeness and regard to me, gives you a claim to my warmest acknowledgements. In brief, dear Mr. President, you will be sorely missed by the nation, the Congress and the author of this too brief letter.

I must confess to you that the prospect of your journey to Boston fills me with misgivings. Although you will travel in the role of a private citizen, our foes nonetheless regard you as the principal architect of our liberties, and would take great joy in your capture. I am taking steps to prevent that unfortunate event. An escort of horse will await you at Bethlehem, and will accompany you to the headquarters of General Israel Putnam at Fishkill, New York. I have instructed General Putnam to provide you with another escort from that place to your home.

I, and our countrymen with me, hope you will soon be re-

stored to health and to the service of the nation, which will miss you during your absence.
I remain, sir, ever

Your obdt. svt.,

G. Washington.

9

Hundreds of citizens, running from their homes and offices, passed the word that the first citizen of Massachusetts had come home for the first time since the beginning of the war. Thousands packed the streets, an impromptu parade was organized, and wave after wave of cheers accompanied the dusty carriage. John made a great effort to respond, but the long ride from York had been so debilitating that he could barely raise a feeble hand to wave occasionally, and his smile was forced.

His only feeling was one of annoyance. Boston was giving him a hero's welcome greater than any man had ever enjoyed, but he was too weak and sickly to enjoy it. Had he been a shade stronger, the knowledge would have infuriated him.

Boston looked bigger than he had remembered it, and seemed surprisingly prosperous. Several large new buildings had risen to replace those destroyed by the British just prior to their evacuation, and the people appeared warmly clad and well fed. Only the absence of young men in their late teens, twenties, and early thirties was a reminder that the capital of Massachusetts and first city of New England was at war.

Scores of men and children, accompanied by a surprising number of women, ran beside General Putnam's cavalry escort as the carriage made its way slowly up Beacon Hill, and John roused himself. His first reaction when he caught sight of the Hancock mansion was that it needed paint. The coating of whitewash on the picket fence was too thin, the grounds hadn't been raked and the long grass should have been burned off earlier in the autumn.

A group of men was clustered at the main entrance, and it suddenly occurred to John that there would be speeches of welcome, to which he would be expected to reply. He tried to think of a brief, patriotic statement that would be appropriate for the occasion, but his mind refused to function. He had needed two days to prepare a short farewell address to the Congress that ordinarily would have required no more than an hour to write, and in his frustration he petulantly decided he would have to repeat portions of it now.

The carriage pulled to a halt, Putnam's dragoons dismounted and two of them helped the former President from his coach. His clothes hung loosely on his bony frame, the silk stock that encircled his neck drooped almost to his collarbones and only his feathered tricorn was jaunty. Dolly came forward, and neither demonstrated her sense of shock nor burst into tears.

John clung to her for a moment, then forced himself to stand erect to face the members of the committee sent by the General Court to greet him. Calling on his last reserves of strength, he shook hands with each and murmured a few personal words.

Thomas Cushing realized the welcoming ceremonies would have to be sharply curtailed, however. "Gentlemen," he said, "President Hancock's journey home has taken more than two and a half years, so he's understandably weary. I suggest we postpone our remarks of welcome and call again another day."

"No!" John refused to let his return be marred by a lack of hospitality on his part. "I'll want all of you to come in for a cup of flip. My dear, General Putnam's squadron of brave young men need a hearty meal. And these good people," he added, gesturing weakly in the direction of the citizens who were still arriving on the grounds in large numbers, "must be given refreshments."

Dolly exchanged a helpless glance with Cushing. Entertainment on such a vast scale was ludicrous under the circumstances, but the head of the house of Hancock could not be denied.

Servants were sent scurrying to the kitchens to make a punch for the crowd, the soldiers were led to the dining room and John, supported by Cushing and Dolly, led the members of the General Court into the main parlor. There he was seated in a cushioned chair before the fire, and even before the arrival of the major domo with flip for his guests, he rallied sufficiently to launch into a discussion of local politics.

"Have you named the Whig candidate for town moderator yet?"

William Winthrop, a descendant of the founder of the Massachusetts Bay Colony, ignored Cushing's head shake. "We've been hoping you'd serve in the post as well as accept re-election to the Congress."

John beamed. "I'll be delighted, Billy." He looked up as his wife came into the room after completing her hasty arrangements for the various entertainments. "Dorothy, with the weather this cold in December, Boston will have a most unpleasant winter. Arrange with the major domo, if you will, to have one hundred and fifty cords of firewood made available to the poor." He could see his guests were impressed, and couldn't resist the temptation to enlarge on the theme. "We'll store it in the stable sheds, as we did in the years before the war, and anyone in need of wood can help himself to a supply."

The crowd in the yard outside gave three cheers for President Hancock as servants in livery appeared with bowls of punch, and then began to sing "Yankee Doodle."

Another broad smile crossed John's pale, lined face. But, no matter how pleasant he found the adulation of his fellow citizens, there were more important matters on his mind. "Did any of you bring me the secretary's record of the General Court proceedings?"

His guests were unable to conceal their surprise. None of them had dreamed that a man forced to resign from the Presidency of the Continental Congress because of ill health would be concerned about recent activities of the Massachusetts legislature.

"I want to see the secretary's minutes for the past six months, including the full voting records of every member."

The gentlemen were forcibly reminded that, healthy or ill, the request was being made by the head of the Whig party.

"I also want the Boston town meeting accounts, and I'll be obliged to the town meeting moderators of the smaller towns for all figures on finances, taxes, and militia recruiting."

Winthrop coughed discreetly behind his hand. "They're very

cautious about the release of recruiting totals to anyone except the military."

There was no humor now in John's smile. "In case you've forgotten it, Billy, I'm the highest-ranking officer in the Massachusetts militia. The senior brigadier has been acting in my stead, but I'm the commander. While I'm at it," he added after allowing the gentle rebuke to sink in, "I want a full report from the General Court monetary committee on the amounts of paper currency printed and the silver reserves in the vaults."

The guests were silent.

"I presume we do have a silver reserve?"

"Of course, John." Cushing was half-apologetic, half-defiant. "We simply didn't know that an invalid would want to make such a thorough survey of the state's affairs."

"I have no intention of rotting like a discarded ship's timber while I regain my strength. Tom, I'm not sure I approve of the bond issue you plan to float in order to raise funds. Your note to York telling me about it was sketchy, and I'd like a full explanation so I can explore the idea in detail with you. Perhaps you'll be good enough to call on me here tomorrow. Oh, yes, and before I forget it, I'll need the services of two secretaries. One of them should know enough of political affairs to prepare correspondence on his own initiative for my signature."

Dolly was becoming visibly upset. "Dr. Rush wrote me that you're to have a complete rest," she protested.

"So I shall," her husband replied genially. "I intend to sleep until six-thirty every morning, an hour later than usual, and I'll spend most of my days right here at home. I hope we have enough horses for me to ride for an hour or two every day. I'm badly in need of stretching my muscles."

Cushing hastily drained his cup of flip, and at his signal the others did the same.

John was disturbed when they stood simultaneously. "Not so fast, lads. I'm anxious to learn about progress on the new frigate that will replace the captured *Hancock*."

Winthrop edged toward the door. "She was on schedule the last time I stopped in at the yard."

"How long ago was that?"

"About two weeks."

"A great deal can happen to a warship in two weeks. Ask the yard superintendent to stop in here at around three tomorrow afternoon, will you, Billy? He might bring the naval architect with him. I haven't yet seen the detailed plans of the frigate, and I might want to suggest some modifications."

Massachusetts' political leaders finally managed to escape, and John was alone with his wife.

"Welcome home, dear," she said.

He allowed himself a small sigh.

"I've arranged to have dinner served upstairs tonight." Dolly helped him to his feet, showing more firmness than gentleness.

"I can walk without help," John muttered.

She paid no attention, and kept an arm around him. "Lean on me."

They moved slowly to the staircase, and he held on to the railing as they climbed to the second floor. Pausing for a few moments at the landing, John started toward the stairs that led to the third floor, but Dolly halted him. "To be sure," he said with a faint smile, "we'll be sleeping in the master suite now." He let her lead him toward it, and halted at the entrance. "For the first time, I realize how badly I miss Uncle Thomas and Aunt Lydia." Shaking off his feeling of depression, he smiled at his wife. "You're the mistress in this house at last."

There was such emotion in his voice that she refrained from reminding him that she had spent many weeks in the house since returning to Boston from Philadelphia.

He gazed at the familiar sitting room and, beyond it, the chamber dominated by a huge four-poster bed. "What happened to the cushioned chair that faced the fireplace here? It was of cherry wood, and Aunt Lydia embroidered the covers for the back and seat herself."

"I moved it downstairs. It was far too large for this room."

"Please have it moved back, Dorothy. It's the most comfortable chair in the house. Uncle Thomas always sat in it, so I didn't ask for it after he died, but now that Aunt Lydia is gone, too, it's mine." Something else puzzled him for a moment. "Ah. There was an old blunderbuss over the hearth."

"The tapestry I've put there is much prettier," Dolly said defensively, "and in summer I want to keep bowls of fresh flowers on the mantel."

"Fill the whole house with flowers, if that will make you happy," he told her, "but I want the blunderbuss here."

She supposed she shouldn't argue with a man in ill health, but she wasn't ready to give in so quickly. "It's ugly. And it's a reminder of wars."

"It belonged to my great-grandfather, and the proper place for it is right here." He spoke more softly when he saw her lower lip tremble. "Decorate your sewing room as you please, my dear. I think I can spare five hundred dollars for anything new you might want to get."

Dolly knew he was buying her assent, and realized she had to take a stand. "This suite is ours, John—it's mine as much as it is yours."

"Naturally." He thought it wise to miss the point she was trying to make, and hurriedly changed the subject. "You wrote to me that you engaged men to paint the inside of the house. When are they coming?"

"I've made tentative arrangements for week after next, but I can delay them—"

"No, that will be perfect. By then I'll have my headquarters set up in the Hancock offices again. By the way, be sure they keep the same colors in these rooms. Green in the bedchamber and gray in here."

She had planned a different color scheme for the suite, and had already ordered new drapes and bed curtains made in blue to match the blue she wanted for the walls. But it was useless to tell him what she had intended, just as it would be a waste of breath to explain that the sitting room had been white, but that smoke from the hearth had smudged it through the years.

John had no idea what was going through her mind, and sank gratefully onto a divan. "Now I'm really home," he said.

"I'm very happy, dear, for both of us." She decided to go ahead with her own plans for the suite. He would raise a storm, of course, because he was congenitally incapable of leaving decisions to anyone else, even in the most picayune matters. But, no matter how loudly he protested, the suite would be redecorated as she wanted it, and he would soon become accustomed to the changes.

Dolly moved to a bell rope and, as she rang for a servingmaid, decided not to tell John what she had ordered for dinner. If she gave him the chance, he would insist that the entire menu be altered. In the rented lodgings that had been their dwelling places in Philadelphia and Baltimore she had found it easy enough to give in to his whims, as she really hadn't cared about the details of living there. But this house would be her home for the rest of their lives, and it was high time that the master of the Hancock mansion, whom no man dared dispute, learned that she was its mistress in more than name.

10

The Long Room Club had changed so drastically in spirit, purpose, and even physical appearance that only its name remained the same. Ousted from the premises of the rapidly expanding *Gazette*, it now occupied its own building adjacent to a tavern, the Patriot. A connecting door linked the two establishments, and club members could order food and drink from early morning breakfast to late night supper. The furniture in the club's quarters was substantial, comfortable, and decorative, most of it having been contributed by its wealthiest member, who had been elected president soon after his return to Boston from York.

Shipowners, merchants, and bankers had joined in large numbers, and independence was now taken for granted. Occasionally the atmosphere was martial, and prominent Bostonians were pleased to attend a reception that John gave for a German adventurer-officer, Baron Friedrich Wilhelm Ludolf Gerhard Augustin von Steuben, who had come to the United States to offer General Washington his services. But profits were as important to the gentlemen as the progress of the war, now that a French fleet had arrived off the coast to help protect Yankee shipping. So the members contented themselves with paying their respects to the Baron, who had been promised the post of Inspector General of the Army, and let John assume some thousands of dollars' worth of bills for baronial wages, horses, equipment, and other expenses.

Politicians, including virtually all representatives who sat in the General Court, made the Long Room Club their unofficial headquarters, and John reigned supreme in their company until the Adams cousins returned to Boston when the Continental Congress adjourned. Rivalries were temporarily forgotten when a formal treaty of alliance was signed with France, however, and a new round of social activities began when a powerful French fleet commanded by Comte Jean Baptiste d'Estaing arrived at the city.

Sam Adams, who still felt ill at ease at receptions, sourly criticized a party for five hundred that John gave at the club in the French commander's honor, and refused to attend a still larger affair the following day at the Hancock mansion. But John ignored his old friend's shortsightedness, and his generous enthusiasm paid enormous dividends. D'Estaing had been squabbling with American commanders jealous of their prerogatives, tempers became short when a joint Franco-American campaign to liberate British-held Newport, Rhode Island, failed, and the naval officer refrained from carrying out a threatened return to France only because John's hospitality overwhelmed him.

Major General the Marquis de Lafayette, a noble young French volunteer who had become one of Washington's most trusted senior officers, wrote to the commander-in-chief that only the tact and lavish expenditure of vast sums on the vain D'Estaing had prevented the rupture of the new alliance.

John appreciated the warm letter of thanks he received from General Washington, but matters of far greater concern than the soothing of ruffled feelings occupied his mind in 1778. Even though the military situation was improving, and Washington led a hardened, disciplined corps into the field after spending a winter of terrible hardships in his winter quarters at Valley Forge, the country was in danger of disintegrating just when the goal of real independence was at last within reach.

The states were refusing to grant the Continental Congress enough power to coordinate the war effort and carry the struggle to a successful conclusion. The country looked to Massachusetts for leadership, as everyone had done in the years prior to the break with England, and Sam Adams brought the crisis to a head by writing a long, impassioned editorial in the *Gazette* condemning the principle of centralized authority.

John read the newspaper at breakfast, and immediately sent Sam an invitation to join him for noon dinner at the Long Room Club. They met in the taproom, but merchants and politicians alike were so anxious to eavesdrop on their conversation that, at John's insistence, they adjourned to a small, private chamber, where they were served oyster chowder, fried bear steak that had been marinated for three days in wine and grilled lambs' kidneys.

Sam, seedier than ever, knew this was no social occasion, and not until he finished his second pint of ale did he relax his wary vigilance enough to observe a few amenities. "Elizabeth tells me Cousin Dorothy is going to have another baby."

John worried more about his wife's pregnancy than he was willing to admit. "Yes, we're very pleased and excited," he said, speaking too quickly and casually.

"I hope you have a boy, and that he'll show a liking for your business."

"My only business is that of the United States. I'm not reopening the merchant house."

Sam raised an eyebrow, bracing himself.

"Right now," John continued, coming straight to the point, "my concern is the ratification of the Articles of Confederation by the states. The Congress needs the power to fight the war and negotiate the peace after we've won. Congress is the only body that can send ministers to foreign countries and direct their work. It's damned foolishness to think that a committee of state legislature representatives could manage. We need a national currency—and only a national currency. Right now each of the states is printing money—and so is the Congress. Our credit will be ruined if we don't organize more efficiently. Yes, and the Congress must have the exclusive right to borrow from foreign governments. It was outrageous last month when New Jersey and Delaware tried to negotiate independent loans with France."

"There's no need to tell you where I stand," Sam replied. "I made my position clear in the *Gazette*."

"I also believe," John said firmly, "that the Congress must have the right to tax the people. A government that can't levy taxes is no government."

Sam's face darkened.

"Oh, I realize it will be a few years before we persuade the legislatures they've got to give the national government the right to tax. And I'm willing to be patient a little longer—on that one subject. But if the Articles of Confederation are rejected, we'll have thirteen countries, not one. And England can gather us back into the fold, one at a time."

"If you're trying to persuade me to change my mind, John, you're wasting your breath."

"I know you too well for that. I'm in your debt, Sam, as long as I live. We've been good friends as well as associates. But I'm going to fight you in the open on this issue, if I must."

"Then that's what you'll have to do. What's your battleground?"

"The General Court. I'm going to use every means at my disposal to push through approval of the Articles of Confederation. The other states are waiting for Massachusetts to show them the way. And show it we will." He smiled and pushed a platter across the table. "Try some more of this bear steak. It's a recipe I learned from some of the German settlers at York, but our cook at home added some herbs to give it still more flavor."

Sam had completely lost interest in food. "Do you think you can get a majority in the General Court to go along with you?"

"I can try, although I hate letting the British see that you and I have fallen out. But it can't be helped."

"It seems to me," Sam said, his temper flaring, "that you're trying to impose your ideas of government on the whole country."

John helped himself to another slice of steak. "Isn't that what you're doing?"

"But I'm right!"

"In a democracy, the majority is right. The issues must be presented clearly and honestly, so people can decide for themselves. You gave your views sharply in the *Gazette* today. Will you give me space to present mine?"

Sam laughed wryly.

"Then you force me to inform the electorate in other ways." John was tempted to say something about Sam's criticism of the entertainments for the Comte d'Estaing, but decided their friendship was already being subjected to a strain that might destroy it. "Let me tell you just one thing. I've spent the better part of my fortune on the United States and risked my life in the bargain. I value money, and I respect human life. But my sacrifices have been minor. Thousands of our soldiers have been killed and wounded. Merchants in occupied cities have been ruined. I believe I'll be disloyal to my trust if I don't fight you with every weapon I can get my hands on. These kidneys are delicious, if you're partial to garlic. I am."

11

A pamphlet entitled *Your Articles of Confederation* was distributed by the thousands in Massachusetts, and created such a favorable impression that members of the Continental Congress in other states requested copies. John had more printed, and sent them to his colleagues at his own expense. As the population of the United States had now grown to approximately two and one-half million, he estimated that four hundred thousand copies were needed, and he spent twenty-five thousand dollars on the project.

The *Gazette* ridiculed the pamphlet and its sponsor, but John made no reply until, suddenly, a new newspaper, the Boston *Patriot*, made an unexpected appearance. It was published twice each week, and devoted all of its editorials to the need for a strong national government. Readers were urged to direct their representatives in the General Court to vote in favor of the Articles of Confederation, and the editorial arguments were presented calmly and dispassionately.

Sam Adams made the mistake of directing a violent campaign of vituperation against John Hancock, whom he accused of wanting to set up his own royal dynasty in Massachusetts. Readers of the *Gazette* refused to believe such nonsense, and public sympathy for John—and for his cause—increased immeasurably. Sam changed his tune and concentrated on the actual issues for and against Confederation, but by then the damage was done.

Refreshments were served nightly on the grounds of the Hancock mansion to all citizens, and John mingled freely with his guests, drinking cups of punch with them and eating strips of smoking venison with his fingers. He made no formal speeches in favor of the Articles, but missed no opportunity to discuss them with the men from all walks of life who accepted his hospitality.

The Boston clergy united in support of the Articles, and each Sunday impassioned sermons were made on the subject. Sam Adams' most faithful supporter in the General Court, James Bowdoin, conducted a quiet investigation, and discovered that the ever-generous John Hancock had made a substantial contribution to every church in the city. He had been careful to ask for nothing in return, however, so the fuming Sam could not claim that the clergymen had been bribed.

Finally, only two days before the question of the acceptance or rejection of the Articles was to be decided in the General Court, John gave a garden party for all members and their wives. A display of too much extravagance was considered in bad taste when the country was at war, but John blithely dazzled his guests, lavishing them with a bewildering variety of foods and wines served by footmen in livery. Dolly, who was expecting her child at any time, appeared at her husband's side when he asked for silence and begged the indulgence of the company to make a few remarks.

Sam Adams had predicted that John would make a speech begging for support, and his adherents, who did not object to eating John's delicacies or drinking his French wines, laughed cynically. The host, standing on a chair, favored them with a benign smile, however, and seemed undisturbed.

"Ladies and gentlemen," he said, "the time has come to reveal the purpose of this little gathering. I have asked you here to celebrate two events of great significance. Sir Henry Clinton, the new British commander-in-chief, has evacuated Philadelphia."

The company started to cheer, but he raised a hand for quiet.

"Only this evening," he went on, "I have received word that General Washington attacked the enemy at Monmouth, New Jersey, while Clinton was trying to withdraw his forces to New York Town. Our victory was not complete, but it is the greatest we've yet won. The Continental Army is now a force worthy of the United States."

He stepped down from the chair as the guests applauded, and the anti-Confederation men were dismayed by his shrewdness. The British withdrawal from Philadelphia and the American victory at Monmouth were far more effective than any speaker in proving that a national government could achieve more than the individual states could accomplish.

Dolly went back into the house, and her husband strolled around the garden, playing his role of host perfectly as he sipped Madeira from a silver cup. Even Bowdoin was forced to admit that Hancock luck seemed to be unfailing.

The party continued far into the night, but John vanished into the house when a servant came to him and whispered something in his ear. No one thought his disappearance unusual until messengers were seen hurrying off down Beacon Hill. Within the next half-hour three physicians arrived at the mansion, the ladies guessed correctly that Mrs. Hancock was in labor and the party came to a quiet, rather abrupt end.

Bowdoin reported the news to Sam Adams, who raised his hands in despair. "John couldn't have done better if he'd arranged all this himself," he said. "Philadelphia, Monmouth—and now a new baby to win him still more support. And damn my soul, he was the one who wanted a vote on the Articles decided on the merits alone. He's done more in one night to play on the feelings of the members than I've done in all the time I've been back in Boston."

John was unable to appreciate the improved potential of the political cause he favored, however. Unwilling to let others see him in a time of stress when he might give way to his emotions, he rejected the suggestion of the physicians that he ask a friend or two to wait with him. He tried to keep busy by working on the account books of Harvard College, but could not concentrate on figures. As treasurer of Harvard he was responsible for the school's funds, and he knew he had long neglected his duties there, but every sound he heard from the room directly above his library caused him to stiffen, and he soon abandoned his fruitless task.

He paced the library endlessly, twice accepted mugs of coffee from a servant but forgot to drink them and, as dawn approached, discovered he was ravenously hungry. He was ashamed to ask for food while his wife was still in travail, however, and stubbornly refused to order anything for himself when he had platters of meat and bread sent up to the physicians and the two midwives assisting them.

The sun was rising when a servingmaid came to the library door and beckoned.

John abandoned his dignity and bolted up the stairs two at a time. He had heard no welcome cry from a newborn infant, and he was filled with dread as he pushed open the door of the master suite and hurried to the threshold of the bedchamber. Dorothy's blue drapes were tightly closed, and he held his breath for a moment when he saw that the blue curtains hanging from the frame of the four-poster were shut, too.

Several women were standing together near the bed, speaking in low tones, and John drew a deep breath as one of them, a midwife, came to him.

"Congratulations, Mr. Hancock," she said.

He didn't hear her, and pointed toward the closed bed curtains.

"Mrs. Hancock is sleeping now, sir. The doctors gave her a strong drink of laudanum, and I don't believe she'll awaken before tonight."

He was incapable of grasping more than one fact at a time. "She's in no danger, Mrs. Walters?"

"Her health is perfect, sir."

"Where in blazes are the doctors?"

"I believe they've gone down to the dining room for some breakfast. They'll wait for you there, Mr. Hancock."

He turned and started out of the room, but paused when she put a detaining hand on his arm. "Don't you want to see the baby?"

John grinned sheepishly as he accompanied her to a nursery that had been prepared on the far side of the corridor. A middle-aged woman sitting beside a tiny bed smiled at him, and John nodded absently as he peered down at an infant with a wrinkled face. He knew what was expected of him, and managed to say, "She's very pretty."

The two women looked at each other in surprise. "Didn't they tell you, sir?" Mrs. Walters asked. "You have a son."

John thought he would faint, but recovered sufficiently to gasp his thanks before running from the room. He hurried down the stairs, and from the ground-floor landing could hear the physicians chatting in the dining room. But he wasn't ready to face them yet, and went straight to the library, carefully bolting the door behind him.

For a long time he stood still, looking up at the portrait of Uncle Thomas over the hearth. Then, unable to control himself any longer, he wept silently, letting the tears roll down his face into his neckcloth. This was the most important day of his life, yet he could feel no elation, no triumph. It was startling to discover that his only emotion was one of sadness. Uncle Thomas and Aunt Lydia weren't here to share this joy with him, nor was his own father, who had been absent from his mind for years. Later in the day, when he wrote to Dolly's family, he would send a courtesy note to his mother in Braintree.

He needed a dram of brandywine to stop the shaking of his hands, and he straightened his powdered wig, buttoned his velvet coat and put a clean lace-edged handkerchief in his left cuff before going to meet the doctors.

They stood as he entered the dining room, offering him their congratulations simultaneously.

John instantly slipped back into his role as a man of affairs, and no one in the room could have guessed that he was oppressed by a crushing weight of loneliness. "Gentlemen," he said in his best oratorical manner, "I am grateful to you for preserving the life of my lady, and for successfully bringing John George Washington Hancock into the world."

It didn't cross his mind that Dolly might have wanted a voice in naming the baby.

12

The General Court began its final deliberations on the Articles of Confederation at nine o'clock in the morning. Sam Adams, James Bowdoin, and three of their supporters made speeches opposing ratification, and even their foes courteously applauded them. But Thomas Cushing, the acting Whig leader, made no reply, and John Pickering, the Speaker, adjourned the meeting for two hours without explanation.

At one o'clock in the afternoon, an hour when legislators' appetites were sharp, the General Court reconvened, and the reason for the delay became evident when John Hancock sauntered down the center aisle, pausing to exchange a few words here and there with friends and to shake every outstretched hand. Pickering gaveled for order, and John, who hadn't yet bothered to take his seat in the front row, asked for the floor.

"The chair recognizes the Majority Leader."

"Mr. Speaker, fellow representatives, I'm sorry that affairs of a family nature detained me today."

The members heartily applauded the birth of a Hancock son and heir.

"I also realize you want your dinner, so I have no intention of delaying you further by making an address. The arguments on both sides of this debate have been presented in detail over a period of many weeks. I therefore move the ratification of the Articles of Confederation."

"I second the motion," Cushing said as John sat down.

The Speaker had been carefully rehearsed. Not looking in the direction of Sam Adams and his cohorts, who were clamoring for the floor, he rapped his gavel on the rostrum. "The Clerk will take a tally," he directed.

The voting began immediately, and it quickly became clear that an overwhelming majority favored the national government. The final totals were sixty-nine in favor of ratification and twelve opposed.

Then Cushing moved that the assembly adjourn for the day, and a few moments later John crossed the aisle to Sam Adams, who sat alone, stunned and confused.

"Sam, I have few talents for newspaper publishing, so I've decided to give up the *Patriot*. I'll sell you the assets for one Continental dollar, and you can merge it with the *Gazette*."

Shaking off the hand on his shoulder, Sam blinked angrily. "We criticized Lord North for building a party of puppets he controlled by pulling a few strings. We even went to war against

England because the artillery fire of tyrants silenced the voice of the people. And now you're guilty of the same offense, Hancock. Damn you!"

John took no offense. "Here are the legal papers putting the *Patriot* in your name. The real reason I was late for today's session was because I was busy with the lawyers, drawing them up."

Sam refused to accept the documents. "Maybe you've won this fight, but there will be others. You know as well as I do that the states, not the Congress, control this country. For the present you've taken possession of Massachusetts—just like you take anything you want. But I'm not giving up."

"I'm sorry you feel that way," John said quietly, "and I hope you're not trying to scare me. I've never yet run away from a fight, and I don't intend to start now." Dropping the papers making Sam the *Patriot's* proprietor into the other man's lap, he walked quickly from the chamber.

13

"If every invalid accomplished as much as you did," Henry Laurens said, "we'd be negotiating the peace treaty with the British by now. Seven states have followed Massachusetts' lead. Ratification of the Articles is assured, John."

"Yes, I think we can safely say that question is settled. But there are others. We've got to force stronger state action to triple the size of our Navy. Only the states can build merchant fleets, and we've got to depend on our own commercial shipping if we're to survive after the war ends. For that matter, we need more manufacturing plants, hundreds of them, so we won't have to rely on England again in peacetime. Or on France, for that matter."

The President of the Congress shrugged. "I'm a planter, not a merchant or banker. How do we persuade people to open plants?"

"The states must do it," John replied. "I've been thinking a great deal about the problem. If a state grants a loan to a man who wants to open a plant—and will offer him the added incentive of low taxes on his product, men all over the country will be eager to go into business for themselves." He looked around the large, well-lighted room. "These are very comfortable quarters, Henry, and they add to the prestige of the President. The builders were busy while I was away from York."

Laurens smiled. "This office will be yours. I'll resign as soon as the new session starts, and I have no doubt that your re-election will be unanimous."

"I won't be available for the Presidency, and this is my last term in the Congress."

Laurens was startled. "But you appear to be healthier than I've ever seen you."

"I'm feeling fine, thanks. Even Rush can't find anything wrong with me. But I don't think my place is in York for the next few years. I spent two days with General Washington on my way down here from Boston, and he's sure it's just a matter of time now before we win the war. The Lobsters are on the run, and we civilians must start thinking of organizing the peace. I've just mentioned a few instances that require origination on the state level. There are scores of others. Well, we're going to start electing our own governor in Massachusetts this coming January, so I intend to run for the post."

"I'm sure you'd make an able governor." Laurens hesitated briefly. "I just hope you haven't taken umbrage because the Congress hasn't paid your salary. Some members are retiring because we have too many bills to pay ourselves."

John leaned back in his chair, laughed and took a pipe and deerskin tobacco pouch from his pocket. "I've been a member of the General Court for a good many years, but Massachusetts has never paid me a ha'penny, either. Oh, I'll put in a claim for wages and expenses before I leave York, and someday, when the United States can afford to pay me, I'll get what's due me. In the meantime I don't expect a profit from government service. I just want to go where I can do the most good, and these days I think there's more need for me at home than there is here."

14

It was bitterly cold in the Braintree churchyard, a raw wind blowing out of the west cut through Mary Hancock Perkins' cloak and she shivered as she held her brother's arm to avoid slipping on the ice underfoot.

There was no sound but the crunching of John's boots and the lighter tap of his sister's footsteps. "Thank you for coming with me, but you should have stayed indoors," he said.

Mary tried to smile at him as they made their way to the far side of the graveyard, but the cold was too numbing. "I had no intention of letting you come here alone. I'm sorry Dorothy couldn't make the trip from Boston with you."

John was unable to meet her gaze. "Dorothy's health has been delicate since the baby was born."

Mary sniffed audibly. "You've taken the time from your campaign to ride down."

"I'm not campaigning actively. It wouldn't be seemly for a man to make speeches and attend dinners so soon after his mother's death. If I hadn't been off in Springfield," he added suddenly, "I could have been here in time for the funeral."

"I understand, John. So does Dick."

"Do you?" he demanded fiercely. "Or do you think I loitered on the road?"

She continued to grip his arm firmly. "Don't shout, John. Not here."

"Sorry." He allowed her to lead him to a new tombstone of white marble.

Mary released him, and John walked alone to the head of the grave. He removed his bicorn and the cold bit into his scalp, but he ignored the discomfort as he stared bleakly at his mother's grave.

For as long as he could remember, until ten days ago, he had secretly nourished the slender hope that someday he would win her approval, that someday she would tell him she loved him and was proud of him. Now it was too late.

Tears stung his eyes, then froze on his cheeks, but he was uncertain whether he was weeping for her or for himself.

Perhaps she had been indifferent to him because she recognized him as pompous, ruthlessly ambitious, and self-centered.
Perhaps it was his own inability to give love freely that had
turned her against him when he had been a child. Their estrange-
ment had become so great that, in recent years, he had made only
token visits to Braintree and hadn't known what to say to her.
She had shown no interest in the affairs of the country or his
own role in helping to shape the future of the United States.
She had approved of no vocation except that of the clergy, and
he suspected she had merely tolerated him as a merchant. She
had never voiced political views of any sort, but he suspected she
had been ashamed of his life as a public figure.

Strangely, now that she was dead, he felt closer to her than he
had through all the frustrating years of his life. The desire to
wring praise from her no longer consumed him, and he was able
to think of her as a human being who had known pleasures and
pains of her own rather than a symbol, that of the mother who
had wanted to be rid of him.

He had always been quick to find flaws in her, yet he knew
no one who was perfect, least of all himself. Having learned
something of the agonies a woman suffered in childbirth, he felt
a greater sense of gratitude to her for bringing him into the
world. His father had loved her, and his father had been a wise
and good man who, obviously, had seen admirable qualities in
her. Loving a wife was not easy, and he wished he had been able
to see his mother from his father's perspective, with his father's
eyes.

Bowing his head, John prayed, but could not put his plea to
the Almighty on his mother's behalf into words. He knew only
that, if there really was such a place as the Hereafter that the
clergy believed in, he wished her everlasting peace and joy there.

"Amen," he said aloud, and when he lifted his head he saw
that Mary was surprised. No one in the family had ever considered him devout and, by their standards, he supposed he was
virtually an atheist, the direct result of his contempt for a sanc-
timonious stepfather.

Settling his hat firmly on his head, he took Mary's elbow, and they made their way back through the yard to the street, then set out for the Perkins' house. Both were silent on the walk, but Mary's spirits rose when she saw that her husband had made a roaring fire in the parlor hearth.

Dick had sent their children out to play, and the three adults were alone before the crackling logs. "Can I give you a mug of flip, John?" his brother-in-law asked.

John shook his head and stared morosely at the flames.

"Our local ale is good, and I mix it with the sack you send us."

"I don't feel in the mood for a drink."

Husband and wife looked at each other, and Mary put a hand on her brother's shoulder. "Don't blame yourself."

"How do you know what I'm feeling and thinking?"

"We're more alike than you realize. Mother and I weren't very close or friendly."

"At least you saw her often. Every day."

"That made less difference than you'd imagine. She was always aloof."

John clasped his hands behind his back, concealing them beneath the tail of his coat so they could not see how tightly his fingers were intertwined. "The eldest of her children takes after her."

They were interrupted by the arrival of the Perkins' one servingmaid with a pot of tea for Mary and two mugs of steaming flip for the men.

John had time to compose himself, and by the time the woman left the room, some of his tension had drained away. "Mother and I were always strangers," he said, "so it's useless for me to explain how I feel now. It's as though I were being pulled in two directions at the same time."

Mary rose from the settee to kiss him on the cheek.

He made an attempt to change the subject. "Dick, have you given any further thought to my suggestion that you practice law in Boston?"

Perkins ran a hand through his graying hair. "I wouldn't feel at home in the city, John. Mary and I have spent all our lives in the same town, and we've made a permanent place for ourselves here. My clients know me as well as I know them, and I earn enough to live here comfortably. With all the gifts you send us, we're more than comfortable. I appreciate your many offers to help me establish a larger practice, but I have no real desire to become wealthy or famous or powerful. Public office doesn't appeal to me, either. Perhaps I sound lazy or stupid, but there are many of us who are satisfied to be governed, and have no desire to become rulers ourselves."

"I envy you," John replied bluntly, and wondered whether he himself might have been happier had so many ambitions not consumed him.

"I've made four speeches for you, though. And even though the whole Adams clan is supporting Sam's candidate, Bowdoin, I think you'll get most of Braintree's votes."

"Thank you, Dick. I have no idea how well I may do. Sam would love the chance to criticize me for campaigning at a time like this, so I've got to sit back quietly, make no appeals to the voters and let them decide—without my help—whether they want Bowdoin or me. In the past week I've done almost nothing except catch up on my correspondence with friends in the Congress and the Army—and play with my son."

Dick chuckled, finding it difficult to picture John as a fond father.

Mary poured herself a fresh cup of Dutch tea and stirred it vigorously. "I do think," she said, her voice strident, "that Dorothy could have made the effort to come here with you."

"I agree," John replied flatly, but had no desire to elaborate on the domestic discords of recent days.

His candor surprised and encouraged Mary. "Dorothy was always an ambitious flirt who set her nose too high in the air. And now that she's the first lady of Massachusetts—"

"I haven't yet been elected," John cut in. "Nor am I as wealthy as I was at the start of the war. Property values will go up when the war ends, of course, but even if I include a reasonable increase, I'll have lost at least half my fortune."

Dick seized the opportunity to veer away from the embarrassing subject of Dorothy. "You'll earn another."

"That will depend on the voters. If they'll elect me as governor and keep me in office, I'll be satisfied to work for the public good until I retire. I'll still have enough money for my son to make whatever life he may want for himself."

"I can remember when Hancock and Company was your whole existence. What magnet keeps drawing you to politicking?"

John tried to be honest with his relatives as well as with himself. "I'm not sure. In part it's an enjoyment of power, knowing I can put my ideas of what's right for Massachusetts and the United States into law. I like the being known, too, and I won't deny it. I find it pleasant when a crowd cheers me, which makes me vain and foolish, I suppose. But there's something else that pulls me to public life. I can't define it and I can't explain it, but it's a disease that attacks everyone I've ever met in the Congress, the General Court and the legislatures of other states. I saw it in members of Parliament when I was in England years ago, too. A man who has held office can never find contentment in anything else. It becomes his whole life." He turned away from them and gazed into the fire. "Right now I'm taking a far greater gamble than I did when I opposed the Crown and took a stand for independence. If the voters reject me, I'll never find real satisfaction in this world again."

15

"Governor Hancock," Thomas Cushing said, "as chairman of the election board for the Commonwealth of Massachusetts, it's my great honor to notify you of the final election returns. You received 9475 votes. Bowdoin got 888. Ten votes were given to other candidates. The size of your victory, sir, staggers the imagination."

The members of the election board applauded, and each stepped forward to shake John's hand. The last of the group to approach was Sam Adams, and the others hurriedly left the Hancock library, obviously by prearrangement. Sam was dressed in a freshly sponged suit and a new cloak, his linen was clean and he had even consented to wear his powdered wig for the occasion. John was duly impressed.

"I fought you as hard as I could," Sam told him, "but the voters didn't agree with me. If you prove that they've chosen a wise and virtuous governor, only a few will be disappointed. If they discover they were wrong, they'll turn you out of office next year."

"Thanks for your good wishes, Sam. Join me in a drink."

"The miracle of this new form of government we've set up in the United States is that the ultimate wisdom of the people is infallible. I was beaten on the ratification of the Articles of Confederation, and I accepted my defeat. The people have chosen you as the leader of this state, and I must support that decision. I do support it, and I'll do everything in my power to help you. I wish you all that I wish for Massachusetts and for the country."

John was surprised to see tears in the eyes of his former mentor. "With your help, I won't need others."

"You'll need every able-bodied man in the state, lad, and don't forget it!" Sam's manner changed abruptly, and he glared at John across the rim of his glass. "My head spins when I think of all you'll have to do in order to make Massachusetts prosperous and secure."

"You're quite right, of course." John sat down behind his desk. "I suppose you recommend that I ask the new Senate and House to elect Bowdoin as lieutenant governor."

"I refuse to interfere. It's your prerogative." Sam took a chair, too, and stared thoughtfully at the ceiling. "He'd appreciate the gesture, but he wouldn't accept after being defeated so badly. Think of it from his point of view. He doesn't have the public's confidence."

"All the same, I'll recommend him." John believed it essential that men of every persuasion close ranks now.

"That will be good politicking. Then I reckon you'll elect Tom Cushing?"

"Well, I have had him in mind."

Sam laughed and, after a moment's hesitation, John joined in. They understood each other perfectly, and their feud was ended.

16

"I'm not sorry for you in the least!" John shouted as he stood in the center of the master bedchamber in the Hancock mansion. "You wanted to make this room blue, and you can't change it again!"

"Please lower your voice so you don't wake up Johnny." Only

a nervous tug at the sash of her dressing gown revealed that Dolly was somewhat less than calm. "The new peach-colored fabrics that have just arrived from France are beautiful, and they'll make elegant drapes."

"I wonder if you've stopped to count the cost. We'll have to spend four thousand dollars for the material alone!"

"In paper money. That's only forty dollars in silver."

His rage was so great that he could feel his temples pounding, so he forced himself to sit down. "The paper money is real, unfortunately, as I've tried to tell you hundreds of times. Do you know what we paid for the beef we ate at dinner last night? Eleven dollars per pound! Butter costs sixteen dollars per pound! The two barrels of flour that were delivered on Tuesday cost us more than three thousand dollars. I wanted to order myself a new suit, but my tailor told me it would cost three thousand— without the waistcoat. This is no time to talk of decorating the house again!"

"I can't for the life of me see why you're so excited. All our money is in good silver and gold, so we aren't paying these insane prices."

Her logic was maddening. "The United States can't survive on English silver and French gold. All our victories in battle will mean nothing if we can't create public confidence in our own money. Damnation, Dorothy, I spend half my waking hours trying to devise new ways to improve our finances. And I refuse to let the governor's wife be accused of extravagance."

"You're deliberately denying me even the simplest pleasures. We haven't given a single dinner party since you were elected, you lose your temper every time I have a new dress made and now you want me to live with furniture that's grown shabby."

John pressed his hands to his temples. "Thousands of our citizens can't afford to buy corn or meat. I was forced to ask the farmers for voluntary contributions of food and establish distribution centers for the poor. Only last week in Salem two men were sent to prison for stealing a five-pound piece of beef. Do you know what they had done? They were a father and son too poor to buy food for a family of eight. The son was wounded at Monmouth, and the father fought on Long Island. These people are patriots, the finest Americans in the land. But hunger makes men desperate."

"You're thinking only of being re-elected. You have no idea how many of our friends are laughing at you because you think of nothing except trying to win popular support with your free gifts of food, releasing dangerous criminals from the jails—"

"Your friends are entitled to believe what they please, and perhaps they can persuade their husbands to vote for someone else. But I'll continue to do my duty as I see it. And my wife will either curtail her expenses voluntarily or I shall be forced to notify the merchants of Boston that you no longer have credit— anywhere."

Dolly opened her mouth to protest, but John rose swiftly from his chair and stalked from the room.

He glanced at his watch and realized he would have to ride to the office rather than walk. He had called a meeting at eight o'clock with a half-dozen subordinates to discuss possible ways to raise a new regiment of militia that General Washington had requested. Massachusetts had grown weary of the war, and it would be difficult to find eight hundred new recruits willing to serve for a minimum of twelve months. Yet it was essential that the commander-in-chief's needs be met. They were as urgent as the need to feed the hungry, bring down prices and establish confidence in the dollars the Continental Congress was still printing. Work had been found for hundreds of men in shipyards and at least fifty farsighted entrepreneurs had been persuaded to open factories, but the governor's task had just begun.

Settling wearily in the back of his coach, John braced himself for the beginning of a new day. Remembering his talk with Mary and Dick Perkins about the mysterious magnetism of public office, he laughed aloud, wryly. The drawing power was even more perplexing than he had been willing to admit, and he wondered if all statesmen were a trifle mad. There was no other explanation for his willingness to accept a new term as governor and, probably, still others in the years ahead.

All he knew was that there was a job to be done, and he believed with all his heart that he could do it better than anyone else in Massachusetts.

17

Oil lamps burned late in the building that had once been the home of the Crown deputy for the colony of Massachusetts Bay. But the nasal twang of New England was the only accent heard as busy, harried men went from office to office, conferring, and in the large, inner chamber that had once been the sanctum of viceroys, no hint of Bernard, Hutchinson, or Gage could be found. A portrait of General Washington was hung over one of the twin fireplaces, and his austerity was matched by the elegance of Governor Hancock's likeness over the other hearth.

Miniatures of Dolly and little Johnny crowded the desk on which royal edicts had been signed in bygone days, and small replicas of a half-dozen frigates and merchant ships lined the edges of a table piled high with papers. Everywhere there was evidence suggesting that the man who occupied the office was cruelly overworked. Stacks of papers filled the better part of his desk, and the overflow had been deposited on chairs and a sagging divan.

But John looked completely at his ease, in spite of the hollows beneath his eyes. His suit of canary-colored velvet was cut in the latest French style, the silver buckles on his shoes gleamed in the light of the lamps and his wig looked freshly powdered. His smile was cordial and, as always, his hospitality was overwhelming as he poured his guest a generous cup of sack.

Major General the Marquis de Lafayette protested in vain. "Please, Governor, I've had little to eat since breakfast, and spirits will make me ill." He spoke English with only a trace of what had been a heavy French accent when he had first come to America.

John rang for a servant and ordered a platter of biscuits, two dozen shelled oysters and a dish of cold ham for his visitor. "So few military men come to Boston these days that I'd be guilty of neglect if I failed to look after you properly, General. What brings you to Boston? How goes the war in Virginia, and has the French fleet in the West Indian Islands brought Washington the reinforcements he needs? You'll stay here with Mrs. Hancock and me? I shall take it as a personal insult if you refuse!"

Lafayette straightened the coat of his travel-stained blue-and-buff uniform. "If it won't inconvenience you, nothing will please me more than to sleep under your roof, Governor." A mischievous smile spread across his youthful face. "You've heard no recent news of the war?"

"The last I heard was that the Comte de Grasse had driven off a British squadron trying to carry relief to Lord Cornwallis' corps by sea."

"Ah, then I'm in time. General Washington sent me as his personal emissary to bring you the news." The Marquis paused, and his smile faded as he said, "October 19, 1781, is a date that Americans will remember for all time. Cornwallis surrendered his entire corps to General Washington at the village of Yorktown, in Virginia. On my journey north I learned that Sir Henry Clinton is planning to evacuate New York Town and will sail either to England or Halifax with his remaining troops."

For all practical purposes the war was ended and American independence had been won. John was so stunned by the news that, for the first time in many years, he was speechless.

Lafayette saw that he had no glass, and handed his own cup of sack across the desk.

John took a great gulp, coughed and gasped for breath. "I've hoped. I've prayed. But I didn't think it would happen—as suddenly as this." Overcome, he could say no more, and walked to the windows, staring out at the dark street until he could regain his self-control.

"I can't verify this," the Marquis said quietly, "but I've been told General Washington wept, too, when he retired to his private quarters after the surrender."

"After all these years, I find it hard to believe we're truly free." John continued to peer blindly into the street.

The servant returned with a tray of food, which Lafayette accepted with the eagerness of a soldier who hadn't eaten regularly for a long time.

John turned back to his desk. "Make yourself at home," he muttered as he sat down, took a quill from a jar of sand and began to write rapidly. Then he sat back and read aloud. "Let freedom ring throughout the Commonwealth. The war is won, and the United States of America is an independent nation." He jumped to his feet, started toward the door and halted. "Boston will hear the word from town criers, and couriers will carry the news to the streets of every town and village. You'll address a joint meeting of the Commonwealth House and Senate, General? I insist!" Too excited to remember that he could ring for an aide, he opened the door and shouted at the top of his voice.

Men came running from every office, and stopped in astonishment. The imperturbable Governor Hancock, his wig askew, was laughing and weeping, but appeared sober. And before anyone could question him, he began to prance around his office, paying no heed to the gout that had been causing him pain in his left foot. The staff members were even more amazed when the dapper Marquis de Lafayette entered into the spirit of the occasion by sweeping the papers on the desk to the floor, jumping up with such force that he knocked over a jar of ink and, indifferent to the damage, started to sing "Yankee Doodle" in a hoarse, triumphant bellow.

EIGHT

1783 — 1789

1

John opened the peach-colored silk drapes that covered the windows of the master bedchamber, jerking the cord so violently that it broke. "The way I invest my money is my own affair, and I'll tolerate no interference from you, madam!"

Dolly sat up in bed, slipped into a quilted jacket that matched the curtains and the drapes, and faced her husband defiantly. "Everyone in Massachusetts worships at the shrine of the great Governor Hancock. His ears and mind are filled with such praise from dawn until midnight that he believes himself the wisest of men. You're gambling with my future, John! Can't you understand something so simple that a child can grasp it?"

"Under the terms of my will, you're being left this house—which is worth at least five thousand pounds in British sterling, and the Hancock Wharf, which is worth another ten thousand. Even if I cut you off without another penny, you'll never starve."

Refusing to be cowed, she changed tactics. "I don't care for myself. I've never been greedy."

His contemptuous look expressed his feelings better than anything he might have said.

"I'm thinking of our son!"

"You may take my word for it, Mrs. Hancock, so am I!"

"Then be sensible, I beg you. Fifty thousand pounds in good

English silver is a huge fortune. With that amount of money, Johnny can do whatever he wants in this world. He can buy a plantation in Virginia, a manufacturing plant in New York Town, a fleet of merchant ships here in Boston. With that sum he can buy all three—and still have enough left to live like a great lord— or like his father."

John ignored the slur. "I'm doing what I believe best for the protection of my son's future."

"It's madness to put that huge amount into bonds issued by a weak, foolish government. The whole world knows the United States is bankrupt!"

He saw that her concern was genuine, and unbent sufficiently to explain. "It's true," he said, "that the Confederation owes great debts to France and Spain and the Dutch bankers. But the potential wealth of this nation can pay off our foreign creditors, repay the loans of the individual states and still show a national profit. There are many prosperous men in this country, Dorothy, and now that the peace treaty with Great Britain has been signed, there will be new fortunes made every day."

"Reopen the doors of Hancock and Company, then! Put your money into shipping, something you know, and your fifty thousand pounds will soon become one hundred thousand!"

He eyed her coldly. "This nation made great sacrifices to attain her freedom. We who love her must prove now that we have faith in her future. That's why Dr. Franklin, General Washington—all of us who are fortunate enough to have funds—are buying Confederation bonds. If we do it, others who are fearful and reluctant will follow our example. But if we who created this nation stand back, who'll believe in America's future?"

"You're throwing away Johnny's heritage!"

"On the contrary," he said, drawing himself erect, "I'm making certain he has a future. Do you think the British agreed to generous peace terms because King George loves us? He's convinced we can't survive as a free and independent nation. He's waiting for us to falter, and then he'll send another horde of Lobsters across the sea to reclaim his lost colonies. We can't let that happen, and we won't. I intend to do everything in my power to insure that my son grows up to be a free man in a free nation. If the United States fails as an experiment in democracy, a fleet of merchant ships and a manufacturing plant and a Virginia plantation will be worthless. The British will claim all property. And under those circumstances, I'm afraid, a young man bearing the unfortunate name of John George Washington Hancock wouldn't fare too well. His new masters wouldn't show him much mercy. That's why—if I have anything to say in the matter, and I have—the United States will be as strong as I can help make her."

Dolly began to weep in futile rage as he started toward the door.

John paused at the threshold. "I'm doing more than buying Confederation bonds. I'm announcing today that I'll trade British sterling for Continental dollars. I intend to offer ten thousand pounds in silver to any veteran of the Continental Army who wants hard cash in return for his discharge pay."

She thought he had lost his wits. "Then we'll be penniless."

"Not quite. I'll have five or ten thousand pounds left, enough to see us through the next few years. By then," he added gently, "the United States will live up to her potential—or life itself will lose its flavor."

2

Captain James Scott had served his country with distinction throughout the war, serving as master of his own privateer, and it was his proud boast that he could handle a ship in any weather or fight any foe on the high seas. But he felt distinctly ill at ease in the office of Massachusetts' first citizen, and he glanced fitfully at the portrait of General Washington above the hearth on the left side of the room.

John tried to make his former employee more comfortable. "Let me give you a glass of West Indian rum, Captain. It's the first we've brought up from Jamaica since the end of the war."

Scott smiled shyly. "I probably carried that jug in the hold of the *Carrie Ann*, Governor."

John filled the glass almost to the brim, then poured himself a few drops of sack, which he diluted with water. He hated to admit that his doctors might be right, but he found that the gout in his left foot was less painful when he drank sparingly. "To the United States," he said. It was the only toast he had offered in years.

Scott neither coughed nor blinked as he downed half the contents of his glass in a single gulp.

At least a dozen visitors were waiting, so John had no time for extended amenities. "I hear you're sailing to England next week, Captain."

"You're well informed, Governor—as always. And if you ever decide to go back into shipping yourself, I'm always interested in sailing under the Hancock flag."

"Thank you, Captain. There's no one I'd approach before speaking with you. A merchant's life is so pleasant and uncomplicated that I'm often tempted to return to it." John stifled a sigh, then picked up a long sheet of paper. "In the meantime, Captain, I wonder if you'd be willing to accept a little commission from me to buy a few odds and ends in London that I need. In return for a fee, of course."

"I'll be delighted to take care of your purchases, Governor, but I'd rather not accept money from you."

"I insist you take five percent of what you spend. The items are minor, but it will be something of a nuisance going from shop to shop." He handed the man his list.

Scott read aloud from it. "A new coach."

"Yes, I need something large enough for two servants on the box, something I can use on occasions of state. You'll note I want my crest on the doors, a lamp at each side and a leather trunk that will fit snugly on the roof. It should be lined in crimson silk, and I'll give you a swatch of the material I think will be suitable."

"Six dozen of the very best pewter plates, with oval dishes for Saturday's salt fish." Scott tried not to reveal that he felt overwhelmed.

"They should bear my crest, too."

"Seventeen chairs, five settees, nine tables, all according to attached designs, three new double fourposter beds."

"I believe a silk and worsted upholstery will be good enough for the furniture. I want something that will last long enough for my son to enjoy when he comes of age."

The merchant seaman drew a deep breath. "Thirty-two pairs of silk window curtains, with cushions to match, and a sofa of the same."

"For Mrs. Hancock, you know. She's been a little restless lately, living with furnishings that are either shabby or Boston made, and I'd like to surprise her." Then, John thought, Dorothy might give him a semblance of domestic peace.

Scott couldn't help blinking. "Forty-eight woolstuff-back chairs?" He found it difficult to believe the words on the paper.

"For the dining room," John explained. "Our monetary system should become stable soon, so we'll have to do a bit of informal entertaining."

The mariner gulped and nodded. "Two Wilton carpets, one of them thirty feet by twenty-four, the other twenty-four by twenty-four."

"Yes, the carpets in the master bedroom suite are becoming a shade threadbare. Sir Henry Clinton was careless with his spurs when he lived in the house during the occupation."

Scott was becoming increasingly overwhelmed. "A forty-inch sword of Toledo steel, if available, or of Sheffield, if not. The hilt and scabbard must be of gold leaf."

John brightened. "A birthday gift for my son. In another year or two he'll be ready to wear a dress sword. You'll find a pair of small dueling pistols on the list somewhere, too. By next year I can begin teaching him the use of firearms. French pistols are superior, but an English pair will be good enough for a child. I don't want to spoil him or lay myself open to a charge of extravagance."

The sea captain stifled a grin. "A tea urn of solid silver."

"For Mrs. Hancock's exclusive use. I lost my taste for the filthy stuff during the unpleasantness with the East India Company just before the war. You'll find a few more odds and ends there, too, Captain, but none of them will give you any trouble, I'm sure."

Scott was relieved that Governor Hancock had insisted on paying him a fee. Shopping for the items on the list would keep him busy for a full week, but his percentage would pay all his expenses in London, and he would be surprised if he didn't show a handsome profit as well. It might be true, as all Boston believed, that Governor Hancock had invested his entire fortune in Confederation bonds and Continental dollars, but he was still living as though he had pounds sterling to burn.

3

"Don't fight the recoil, Johnny. You know there will be one the moment you pull the trigger, but if you anticipate it, your aim will be spoiled." John stood with his son behind the Hancock mansion, both in shirtsleeves, facing a tree, to which was pinned a crudely drawn figure of a redcoat.

The little boy looked dubious, but was accustomed to the acceptance of his father's orders without question.

"Here, I've reloaded this one, so try again."

Johnny took the pistol, but held it as though he feared it might explode in his hand.

"Point it away from your foot, boy."

"Yes, Papa."

"That's better. Now, take the stance I showed you, hold out your arm and look down the barrel at your target."

Johnny tried to follow directions.

The critics of Governor Hancock who claimed he was quick to lose his temper would have been astonished had they seen his demonstration of patience. "Straighten your arm. And don't close your eyes, Johnny. I give you my word that you'll do better if you keep your target in the center of that little notch at the end of your muzzle."

The child bit his lower lip, but opened his eyes wide.

"Good. The enemy is approaching, Colonel Hancock. You may fire when ready!"

"Ready, General Hancock." The little boy remembered to squeeze the trigger rather than jerk it.

There was a flash of flame, a sharp cracking sound and then smoke poured out of the barrel.

Johnny peered at the figure of the British soldier in awed wonder. "Papa, I hit the helmet!" His shriek of glee was unrestrained.

John swept him off his feet and, paying no attention to the tenderness in his swollen left foot, danced around the yard.

"I want to do it again, Papa!"

John deposited the boy on the ground, hurriedly reloaded the second dueling pistol and handed it to him.

At that moment they were interrupted by Dolly, who ran toward them from the house, holding up her skirt and petticoats so she wouldn't stumble. "What happened to my baby?" she cried.

"Our son is a marksman. He'll soon be able to apply for a commission in Morgan's Rifles."

She was not amused. "Dan Morgan has returned to civilian life—as has everyone else." She peered anxiously at the child. "Are you quite sure you're all right, Johnny? Your scream froze the marrow in my bones."

"I hit the target, Mama," the boy said breathlessly, "and now I'm going to do it again. Watch me!"

"I'd rather not. I don't approve of such barbarism."

John felt a flush of anger when he saw his son's face fall. "Stay, Dorothy. He's proud of his achievement, as he should be, and he wants to share it with you."

"It shouldn't be necessary to remind you, of all men, Governor Hancock," she replied coldly, "that we live in the year 1786. The peace treaty was signed a full three years ago. There won't be another war in Johnny's lifetime, and I think it's disgusting—as I've told you again and again—to teach him the use of weapons that can kill his fellow humans."

John didn't want to argue with her in the boy's presence, but felt it necessary, for his sake, to correct her. "No one knows when we may be attacked by a hostile power, and I can assure you that the good people who live in the wilderness settlements and are in constant danger from Indians wouldn't appreciate your belief that we're at peace."

"We live in Boston, not the Ohio Valley!"

"What's more," he continued, "the day may come when he'll find it necessary to defend the honor of his mother or his wife. Colonel Hancock, the enemy is approaching. You may fire when ready!"

As far as Johnny was concerned, the problem was settled. "Ready, General Hancock!"

Dolly gasped and her hand flew to her mouth when the child fired the pistol.

Again Johnny screamed in delight. "Look, Mama, look! I hit his chest!" In his excitement he threw the weapon into the air.

It landed with a thud a foot or two from Dolly, and she drew back from it as though it were a snake.

"Colonel Hancock, I salute you," John said solemnly. "You've proved you can really handle firearms, and you deserve a reward. What would you like—more than anything in the world?"

Dolly intervened quickly. "A spinnet, and music lessons from the best teacher in Boston, Mr. Gregory."

The boy looked anxiously at his mother, then at his father. "I want a pony of my own," he said, defiance and fear in his eyes.

"You shall have it today." John looked at his watch. "In fact, we'll cut short your pistol practice and go down to the horse market right now, before my meeting with the leaders of the General Court." He turned to his wife without apology. "We can discuss the subject of a spinnet on another occasion."

Dolly's fury gradually subsided as she watched them clean the pistols and pack them away in their silk-lined case. She had been defeated again, but all the same she couldn't help being grateful for John's close attachment to their son and Johnny's obvious adoration of his father.

John was less than perfect as a husband, and she would never forgive him for the hideous carpets in the master bedroom suite, which were so strong and so magnificently woven that they would last for a quarter of a century. Nevertheless, she recognized the close bond that tied father and son, and even though John was turning the child into a male savage, she appreciated the interest and devotion he lavished on Johnny. Few men who were as busy wrestling with seemingly insoluble problems gave their families that much love.

4

Robert Morris stretched his gold-buckled slippers toward the fire of hemlock logs. "A magnificent dinner, the wines were excellent and this brandywine is better than any in my own cellar."

John beamed at his guest. "You shall have a dozen bottles of it when you leave."

"I wouldn't dream of depriving you. This is superior to the pipe of brandywine that Jefferson sent me from France."

"Mine came from the Cognac country. Jefferson sent me several bottles from Languedoc, but it was too fiery for my taste. Strictly between us, I think his reputation as a judge of wine is undeserved."

"I agree, but please don't quote me."

They raised their glasses to each other, sipped their drinks and lapsed briefly into a companionable silence.

"Have you heard from Alex Hamilton lately?" Morris kicked off his slippers.

"Don't leave them too close to the fire. You may harm those buckles. Yes, he wrote me in September, urging that Massachusetts arrange her financing through your new Bank of North America, as the Congress and Pennsylvania have done. I'm in favor of the idea myself, but my legislature will balk. New England provincialism is still too strong a force, and the General Court would be sure to reject such a proposal out of regional pride."

Morris sighed deeply. "I can sympathize with you. I served for a couple of years in the Pennsylvania legislature."

"I'll support any project that will put us on a sound financial basis. Nearly all my assets are tied up in Confederation bonds and those infernal Continental paper dollars."

"So are mine, and that's why I'm here. Alex said nothing to you about his plans for forming a stronger national government?"

"He mentioned it briefly, and I've been corresponding with John Adams on the subject since he went to London as our minister there."

"What do you think of the idea?"

"I approve, naturally," John sounded hurt.

"I ask for only one reason. The Congress notified Massachusetts that your share of the national deficit for this past fiscal year amounted to almost two million dollars. But you sent about five hundred thousand less than the requested amount to Philadelphia."

"I made a personal appeal to both houses of the legislature in a joint session. But the members, in their collective wisdom, ignored the Congress' figure, and elected to send a smaller amount. That's precisely why I favor a stronger national government. We have obligations as a country, legations abroad to maintain, a crying need for a national, standing Army and Navy. If the government of all Americans must depend on the charity of the states, we were better off as British colonies. Our national paper money must be supported by a reserve of silver and gold, and until it is, our currency will be worthless."

"I've been saying the same thing for years."

"Above all," John went on, "the national government must have the right to levy taxes, dispense justice, and coordinate the activities of the states. It's absurd, you know, that Boston, Philadelphia, and New York Town levy different import duties on the authority of their state legislatures. And Charleston, which is trying so hard to become a more important commercial port, imposes no tariffs at all. Some of our merchants are finding it cheaper not to bring goods to Boston direct from Europe. They're having cargoes sent to Charleston and then transferring them to coastal brigs."

Morris put on his slippers. "We can rely on your support and your influence in Massachusetts?"

"Certainly, and although I have no right to speak for John Adams, I know you'll find him receptive, too."

"Will Sam stand with us?"

John shrugged. "I doubt it. He's becoming more and more unpredictable as he grows older, but his belief in state rule is consistent. He's afraid a nationally elected president might be so powerful he'd try to make himself a king." John chuckled.

"A great many people will share that fear."

"Unfortunately, Bob."

"That's why, assuming we can persuade the states to accept a stronger national government, we must be careful in our choice of our first president. He'll set the standard, the tone, for his successors, so we'll have to select someone the people of every state trust."

An anticipatory chill moved slowly up John's spine. Morris was looking straight at him, and the Philadelphian's meaning seemed clear. "I'm sure the citizens of the United States can be trusted to make a wise choice." He hesitated for an instant. "Who is working on the project?"

"Virtually every member of the Congress, past and present. Alex is acting as something of a coordinator, but others—Jefferson in

Paris and young Madison in Virginia—are working on their own ideas independently. Any number of Confederation bond holders who are in retirement are giving us their full support. General Washington is enthusiastic—"

"Ah!"

"—and so is old Dr. Franklin. His mind wanders occasionally, but he can still concentrate when a subject interests him. But there are some leaders who are opposed to us, I'm sorry to say. Sam isn't the only one. Governor Henry of Virginia swears he'll do everything in his power to fight the formation of a stronger national government."

"I've never met Patrick Henry," John said. "but from what I've heard, he's one of those rebels who doesn't realize we won our war. How does he propose that we pay off our national debt and support our paper money so merchants here and in Europe will respect it?"

"There are few merchant companies and fewer banks in Virginia," Morris said dryly.

"Planters and farmers have as great a need for money as townsmen. But we needn't worry about Henry. The influence of General Washington and Jefferson must outweigh his."

"Washington is respected everywhere."

"Winning generals always have an enthusiastic following. Marlborough more or less set the standard for our century." John felt a slight twinge of uneasiness when he recalled that the Duke of Marlborough had risen from his post of military glory to become, in effect, Queen Anne's First Minister.

"General Washington has no interest in holding public office. He wants to spend the rest of his life on his farm."

A feeling of relief flooded John. "Too bad, but I can't blame him. I often wonder why those of us who still hold public office don't retire, too. I suppose it's because we know there's no one efficient to take our places."

5

"Hurry, Papa, or the pond will be crowded before we get there." Johnny tugged impatiently at his father's arm.

With his free hand John leaned heavily on his walking stick

as he limped painfully down the Mall toward the skating rink at the far end of the Common. "Run ahead, Johnny."

"No, you'll have to help me put on my skates."

Tom Cushing shook an admonishing finger at the boy. "Then you'll have to be patient, youngster. John, I'm sorry. I wouldn't have bought him the skates had I known you intended to walk all the way down yourself."

"My gout has been worse, Tom. The real reason I'm going with him is because Dorothy hasn't wanted him to have skates. I feel I should keep watch over him myself."

"I wish I'd known. The lieutenant governor has no desire to come between the governor and his lady."

"Johnny has a fine sense of balance, and he's wanted skates so badly that he's been sliding around that frozen patch next to our vegetable and pastry kitchen for the past month. I know of nothing you could have given him that he'd enjoy more." John smiled in spite of his discomfort. "Next year I'm going to have a small version of a long rifle made for him, but I don't want to push too fast. I still have to live with Dorothy."

Cushing's laugh was uncertain.

John didn't want to embarrass his old friend, and hastened to explain. "She doesn't mean to hover over him, but she can't help it. The death of little Lydia was partly responsible, and Dorothy knows that Johnny is her last child. We should have been married much younger, and we'd have had a whole brood."

Johnny raced ahead to the pond, sat down in a patch of snow near the bank and began to fumble with the skates.

The two men dropped to their knees to fasten the blades to his shoes, and other parents, who had accompanied their children, were awed by the spectacle of the governor and lieutenant governor dirtying and wetting their knees.

"Not yet, son," John said. "Let me make this clamp a mite tighter. That's it."

Johnny acted as though he had been born on skates as he took a few experimental steps and then began to glide across the ice.

His father, ineffectually brushing his knees, pulled up the beaver collar of his long cloak and smiled proudly. "I worried a great deal about him when he was a baby. I was afraid the combination of city living and his mother's influence might make him too soft, but I needn't have been concerned." He saw his old friend looking at him strangely. "The heir to a fortune must learn self-reliance, Tom. He needs to be more resilient than other boys."

"If he takes after his father, he'll have no problems."

John started to reply, but gasped when he saw Johnny and another child collide violently. Both tumbled to the ice, and Johnny bumped his head hard, then sprawled on the frozen surface of the pond, unmoving.

Several adults started toward him, but his father was the first to reach his side.

"Johnny!"

There was no reply.

"It looks to me," Cushing said over John's shoulder, "as though he's been knocked unconscious."

John silently gathered the limp figure of his son into his arms and, the pain in his own foot completely forgotten, carried him off the pond and began to walk through the Mall in the direction of Beacon Hill.

"John! This gentleman will give us a ride in his carriage."

"I'll be glad to oblige, Governor," the well-dressed young man said.

John didn't hear him, and Cushing repeated the offer, then gently led his friend to the coach.

As soon as they were inside, John bent close to his son's face. "Thank God he's breathing."

"Of course he is." Cushing could understand John's alarm, but felt certain the accident was minor. "After you take him into the house, I'll fetch a doctor, just to be on the safe side."

"Please do. Get Ned Pringle, if you can. Dorothy has great faith in him. But if he isn't in his office, bring Isaiah Baker."

The horses skidded to a halt at the main entrance of the Hancock mansion, and John climbed out, still cradling the unconscious child in his arms. He knocked his hat to the ground as he stepped down, but didn't realize it, and when two servants came out of the house to relieve him of his burden, he shook his head.

"No," he said. "I'll permit no one to touch him. Fetch Mrs. Hancock at once."

Dorothy came into the main drawing room as her husband gently lowered the boy to a sofa. She was pale but composed, and as he told her what had happened she opened the collar of Johnny's greatcoat and loosened his neckcloth. She turned to a trio of servingmaids hovering just outside the door, and spoke for the first time. "Bring the silver phial of smelling salts from the table in my dressing room." She sounded calm, in command of herself and the situation.

John's dread became a trifle less intense, but he paced the room restlessly. Dorothy was kneeling at the sofa, and he did not disturb her.

One of the servingmaids ran into the drawing room and thrust the silver container of salts into Dorothy's hand.

John drew nearer and watched anxiously as his wife held the phial under Johnny's nose.

The boy did not stir.

Dolly looked into John's eyes for the first time, and her fear was so intense that a wild panic surged up in him, but he curbed it instantly. But he was afraid his voice might betray him, and tried to soothe her by stroking her arm and shoulder.

They waited for what seemed like an eternity before Cushing came into the room with Isaiah Baker, a fashionable young physician much in demand since his return from service with the Continental Army.

The doctor went straight to the child on the sofa, and Cushing drew John aside. "Pringle will be here at any moment, too," he whispered. "His carriage was just turning into the driveway as we came to a stop at the door."

John was watching Baker closely, and scarcely heard him.

When Dr. Edward Pringle appeared, it was Cushing who hurriedly explained the situation to him. Pringle, a prematurely white-haired man who had escaped to Massachusetts with his family during the British occupation of New York Town and had decided to remain in Boston, joined his colleague.

He and Baker exchanged a few words, then he bent over Johnny to conduct his own examination.

Tom Cushing slipped unnoticed from the room.

John went to his wife and put an arm around her.

The two physicians muttered to each other again, then turned to the anxious parents. "The accident was unusual," Pringle said.

"In most cases of this sort, the buoyancy of the body humors is restored within a matter of a few minutes."

John could tell by his eyes what was coming next, and planting his feet apart, gripped Dorothy more firmly.

"Mrs. Hancock, Your Excellency, I'm afraid there is nothing we can do for your son. He's beyond our aid."

John found himself incapable of accepting the incredible news.

Dorothy sagged for a moment, then straightened and tried to shake off her husband's hold. "I've always known," she said in a strained, high-pitched voice, "that something like this would happen."

John tried to lead her from the room, but she resisted strenuously, and only when Pringle intervened did she consent to go.

The only way to avoid madness, John knew, was to remain active, and he insisted on making immediate funeral arrangements himself. He vetoed Cushing's suggestion that there be a parade through the streets of Boston, with Continental Army and Massachusetts militia veterans participating, and he flatly refused to permit any official recognition of the tragedy. Services would be private, he decreed, and would be held within twenty-four hours. He wanted no eulogistic sermon, and insisted that the graveside ceremony be brief, instructing Cushing to find a cooperative clergyman who would defy tradition and take an oath not to speak for more than five minutes.

By the time he wearily made his way upstairs, his left foot hobbling him, Dorothy had already taken a strong dose of laudanum that Dr. Pringle had given her. The opiate was just beginning to take effect, and her eyes were bright as she prepared for bed.

She stared at her husband, but could not focus on him. "It was your fault," she said.

John's grief was so intense that, compounded with a sudden rage, he scarcely knew what he was doing. The only conscious thought in his mind was that he wanted to kill Dorothy.

She took a step backward. "I'm sorry. You loved him as much as I did. Even more, I think."

His anger dissipated, leaving him so weak that he collapsed into a chair.

"Dr. Pringle left you a glass of laudanum, too. Drink it, dear. Please."

He didn't hear her, so she took the glass from his bedside table and handed it to him.

John accepted it mechanically, and the bitter concoction burned his mouth and throat.

Dorothy was becoming groggy now, and staggered to the bed. She stumbled and almost fell, but managed to climb into it, and whimpered quietly as she slowly lost consciousness.

John continued to sprawl in the chair, his anguish so great that it robbed him of all feeling. When the drug began to take hold he fought it, but the battle was a losing one, and eventually he fell asleep in the chair, his fists clenched.

6

Governor Hancock had made it a practice to address joint sessions of the Massachusetts Senate and House a number of times during each session, but the members knew this occasion was different, and no one cheered as he made his way slowly down the center aisle and mounted the rostrum. He shook hands with Lieutenant Governor Cushing, the presiding officer of the Senate, and General William Heath, Speaker of the House, who were seated behind him on the rostrum, and then turned to face the legislators.

He took no notes from his pocket, but put on his steel-rimmed spectacles. When he bent to take a sip of water, many members realized for the first time that he was wearing no wig, and they were surprised that his hair was so sparse and white.

John looked out at his audience, and it occurred to him that he knew everyone present by his Christian name. Some had been close to him for more than twenty years, and all were his friends. The sympathy he saw in their faces choked him, and he had to drink more water before he began speaking in the cracked, dry voice of an old man.

"Gentlemen," he said, "I have not come here to discuss recent events which have shattered my private life. The General Court is obliged by law as well as by principle to confine itself to matters concerning the public welfare. My present personal situation is such, however, that various rumors harmful to the stability of the Commonwealth have been repeated throughout the state during the past month. I believe it my obligation to silence these rumors by speaking to you with candor.

"The state of my health is infirm, and I am handicapped by an incapacity to render that service which is expected from one in my position. Justice to the public, to you and to myself loudly call upon me not to prejudice the community, but rather to promote its benefit.

"Gentlemen, in order to effect this end, I am obliged to inform you that my physicians have ordered me to find relaxation and surrender my cares. Therefore I must give up all attention to public business. With a sorrowing heart I must request to be indulged with a resignation of the stewardship of this Commonwealth.

"This will necessitate the holding of an election for the position of governor some four weeks earlier than has been the custom of this state since the end of the war. I will remain in office until that election has been held and its results certified, if that be the desire of the General Court. It would grieve me to be derelict in my duties after so many years of service in the public trust.

"My decision has been difficult, and the pain I feel at taking leave of you will abide with me for the rest of my days. I shall retire into seclusion, and beg only one favor in the name of personal friendship. For Mrs. Hancock's sake, and for mine, leave us alone in our grief. We are grateful for your many calls of condolence, but we feel inadequate to cope with visitors at present.

"I shall forever be grateful to you for your help in guiding the ship of state of this Commonwealth. No captain has ever been served with greater devotion and loyalty by his officers. Through you, I take leave of our people, and hope you will express to them my appreciation of their trust in me.

"Within the week I shall submit to you, in written form, my recommendations for the future public good, and I hope you, as well as my successor, will give them serious consideration. They represent an accumulation of all the knowledge I possess concerning the welfare of the Commonwealth and her people.

"Gentlemen, I must now bid you farewell. May Almighty God

protect and preserve Massachusetts and the United States of America."

No one applauded, but the representatives stood in silent tribute as John, using a thick new walking stick, descended from the dais and limped slowly up the aisle. Only after he had disappeared at the rear of the auditorium and the double doors had closed behind him did the members of the General Court cheer him.

7

John Adams, who had just returned home from England, was wearing a conservative but handsomely cut suit made for him by a London tailor, and looked better dressed than ever before in his life. The hair at his temples was gray, the life of a diplomat had given him a suave air of self-possession that, at best, had always been no more than latent, and he was crisply alert as he preceded his host into the Hancock library.

John had changed even more drastically during his year of retirement. He had gained at least twenty pounds, his face was florid and puffy, and his gout had swollen the joints of both legs and arms. But he still retained a trace of his flamboyant manner as he splashed brandywine into two glasses. "The ladies can look after themselves for an hour or so, and I'm sure they'd rather gossip with each other than listen to us. It's good to have you home, Johnny, even on a short visit. To the United States—and your health." He emptied his glass and refilled it.

Adams sipped his brandywine with the caution of a man who secretly disliked alcoholic spirits. "Retirement," he said bluntly, "doesn't become you."

John flushed, and would have resented the remark had it come from anyone else. "It hasn't been a complete retirement, you know. The people insisted on electing me as a delegate to the Continental Congress again. Not that the Congress accomplishes anything these days. To be honest with you, I made one brief visit to the sessions in New York Town, and was so disgusted I came straight home again."

"The new Federal government that the Constitutional Convention will start drawing up in Philadelphia next month should be much stronger and more effective."

"It will have to be, or there won't be much left of the country. The revolt of Dan Shays and his friends in the western part of the state last year is a symptom of what will happen everywhere. I felt sorry for those devils, and if I were governor, I'd pardon every last one of them. Oh, I realize that Bowdoin had to put down the rebellion with troops, but what can a poor debtor do except revolt? His situation is hopeless."

"I've heard it said by men who aren't your greatest admirers," Adams replied with a faint smile, "that it was typical Hancock luck for you to be out of office when the rebellion broke out. You'd have had to suppress it if you'd been in Bowdoin's boots, and the people would think of you as the villain now."

"It probably would have been better if I'd been governor, Johnny. Bowdoin wants to run again, but I don't aspire to public office any more. Tell me more about the problems you had in London."

"I think I summed them up before dinner. The Congress was able to give me no authority, and although the British were cordial—surprisingly cordial—I've had no real powers to negotiate with them."

John nodded gloomily, drank more of his brandywine and wiped his mouth with a silk handkerchief. "Who said that the bond holding the country together is a rope of sand? I like the phrase. If it weren't for my real estate properties—which are worth three times their value at the start of the war—I'd be a pauper today. I still own those worthless Confederation bonds, not to mention stacks of Continental dollars. Alex Hamilton told me his plans for a Federal Treasury with powers to act, and it's our only financial salvation."

"Then you favor a Federal government for personal as well as patriotic reasons."

"Well, Dorothy and my sister and brother would be far wealthier after I'm gone." A shadow crossed John's face as he thought of his son. "But I don't expect to enjoy any benefits in my lifetime, so my concern isn't personal. I have enough left to let me live in comfort for the short time I'll still be here."

"It isn't like you to wallow in self-pity."

"I'm being realistic."

Adams took a deep breath. "The United States," he said sharply, "still has a need for your services."

"I've been corresponding with Washington and Bob Morris and Dr. Franklin, and I approve of the basic outlines of the new Constitution the Convention will prepare. But Philadelphia will be a place for lawyers and bankers. They don't need a retired merchant and politician."

"Are you so insulated from the world that you don't know there's tremendous opposition to a Federal form of government right here at home? Cousin Sam is stirring up trouble with his printing press again. Bowdoin stands with him, and so do people like Gerry, who should know better."

"I've heard the thunder rumbling."

"It's more than thunder, John. The Constitution will be washed away by the rain of an old-fashioned New England line storm unless the Federalists band together and start fighting. Above all, they need a leader."

"You're ideally suited for the post."

"I'm still minister to England, and I'll be back in London by the time the Convention meets. There's only one man who can rally the Federalist forces. The most popular man in Massachusetts."

John became evasive. "Gerry is going to be a delegate to the Convention. That should destroy Sam's influence on him rather effectively."

"Massachusetts won't accept a Federal form of government unless you organize the supporters of a strong national government, educate and rally the people—and work even harder than you did for the Confederation."

John was silent for a moment, looking at him. "Is all this your own idea?"

"Massachusetts is still the most popular and wealthiest state in the Union. If we show that we're not afraid an executive branch will want to make the president a king, if we refuse to prove we believe in a judicial branch that will operate independently and a legislative branch that will deal fairly with every section of the country, the smaller states won't accept the Constitution. We'll be saddled with the Confederation's inadequacies for another year

or two, which is an optimisic estimate, and then the wheels will
fall off the coach of state."

"I'm not disputing the substance of a single word you're saying,
Johnny. I just can't help wondering why you, my oldest friend,
should happen to approach me on this subject during a very short
visit to Boston and Braintree. Your very evasiveness makes me suspect you're a party to a conspiracy."

"A benign conspiracy."

"You've never been a good liar. The Congress should have sent
someone far more glib to London."

"Bob Morris thinks you're indispensable, as do Roger Sherman
of Connecticut and General Pinckney of South Carolina."

John couldn't help preening.

"I've exchanged very little personal correspondence with young
Hamilton, but I know he desperately wants your help. If it will
influence your decision, I'll gladly show you letters I've received
from Washington and Dr. Franklin—"

"Franklin, and the General, too." John was overwhelmed.

"The leaders of every state are praying you'll accept this assignment. Governor Randolph of Virginia, John Dickinson of Delaware, even Bill Paterson of New Jersey, who trusts you so much
he's convinced you'll only support a Constitution that will protect
the interests of the smaller, weaker states."

John was silent for a long time. "I'm flattered that my friends
think me capable of exerting influence, but I don't think they
realize how quickly a man who retires from public life is forgotten. The voters are fickle."

"Try them."

"Maybe I will. I'll have to think about it."

8

"That's the gist of our conversation, my dear." John felt a little
guilty as he lighted his pipe with a spill from the sitting-room
hearth. Dorothy objected strenuously when he smoked in their
bedchamber, and she wasn't pleased with the odor of tobacco
fumes here, either.

But she was thinking too hard about what he had said to notice.

"It's wonderful that so many men believe I can make an important contribution to the cause. On the other hand, I think Massachusetts prefers the leadership of younger men now, and I'd hate
to be beaten in an election after giving up the privacy I cherish."

Dolly poured herself a steaming cup of tea, but knew better
than to ask if he wanted one.

"It's essential that the United States establish a more effective
government. That's sufficient reason for me to accept this new
challenge." John deliberately refrained from telling her their own
financial situation would be enormously improved under such a
government, as the knowledge would destroy what little objec-
tivity she possessed. "But I'd do more harm than good if I should
come out of retirement, run for governor—and lose. I've often
been called a jackass in the past fifty years, but I'd hate to be
called a damned fool."

She realized how rarely he had ever hinted to her that he felt
unsure of himself behind the façade, and knowing how badly he
sought her help, she gave him her warmest smile.

"What should I do?"

Never before had he asked her advice in political matters, and
Dolly was surprised. She knew how miserable he had been in retirement, and she had seen boredom as well as grief age him. But
she felt incompetent to make his decision for him.

John saw her hesitation, and spoke again, quickly, before she
could reply. "I'm being unfair to you."

"I'm sure you'll do what's best for the country—and for us."

"The two aren't necessarily the same. Suppose I should succeed,
and we set up a new government. Would you mind spending four
years in Philadelphia—or in New York, if the national capital
should be moved there?"

Dolly was mystified, but answered as honestly as she could.
"This is our home, and I love it. But for the past year I haven't
felt rooted anywhere."

They avoided looking at each other, and John puffed hard on
his pipe, trying to put the image of the small, limp figure of their
son out of his mind.

"Will the government be moved to New York Town?" Dolly
found it hard to speak.

"There's been talk of it since the Congress met there this past year. It's growing faster than Philadelphia, and may become as large as Boston someday. They've even stopped calling it a town." John had mastered his emotions now, and was able to smile. "We've discovered a need for a head of government, and under a Federal system we'd have a new type of presidency. The man who'd serve as president wouldn't be just the chief of the Congress, but of the nation."

Something in his tone made her look at him more closely.

"It would be undignified to conduct a campaign for a position of such great honor," he said carefully. "No man would seek it openly or actively. But, in the strictest of confidence, I believe that the leaders of every state are thinking of me for the post."

"They should, dear. No one has served the United States more faithfully than you."

John reddened. "You're prejudiced in my favor, of course, but I'm lucky to have friends who seem to feel as you do, Dorothy. It's strange, but there's a difference between national and state service. A politician must remain constantly in the public eye to hold an important elective position in a state, but there are so few men of stature who are known throughout the whole country that a retirement of a year or more is less important on that higher level."

"Living conditions were so unpleasant in wartime that I couldn't enjoy being the wife of the President of the Congress, but I know I'd enjoy being the wife of the President of the United States."

"That's what I wanted to hear you say." John beamed at her, but his smile quickly faded. "However, a cod must be caught before it can be salted and eaten."

9

John Hancock's declaration announcing his emergence from retirement was so brief that Sam Adams said he couldn't believe such a verbose man had written it himself. More than one hundred thousand copies were printed, under John's signature: "The chaos in the Commonwealth compels me to announce my candidacy for the governorship in the forthcoming election. If returned to that august office, I will press with all due earnestness for the adoption of a new Federal system of government, being convinced that the prosperity of Massachusetts and of the United States depend one upon the other, and that the future welfare of the two are inseparable."

The voters expressed their views emphatically, and John was elected, receiving nearly 19,000 votes to Bowdoin's 6000. With the help of Tom Cushing, who was returned to office as lieutenant governor with him, he spent the summer flooding the state with pamphlets and other literature explaining the need for a national government that could deal with other nations, settle disputes between states and establish a sound currency. Marking time in state affairs, he left routine business to subordinates and traveled incessantly, making speeches throughout Massachusetts to crowds that demonstrated his unquenchable popularity by turning out in vast numbers to see and to hear him.

By the time the Constitutional Convention completed its work and adjourned on September 17, 1787, he had lost most of the weight he had gained during his retirement. The John Hancock of old returned to Boston, the applause of the state's citizens still ringing in his ears, and he rode in triumph in his most elegant carriage at the head of a long parade, accompanied by three fife and drum corps. That evening the grounds of the Hancock mansion were thrown open for the first time in almost eighteen months. The throngs attending the reception were so large that Dolly twice ran out of punch and had to send servants to borrow pies, cakes, and other pastries from her neighbors.

The Convention had proposed that the new Constitution be ratified by state conventions elected by the citizens for the purpose, and Sam Adams opened fire on the suggestion with all of his guns. "The would-be tyrants," he thundered in the *Gazette*, "are already conspiring to rob us of our rights."

John's reply, which was printed by every newspaper in the state except the *Gazette*, was crisp. "My esteemed friend," he wrote, "sees ghosts where there are none. Delegates to the Massachusetts convention will be elected by the same districts that send representatives to the General Court. In most districts, members of the General Court stand as candidates for seats in this new meeting. Therefore I think it likely that the composition of the convention will be much the same as that of the legislature. Surely my good friend finds no tyrants sitting in the General Court!"

The Antifederalists continued their barrage, and Elbridge Gerry, who had not changed his position in spite of his service as a delegate to the Philadelphia Convention, duplicated John's tour, making speeches everywhere in the state and explaining in detail why he opposed ratification. Sam Adams adopted new tactics to meet new times, and held hundreds of private meetings with plant, dockyard, and shop foremen, master craftsmen and the proprietors of small business enterprises. He visited the leading farmers of each area, too, and argued until he was hoarse.

John was elected without opposition as the delegate of the Beacon Hill district of Boston, and although he professed to feel confident that the Constitution would be approved, he and his supporters were beginning to feel private doubts.

"I hate to say it," he told Tom Cushing after noon dinner at the Long Room Club one day, "but Sam has a telling point we can't answer. I've studied the Constitution with great care, and it's as remarkable a proposal as we claim. But—damnation—there are no guarantees of the personal liberties that sent us to war in '75. Every time Sam and Gerry say that freedom of speech and worship and assemblage are in danger, they win converts. And when they ask whether the Federal government or the states will exercise the specific powers not mentioned in the Constitution, I begin to feel uneasy myself."

Sam demanded that a new census be taken, and John, who was trying to be scrupulously fair to his opponents, complied. When it was discovered that some districts had grown larger than anyone had realized, new delegates had to be elected from them. The Adams-Gerry men had done their work well, and Antifederalists won these seats.

The convention met at the Statehouse on January 9, 1788, but there were so many delegates that thirty were forced to stand at the rear of the hall. The credentials committee, acting on John's suggestion, obtained permission to hold the sessions in the Brattle Street Church, where the Hancocks had owned a pew for generations. But some delegates were forced to sit in the choir loft, where the acoustics made it difficult for them to hear what was taking place below. The convention adjourned indefinitely, and did not reconvene until January 17, when the members gathered at the Congregational Church on Long Lane.

The first order of business was the election of a permanent president, and Cushing loyally proposed the name of John Hancock. To the surprise of the Federalists, Sam Adams seconded the motion, and John was elected by acclamation.

That night John worked long and hard writing a brief speech of acceptance, and finally realized the cleverness of Sam's support. No man understood his conscience better than Sam, who knew he could not give the Constitution his unqualified support.

So many guarantees were lacking, and although he thumbed through the essays written by Hamilton, Madison of Virginia, and John Jay of New York explaining the Constitution, he could find no Bill of Rights. A Federal government could, at its pleasure, withhold the right to assemble. The press was subject to Federal censorship, and a tyrant could, as Sam claimed, deny men the right to worship as they pleased.

Proponents of the Constitution had armed John with a list of proposed amendments, some of which had already been offered by Delaware, Pennsylvania, New Jersey, Connecticut, and Georgia, the five states that had already expressed their approval of the new form of government. He liked several he considered eminently sensible, the most important being the provision that all powers not specifically delegated to the Federal government be reserved by the states.

Writing slowly, he added this provision to the Bill of Rights, along with several others. He heartily agreed that no Federal officeholder should accept a title of nobility from a foreign nation, and he included an amendment protecting the rights of individuals in criminal cases. In all, he spelled out nine amendments before he felt satisfied and put down his pen.

It occurred to him as he limped off to bed that his own position in the struggle had changed. Although he was still a champion of the Constitution, he was trying to bridge the differences between the document's friends and enemies, and thus had become more of a conciliator than an advocate. Aristotle had been right when he had contended that men tended to become more conservative as they grew older. The philosopher should have added that the responsibility of high office did far more than advancing age to make a leader cautious.

Dolly stirred as her husband climbed into bed beside her and gratefully stretched his aching body.

"What time is it John?" she asked sleepily.

"Four o'clock."

"You'd have done far better to go back into business. Politics will be the death of you."

John was inclined to agree when, immediately after the delegates convened only five hours later, he read his speech. The Federalists were disappointed by his support for amendments, and the Antifederalists were angry because he didn't lean far enough in their direction. Both sides agreed that his suggestions, which came to be known almost immediately as the Conciliatory Proposition, created more problems than they solved.

Apparently Sam Adams thought otherwise, however, for he came to John and suggested they meet privately. Most of the delegates went to the Long Room Club at noon, so the pair who had done more than any other men in the nation to spark the movement that had resulted in American independence adjourned to the Bunch of Grapes.

"The luxury of this place is overwhelming," Sam said as they sat down in a curtained booth. "They've spent more money on new decorations than I've earned since the end of the war."

"Surely this isn't the first time you've been here since the war?"

"You know I can't afford places like this, John."

"What you mean is that you don't like ostentation." They grinned at each other.

Then, as a silver bowl of oysters in the shell was placed between them, Sam got down to business. "While you were talking this morning, representatives of eleven hundred Boston artisans appeared at the meeting with a petition. Were you responsible for it?"

"This is the first I've heard of the matter."

"That's what Tom Cushing told me, but I wanted to be certain. John, they urge the adoption of the Constitution, provided personal liberties are safeguarded. And when citizens take that kind of action on their own initiative, I've got to revise my own thinking."

John opened an oyster and sprinkled it with vinegar and powdered West Indian peppers. "Just as I changed in trying to con-
ciliate men on both sides."

"I approve of your suggestions, but you should have made
more. There should be an amendment guaranteeing individuals
the right to own firearms. We need stronger safeguards to prevent the seizure of any person or his property—"

"Then you're veering toward support of the Constitution?"

"Hold on, lad. I haven't gone that far."

"Sam, this country is doomed if you don't. Let's not fence with
each other. You and I have spent too many years counting noses
in town meetings and legislatures and the Congress. Right now
you can muster enough strength to reject ratification by fifty to
seventy-five votes. If Massachusetts refuses, where does that leave
the rest of the country? New York is waiting to see what we do,
and you know blamed well that the United States will collapse
if the two strongest states turn down the Constitution."

"I know the Constitution will become a useless scrap of paper,
but I'm not so sure I agree with your prediction about the country. What does impress me is that there's a genuine growth of
feeling in favor of a Federal government on the part of the people themselves. We've got to be sensitive to their wishes. That's
what will decide whether democracy itself succeeds or fails."

John ate another oyster and waited.

"I think we can work out a compromise."

"How?" John remained wary.

"If we incorporate our amendments into our ratification, I'll
be content, and so will everyone who stands with me."

"I wish I could oblige you, but you're forgetting we're under
strict instructions from the Philadelphia Convention to accept or
reject the Constitution without changes. Hamilton is adamant on
the point."

"To blazes with the lawyers who wrote the original! And who
does Hamilton think he is? You and I were risking our lives for
liberty when he was still a schoolboy. I can't stomach these tyran-
nical orders from the mountaintop!"

"The Federalists have a valid argument, Sam. If every state in-
cludes amendments—and they'll be different, you know, with
different wording—it might take years before the Constitution is
adopted."

"Let it."

"We can't afford to wait. Be fair, Sam. Nobody is dictating to us. Hamilton and Madison and the other young men who are in charge of this Federalist drive have made it very clear that amendments proposed by the states will be incorporated in the Constitution—by Constitutional means provided in the document itself—as soon as the first Congress convenes."

"How do we know that the men elected to a Federal Senate and House will agree to amendments?"

"You believe without reservation in the democractic process of government, Sam."

"I do! But what connection—"

"The members of the Federal House and Senate will be elected by the states. Members from Massachusetts will be pledged to support our amendments. The same will be true of members from other states."

"They might bicker and water down wordings—the way we did in the Continental Congress."

"What's more, we've had the promise of Federalists in every state to support amendments constituting a Bill of Rights. I see no danger."

"You're more trusting than I am, John."

"They're honorable men!"

"We've both seen circumstances that prevent honorable men from keeping their pledged word." Sam hesitated for an instant. "You're still an ingenuous merchant playing at being a statesman, and I'm going to prove it to you, although neither of us is going to like this. I've heard rumors that various Federalist leaders have hinted you stand a good chance of being elected president of the new Federal government. Have any of them been in touch with you?"

"I find I have friends in every state." John became uncomfortable. "But this is premature, you know. The Constitution will have to be ratified and the new government organized before we can think seriously in terms of electing someone who'll be president of all the people."

"If my fight to reject the Constitution fails," Sam persisted, "you'll have my support for the presidency—provided you become a serious candidate." His smile was cynical. "You look surprised. Your so-called friends have been telling you that Virginia is badly split because Governor Henry has taken a stand even stronger than mine against Federalism. According to this reasoning, General Washington wouldn't win the support of his own state, so you could count on the votes of the Carolinas, Georgia, and Maryland as well as Virginia."

"I've been told something of the sort." As Sam already knew so much, John decided to speak more frankly. "I feel reasonably certain I could count on the help of the New England states, so my election would be insured, no matter what New York and Pennsylvania and New Jersey might do. And Delaware, for that matter."

"John, you're being used. The Federalists are deliberately flattering you. They'll promise you anything to win Massachusetts' ratification, but they'll be in no position to keep their word to not?"

The oysters suddenly developed a bitter, metallic taste. "Why not?"

"Because the whole country will want Washington as president. Don't forget he was chosen unanimously to preside over the Constitutional Convention."

"At the risk of sounding immodest, Sam, I wasn't a delegate to Philadelphia. People always tend to regard a successful military hero as the man who won the war. But anyone who knows that the process of defeating an enemy is very complicated certainly understands the contributions made by civilian leaders. For instance, Bob Morris' work was brilliant. And I think I did my share."

"You did far more than most of our citizens realize. But you fool yourself if you think you're as popular as the general."

John was nettled. "He has no interest in holding elective office. In the past few weeks I've had three letters from his friends and neighbors, men in a position to know his thoughts, and they assure me he wants to live out the rest of his life on his plantation."

"You're even more naïve than I thought." Sam cut open the meat pie that was set before him and slit it open with his knife to let the steam escape. "The mere fact that you've received three such letters is proof—to me—that the Federalists are engaging in an active conspiracy at your expense."

"I can't believe it! I've known General Washington for more than twelve years, and I know something about human character. He's the most honorable person I've ever met, and I'm positive he'd be no party to a conspiracy!"

"He isn't," Sam replied mildly. "I dare say he has every intention of wanting to remain in private life. You and I know that public service is wearing, and that the rewards become fewer as we grow older and more tired. But not even Washington could be entirely lacking in vanity. When he's told the country needs him, will he refuse to accept a post as powerful as a king's? No man could be that strong or stubborn!"

John stopped deluding himself. The argument made sense, and he faced the issue without flinching. It was true that Washington, if he agreed to accept the presidency, would be the overwhelming choice of the entire country. Even Massachusetts would prefer him, and John, proud of the fact that he had never lost an election, had no desire to spoil his record by entering such a contest.

He fell silent as he began to eat his beef and vegetable pie, and was grateful that Sam was giving him a chance to put his thoughts in order. If the Federalists were actually using him, it would be difficult to control a feeling of resentment against them. What bothered him was the realization that they completely failed to understand him, and gave him no credit for patriotic motives. It was incredible, in view of the many sacrifices he had made, that they should deem it necessary to offer him the bait of what would become the nation's highest office in order to win his support.

However, as he learned during the turbulent days just prior to the war, principles were more important than the men who believed in them. Freedom for all was a shining ideal, but many supporters of the cause of liberty were weak and muddle-headed.

At last John raised his head and looked across the table at his old friend who had so often been his political foe. "Even if I'm forced to retire permanently from public life the day our convention ends, I'll still fight for ratification of the Constitution and for the amendments that protect personal liberties. The new form of government is more important than the men who may be playing me for a fool. You and I have been dreaming for many years of a free and independent United States that will become great. I think a strong Federal government in which each of the three major branches is checked and balanced by the other two assures us of that greatness. No matter what may become of me—or of the men who may be trying to tempt me with an offer they don't mean—I favor the Constitution, Sam."

"I wish you weren't so honorable, John, and so obstinate. I've got to fight, too, and I intend to do everything in my power to beat you."

10

Virtually every delegate to the Massachusetts convention wanted his views entered in the formal *Debates and Proceedings* that would be put into print after the task was completed. Speechmaking began early every morning and invariably lasted far into the night.

But John was seldom on the podium, relinquishing his place as presiding officer alternately to Federalists and Antifederalists with strict impartiality. He believed he had more important things to do, and taking over the office of the minister in a wing of the church, systematically held private meetings with each delegate in turn. He encouraged the Federalists to hold firm, and gave them copies of the pamphlets that Hamilton was printing in New York. But he spent far more of his time with the delegates opposed to ratification of the Constitution, trying to win over the weak and wavering, beat down the arguments of the recalcitrant and overwhelm the impressionable.

He made the same, unequivocal promise to everyone: he would support the amendments voted by the convention and, if necessary, would continue to serve as governor of Massachusetts in order to use his influence on the men elected to the first Congress under the new system. He made no secret of his own desires, explaining frankly that the governorship had become tiring and something of a bore, but he swore he would not retire or take a lesser public office until the mission was accomplished.

He made his personal position clear, too. He was not interested in becoming a Senator or a Representative, he said, and was not qualified to accept a seat on the Supreme Court. Nor did he want a Cabinet post as head of one of the new departments to be set up under the Executive branch. Younger, more malleable men, he usually added, would be better suited for places abroad in the diplomatic services. It was evident, by a simple process of elimination, that if he could not be elected as president or vice-president, and from these pinnacles exert his power and influence to make certain the amendments proposed in his Conciliatory Proposition were made the law of the land, he would stay as long as necessary in his present office to achieve that end.

The more stubborn of the Antifederalists were exposed to the Hancock charm. Dolly informed the cook that there would be at least twenty guests at dinner every night, and men who had never seen the inside of the mansion on Beacon Hill were entertained royally, eating the finest foods and drinking the most subtly potent wines in Boston.

A close count was kept on both sides, and Sam Adams remained confident that he had enough votes to defeat the proposed Constitution. John made no predictions, but sent brief, vaguely optimistic letters to Hamilton in New York and Washington in Virginia. February 6, the day on which the balloting would take place, he wrote, would be a definitive turning point in American history.

He was on hand an hour before the session began that day, and conferred busily with friends before mounting the podium and calling the convention to order.

"The chair," he told the delegates, "will permit no speeches, no applause, and no demonstrations. Any member of either faction who tries to win converts to his cause after the balloting has begun will be escorted from the hall by the sergeant-at-arms and his vote will be invalidated."

A number of men started to protest.

The crack of John's gavel echoed through the church. "The chair's decision is within his prerogatives as president of this convention and is final. There will be no discussion of the ruling. Balloting will begin on the amendments."

There had been general agreement that the Conciliatory Proposition should be passed as an expression of Massachusetts' opinion, in order to serve notice on the other states that a Bill of Rights was regarded by both factions as essential. Only a few diehard Antifederalists refused to accept the principle, and the convention voted in favor of the amendments by an overwhelming majority.

The hall became silent as voting began on the Constitution itself, and John, unwilling to wait for the secretary's count at the end of the balloting, kept his own tally.

His tension soared as one delegate after another stood to announce his "Aye" or "Nay." The voting was closer than he had anticipated, and it did him no good to see that Sam Adams, sitting at the end of the first row, was worried, too.

By the time three hundred votes had been recorded, the Federalists had a slender lead of eleven. But with fifty-five more votes yet to be announced, the tide could be reversed with ease.

Sam stood and went to the back of the church, where he walked up and down while keeping count on a slate. John felt an urge to join him, but could not leave the rostrum.

The Federalist lead crept a little higher, but John refused to trust his own tally. On several occasions he had made mistakes when presiding over the Continental Congress, and had learned to trust only the secretary's final count.

At last the voting came to an end, and the secretary went over the lists name by name with two assistants, who had kept separate tallies. Sam returned to his seat, and John tried to grin at him, but his face felt too stiff. Then the secretary raised his head, and no one moved.

"Mr. Belknap," John said, "be good enough to read the final result."

"In favor of ratification, one hundred and eighty-seven votes. Opposed to ratification, one hundred and sixty-eight votes."

The Federalists started to applaud, but John gaveled for order. "This convention," he said, "has ratified the proposed Constitution of the United States. Mr. Belknap, prepare the documents of certification, if you please. Gentlemen, under the democratic process in which all of us believe, this state has now gone on record in favor of a Federal system of government, with amendments to be added to the Constitution on the initiative of the first Federal Congress. Let me urge all who opposed ratification to give it their full and unqualified support."

Sam Adams led the applause, although his face was grim.

John concealed his joy. The victory had been won by a narrow margin, but Massachusetts had spoken, and New York would be certain to follow her example. Ratification by all states was now assured, and soon a new era would begin.

11

New Hampshire became the ninth state to ratify the Constitution, on June 9, 1788, assuring the reorganization of the American government. The whole country immediately plunged into a campaign, the first of its kind, to select its President and Vice-President. Even though the first Federal Congress had yet to be elected, the states reached an informal agreement to the effect that the voters would name the members of the Electoral College in January, the President would be chosen in February and the first Federal administration would take office in March.

It was plain from the outset that there would be no contest worthy of the name for the highest place in the land. Newspapers in every state sang the praises of General Washington, and citizens of every class gave serious consideration to no one else. The real contest would be for the office of Vice-President, and the politicians became feverishly busy.

John quietly stole a march on his competitors many weeks before New Hampshire's ratification of the Constitution. Keeping his pledge to the state convention delegates, he entered the lists for the governorship of Massachusetts again, and adroitly mended his fences by persuading Sam Adams to run for the lieutenant governorship on the same Conciliation ticket.

The citizens responded with their usual loyalty, and John was re-elected by a landslide, winning more than eighty percent of the vote and sending his two opponents, Bowdoin and Gerry, into oblivion. He was not strong enough to carry Sam into office with him, though, and General Benjamin Lincoln, who had smashed the farmers' rebellion in the western part of the state, became lieutenant governor.

The *New Hampshire Gazette* wasted no time, and published an editorial on its front page urging its readers to support John for the vice-presidency. Other newspapers throughout New England echoed the call, and John soon won newspaper support in Pennsylvania and New Jersey, too.

Political-minded men in all parts of the country agreed that as a Virginian would in all probability become President, the second highest office should go to someone from one of the big northern states. Robert Morris took himself out of the running, New York had no eligible candidate who was sufficiently well-known nationally, so all eyes turned to Massachusetts, the cradle of American liberty.

Dolly Hancock confided to friends that it would be a wrench to leave Boston for four years, and Sam Adams' *Gazette* boldly declared, "In a few months we shall have to hold another election for governor, as soon as it becomes official that Vice-President Hancock goes to New York."

But the Antifederalists had other ideas. Unable to forgive John for the role he had played in bringing about ratification of the Constitution, they formed an alliance. Henry of Virginia, Gerry of Massachusetts, and the wealthy Hudson Valley landowners of New York who were angry because they soon would have to pay national as well as state taxes on their property, started to search for another candidate.

The Albany *News* was the first to find one. "Hancock," the newspaper declared, "isn't the only man in Boston who has served his country with distinction. No man has been a more efficient and devoted a contributor to the establishment and maintenance of liberty than John Adams."

John read the editorial, which had been mailed to him, while eating his noon dinner at home one day, and promptly lost his appetite. Pale and shaken, he handed the newspaper across the table to his wife.

Dolly became angry. "This is so unfair! Cousin John has been out of the country so long he knows nothing of the problems we face here."

"Our distinguished Minister to England is lucky," John said, sipping a glass of watered Madeira. "By living abroad he's made no enemies at home."

"Surely he has no real chance of beating you?"

"He has a better chance than anyone else in the entire United States, my dear. The Antifederalists have made a shrewd choice. Sam will support him—"

"He won't!"

"He must. Sam may be a rebel who hates conforming to rules, but he's got to stand behind a relative. No one would have any respect for him if he deserted Johnny. But he's only one of a dozen who'll leave me. General Henry Knox is my friend, but he's always been much closer to Johnny than to me, and he can swing Cambridge into line behind the Adams name. Ben Lincoln has no love for me, so I'm sure Johnny can count on his support." His mouth tightened. "What they're trying to do is destroy my home base of power. If they can cut the ground out from under me here, they can ruin me. Once they've done that, they can even discard Johnny if they really prefer someone else. It's a clever maneuver, as shrewd a trick as I've seen in years."

"Can't you do something to stop them, dear? I'm sure General Washington will send you his endorsement if you write to him."

Ordinarily John would have resented her ignorant intrusion into a field about which she knew literally nothing, but the suggestion was so absurd that he laughed.

She took offense immediately. "I'm glad you find me so amusing."

"Dorothy, the last thing in this world Washington can do is offer me his support."

She became still angrier. "You worked together, and you had great respect for each other. He knows what you think of him."

John realized she was referring to their son's name, and tried to be even more tolerant. "A year ago I couldn't believe Washington would accept the presidency. Now I know he wants the position. All he's needed to do—at any time—is to tell some of his supporters he doesn't intend to leave his plantation. But he's kept silent, and his whole strength lies in taking the stand that he's above politics."

"I'm just a woman, but I've been married to a man in public life for thirteen years, and I know that no politician is really above politics."

Her unexpected insight made him laugh. "You're quite right, my dear, but it's an effective pose."

"People will see through it! After all, he made no secret of his support for the Constitution."

"That was different. He fought for it on principle, as I did—as a great many men did. But he hurts himself, particularly now, before he's actually been elected, if he shows partiality to any one man. I do the same sort of thing on a state level, and I wouldn't embarrass him—or myself—by asking for his help."

"Surely you're going to fight this threat!"

John eyed her for a moment. "I've often heard you complain about the impositions that public life force on an official's wife, but I've always suspected that was just a pose. You really enjoy our sort of life, don't you?"

"Yes, because it is a pattern we've made for ourselves. If you were a different kind of man, I wouldn't care for it."

"Meaning?"

"It's not easy to explain." She sighed and tried again. "Women can change their natures as they change their dresses. Martha Washington was content with her plantation life, but she had to change completely when her husband became a soldier. At first she hated it. I know, because she told me she did. But gradually she became accustomed to it. I'm sure she was relieved to go back to the plantation at the end of the war, but now she must start a whole new way of living because it's what her husband wants."

John was thoroughly confused. "Would you have preferred to have me become a merchant again?"

"No, you wouldn't have been happy, and the strain would have hurt our relationship. I haven't been the best of wives, I'll admit, any more than you've been the best of husbands, John. We have the same faults, you know—we're both quick-tempered and intolerant of mistakes. And we take umbrage at the slightest insult. But I've learned one thing in the past thirteen years. A wife can't find happiness unless her husband is satisfied with his work."

He reached across the table and took her hand. "That's the nicest compliment you've paid me in a long time."

Dorothy smiled. "How odd. I was just stating facts, not complimenting you. If I were married to a sea captain—or a fisherman—he'd have to be happy as a sea captain or fisherman in order for us to achieve a successful marriage together. I know you have your heart set on holding an office in the new government—"

"Not just any office. I won't settle for less than the vice-presidency, which will put me first in line to succeed Washington as President."

"All right, high office. You want it, so I want it for you. For us. And I'll gladly work to help you get it, if you'll find something useful for me to do."

John smiled grimly. "There's going to be a great deal for both of us to do." He held her hand more tightly, and suddenly he smiled. "But we'll be doing it together, and that will be half the battle."

12

A fife and drum corps in the blue, scarlet trimmed uniforms of Massachusetts militia played "America" and "Yankee Doodle," and the crowd gathered at the Hancock Wharf joined in the singing of "The Liberty Song:"

> *"In freedom we're born,*
> *And in freedom we'll live;*
> *Our muskets are ready,*
> *Steady, friends, steady,*
> *For freedom we'll die,*
> *And for freedom we live!"*

A small but handsomely appointed open carriage approached the Wharf, and a large crowd began to cheer. The commander of a militia honor guard called an order, the troops stood at attention and the musicians played a stirring version of "Ruffles and Flourishes," which had always heralded the arrival of royal viceroys for the colony of Massachusetts Bay.

Several officials stood near the far end of the Wharf, watching with interest as John and Dorothy smiled and waved as the carriage moved slowly toward them. Both looked striking, Dorothy in a pale green gown and tiny hat, John in a suit of white silk with rust-colored revers and a rust waistcoat. No one paid any attention to a ship's boat moving across the harbor toward the Wharf from a brig that had just cast anchor.

"Governor Hancock's genius," Lieutenant Governor Ben Lincoln said in an undertone, "is that he knows how to steal attention. If Beelzebub were to come here, Hancock would greet him wearing a scarlet suit—of velvet, of course. And, so help me, he'd carry a flaming torch in one hand and a pitchfork of sterling silver in the other."

Sam Adams chuckled. "John has made popularity his business, and no one is better at it."

The crowd's applause reached a peak as Governor and Mrs. Hancock alighted from their carriage. At almost the same moment the boat drew up alongside the Wharf, and the tall, soberly dressed man and plump, sensibly attired woman who stepped ashore were virtually unnoticed. The United States Minister to Great Britain and Mrs. John Adams had come home.

Dolly, looking younger and prettier than she had in several years, embraced Abigail Adams, and the crowd had no difficulty in deciding for itself which was the more attractive.

Governor Hancock and Minister Adams shook hands with a formality that was endangered when they looked at each other. It wasn't easy for friends who had gone fishing together at the age of five to behave like statesmen, but both made the effort.

"On behalf of the Commonwealth of Massachusetts and her people, Mrs. Hancock and I extend a hearty greeting to you and Mrs. Adams, sir, and welcome you to your home."

"Mrs. Adams and I are sensible to your greeting, sir, and are grateful to the people of the Commonwealth for this greeting."

The fife and drum corps began to play again, Dolly brushed John Adams' cheek with a kiss and Governor Hancock bent low over Abigail's hand. The crowd continued to cheer.

"First we'll go down the line of troops, Johnny. You're supposed to inspect them. Then we'll go over to the notables who are waiting to say a few words of welcome to you."

Adams allowed himself to be led toward the honor guard. "I've been a civilian all my life, and I never know whether I'm supposed to inspect their muskets or find lint on their coats." He assumed an appropriately grave manner as they reached the front rank of militia. "You're putting on a rather spectacular welcoming ceremony, John."

"You've become one of the most important men in the country, Johnny. Your name is mentioned constantly in connection with high office in the new Federal government."

"As is yours," Adams replied quietly.

John glanced at him.

"My correspondence was unusually heavy in the weeks just before we left England. And when the ship put into New York on Tuesday, someone was kind enough to bring all of last week's newspapers on board for me."

They reached the end of the first row of militia and started down the rear rank. The crowd could not see them now, and only John's plumed hat was visible above the burnished helmets and muskets of the soldiers.

"I was rather surprised," Adams continued, "to see how much space was devoted to me, and I was intrigued by the speculation concerning my future. A man who has been out of the country for years really doesn't expect to be remembered so lovingly by the press. I couldn't help wondering whether you might be responsible for the editorial applause."

"I, Johnny? I have no connections with the press." John contrived to look blank.

"The newspapers that went into detail about me are owned by men who have always been exceptionally friendly to you."

John hoped he looked as though he thought the coincidence unusual.

"And the identicality of their views was startling, too. Seven newspapers from New Hampshire to Pennsylvania suggested me for head of the new national Supreme Court."

"You'd be a good one, Johnny."

Adams met his old friend's gaze squarely. "I disagree. I've practiced no law in years, and I know far less about the intricacies of the Constitution than the lawyers who have been devoting all their time and thoughts to it for the past year and a half. Jay of New York would be a better chief justice than I, as I've already written General Washington. So would Madison and John Marshall of Virginia."

331

John's cleverly devised scheme had failed, and he hid his disappointment.

They came to the end of the rear rank, and Adams paused, still looking at John. "I have interests in another direction. I believe you and I want the same place in the new government, no doubt for the same reasons."

John accepted the jolt with a surface calm. "How strange that two urchins from Braintree should find themselves at the same spot on the road after more than a half-century." He extended his hand, Adams shook it and both knew the campaign would be hard and bitter.

13

Colonel Joshua Wentworth's escort of light horse kicked up a thick cloud of dust at the head of the parade through the dirt streets of Portsmouth, New Hampshire, and waves of it rolled back along the line of march.

"I'm suffocating," Dolly said, sitting high in the open carriage directly behind the troops.

"Don't hold your handkerchief to your face," John said sharply. "Keep waving to the crowd with it. And smile."

She obeyed, but was still miserable. "The food at the William Pitt Tavern was inedible. I don't understand how you could pretend to enjoy it."

He waved energetically to a group of workers from the shipyards who cheered him enthusiastically. Many Hancock merchantmen had been built in Portsmouth before the war, and the craftsmen hadn't forgotten it. "I was sitting between Governor and Mrs. Langdon," he replied as he smiled and bowed. "Every dish we ate was their personal selection, and Mrs. Langdon told me some were prepared from her own recipes. If you're feeling badly, my dear, try to sympathize with me. I'm suffering an excruciating attack of gout as a result of that accursed meal."

Dolly stifled a sigh and beamed at a contingent of fishermen. "How soon may I leave for the tea that Mrs. Wentworth is giving for me?"

"You'll have to ride with me until the parade ends."

"But I heard Governor Langdon tell you that the line of march goes all the way to Fort McClary across the river!"

"Militiamen," he replied firmly, "cast their ballots for members of the Electoral College under the new system. A soldier's vote is as good as anyone else's."

"But this sun is blistering, and I'll be a mass of freckles. I should have worn a larger hat."

"Then the people wouldn't be able to see your face."

"I think this is dreadful, John."

"I'm afraid it's only the beginning, my dear. We're going to visit every town of any consequence in New England on this tour. John Adams may be undermining my hold in Boston, so I'll make the whole region my base. We can't afford to think of our personal comforts and conveniences." He doffed his hat to some farmers who had come in from the remote hill country to see him. "Be sure to change your clothes before tonight's banquet. It will be expected of you. And please, applaud my speech at the torchlight rally."

"But it will be the same speech you made at Marblehead and Salem. I know it by heart."

"That doesn't matter. A candidate's wife is expected to show enthusiasm, and so you shall. If I lose, we must at least have the satisfaction of knowing we tried."

14

"Your mistake," Sam Adams said as he made himself at home in the governor's office, "was that you tried too hard, John."

"If anyone had to beat me, I'm content that it was Vice-President John Adams. But I can't understand why I placed fifth, nor why I didn't get the vote of a single Massachusetts elector. It makes no damned sense, Sam. The same voters have re-elected me as governor by the biggest vote I've ever had, and this time—because I begged and cajoled and pleaded with them to restore harmony in the state—they've even made you their lieutenant governor." John spoke in a voice drained of all feeling.

"Try a glass of sack. You look faint."

"I don't like the taste any more."

"You've eaten nothing for the past two weeks."

A dull gleam of anger appeared in John's eyes. "I sent a letter to President Washington promising him the full cooperation of Massachusetts in all things. I've twice congratulated Vice-President Adams publicly and have attended four banquets in his honor. If I choose to have no appetite for food, that's my own affair."

"You've enjoyed Hancock luck all your life. It isn't easy to lose an election for the first time in a long career." Sam's rasping voice actually sounded soothing.

"Why did it happen? Why did the voters of Massachusetts reject me—and then turn around to re-elect me their governor in almost the same breath. It defies reason!"

"The people follow their instincts in an election. They use their common sense, which isn't necessarily logical."

"Spare me your enigmas." John painfully hoisted his left foot onto a padded stool behind his desk.

"You've asked me for an explanation, and I'm trying to give it to you as best I can. The whole Commonwealth knows and trusts Governor Hancock. They appreciate what you've done for them. They've seen you battle to stabilize the currency and reduce prices. They know you won't tolerate disorders, and householders are grateful for the protection you give them. They're pleased at the growth of industry, at the new schools—at all the things you've done for Massachusetts. Yes, and they know you'll insist that the Federal Congress amend the Constitution to include a Bill of Rights. You're a man of your word, and you do what's right and good for the Commonwealth."

"But they don't like or trust me enough to support me for the office of vice-president of the United States!"

"Running for a high Federal office isn't the same as campaigning for a state office. I don't think you realized it, and even if you had, I can't imagine how you could have changed your personality."

John glared at him in frustrated bewilderment.

"Washington set the tone by holding himself aloof and standing on his dignity. Whether we agree or not—and I still have no love for the Federal system—he created a stature for the presidency. It's my opinion that Cousin John won the vice-presidency because his own nature is stern and retiring. Without realizing it, his own dignity fitted the concept that Washington created. So the people sent their representatives to the Electoral College with instructions to vote for him. It's that simple, I believe."

"You're telling me I'm a minstrel, a vagabond?"

"No, you're an exuberant and colorful man who can't contain or hide your enthusiasms. You live well. You—"

"Am I to be penalized because I'm wealthy? Washington is no pauper, but that hasn't hurt him!"

"Hear me out, I'm sure Washington lives well, too, but he does it quietly, rather modestly. He reminds me of the English aristocrats we saw here before the war. He seems to take his fortune for granted, and he behaves like a man of much lesser means."

"But I don't," John said bitterly. "I live in the biggest house ever built in Boston, and on the most conspicuous site. I wear gaudy clothes, I ride in expensive coaches and my entertainments are anything but niggardly. I'm so fond of good food and drink that I'm crippled for the rest of my days by this damnable gout. Is that what you're trying to tell me?"

"In part. Other men are content to marry ordinary women who'll look after their needs and make them comfortable. You married the most beautiful woman in the Commonwealth. You don't walk quietly into a room, John, you make a grand entrance. I honestly don't believe you're capable of committing an unobtrusive act."

"So the people I've served for more than twenty years have been willing to eat my rich bread and drink my foreign wine, let me spend my fortune on the United States and work myself into an early grave for the good of the country. But they're ashamed of me."

"Not at all, and stop feeling so sorry for yourself!" Sam's patience snapped. "You've been rewarded with the governorship year after year, and you can stay in office until the day you die. They simply want a different sort of man in high Federal position, someone less flamboyant.

"Think of how far Massachusetts and the United States have traveled on the road to freedom and security, John, and how much is due to your own efforts."

John's fist crashed on the desk. "I have no false sense of modesty, Sam! I'm proud of my record, and I refuse to wear a mantle of humility to satisfy the voters' whims of the moment."

"Don't. That's what I've been trying to tell you."

"Styles in Presidents will change. The people will grow tired of icicles, but I won't be here any longer when they'll demand someone with more of a zest for life. Mark my words."

"I shall, but I advise you to stop worrying about what will happen to public tastes after you're gone."

"Oh, I've reconciled myself to spending the rest of my days right here, and so has Dorothy. There's still work to be done for Massachusetts, and as long as the people will have me as governor, I'll do it."

NINE

1793

1

In April 1793, for the third year in succession, no candidate for public office was courageous enough to oppose Governor Hancock at the polls, and he was re-elected without opposition. Even the dwindling handful of men who disliked him admitted that he was the undisputed master of Massachusetts. The Commonwealth's Senators and Representatives were his spokesmen in the Federal government, the General Court accepted his legislative program without question and, as a rule, the mere threat of a veto was sufficient to kill any measure he disapproved.

Life on Beacon Hill was serene but circumscribed. John's persisting gout had weakened his health, and he now needed two canes when he walked. The third floor of the mansion had been closed off, and only three parties had been given in more than a year, a small dinner in honor of President Washington soon after his re-election and two receptions for visiting French dignitaries. The staff had been reduced by more than half, and there were only eleven servants in the employ of the governor and his lady now, not including the two sergeants of militia who drove the official carriage, or the secretaries, also hired by the Commonwealth, who lived at the house because John wanted them close at hand.

The huge dining room on the ground floor was used only at

night. John ate breakfast with Dolly in the sitting room of their private suite, and often found it convenient to spend his mornings working in a new study set up for him in what had been their son's room across the corridor. It had become an effort for him to go to the Long Room Club or the Bunch of Grapes for his noon dinner, and he usually retired to the sitting room for a light meal, sometimes inviting Sam Adams or another old friend to join him.

He found the preparation of his annual inauguration address to the General Court more of a chore than usual, and for several days he was in a foul temper. The management of the household displeased him, he found the work of the gardeners slovenly and, hating the plain diet to which Dr. Pringle and Dr. Baker restricted him, he complained at length about the talents of the cook.

Dolly wisely avoided him when he was in a bad mood, and deliberately slept late each morning, joining him for a token cup of tea as he was finishing his breakfast. When she appeared one morning late in April, however, he startled her with a boisterous greeting.

"My love, you're a feast for tired old eyes."

She blinked sleepily, then stared at the mug beside his plate. "John! Have you been drinking?"

"Join me in some fifty-year-old rum that Uncle Thomas saved for special occasions."

"I disapprove of spirits this early in the day," she replied primly, taking her seat and ringing for her pot of tea. "And you know what Dr. Pringle will say."

"Ned Pringle may barbecue in Hades, for all I care. Look here!" John waved a sheet of paper.

"What is it?"

"Alex Hamilton has put the Treasury Department on a paying basis at last. He's paying compound interest on the old Confederation bonds, and he's redeeming Continental paper money, one hundred cents on the dollar. The United States is solvent— and so are we."

She was pleased, but that didn't prevent her from reaching for his mug.

He snatched it away. "I think I've earned a quiet celebration."

"You've been eating mutton chops again, too. Dr. Baker says there's nothing worse for you."

"We have enough funds now to invest in Jim Scott's new shipping company—in your name, of course. If word spreads that I'm becoming his silent partner, he'll have more investors than shares of his stock for sale." John grinned at her. "And if I keep eating mutton chops and drinking rum for breakfast, you'll be rich enough to bury me in a golden coffin."

"Your sense of humor is misplaced, Governor Hancock!"

"If my conduct is a trifle unseemly, forgive me. But I'm as excited as I was back in the days when we were thumbing our noses at King George. What a pity he's lost his wits and can't swallow the gall of our new triumph. Don't you see, Dorothy? I was right! Our Federal system of government is a succes. We've come a long way from the Boston Tea Party. We gambled—and won."

"Why don't you ask Cousin Sam to dinner this noon, after you deliver your inauguration address?"

"A good idea. I shall."

She began to open her own mail. "Perhaps we can visit New York after the General Court adjourns."

"The trip tires me too much, but I'll gladly make arrangements for you."

"I don't want to go without you, John."

"Thank you, but I hate to think of you being tied to an invalid in Boston."

"You're not an invalid!"

He sighed and shook his head, but made no reply. Even routine work exhausted him these days, and Dr. Pringle became evasive whenever he asked whether his health was failing. But it would be cruel to alarm Dorothy prematurely. "I saw you have a letter from Abigail Adams."

Dolly glanced up from her mail. "Yes, the poor dear is depressed over the life they'll lead for the next four years. Cousin John has nothing to do but preside over the Senate, and he becomes terribly crotchety."

John chuckled. "It serves him right for accepting a second term as Vice-President."

"Don't be vindictive, dear. It doesn't become you."

He sobered. "John Adams will win his reward. His post is regarded as an apprenticeship, and he's almost certain to succeed

Washington as President. He'll have what I wanted, but I'll give him my support."

She looked at him anxiously. "Does it still hurt—when you think about it?"

"No, not really. I've made my own niche, and I'm satisfied with it. Every man wants to be remembered after he's gone, and I think I've earned my place in history."

2

"As I begin my eleventh term of office, I want to share some of my thoughts with you, gentlemen. I believe it fitting that I do this at a time when our Federal government has proved its stability, demonstrated its strength and convinced its foes, both domestic and foreign, that the United States of America will flourish. The problem of how to distribute the powers of government in a democracy has been solved, and that brings me to broader, deeper questions which I have been pondering of late." John gripped the sides of the rostrum and looked out at the newly elected members of the General Court.

The scene was familiar, as were many of the faces in his audience, but he felt a sense of challenge, as he always did when meeting for the first time with a legislature at its opening session. "Gentlemen, some of you were small children at the time our nation was being formed, but our concept of self-rule is still so fresh, so unusual that I feel certain you share with me the excitement of our continuing growth. Two years ago Vermont became our fourteenth state, and since I last addressed you in this hall Kentucky has joined the sisterhood of states. The settlement of our western lands is so rapid that, I know, other bright stars will soon be added to our national ensign.

"There are trends in our development that I deplore, none more strongly than the formation of political parties within recent months. I have no doubt that some of you stand with Mr. Hamilton in favor of strengthening the Federal government, while others of you share the view of Mr. Madison that the states must remain supreme in their own spheres. For myself. I see merit in both positions, and prefer not to pass judgment. I do know, however, and emphasize to you that democracy will prevail. We, the people, established the Constitution, as its preamble states. We, the people, ordained it, and we, the people, sustain it. I am confident that democracy will not be destroyed by the formation of political parties.

"In some areas the Federal government is and must be supreme. The establishment of tariffs at our national barriers and of excise taxes within our borders has enabled the United States government to become solvent, absorb the debts assumed by the separate states during the war and the period of the Confederation, and pay off those obligations.

"This leaves the states with a problem, and nowhere is it more pressing than in this Commonwealth. Where shall we obtain the revenues necessary for our own operations? My solution is a simple one. I propose that we extend and tighten our system of property taxation. Lest any of you protest that Governor Hancock goes too far, let me remind you that I, as the owner of more property than any other person in the Commonwealth, will be obliged to assume a far greater burden of taxation.

"I shall assume it gladly. So will all of our citizens who shared with me the unfair system of taxation imposed upon us by our British masters in our colonial days.

"But there is one form of revenue raising I will not tolerate. It has come to my attention that some members of this body intend to submit legislation to the General Court establishing a state lottery. They argue that it is an 'easy' way to raise money. So it is, insofar as all of Satan's ways are easy.

"You will recall, gentlemen, that last year I forced a theatrical company to close its doors in Boston after the aliens who were members of the mummers' group openly breached our laws and contemptuously insulted our powers of government. The traditions of Massachusetts cannot be broken with impunity.

"A lottery would breach our traditions. Let us call this evil by its true name, gentlemen. A lottery is a cheap and sleazy form of gambling. Like theatrical performances, gaming is an evil, and has no place in the Commonwealth. I will veto any legislation that proposes the establishment of a state lottery, and will fight this concept with every other weapon at my command.

"Let me now proceed to that matter which has been my primary concern of late. A new generation is growing to manhood, a generation too young to remember the degradation of colonial rule or the horrors of war. This generation will take democracy for granted, and thereby weaken its fabric, unless we define its meaning in terms that every citizen can understand.

"What is democracy?

"A free government founded in the natural, equal rights of all the people is within the reach of human ability. It is to be prized as a principal support of human happiness. It is an idea which has been long established in the minds of the greatest and wisest men in the world."

John paused and spoke slowly, in his most solemn and emphatic manner. "That government may be considered as truly free where all the people are, by the constitution and laws, upon the same rank of privilege and have an equal security for their lives, liberties, and property—where the laws do not create, but are calculated to prevent, all exclusive rights to fame or wealth, and leave each citizen upon his own merit for the honors of his country and upon his own honest exertions for the acquirement of property."

A storm of applause interrupted him.

He waited until his audience subsided. "There is, in this democracy, one sensitive area which requires the vigilance of all elected officials to prevent abuse of power and injustice to our people. Governments, by their nature, try to acquire more power. That is true of state and town governments, as it is of the Federal government. Each is eager to acquire the rights and prerogatives of the others.

"We, the people, must be the constables who keep watch over all our various governments to make certain our liberties are not stolen from us. It is not enough that the Tenth Amendment to the Constitution reserves to the states those rights not specifically granted to the Federal government by the Constitution. Who shall prevent the states from stealing our liberties? We ourselves must do this, perhaps by granting constabulary powers to the Federal government.

"The balances within the framework of the Federal establishment appear to be effective. Our next great task is the creation of balances that will enable the states to work in harmony with the nation. I propose no simple formula for this purpose. But you and I, and our citizens everywhere, must devote themselves to this purpose so that our precious freedoms shall not be endangered.

"It has been my custom in my annual address to recommend new legislation that, if passed by the General Court, will benefit the people of the Commonwealth. I make several such recommendations at this time.

"The whipping post is a cruel and primitive device, and should be abolished. Surely we can find ways to punish our criminals less barbaric than beating them like dumb animals. They are fellow humans, not brutes. I should also like to see the practice of branding criminals discontinued for the same reason, and believe that the cropping of criminals' ears for certain offenses is a degradation unworthy of a democracy. It is also my personal opinion that the death penalty is too severe a punishment for the crime of burglary, and I suggest that each house of the General Court appoint a committee to work with Lieutenant Governor Adams toward the establishment of a new and enlightened penal code.

"Great controversy has been caused throughout the United States by the recent request made by Secretary of the Treasury Hamilton for the creation of a national bank. Such a bank, in my belief, would insure our continued financial stability, and is much to be desired. I urge the General Court to elect special groups from the banking and finance committees of both houses to confer with me. It is my hope that, working together, we can give the national bank idea the support it deserves from this Commonwealth.

"Dear friends, I shall not be with you much longer. Often, of late, I have seen the Great Ruler of the Universe call me closer to His eternal realm."

Cries of "No!" interrupted the silence, and John waited until they subsided.

"I speak of this matter sensibly, dear friends, so you will be ready to carry forward the torch of freedom when I am forced to lay it down. But I'm still here, and I can assure you that I love my country today as I loved her when she and I were younger. I will not give up my liberties to my last drop of blood. I may have become infirm, but you will always find me prompt to plan for the defense of freedom and ready to execute when necessity requires. I remain devoted to the principles on which this nation is founded, and will fight for them until the last breath is squeezed from my lungs.

"May the Almighty bless and keep you, now and forever. Amen."

The unexpected solemnity of his closing words stunned the legislators, and they stood in silent tribute as, assisted by the sergeant-at-arms and a husky young militia officer, he slowly made his way to the rear. Everyone who saw him realized he had not exaggerated or dramatized his situation. It was obvious from his feeble walk, his color, and the weakness caused by the least physical exertion that his days on earth were numbered.

3

On the evening of October 7, 1793, Governor and Mrs. Hancock gave a small dinner party in honor of Vice-President and Mrs. Adams, who were paying a brief visit to Massachusetts. Only a few relatives and old friends were present, and John was the perfect host, insisting that everyone eat the delicacies prepared for the occasion and opening several bottles of his most precious wine. Dolly had been afraid he might be tempted by the rich food and spirits, and wisely included Dr. and Mrs. Pringle among the guests. The physician sat near John, who restrained his appetites, ate only the plainest of fare and drank sparingly. The affair ended shortly before midnight, and the host and hostess retired.

Sometime later that night or in the early hours of the morning, John expired in his sleep. The man who had lived spectacularly died so quietly that, as John Adams sadly remarked, the event was anticlimactic, and the victim had been cheated of the opportunity to bid the world a last, dramatic farewell.

In a conversation with one of Dolly's sisters only two weeks earlier, John had said he wanted to be buried without public display or ceremony, but Acting Governor Sam Adams ignored the request.

"A man who lived as John did," he said, "can't steal off unnoticed to his grave."

The widow agreed.

For five days the body rested in state in the main drawing

room of the Hancock mansion, guarded by an honor contingent of troops drawn from every battalion of the state militia. From daybreak until late at night thousands of citizens filed past the bier and, as the weather was unseasonably pleasant, punch, cakes and other refreshments were served on the lawn.

"My husband," Dolly said, "wouldn't have wanted anyone to leave his house hungry or thirsty."

On October 14 the bells of every church in Boston and Cambridge began tolling at sunrise, and rang for two hours. Cannon boomed at the Castle, the old fort that guarded the entrance to the harbor, and every ship at anchor lowered its flag to half-mast.

Shops and other establishments serving the public were closed at noon, and for the first time in the history of Boston the taverns and inns refused to serve customers either food or spirits.

Two thousand state militia commanded by Major General William Hull formed in the Common, and five massed bands played dirges as the funeral procession formed. Directly behind the troops and on foot, at his insistence, was Sam Adams. Behind him came the coffin, with members of the Boston town council at either side of the cart as honorary pallbearers. Next, draped in black velvet, was a cannon that had been smuggled out of Boston a few days before the start of the war in 1775.

Dorothy rode in the first carriage with John's sister and brother-in-law, and other members of the family followed in another. Vice-President Adams led the official mourners. All Federal judges from New England were there, as were members of the Congress and General Court, the governors of New Hampshire, Vermont, Rhode Island, and Connecticut. The foreign envoys stationed in New York had come to Boston for the funeral, as had a score of members of the Federal government. Clergymen of every denomination in the city forgot their differences and rode together.

The funeral parade lasted more than an hour as it moved through the silent streets, and Sam became so tired that Dorothy insisted he ride with her. The most astonishing aspect of the procession was not the presence of so many notables, but the fact that the citizens spontaneously joined in the march. Newspaper estimates of the number who participated differed somewhat, and ranged from thirty to forty-five thousand, all walking four abreast in a line that stretched out for more than two miles.

The *Chronicle* thought it significant that the population of Boston was slightly less then thirty thousand. "Nearly everyone in town took part," it said, "as did thousands from other places."

Brief prayers were offered by two clergymen after the cortege reached the Old Granary Burying Ground. Sam Adams had demanded the right to deliver an oration, but when the time came for him to speak, he could say nothing. Tears came to his eyes, he choked and finally shrugged helplessly.

Returning to his place beside the widow, he signaled the massed band of musicians as the coffin was lowered into a place beside that of John's son.

To the astonishment of nearly everyone present, the musicians began to play "Yankee Doodle."

Dolly clung to Sam's arm, and they laughed together through their tears. "Thank you," she said.

"Wherever John is," he replied, "he's enjoying this. He'll be glad we're reminding all these people to take pride in being American, and he always liked a lively air."

A Postscript

Few men in American history, if any, could boast characters as complex and contradictory as John Hancock's. The wealthiest man in Britain's North American colonies, he had more to lose than anyone else if the American bid for independence failed, yet he led that fight. Rather than retire to private life after the war to repair his private fortunes, he not only remained in public life, holding high office almost continuously until the time of his death, but invested what was left of his wealth in what appeared to be worthless scraps of government paper.

Hancock loved liberty, and his faith in the future of his country never wavered. These were his finest qualities, and it is still astonishing, today, that a man who fought as he did for a free, secure America could have been so pompous, luxury-loving and, in unexpected ways, so narrow-minded.

I would like to add a few words here for the serious student of biography. Two incidents in John Hancock's life have been omitted from this novel. His brief venture into military life as a Major General, when he accompanied General John Sullivan on the expedition to free occupied Rhode Island, was abortive and accomplished literally nothing. Hancock spent a few dull weeks in the field, saw no active fighting and, when the expedition collapsed, quietly returned to Boston.

I saw little to be gained, either, by dramatizing the curious table-tennis match over protocol waged by President Washington and Governor Hancock shortly after the creation of the Federal government in 1789. Washington paid a brief visit to Boston, and insisted it was Hancock's place to call on him first. Hancock was hurt, and felt the President should call on him. Washington held out longer, and Hancock capitulated, knowing he was in the wrong and that had he been President, he would have demanded respect from a mere governor, too.

In any event, ruffled feelings on both sides were smoothed, and several calls were exchanged during the remainder of Washington's visit. There was a great deal of gossip about the incident

347

at the time, but after the passage of 175 years it seems trivial. Both men were tired and overburdened, and the flurry in no way spoiled their friendship. I found it so lacking in significance that I was reluctant to give it more space in these pages than I felt it deserved.

Another novel could be written about the tempestuous Dorothy Quincy Hancock, who became the wealthiest widow in New England after her husband's death. To the dismay of her relatives and friends, she took a second husband in 1796, marrying Captain James Scott, Hancock's former employee and favorite ship's master.

Boston society immediately snubbed Mrs. Scott, but she thumbed her nose at the patricians and, at the age of forty-nine, went off to live with her new husband in Portsmouth, New Hampshire. Scott was a proud man who refused to live on the Hancock fortune, and Dolly was forced to adopt a new scale of living. They took a small house, and instead of supervising the labors of twenty or more servants, she considered herself lucky to hire one. She did most of her own cooking and housework.

Scott apparently made her happy for thirteen years. At any rate, she made no comments about her marriage other than to mention his passion for Madeira, a love he shared with Hancock, in occasional letters to her sisters.

Immediately after Scott's death in 1809 Dolly returned to Boston and took up residence once more in the Hancock mansion, but it was too large for her needs, and she sold it, moving to a smaller house. The Hancock money and name made it impossible for the aristocrats to keep their doors barred to her, and she resumed her old place in their ranks.

Only one event in her later years was newsworthy. The Marquis de Lafayette made his last visit to the United States in 1824, a journey which created enormous excitement when he deliberately sought the company of General Andrew Jackson, the frontier hero who was to become President four years later. Lafayette was greeted everywhere by mammoth crowds, and Boston gave him a riotous welcome. He further endeared himself to the people of Massachusetts by paying his first call in Boston on Dolly, and he insisted that she be present at all banquets and other festivities in his honor.

She died in 1830 at the age of eighty-three, and her relatives, pretending Scott had never existed, buried her beside John Hancock and their son.

N.B.G.

Waterford, Conn.

Adams, Abigail, *Letters*, Boston, 1841.
Adams, Charles Francis, Jr., *History of Braintree, Mass.*, Boston, 1891.
Adams, Henry, *Documents Relating to New England Federalism*, New York, 1905.
Adams, John, *Letters Addressed to His Wife*, Boston, 1841.
——, *Life and Works*, Boston, 1850–56 (10 vols.)
Adams, Samuel, *Writings*, New York, 1904–8.
Allan, Herbert S., *John Hancock, Patriot in Purple*, New York, 1953.
Austin, James T., *Life of Elbridge Gerry*, Boston, 1828 (2 vols).
Ayer, Mary F., *Early Days on Boston Common*, Boston, 1910.

Baxter, W. T., *The House of Hancock*, Cambridge, Mass., 1945.
Beard, Charles A. and Mary R., *Rise of American Civilization*, revised, New York, 1932.
——, *The Open Door at Home*, New York, 1935.
Becker, Carl, *The Declaration of Independence*, New York, 1942.
Boston *Evening Post*
Boston *Gazette*
Boston *Herald*
Bridenbaugh, Carl and Jessica, *Rebels and Gentlemen*, New York, 1942.
Brown, Abram, *John Hancock: His Book*, Boston, 1898.
Burnett, E. C., *The Continental Congress*, New York, 1941.

Carlton, Mabel M., *John Hancock*, Boston, 1922.
Continental Congress, Journals of, Washington, 1905–7.
Convention of the Commonwealth of Massachusetts: *Debates and Proceedings*, Boston, 1856.

Drake, Samuel G., *History and Antiquities of the City of Boston*, Boston, 1854.

Fast, Howard, *Citizen Tom Paine*, New York, 1943.
Faulkner, Harold U., *American Economic History*, revised, New York, 1943.

Forbes, Esther, *Paul Revere and the World He Lived In*, Boston, 1942.

Franklin, Benjamin, *Writings*, New York, 1906–7 (10 vols).

Gibbs, George, *Memoirs of the Administrations of Washington and John Adams*, New York, 1846 (2 vols).

Hamilton, Alexander, *Works*, New York, 1903 (12 vols).

Hancock Letters, Baker Library, Harvard University, Cambridge, Mass.

Hancock Papers, New York Public Library, New York.

Hazleton, John H., *The Declaration of Independence*, New York, 1906.

Higginson, Stephen, *Ten Chapters in the Life of John Hancock*, New York, 1857.

Hunt, Freeman, *American Anecdotes*, Boston, 1830 (3 vols).

Hutchinson, Thomas, *Diary and Letters*, Boston, 1884–6.

Jensen, Merrill, *The New Nation; a History of the United States During the Confederation, 1781–9*, New York, 1950.

Jernegan, Marcus W., *The American Colonies*, New York, 1930.

Lafayette, General, Marquis de, *Memoirs, Correspondence and Manuscripts*, Philadelphia, 1837 (3 vols).

Larabee, Leonard W., *Royal Government in America*, New Haven, 1930.

Loring, James S., *Boston Orators*, Boston, 1852.

Miller, John C., *Sam Adams, Pioneer in Propaganda*, Boston, 1936.

Musick, John R., *John Hancock*, Dansville, New York, 1898.

Myers, Ralph T., *Dolly Hancock, the Beauty of Her Age*, New York, 1927.

New England Independent Chronicle
New Hampshire Gazette

Pattee, W. S., *History of Old Braintree and Quincy*, Quincy Mass., 1878.
Pennsylvania Gazette
Pennsylvania Ledger

Quincy, Martha A., *Our Country*, (Reminiscences of the Hancocks), revised, Baltimore, 1867.

Rush, Benjamin, *Autobiography*, New York, 1948.

Schachner, Nathan, *Alexander Hamilton*, New York, 1946.
——, *Thomas Jefferson*, New York, 1951.
Sears, Lorenzo, *John Hancock, the Picturesque Patriot*, Boston, 1912.
Sparks, Jared, *Correspondence of the American Revolution*, Boston, 1853 (4 vols).
——, *Writings of George Washington*, Boston, 1859 (12 vols).
Sullivan, William, *Familiar Letters on Public Characters and Public Events*, Philadelphia, 1834.
Sullivan, William S., *Dorothy Quincy Hancock, a Portrait*, New York, 1919.

Taylor, Frederick Edward, *Crown and Colonies*, 1763–83, London, 1935.
——, *King George III*, London, 1948.
Trevelyan, George O., *George III*, London, 1912 (3 vols).

Umbreit, Kenneth B., *The Founding Fathers*, New York, 1941.
Underwood, Chester L., *Sam Adams and John Hancock, the Unholy Alliance*, New York, 1959.

Van Doren, Carl, *Benjamin Franklin*, New York, 1938.

Wells, William V., *Life and Public Services of Samuel Adams*, Boston, 1865.
Wharton, Anne H., *Social Life in the Early Republic*, New York, 1902.
Winsor, Justin, *A Narrative and Critical History of America*, Boston, 1887 (8 vols).